Seith and Sword
by: Chris Challice

Published by Pendelhaven 2015

Pendelhaven
121 2^{ieme} Bourbonniere
Lachute, Quebec, Canada
J8H 3W7
www.fateofthenorns.com
www.pendelhaven.com

Based on the Fate of the Norns world created by Andrew Valkauskas

Cover artwork by Natasa Ilincic

Map artwork by Soni Alcorn-Hender

Editing: Hepzibah Nanna

ISBN 978-0-9940240-4-6

Published in Canada
Printed in the USA

Dedicated to my mother- Sue Challice

CHAPTER 1

Chattel, I was. | A mere refrain to Dorte's song.
Harsh was my service, I had no wages.
Cunning, I used. | To avoid the embrace of the gods.
"Thralls enjoy their lot." is the vilest of lies.

Vanadis watched Dorte's move with trepidation. Her opponent slid her white piece down the board, paused, and carefully set it.

Vanadis was a tall, willowy young woman. She had sharp, regal features, and long brown hair that was bound by a simple leather string. She wore a rough, but clean brown woolen dress. She had no jewellery. Her keen grey eyes locked with Dorte's, she sighed and considered her next move.

Dorte was the same age as Vanadis. She was shorter but trim and fit in build as well as, complexion. Her brilliant golden hair was tied in a braid with a silver thread. Her features were soft, with a hint of pride. She wore an expensive blue dress with silver trim. Around her neck was a golden chain, around her wrists were silver and gold bangles. She bit her lip and watched for Vanadis' next move.

They played on a white tiled hnefatafl board. The pieces were smooth black and white marble; the white king wore a tiny gold crown.

The board sat on a small, smooth table. The maids sat across from each other on stools. They played in the centre of the Great Hall, sunlight streamed through the timbers and open front door.

Clustered around them were a crowd of well-dressed young women. They watched the match with baited interest. A few whispered, but none dare giggle.

Halldora, Dorte's mother, sat at her bench at the western side of the hall. She was matronly, and her blonde hair was streaked with grey. She wore a fine dress of red. She paused from her weaving and watched Dorte with a measure of pride.

Outside could be heard the sound of their town Kelifar; the clopping of horses, the gaggle of citizens, the ring of the forge and the rolling of the sea.

"Will you not move?" Dorte huffed.

"Yes, mistress." Vanadis' thoughts clicked and she slid her black piece to land beside one of Dorte's. The white was bordered by the black and so the thrall snatched it away.

The girls murmured in surprise and amusement.

"Hush." commanded Dorte and they fell silent. She glared at Vanadis and then, she put her full attention on the board.

Vanadis sat straight and calmly assessed the game, yet inside her was a knot of worry. This knot twisted as Dorte's delicate hand hovered over each white piece in turn. Would her mistress see through her gambit? She wasn't sure. The thrall mastered the board as best she could but Dorte's victories and follies had surprised her. Everything came down to this. One move would determine the winner.

Finally, Dorte seized her piece.

Vanadis' grey eyes flashed. 'Yes, that's it.' she cheered silently.

Dote swept her hand and placed the piece with a click.

It was all the thrall could do to keep from shouting for joy. Instead, in a reserved manner she tapped her lips and pretended to plot her response. She could now force the outcome.

Their play continued. Marble on tiles clicked. White and black warriors fell. With each move Dotre's expression brightened and Vanadis drew a deeper 'mask of concern'.

"Oh, you were clever, but I have you now." laughed the mistress. A few swift manoeuvres later and Dorte's king was in his corner.

Vanadis sighed in defeat, though, in truth, it was a sigh of relief. As the girls cheered and Dorte's mother clapped, all feelings of fret left the young thrall.

After basking in her peers' adulation Dorte regarded Vanadis beneficently, "Quite the match Vanadis, I dare say you could beat anyone on this island, excluding myself of course."

"I am no match for Gerd mistress." Vanadis lied humbly.

The young noble tittered proudly, "You shall watch our match, this time I shall trounce her soundly."

"As you say, mistress." Vanadis was confident of Dorte's claim for she had tailored their game to prepare the young lady for said inevitable confrontation.

Suddenly, a jovial voice called out, "What's this? Leisure in the middle of the day? I won't have it."

It belonged to Steinarr the Rogue. He was a short, burly man. His head was as bald as a rock but his light brown beard was thick. He had bright blue eyes and a confident swagger. He wore expensive garb of purple. On each arm was a band of pure gold. With a swipe, he scooped Halldora off her bench. She embraced him and giggled.

Pointing at Dorte and then the matron's weaving he said, "See? Your mother, the fine Lady of this hall, is busy at work. As am I. Sorry for the sweat dear."

"You lout." His wife cupped his cheeks and kissed him.

The gaggle of girls hid their laughter. Dorte made as if she were going to be sick. Vanadis hid her grin behind her fist.

After taking in his Halldora, with a warm smile, Steinarr returned her to her bench and turned on the girls.

"Elina, Ingeborg, Bote, Nikolina, festival preparations, now. Camilla, Solevieg off to sword practice. Petra, your father needs water at the forge."

As one the girls bowed and scattered.

"Dorte fetch Gerd and Ingri. The three of you have been chosen to prepare Freya's alter."

At the mention of Kelifar's patron goddess Dorte's annoyance turned to duty. "Yes, father. Come Vanadis."

Steinarr gripped the thrall's shoulder. "No, I have need of her."

Vanadis said nothing but her heart leapt to her throat.

Dorte paled. "Father, surely you're not thinking..."

Steinarr chuckled. "Not at all. We draw for the blot tonight, not a moment sooner. I need your handmaid to deliver a message."

Vanadis closed her eyes and issued a silent prayer of thanks.

Dorte eyed her father for a moment. He motioned her to carry on. She humphed left.

"Come along." Steinarr said to Vanadis.

He walked over to Halldora's bench and sat beside her. Vanadis, followed and stood obediently before them.

"Husband?" the matron asked with a hint of concern.

Steinarr glanced around the now empty hall and whispered to them both. "I have word that Hardegon's in Neshraun."

Halldora looked quizzical on that. "Why the hush? This is good news. He must come to the festival."

"He may be with Starkad." Steinarr pressed.

"Oh." his wife replied grimly.

Steinarr grasped Vanadis by the collar and pulled her close enough to smell the breakfast mead on his breath. "We need torches. I'm giving you this to buy them." He tucked a money pouch into her hand. "Gather one other thrall, not your brother, and borrow a boat. It's alright, the fishermen expect you. Go to Neshraun for the purchase. You're clever enough to find my nephew is there. No one will give a shit about you, let alone a second glance. I trust you won't flee, you know what will happen to Gamli if you do.

If you see Hardegon tell him he's welcome in Kelifar. Mark if you see his brother but say nothing. Return promptly."

Vanadis regarded Steinarr's deadly serious expression and answered, "Yes master." Her eyes expressed that she understood both his instructions and threat.

"Good." The jarl pushed her away. Vanadis bowed and swept out the door.

***

Meanwhile, in the forge, Gamli struck the red hot iron with measured force. Sweat trickled down his powerful arms. Sparks singed his beard.

He was a giant of a young man. His fair red hair was tied back, his beard gruff and wild, it made him look older. His blue eyes watched his work with focus and care. His features were gentile. Under his leather apron he was shirtless.

His work was an axe head, long in neck, suitable for felling trees. Gamli struck the final strikes, guiding his work's final shape.

The smithy was bright, its northern side open to look down on Kelifar. Down the hill was a large harbour. Three longboat houses were along its stony shore. Further around and surrounding it were the well-built and sturdy fisherman halls. Several fishing boats floated on the waters. In the distance, beyond them, were several islands, a few with hearth smoke rising from them. The harbour was crowded with stalls, merchants, and buyers. From the fisherman halls to the foot of the hill were a cluster of tradesmen and warrior halls, these were grand affairs. The murmur of the town, the calls of the merchants were the background to Gamli's hammer rings.

Watching him was Asvard, he was older and broader than Gamli. His hair and beard were grey but well kept. He too wore a leather apron but underneath was a fine white woollen shirt. An intricate silver arm ring hugged his right bicep.

Beside him stood Petra. She was tall, thin, had dark brown hair in braids and a kind features. She wore a red dress. She watched Gamli's gleaming figure work, quite forgetting the water she brought for the forge.

Leaning on a support was Flosi, a thrall about Gamli's age. He was tall, scrawny, had short black hair and the scruff of a beard. His features were sharp and cunning. He watched but more out of obligation than interest.

Gamli seized his axe head with tongs. He turned and paused at the nearly empty water trough.

Petra jumped to action. "Oh my. Sorry."

Gamli stepped out the way, gingerly holding the scalding hot iron out of harm's way. "Not at all, mistress."

"There."

Once the trough was filled and Petra safely out of the way, Gamli plunged his work into the water. Steam hissed from it.

Asvard stepped beside Gamli and when the steam had dissipated, he said, "Hand her over."

"Yes, master." Gamli gave him the tongs.

The blacksmith pulled the axe head out and examined it with a keen eye. He took it over to his work bench and held it to others of its like. He carefully placed it on the table, took a tiny hammer from his belt, and tapped it, listening carefully to its ring.

Gamli looked on anxiously. Petra had stood close beside him. Even Flosi was caught up in the moment.

Asvard shook his head and their faces dropped.

"I'm sorry. It's good but not better than my own. You're not a free man, not yet."

Gamli clenched his fist and glared at the floor.

Petra gently touched his arm.

Flosi patted him on the back. "It's a fine attempt. You'll get there."

"The sacrifice's picked tonight. I might not get another chance." Gamli grumbled.

Asvard crossed his arms and levelled an even look at them. "Chins up, none of that. We draw lots, so whoever gets picked, it's Freya's choice. If your rune comes up, it's an honour, plain and simple."

Gamli raised an ashamed look to his master, "Y-you're right. I'm sorry."

Asvard smiled patted him in the shoulder, "Accepted, but don't rest your hopes in escaping my service on an altar of flowers with our goddess smiling upon you." He laughed. "I wager your only chance at freedom is to beat my craft, and I won't make it easy for you."

Gamli grinned fiercely, "Wouldn't have it any other way master."

"When my brother beats you, and he will, will he have to forge his own arm ring?" Vanadis asked.

They turned to find her at the southern corner. She had a rough green cloak pulled over her shoulders.

"Aye, that he will. Though, I'll supply him the silver." Asvard answered with a toothy smile.

Flosi was suddenly leaning beside her. "Dorte let you off her leash?" he asked.

Vanadis tossed a money pouch into the air and caught it. "We're out of torches. The jarl asked me to fetch some." She poked Flosi in the chest. "You'll do the rowing and the carrying."

"That's hardly fair."

"You'll have the joy of my company."

"We could use more ore. May I go?" Gamli asked his master.

"Sorry," Vanadis shook her head, "but no, jarl's orders. "You get to play hostage so we don't run off. I trust you can keep yourself useful while I'm gone?"

"I could use a strong set of arms to haul the mead to the Great Hall." said Petra with a sweet smile.

"Right, of course." Gamli answered, with barely hidden disappointment.

***

A half an hour later Vanadis and Flosi were on a small boat that cut through choppy, dark waters. Around them were small, rocky islands. To the north was Neshraun.

Neshraun sat on the rocky edge of her island. Her halls were short and squat. A wide road led beyond into the isle's rocky interior that was thick with a pine forest. Her harbour was small. Two merchant knarr's were pulled onto the beach, one fine, the other worn and used. About the town were a mere smattering of people, a few eyed their approach with suspicion.

"We should seize a prisoner in Neshraun and trade him in for our sorry hides." Flosi suggested between heaves on the oars.

Vanadis snickered and chided, "We're supposed to buy, not raid."

"Why not both? Buy the torches, for honor's sake, then steal away a noble."

"Even if you succeeded, Steinarr would get the ransom and one of us would still meet Freya on the morn."

Flosi lifted the oars and paused, a thoughtful, grave look suddenly about him. "How much did master give you anyways?"

Vanadis glowered at him.

Flosi sighed and explained, "Gamli's the son Asvard never had, everyone knows that. Steinarr won't risk his ire."

"25 skatt, enough for you to be king of the cups for a night. Is that worth robbing me for?"

Flosi threw up his hands in frustration.

"I'd never leave my brother." Vanadis added with an edge of steel in her voice.

"Of course you wouldn't." Flosi sighed. Then, after a moment he asked, "If Gamli is freed do you honestly think Steinarr would let you go?"

"Of course not." Vanadis stated flatly.

"Then, don't lose Dorte's favour. Ever."

Vanadis' expression twitched with painful memory. "I don't plan to."

Flosi continued rowing in silence.

After they pulled their boat into the harbour and paid off a ruffian, who threatened them. Vanadis drew the money purse from her sleeve and handed it to Flosi.

"Buy as many torches as you can, then, meet me back here."

The thrall raised an eyebrow. "Where are you off to?"

Vanadis tugged her hood over her head. "Business of the Rogue. You sure you want to know?"

Flosi paused, pondered and answered, "No. Torches it is."

As Vanadis turned to leave Flosi grabbed her arm. "A moment."

"Yes?"

His brown eyes gazed into her grey. "Be careful."

Vanadis hugged him. "You too, don't start trouble you can't get us out of."

They parted ways, Flosi headed up the main road and Vanadis walked along the beach.

She made her way around the western outskirts of town, taking a good look at every hall she passed. When she reached the northern border she spied two guards sitting in front of a large home. They wore leather armour and carried spears. Vanadis cocked an ear and heard their conversation about the summer's raid. When they weren't looking, she dashed behind the hall and snuck around, eyes wide, ear to the wall. A scream from the other side made her jump.

***

"We cannot stay here."

"Master yourself, brother." Hardegon hissed. "Skili, my patience wanes, when will your men have the longboat?"

Skili was a round man dressed in faded finery. "Any moment now."

"I hope so." Hardegon looked as if he'd strode out of a Nibelung fable. His warrior's build carried his leather armour perfectly. The longsword at his hip bore an intricate hilt. Around his neck was a talisman of Thor. His blue eyes were eagle like. His blonde hair and beard neat and trim. His voice, low and confident.

Starkad was his opposite. His black locks fell in his face and over his shoulders. His beard was tangled and greasy. His dark blue garments were torn, he was missing a glove. His brown eyes were wide and unfocused.

They sat in a dimly lit room in Skili's hall. The table before them had a half-eaten meal of bread, stew and ale.

Skili regarded Starkad with trepidation. "Hardegon, I'm going against your father here."

"I am aware of that and your help will be rewarded."

"I'm entrusting my sons to you in next year's raid." the karl continued.

"As per our agreement, yes." replied the hero, with a hint of rising annoyance in his tone.

"So, I have a right to know, what's wrong with him?" he finished pointing at Starkad.

Suddenly Hardegon's brother focused a baleful eye on Skili. "You do?"

"Brother..." Hardegon cautioned.

"Yes, I do."

"I'll show you!" roared Starkad. He stepped forward and traced ᛉ in the air. Suddenly the room filled with a hurricane howl and Skili, the table, the chairs, and part of the fire pit were torn up and hurled to the far wall. Before Skili could rise Starkad was on him. He held the older man down and said in a hysterical whisper, "My father's tablet spoke to me. I traded it to Gorm's sorcerer for wisdom and he showed me," Starkad sniffed, "oh he showed me." He pressed Skili's face into the dirt, leaned closer and hissed, "A godless king whispered in my ear. Such terrible things he whispered, will hear them?"

"G-get off me."

"Do you want to hear them?!" Starkad screamed.

Suddenly, the madman paused as he spotted Vanadis' terrified eye staring between the chinks in the wooden wall. Before he could react the guards from outside, along with Hardegon, pulled him off Skili.

"I will not be silenced! I will not sink in a stone! They will not devour me!"

"My apologies, dear brother." Hardegon struck Starkad in the jaw, knocking him out cold.

To the guards, he said, "Take him to our boat. When Skili's vessel arrives, transfer him there." He offered a hand to the fallen man. "I pray my brother's transgressions haven't soured our deal."

"Soured?" huffed Skili seizing Hardegon's hand. "No, strengthened it. I want him away from here, faster than the toy chest you sailed in can take him."

Hardegon smiled magnanimously, "Excellent. I will speak highly of your family with Bjorn Eriksson."

The guards carried the inert Starkad out of the hall.

Skili watched them go. "Where will you take him?"

"To Väinämöinen of Kalevala. I will treat with him to heal my brother's mind."

"Foreign Magic." Skili spat. "It's more trouble than it's worth. Why not take him to Mjoll the Gentle?"

"I already have, this is beyond even her."

"She once brought me from the brink. If she can't help." Skili shook his head. Then, clapping Hardegon's shoulder he added, "You and I, let's have one good pull of my best mead. Then we'll be on our way."

"That offer, I shall gladly accept." answered Hardegon.

***

When Hardegon left the hall Vanadis rushed the outskirts to pull ahead. Thankfully, the townsfolk had yet to return from the mines, no one spied her flight.

When she reached the beach, she pulled her hood back and walked briskly for the main street. She spied Hardegon and Skili swiftly walking towards a longboat that was prepping for sail. Twenty men were onboard. Sitting with his back against the mast was a figure obscured by a dark blue cloak, Starkad Vanadis assumed.

Flosi sat on their beached vessel snacking on some bread and watching the longship with interest. At his feet were a bundle of torches.

As Vanadis trotted past, she singled for Flosi to wait.

"Master Hardegon." she called.

Hardegon and Skili turned as one, looks of annoyance about them.

Vanadis rushed over and took a knee, her head bowed low. "My master, Steinarr the Rogue, has a message for Hardegon the Trusted, if he would deign to hear it."

At mention of his uncle, Hardegon's look softened. "Rise."

Vanadis stood and the hero regarded her.

Vanadis looked attentive yet meek, secretly she regarded him, as well.

Hardegon the Trusted; spoiler of Fair Hair's plot, contemporary of Bjorn Eriksson, pirate slayer, fear of the west, successor of Hogni. His golden hair, his confident blue eyed gaze, the cut of his chest. He did not disappoint.

"Yes, I recognize you. You're Dorte's handmaiden," he said.

"I recognize her, as well." Skili added, suddenly turning sour.

"My apologies, karl Skili. Have I displeased you?" Vanadis asked, her voice in a slight tremble.

The karl glared at her for a long moment, then turned away and answered, "Bah, if you're ever tired of this life ask your master about your mother."

Hardegon glanced at him, puzzled.

"I'll see to the ship." Skili waded into the water to instruct his men.

Lord and thrall watched him for an uneasy moment. Then Hardegon cleared his throat and asked "The message?"

Vanadis composed herself and bowed. "My master Steinarr the Rogue extends to you an invitation to Kelifar's annual victory feast over Kvistr Dusk Torch."

Hardegon smiled at the recollection of past feasts. "Yes, of course. Sadly, I cannot attend." He gestured to the longship, "I have pressing business up north that is of the greatest of urgency." Then, a thought struck him and he said, "Wait here a moment."

"Yes, Master Hardegon." Vanadis folded her hands in front of her.

Hardegon rushed off to the old, worn merchant ship. Most of the cargo had already been moved. A warrior carried the last bag.

"Sorkvir hold, I'll attend that."

His man handed the satchel to his lord and Hardegon returned to Vanadis, rummaging through it as he walked.

"Ah, yes, here." He pulled two circlets and handed them to her.

Vanadis eyes went wide. They were the same size; one was a beautiful twisted silver band. The other was gold with tiny rubies inlaid in it.

"I requested my uncle to lend me one of Dorte's circlets and he obliged." He tapped the silver one. "The reason I asked is I wanted to win something for her in this summer's raid. I trust this," he tapped the gold one, "will suffice?"

"Y-yes. Very much so. I think it will." Vanadis answered, a little breathless.

Hardegon crouched slightly to look Vanadis square on. He put his hands on her shoulders and gripped firmly. "A thrall, entrusted with a mission and sent away from her master. My Uncle obviously trusts you."

Then, in a harsher manner, he said, "Do not prove him wrong. If you do, you'll find the wealth in your hands poor compensation for what happens when I find you."

Vanadis nodded, "I need a cloth, to wrap them up. I don't want them to be stolen while I deliver them to Master."

"Very wise." Hardegon reached into his satchel and pulled out a canvas bag.

Vanadis took it and wrapped it tightly around Dorte's treasure.

"Hardegon, we'd best set sail." Called Skili.

"Give my uncle my best."

"Of course."

With that Hardegon turned and strode for his vessel. Vanadis turned the other way and walked back to Flosi and their boat.

"What was that about?" He asked.

"The Rogue's business. Let's head back to Kelifar."

***

As Flosi rowed, Vanadis sat in the bow gripping the canvas wrap that contained Dorte's circlets. Envy and guilt gnawed at her stomach as she stared across the dark ocean and the line of Kelifar in the distance. The 25 skatt they were given wasn't nearly enough to buy a hiding place and a living. The treasure she now held in the other hand?

These circlets were as much a symbol of freedom as any armband. Sell them in the right place, pay off the right people and she could be free. Free from Dorte's demands, free from the blott, free from a repeat of wretched history.

She was tempted, but the price, it was too high: Her brother.

She glanced over her shoulder at Flosi. She watched him row and pondered. If he had these, he'd flee. He'd be clever enough to sell them in the right place and live at ease. Vanadis pictured him, the King of Knaves, lying on wolf furs, wearing a tin crown and sipping wine, she couldn't help but grin.

Flosi turned to get a measure of land and caught Vanadis' smile. He smirked and mock posed. "Yes, you are right to admire. I am the strongest thrall in Alands."

Vanadis laughed. "Just get us to Kelifar without capsizing." She squeezed the circlets and banished the King of Knaves from her mind. If she couldn't save herself or her brother, there was no way she could save Flosi.

***

Steinarr admired the gold circlet in the light of the setting sun as it shone through the needle evergreen leaves. He sat on a stump, by a warm camp fire. On his lap was a short axe with a heavy head, one for felling men, not trees. At his belt was a velvet pouch.

Vanadis sat nearby on the edge of a bench made from other stumps and a smoothed log. She had finished her report, she had left nothing out. She wrung her hands fretfully.

They were in a small clearing surrounded by tightly clustered pine. A single path lead a long, stony twisty way back to the great hall.

Steinarr tucked the circlet away and turned to give Vanadis his full attention. "Tell me." he said, "You know why I wanted you to be discreet?"

Vanadis opened her mouth and Steinarr gestured for silence. "Tell me the truth. You play my daughter like hnefatafl, but that won't work on me."

"Yes, Master. I was to deal with this discretely because Hardegon's helping his brother Starkad. Starkad's stole a rune tablet from your brother, his father, jarl Truvor."

Steinarr nodded in approval. "Very good. Now tell me, what would be the best way to ensure no one else hears this?"

Vanadis gaze drifted down to his axe and shook her head, "Master, please don't. I swear I won't tell anyone."

Steinarr suddenly stood and hefted the weapon.

Vanadis cried and fell off her stump.

Steinarr, with a wicked grin on his face, stepped forward.

Vanadis fought through her fear, seized his leg and buried her face in his knee. "Please, Master, surely I've proven myself trustworthy?"

"Why don't you run, thrall?"

She gazed up at him in desperation. "Run? Where would I run to? Dorte would side with you, Asvard wouldn't protect me, and you'd just kill Gamli."

Steinarr snorted and then outright roared with laughter.

Vanadis regarded him with outright, stunned, incredulity.

He let his axe drop and patted Vanadis on the head. "At ease. I jest."

Vanadis turned her glare to the forest. Fury rose within her breast "A jest?"

Steinarr stat back on his stump and wiped tears from his eyes. "Aye, you should have seen your face."

Vanadis couldn't help but stare at the axe and picture it in Steinarr's back. She let out a trembling sigh, wiped away her own tears, and mastered herself.

"To be honest," the Karl said, regarding his thrall with a critical eye. "I had half a mind to kill you, but then, you gave me these." He held the two circlets.

He reached over and patted the bench. "Sit, I have a gift for you."

Vanadis obeyed.

Steinarr took the felt pouch from his hip. "You know well our custom of sacrifice to Freya on the anniversary of our victory over Kvistr Dusk Torch. Usually we sacrifice some hostage whose family failed pay a ransom. If we have no hostages, or all the ransoms are payed, then we make due with sacrificing one of our slaves." He beamed a smile at Vanadis "This year has been very good, a small fortune in ransoms."

"Yes, yes it has Master." Vanadis said, she had removed her fury from her tone.

Steinarr shook the bag. "24 thralls are in the lottery. We give each thrall a rune. When a Thrall's rune comes up he or she meets Freya, and a new thrall gets a rune. Hold out your hand."

Vanadis did so.

Steinarr carefully rummaged through the sack, pulled a small stone out form it, one at a time until he found the one he was looking for. He dropped it into Vanadis' hand, on it was carved ᚲ.

"Your brother is not in this sack." He pointed to the rune Vanadis held, "That one's yours." Steinarr caught Vanadis' gaze and said warmly, "You and your brother are still thralls but both of you are out of the lottery, and not just this year but every year, from now on."

Vanadis clutched the stone tightly. She smiled, "Thank you, master."

The jarl winked, "Keep this to yourself. Don't want to earn the ire of your peers." He stood. "Come, drinks won't pour themselves."

CHAPTER 2

To Valhalla, go the worthy dead.| All else must face Hel.
Her plate is hunger, her knife is famine, disease her bed.
I'll tell you a secret. | You don't have to face her.
You can live without skin and dine on hatred.

The autumn wind rustled evergreen branches.

Vanadis wore a fine wool overdress of purple, which was accented with gold turtle shaped brooches. Her long brown hair was bound in a thin golden chain. She'd never worn anything this regal. It felt right.

Walking beside her was an older woman who, aside from her age, was her mirror. "We're coming home and you must be polite." Vanadis' twin suddenly seized her wrist. "You must remember the laws of hospitality. It is vital." The woman glared with a cold fury. "We are very angry. If either of you transgress there will be no forgiveness."

Panicked, Vanadis yanked her arm away, turned and ran. Beyond the forest she spied the palisades and pushed for more speed. Vanadis broke through the tree line and immediately found herself before the Great Hall. She halted in confusion. How did she bypass the river bridge? She paled when she saw what was before her.

At the foot of the door was a black wolf's corpse. Its eyes were open and leering. Its tongue rolled out touching the ground. White rats swarmed it. All was silent except for the chewing of bloody flesh.

Vanadis watched in fascinated horror.

One by one, the rats dropped, until their bodies littered the wolf's hide.

***

Vanadis woke with a gasp, hand over her fast beating heart.

Golden haired Dorte sputtered awake. "Vanadis? How dare you wake me, and on the eve before the feast!?"

"My apologies, mistress. I had a nightmare." Vanadis whispered.

"You awaken me for that?"

"I had a dream of you, mistress. It was on your wedding night and you couldn't find your comb. Ingri had stolen it. I accused her and was thrashed for it." Vanadis seasoned the lie with fresh foreboding.

Dorte snorted at Ingri, who lay sleeping on a bench across the hall. She stroked Vanadis' hair. "You are a child. Go to sleep."

"Yes, mistress." Vanadis curled up on her place on the floor and pulled the thick blanket around her. She closed her eyes. She frowned and shivered. In her mind, all she could hear were the doomed rats smacking down wolf flesh.

Three sharp knocks echoed from the main doors. Dorte shot up. "What now?"

The hall began to murmur and the women began to rise.

Gerd lit an oil lamp and three more knocks could be heard. At the far end of the hall, a man bellowed "I'm opening the door. I have an axe. If this isn't important you'd best run."

The lamp light flickered. The women sat on their benches rubbing sleep from their eyes.

"By Frey!" exclaimed the same voice at the far end of the hall.

"Vanadis, my dress. I would meet this interloper."

The thrall leapt to her feet.

***

The hall's entrance bustled. Torches shone brightly. The dwellers crowded at the front.

"Out of my way this instant." The throng parted for Dorte and Vanadis. They both gaped at what they saw.

A majestic red stag. By far the largest creature Vanadis had ever seen. His very presence invoked a hush.

"What are you waiting for?" laughed Steinarr the Rogue. "Show him in, he's a guest." There was an awkward pause. "Well?" he prompted with a grin, "Show Lord Stag our Nibelung hospitality."

Aaran the Skunk, the stocky man by the door, chuckled and bowed before the beast. "Please enter, my lord bids it."

At that, the magnificent creature walked forward. The crowd made way. The animal sauntered in, walked around the smoldering fire pit, and sat at end of the entrance hall with a satisfied air.

"Vanadis fetch some mead. Gamli bring forth our finest apples. Everyone, up, get dressed. This is a gift from Freya." commanded the master of the house.

At their lord's behest the host rose, dressed and celebrated the stag as an honored guest. There was some apprehension but Steinarr's infectious laugh combined with mead loosened everyone's spirits.

Fiddle, horn and drum played. Dorte danced with handsome Sorli. Vanadis sat beside the stag holding up a dish from which he licked.

Soon enough, Gamli, her brother, arrived; he was dressed in his finest thrall clothes. He carried a golden plate, on which were five apple slices.

The stag turned from his drink and regarded the young man.

Gamli, in turn, regarded back with barely restrained outrage.

Vanadis kicked him in the shin.

Those watching chuckled.

"Why'd you do that?"

"Be polite." Vanadis hissed. She nodded to Master who watched them both with great amusement.

A flustered Gamli mastered himself. To the stag he said, "Here."

A flicker of judgement crossed the stag's face, he then nodded graciously and ate, crunching the crisp apple between his white teeth.

When the guest had finished, at his sister's nudging, Gamli asked, "Would you like more?"

The stag lifted his muzzle from the plate. Gamli glowered, but bowed and strode away.

Flosi, who'd been laughing heartily with the rest, threw his arm around Gamli. The two pushed through the cloth divider towards the back of the hall.

Steinarr casually took his long spear, approached his guest and asked "Are you satisfied Master Forest?"

To everyone's pleasure the stag nodded.

"On behalf of our entire household, I thank you for coming. The feast you bring will be enjoyed by all." The Rogue moved faster than Vanadis could comprehend. For the flash of a second she was vaguely aware of her master's spear point and then it was suddenly thrust into the breast of the beast. The rush of its passage brushed her nose.

The house gasped. Steinarr, with a fierce snarl drove the spear point deeper into the stag. Vanadis shrieked and fell off her stool. The stag let out a rumbling bellow and fell to his side.

The crowd roared in adulation at their lord's perfect strike. The thrall girl stared in fearful awe at the stag's expression. His eyes were wide, his lips pulled back into a manic, malevolent grin.

***

The next afternoon, Gamli and Vanadis strode away from the sacred alter with the rest of the town.

The crowd murmured excitedly; that night was the anniversary of Steinarr's victory over Kvistr Dusk Torch, when they won their town Kelifar. There would be a feast, with enough venison for all.

Behind them, laying on the altar, his throat slit, framed by the grey sky and rolling sea, was the corpse of Flosi.

Gamli had forced himself to watch, it was the only honor he could give. As did Vanadis, neither could hold back their tears. Yet they returned with the rest. Flosi's death was hard but he wasn't the only friend they'd lost to Freya.

Once they passed the gate Vanadis took Gamli's arm and pulled him along the wall. Once they were away from prying ears she whispered, "Whatever you do, do not eat any venison."

"What?" Gamli asked dryly.

"I'm serious." Vanadis pressed. "Don't even taste it."

Gamli pondered, put his hands on his sister's shoulder and said, "I heard Master nearly struck you when he killed the stag."

She shook him off, "That's not it. The stag was welcomed into our hall and then killed! Do you wish to be cursed?"

The young thrall thought on that further but said nothing.

"Just promise me," Vanadis huffed, "swear to me, on Flosi's name, that you won't eat any part of that creature. Please."

The worry and concern in her grey eyes, the way she took his hands and squeezed, it moved Gamli. "Alright, I swear." He answered gently. "But you owe me a meal."

Vanadis grinned, "Then we have a bargain." She kissed him on the cheek.

In the distance Dorte called for her.

"I better go. Stay out of trouble."

***

Vanadis finished Dorte's headdress by candlelight and sunset. It was a green kerchief with silver embroidery, with tiny rubies inlaid throughout.

Vanadis would attend the feast in only a simple green woolen dress.

They were in a 'dressing house.' Dorte never prepared for a feast in front of others, that way her very entrance would strike an impression.

Dorte had been telling Vanadis about her day. How she'd trounced Gerd soundly at hnefatafl. How Haeng was sore at losing such a clever thrall. How the thrall's death made that harlot Ingri most upset.

Vanadis responded with the expected 'of courses', 'serves her rights' and 'yes mistresses' while at the same time allowing her thoughts to drift. Rats tearing wolf flesh haunted her. The stag's leer followed her. A stone of guilt lay deep inside her. Several times that day she nearly shared her nightmare and misgivings with the Master or his daughter. Flosi's sorrow when he was picked, then, his gallows' smirk when he lay on the altar; these silenced her. Heavy rain splattered on the roof, echoing her gloom.

"Vanadis, you look pale. You're not sick, are you?"

The concern in Dorte's voice tugged the guilt deeper within Vanadis. She fought if off. Her dream was just enough nonsense to warn her brother way from the venison but not enough to show her mistress she was insane. "Forgive me, Flosi's death weighs heavily upon me." Which was truth enough.

"Flosi? Who's Flosi?"

"The offering, he was a dear friend of mine." Vanadis answered with a jagged tone.

Dorte stifled her gasp. "I see. My sincere condolences, if he was your friend I am certain that Freya finds him a most agreeable servant."

The thrall finished the last tie. Tucking the storm of emotions away she saidm "It is nearly time for the feast mistress. Do you wish to make haste?"

Dorte, regarded her for a moment and seemed to understand. She then stood dramatically "Yes, yes I do. Come Vanadis."

Vanadis draped Dorte's cloak over her shoulders and they headed for the celebration.

***

This victory feast was, by far, the most splendid yet.

The Great Hall was open to all and lit brightly with candles and torches. Across a huge table lay a cornucopia of food. Apples, berries, pork, seven different kinds of mead. The scent of venison, cooked to juicy perfection, hung in the air. Musicians played lively melodies. Head fishermen sat beside their lord. Aaran the Skunk, his beautiful wife and their seven children attended. Dorte danced with Sorli, much to Ingri's chagrin.

Outside, in the darkness, the wind howled, the sea crashed and sleet pelted the hall. However, this cold and fury were thwarted by music and the fire's warmth.

For Vanadis however, it was as if she were in Hel's Hall. When the venison was uncovered she muffled her stammer behind her hands and her eyes went wide. At the odd looks she stuttered, "I-I've just never seen anything like it." Which was true because, to her, the plate of venison was a clammy human torso with limbs clustered around it. When she was given her plate she thanked the server but refused to look at it directly. In the corner of her eye she spied tit was a heap of boiled fingers. When no one was looking she fed it to the dog. The celebration was a cannibal feast to her. Early on she excused herself and threw up outside, caring little for the storm.

She returned to a worried brother. "Are you okay?"

"Did you eat any of this?" she gestured to the corpse plate.

"No. I'd like to."

"Drive it out of your mind."

"What's wrong?"

"I..." Vanadis couldn't find the will to express her insanity, so she waved him off, found a dark corner, lay there and closed her eyes.

Before Gamli could enquire further young Petra seized his arm and pulled him off to dance.

Meanwhile Vanadis, in her self-imposed exile, struggled with horror and doubt. Perhaps it was she who was cursed?

Outside of her closed eye prison the music died down.

"Quiet, sit, sit." called Master Steinarr.

The hall hushed.

"Now it is time," Steinarr said solemnly "to tell of our victory over Kvistr Dusk Torch."

The smooth, deep voice of Skefill the Skald began:

"May the gods curse Kvistr and his Pohjalander brood. May Freyja, mistress of war and love, smile upon cunning Steinarr and his family.As she has smiled upon them before. I have witnessed it, the works of our Karl and Freyja's bounty.
The victory that won us Kelifar.

Kvistr Dusk Torch. Whose locks were like fire.
Killed Visin Hamalson in a daring raid.
Visin was a hated fool. At his death the Jarl laughed.
Kvistr was given Visn's Kelifar in jest.

A jest he forged into a prize. He wrung great wealth from of our land.
Steinarr offered him fair price for Kelifar, rightfully a Nibelung hold.
Kvistr was wrongful and greedy. He laughed in our Lord's face.
Clever Steinarr laughed along, and plotted justice for the slight.

Steinarr returned to Kelifar. Kvistr saw him not.
Steinarr wore the finery of a merchant prince.
He sold valued goods. While he marked Kvistr's defenses.
With Kvistr's gold he secured traitor thralls, weapons and men to oppose.

Steinarr bought a gleaming sword. He brought it to Mjoll the Gentle.
Mjoll, Maiden of Sif, Lady of peace.
She blessed the blade. The blessing was a curse.
As bright as the blade shone, it would cut not.

Steinarr once again became the merchant. He was welcomed into Kvistr's hall.
He showed the master the blade so bright.
Kvistr was enthralled. He and his hidden foe bargained for the blade.
The blade fetched a hefty sum, which Steinarr slotted for Kvistr's funeral.

On the next sunset Steinarr knocked on Kelifar's gates. His bought thralls let him in.
Steinarr charged the hall and Kivstr's guards cried alarm.
Steinarr confronted his foe spear in hand. Kvistr swung his blade so bright.
It passed across Steinarr like a pleasant breeze, it was the fool's…"

Skefill coughed, as if to clear his throat.

"It was the fool's…" his voice croaked before he finished his words.

Vanadis opened one eye.

Steinarr glared at the skald, but suddenly, he himself coughed. He then brought a hand to his throat and wheezed.

Then everyone in the hall began to choke. Their ragged hissing cries of alarm shrinking to silence.

The storm rattled the very walls of the hall.

Vanadis stood and caught Gamli's fearful glance. His chest heaved, he could breathe.

The rest couldn't. Dishes, cups, chairs and plates were knocked and scattered as the revelers silently convulsed. Those not wrapped in their own struggles clutched their breathless children who shed terrified tears.

Vanadis saw Dorte fall. Without thinking the thrall rushed to her.

The young woman, who was the same age as Vanadis, held her throat, her eyes bulging.

"Dorte." Vanadis gasped.

Dorte mouthed silent pleas. Vanadis took her hand, it was cold and she was quivering.

"I'm sorry." Vanadis said in a trembling voice. "I wanted to warn you but I though you wouldn't believe me. I didn't know it'd be this bad."

Dorte looked scared and hurt. Her face turned purple. Vanadis' heart flooded with regret and she hugged her mistress to her.

***

Gamli watched in numb shock. Did Vanadis do this? How? Why? He surveyed the hall. Hale warriors, farmers, thralls, children, most had fallen off their seats and many lay still.

He spied Master Steinarr, his face a purple mask of rage. He seized his spear and glared at Vanadis who held his dead child to her.

Gamli snatched a knife and called out, "It wasn't her."

Steinarr the Rogue glanced at him incredulously.

"You were poisoned, I turned the spit." Gamli lied, poorly.

However the jarl sought one to blame and Gamli would do. Steinarr charged, the storm's howl seeming to express his fury. The great spear thrust at Gamli, but lack of breath slowed Steinarr's strike. Gamli knocked it aside and jabbed the knife deep into his master.

Steinarr collapsed upon him, his eyes wide, his strength spent.

"I'm sorry." Gamli said in a trembling voice. "I don't know what's going on." Steiner's last look was one of hate, then he fell and lay still.

Gamli let his master drop, but kept the long spear in hand. His gaze was fixed at the falling sleet through the opened great doors. The city gates were also open revealing the dark, rolling sea in the distance. The town's thrashing ceased. Gamli didn't look upon them, still as they were he knew they were not at peace.

In a deadpan, he asked "Vanadis, you didn't do this. Did you?"

"Nibelung Filth!" Vanadis' voice was laced with another's, that of an older woman's.

Gamli turned. His sister had stepped through Dorte's neck. The girl's head rolled off somewhere. Vanadis' foot was drenched in blood. Vanadis' hair fell into her face, her shoulders were hunched.

"Mice! Rats! Worms! You've died like vermin you are." She cackled.

"Sister?" Gamli croaked.

Suddenly she was in his face, her icy hands on his cheeks.

"Oh son." Vanadis crooned, caressing him in her iron grip. "Oh my dear Gamli, how you've grown. You've outshine these rodents by far."

Suddenly she was at the door.

"Come, come with me. Join your sister and I. Be welcome at my table, as you were meant to be." With that she raced out into the storm.

Stunned Gamli watched her go, right out the gate and heading towards the sea.

He shook himself out of his stupor. He threw a gray cloak around his shoulders, seized a lantern and kept the long spear in hand. In the distance he could see the green blur of his sister's dress through the sleet.

"Vanadis!" he cried. "I'm coming!" and with that, he shot off in pursuit.

CHAPTER ⌐

A child is born. | A mother loves her.
Family draws close to protect their own.
But don't rely on this. | Hearts can change
Especially after the flesh rots and malice remains

Sleet pelted Gamli has he rushed out of the hall and slowed him as he raced down the hill. The halls on either side of the road were lifeless, the entire town had attended the feast. All human voices were silent. Finally Gamli reached the docks. He held his lantern against the storm and saw a figure standing waist deep in the frigid, rolling surf.

"Vanadis?"

The reply was a guttural ragged moan.

Gamli stepped into the water. He felt the sharp cold stab up his leg. His light revealed his sister's mousey brown hair, the tips floating on the water. She stood rigged and silent.

Images of the recent dead flooded his mind. Dorte's hideous bug eyed gaze. Asvard's corpse holding dear Petra. The dead weight of his master on his shoulders. Gamli gripped the spear lowering so it pointed at Vanadis' back.

"Please." He had no idea what he was pleading for. That she'd come back? That he'd wake up? That the ragged fear and grief inside him would vanish?

"No, no, no, no, no, no.", Vanadis sobbed without turning. "It wasn't me, it wasn't me."

Gamli dropped the spear and swept his sister up. She let out a horrifying shriek and thrashed in his arms. Her elbows struck him in the ribs. The back of her head smashed into his nose and it crunched. She kicked and thrashed with a fury he'd never seen. But he still held on, his eyes squeezed tight, in silent prayer to any being willing to ease his sister.

Suddenly she went limp.

"Let's get out of here." Gamli carried her out of the frigid water.

***

Vanadis slowly rose out of chaos. Sharp grief, burning wrath, the cold grip of loneliness, bitter envy, these had stirred in her with such ferocity she was lost. Glimpses of conciseness flashed: the smooth feel of Dorte's hair. The sole of her foot suddenly wet and sticky. Sleet cutting into her skin. Floating in ice water. The strong arms of her brother. These chained together as a thought, with this mental anchor Vanadis found her way back to herself.

Her cheek rested against rough stone, she smelt moss.

"Welcome daughter, you're almost home." said a chilling voice.

Vanadis opened her eyes and pushed herself up. She was back in her purple dress. She felt a circlet on her head. A gold chain was around her neck. It was bright day and she was before the open doors of the Great Hall. The crowd before her was strange, she only recognized one person.

Her older twin. She was dressed the same but her manner was different. The way she stood with her hands folded before her, the way her grey eyes, whose corners were wrinkled, settled on her; she had the bearing of a queen.

Beside her was man, he was a head taller than anyone else in the crowd. Over his fine brown tunic, he wore a black wolf fur cloak. His eyes were bright blue. His hair and beard were wild, thick and the lightest red Vanadis had ever seen. His smile was welcoming but had a certain sorrow to it.

The rest of the crowd were hale warriors and townsfolk. They had a sturdy manner, as if they'd just came in from a hard day's work. There was something off about them though, a low level threat, as if they were secretly muggers.

Vanadis stood and regarded them with thoughtful caution.

Her twin opened her arms, "Come, and embrace me like you did when you were a babe."

Vanadis held up her hand to signal patience, "I beg a moment." The woman's words clicked in her mind and Vanadis focused on her, "You held me as a babe...You're my mother?"

Mother's smile grew a little tighter, she refolded her hands. "Who else could I be? You're obviously addled. Take a breath but tarry not. I've waited long enough."

Vanadis' mind raced as she took everything in. The moss was too green, the sky was too blue, the air too still. Without speech all was silent. Vanadis pinched herself.

"Oh this is quite real." Mother said, "Not only real but right." she gestured for Vanadis to step forward, "You and your brother were always meant to be with us."

"Gamli's here?"

After an awkward pause mother answered, "Not yet, but soon. Come, embrace your father."

The giant opened his arms, his smile became slightly warmer. Vanadis took a longer look, the way the sunlight shone off his hair, it contrasted sharply with the darkness of the hall behind him. "Kvistr Dusk Torch." she gasped. Her thoughts laced together like a weave. All at once she remembered the long stares of the older free men upon her. She recalled how Master tormented her. Skili's words 'If you're ever tired of this life ask your master about your mother', echoed in her mind.

She wasn't born a thrall. Anger slowly boiled up from the pit of her stomach. Her grey eyes flashed with fury. She clenched her fists with such force that her nails bit into her palm.

Her mother chuckled. "Yes, now you understand. I hid you and Gamli with our thralls but as you can see you take after me. Steinarr's no fool, he's known who your parents are for a long time. Yet, rather than foster or kill you he kept you as his property. You were supposed to be a free woman but he ground you under his heel." Her voice turned to mocking sympathy, "Poor dear."

"I'm not his anymore." Vanadis said, swallowing her rage.

"No," her mother said pleasantly. "You're ours, it's time you took your rightful place." She pointed to a spot directly beside her.

Vanadis glanced into the hall but stood her ground. The inside was pitch, a vast nothing. A thought struck her, "Mother, why are you the only one who speaks?"

Mother sighed impatiently. "That doesn't matter, Vanadis come."

Those words, like commanding a dog. The former thrall stood her ground. "No."

"Wretched child, do you think you have a choice?" Suddenly, the hall, the hill, and all of Kelifar melted away to reveal the void. Vanadis' twin became gaunt, her eyes rolled back, her skin shrank and ripped and her jaw dropped like a corpse in a tomb. It let out a husky howl, a skeletal hand reached out and Vanadis felt invisible fingers grip her throat.

Vanadis grasped at where the wrist should be but felt nothing. She clutched her throat, a spike of fear running through her. She remembered the silent death of the townsfolk. She'd only be able to get a few words out. She stood, struggling and thought. Finally, she wheezed, "Mother, what about your legacy?"

"It's gone. There's only wrath now." The ghost's hanging jaw did not move, the voice came from somewhere deep inside the corpse.

"Mother please, you still have me, and Gamli." Vanadis gasped. Then her voice was cut off.

Suddenly she was dropped, the pressure on her neck eased and Vanadis gulped in blessed air.

"Stupid child. They'll blame you for this. You'll have the entire wretched Nibelung clan after you. What kind of legacy is your early demise?"

Vanadis glared up at her corpse mother, "Would you have an outlaw legacy or none at all?"

The corpse hung still an ominous silence wrapped around it like a cloak.

Vanadis stood and smoothed out her dress. "At worse your right, we'll soon die and join you. So what harm in letting us live for now? ", she smirked knowingly at her mother, "Besides, if you're wrong, is it really so bad to lead the Nibelung on a chase?"

Mother's flesh rolled back into place, her corpse stench wafted away, in moments she was once again Vanadis' twin. She chuckled. "Yes, that would do nicely. I will allow it." After a moment of thought she locked eyes with her daughter and added "When you leave Kelifar do not fight the current, we'll take you to Mjoll, and it's about time she did something useful."

***

Vanadis woke with a gasp. She found herself on a sheep skin rug, clad only in thick wool blankets that were wrapped around her. She lay before a fire pit, the flames were low, flickering but still warm. Glancing around she recognized the hall, it belonged to the fishermen, nets above and dried fish was stocked in the shelves.

"Vanadis." she was suddenly in her brother's embrace. "You were like a corpse; I thought I'd lost you." he said with shaking breath.

"I'm fine." She hugged him back, her voice was ragged and dry, "Brother, could I have some water?"

"Of course."

A moment later, Vanadis slowly sipped cool water. It eased her throat. She looked at Gamli. His festive clothes, really just a tan shirt and breeches, were scuffed and dirty. His red hair and beard were a mess. There were bags under his blue eyes. He sat on the ground and hugged his legs, as if that was all he could do to stay upright.

While she finished her water Vanadis silently went through the entity of last night. She recalled everything, expect for leaving the hall. "How did I..., no first", she gestured to the benches, "you sit."

"Vanadis, what was this all of that about?"

The young woman snorted, "You're asking me?" Gamli's glare had steel, he was in no mood for jests. Vanadis gestured to the bench again, "Sit. We'll figure out it together."

Once they were both sitting and once Vanadis ensured Gamli had wrapped a blanket around himself, they talked. Vanadis told the entirety of her part, she was concise but held nothing back. Her tidings did not sit well with her brother. He turned and stared into the fire with a look of dull terror and heart ache.

Now that she had said it, the events caught up with her, the numbness gave way to sharp bitterness. The pleading, hurt look in Dorte's eyes. Asvard holding Petra as they died. The children thrashing for life. She tried to speak but choked on her own tears. Covering her face she sobbed into her hands. Gamli embraced her and she hugged him tight, crying into his tunic. His own chest heaved but he controlled his tears.

When she had finished Vanadis leaned on the wall and Gamli composed himself.

"Tell me, brother, how did we get down here?" She asked.

"We can't sleep in the hall." He glanced up in the direction of the hill. "Not with all them, there."

"I don't remember leaving." Vanadis pressed. "Nor undressing myself."

"You were soaked." Gamli replied his tone suggesting to leave it at that.

Vanadis stood and huffed, "Fine, gather what you can. We're going."

"Going?" Gamli asked with a start. "We can't leave them like that."

"Oh, can't we?" Vanadis laughed, suddenly seizing on something to drive her onward. "They were perfectly fine leaving us as thralls."

"Asvard treated me like a son!" Gamli roared. "And Petra, we can't leave her..."

A dozen cutting observations about Asvard came to the tip of Vanadis' tongue. Yes, a son he worked like a dog. Yes, a son he might free one day. Yes, a son whose sister was slapped around by 'father's' friends. She swallowed those memories and harsh words. Still under his glower she sighed and turned towards the door, the morning sunlight streamed through it. "If we delay jarl Truvor's men will find us. When they do they'll blame us. We'll die agonizing deaths. We have to go Gamli." Gamli stared at the floor clearly torn, "The jarl will ensure Asvard and Petra have a good funeral, we can't give them that. I don't want to leave without you. Please."

He stared up at her, his expression hard, but only for a moment. "Get dressed. I'll get supplies."

Vanadis pulled on some fisher woman's clothes. As humble as they were they were finer than anything she had ever worn. She felt a pang of guilt tying on the boots, in old Kelifar she'd have been beaten for daring to wear them. She briefly held a neck-lass of bronze that had glass beads pressed in a cat's visage, a symbol of Freya. She frowned and put it back, the Goddess may disfavour her already, best not rub salt into the slight. "I'm ready, let's go."

Gamli had dressed himself in heavy tunic and breeches. He wore a thick cloak and thick mitts. He carried a full pack off one shoulder and handed another to his sister. He glanced her up and down appraisingly.

"Don't look at me like that, you're stealing clothes as well."

Gamli seized a black cloak from a peg and another pair of mitts and handed them to her. "Keep warm." He urged. Then, grabbing a spear he rushed out the door, Vanadis followed.

***

Early morning Kelifar was abandoned, not even her cats greeted the siblings as they stepped out. They had all wandered to the Great Hall where a feast of flesh was set for them.

"This way." Vanadis lead Gamli to the boat she and Flosi used two days before.

Gamli regarded the other boats and scratched his beard. "Good choice." Vanadis hopped in and he pushed it out into the dark, cold water. Hopping in the back he seized the oars. "Where are we going?"

Vanadis considered this, then, she answered, "Follow the current, I think that'll take us to Mjoll the Gentle."

"Right, 'mother's' suggestion." Gamli spat.

"Don't take that tone with her." Vanadis hissed. Leaning in she whispered, "She might still be here."

Gamli fell into silence and rowed.

CHAPTER 4

History is just words. | Scratched in souls by victor swords.
Its weight is light because everyone ignores it.
This is foolish. | For every cut bleeds.
When enough blood gathers you drown in it.

Gamli rowed with the current and it pulled him northwards. They made good speed and passed a number of small islands, all of them covered in a crust of ice from last night's storm. The weather was cold but clear.

Morning gave way to noon and they soon were within calling distance of a small, rocky island on which stood a hall. The Great Hall of Kelifar was much larger and sturdier than this. However, this hall was more beautiful. Its wooden walls were spotless, her roof was in prefect repair. A dock connected to a grand stairway, which led to the hall's threshold. On each side of the open door hung two tapestries. On the right, framed in a blue sky, was the Goddess Sif, her golden hair falling across her shoulders, she held a basket of bread and fruit. To the left was red haired Thor, thunder clouds loomed behind him and he held Mjölnir aloft. Smoke wafted from the chimney and a haunting voice echoed out, she sang noon praises to kind hearted Sif.

Gamli paused in his rowing to glance over his shoulder. Vanadis pulled off her hood to get a better look and share in his awe. The wholesome nature of this place lifted the previous night's sorrows. The current stilled.

"We should dock." Vanadis suggested in a whisper.

"Aye." Gamli put his back into rowing.

As they got closer they saw a handful of servants sifting about. They were to the right of the hall, searching the ground carefully. One of them spied their approach and nudged his elderly cohort. The old woman nodded and carefully walked down the stairs to greet them.

"One of them's coming down." remarked Vanadis.

"Do you have a plan?" asked Gamli.

Vanadis frowned, and thought. Finally she said, "Sif is Goddess of Hearth and Home, if we ask to spend the night they'll allow it. We start with that."

"Fine by me."

Vanadis sat up further in the bow and called out, "Hoy! We're travellers looking for a place to stay. Will your mistress welcome us?"

The old thrall glanced up. When she saw Vanadis, she staggered and fell, gripping the railings was the only thing the saved her.

"Gamli, get us there faster, that grandmother's going to fall."

Gamli heaved on the oars.

"Stay there! We'll help you."

The old woman screamed and fled up the stairs on her own, at remarkable speed. "It's Hanne!", she shrieked, "Stop searching the field, Hanne's over there! Get Mistress, get Vinglunr! Run!"

Her cohort, a man with grey hair, glanced at her as if she had lost her mind. She gripped his shoulder and pointed at the siblings. They were at the dock and looking up at them in confusion. The old man jumped and shouted "It's true. Into the hall. Mistress! She's come!"

"Should we go back?" asked Gamli.

Vanadis stepped on the dock, curiosity's hooks in her. "No, I want to see what this is about."

"Very well." Gamli jumped on the dock and loosely tied the boat to it. Before Vanadis could ascend he held her back, "No sister. I go first."

Vanadis glared at him.

"No arguments." He hefted his spear and paused, testing its weight, pondering.

"Take it but don't point it at anyone... unless you have to." Vanadis urged.

Gamli nodded and slowly started his climb. Vanadis followed carefully. Above they could hear an excited and fearful murmur. The prayer song had ceased. They could hear bits of conversation "It's her." "Pohjalander brood at the oars." "Calm." "Sif is with us." "Thor protect us."

When Gamli had almost reached the top he motioned for Vanadis to stay. She didn't look happy but held the railing tighter. Gamli walked up carefully and said, "Hello?"

"Greetings, stranger, why do you approach Sif's house with a spear in hand?" The voice was that of an older woman's, it bespoke authority. Vanadis, from her vantage, could see only her brother and rocky cliff.

Gamli dropped the spear. "I-I was afraid we'd be attacked."

"We're the ones who are fearful. Why have you summoned the dead, Necromancer? " cried the old woman from before.

"Easy Ragnhildr..." it was the rich baritone of a young man.

"We saw her with our own eyes, Hanne was with him."

"Only my sister's here." eased Gamli. "She's usually harmless."

Vanadis lightly punched him in the leg. He held the railing to keep balance and glared down at her, "Will you..."

The matriarch giggled. "Let her come up then. Both of you are welcome."

Gamli nodded to the top of the stairs. "You heard her."

When Vanadis reached the top the old thrall who first spotted her covered her mouth and whined in terror. Her companion paled.

The matriarch was as tall and graceful as an old willow. The corners of her grey eyes and thin lips were wrinkled but she wore long golden hair that drifted lightly past her shoulders. She wore a silver circlet. Her elegant dress was blue and white. She was draped in a dove feather cloak. When she saw Vanadis her expression turned to one of shock and sorrow. She staggered but then steeled herself, and levelled a steady eye on her.

Beside her was young man who had pitch black hair and beard. He was fine featured with deep brown eyes. He wore fine garb of green. He also sported a thick knotted leather belt and a worn brown cloak with gold trim, at his side hung a short sword. No fearful recognition lit his face.

Four shield maidens stood beside the matriarch, shields at ready, axes in hand.

The dark handsome one touched the matriarch on the elbow and asked, "Is this is this truly her? Your sister? "

Vanadis had observed their reactions and the truth had come to her. "Hanne was our mother." she explained. "I look very much like her."

Suddenly Gamli stared at the great lady with wonder, "You're our aunt?"

Mjoll signalled her people to stay where they were. She walked over to Vanadis, her keen grey eyes looking inquiring over her. Vanadis was about to say something but Mjoll lifted a hand for silence. She cupped Vanadis' cheek and turned her head. She took Vanadis' hand and rubbed the callouses on her fingers. She stepped over to Gamli and touched his cheek, running her fingers through his beard. She traced his muscular arm. He stood and accepted the prodding with a curious but patient smile. Mjoll stepped back and took in the two of them.

She folded her hands, squeezed her eyes shut, and tears rolled down her cheeks. "It's true. These are Kvistr's and Hanne's children. They are my niece and nephew."

The crowd murmured in surprise.

Mjoll opened her eyes, steadied herself and asked, "Have you come for revenge?"

Vanadis titled her head in confusion.

Gamli flinched. "N-no. Why would we?" He stepped forward and grasped her hands, his manner holding great respect. "We need your help. Will you hear us?"

Mjoll's smile was one of joy out of sorrow. "Of course I will, please come inside"

The shieldmaidens belted their axes and lowered their shields. The freemen cheered. The thralls went inside to prepare a meal.

Vanadis however, looked troubled.

Steinarr bought a gleaming sword. He brought it to Mjoll the Gentle.
Mjoll, Maiden of Sif, Lady of peace.
She blessed the blade. The blessing was a curse.
As bright as the blade shone, it would cut not.

She didn't notice the young man spotted her look and regarded it with suspicion.

Minutes later, they were in the Mjoll's hall. It was clean and cozy. The fire pit was lit and Ragnhildr stirred a stew pot, occasionally staring at Vanadis. Gamli sat on one side of his aunt and Vanadis sat on the other.

The dark young man seized a stool and sat across from them. Gamli offered his hand, "You're my cousin? I'm Gamli, this my sister is Vanadis."

The young man shook with a firm grip. "Vinglunr, Hanne's ward." he answered politely.

"I consider him a son." Mjoll cut in. "Now, before we do anything, tell me of yourselves. Until today I thought you both killed, slain by Steinarr the Rogue."

Gamli suddenly turned anxious. "It's not a nice story..."

"You've had a hard life then?" Mjoll asked hesitantly.

"Are you familiar with the poem Kelifar Won?" Vanadis started.

"Not the words but I know the story all too well..." Mjoll answered, ill at ease.

"Then allow me to fill you in on what you don't know..." Vanadis told their story with attention and deliberation, measuring Mjoll's reactions carefully. She started with their lives as thralls, unaware of who their parents were. She mentioned how Steinarr must have known, when she did the matriarch smouldered with silent indignation. Then she discussed her first dream about Hanne and left nothing out, describing the dream in prefect detail. The house stopped its work to listen. Mjoll didn't look at Vanadis, but held a thoughtful attentiveness to her words. Vanadis continued with the terrifying events of the festival night. Faces paled, a few servants and free men left the hall. Mjoll gripped her dress and endured. Vinglunr was about to call an end but Gamli interceded and Vanadis skipped over the most terrible parts. She then went over the last dream she had with her mother ending with, "So she suggested we come here. We shall be blamed for the death of Kelifar. As a famed healer and holy woman we beg you to clear our names, failing that please grant us sanctuary."

Mjoll was lost in grief and guilt but when Vanadis made her plea her demeanour strengthened. "Sif's Hall is open to all. You and your brother are especially welcome. Your sanctuary is granted."

Both siblings sighed with relief.

Ragnhildr had finished the stew and offered it to hostess and visitors, Mjoll gestured for her to hold. She stood, "Please follow there is something you must see."

Vanadis and Gamli stood. Vinglunr stood by his foster mother. Together they walked out of the Hall.

As they did the old man thrall approached, he carried a skull in his hands. "My lady I..." he paused at seeing their guests.

"It's alright," said Mjoll. Gesturing to the skull, she added "Vanadis, Gamli, your mother."

Gamli took a step back. Vanadis brought her hand to her mouth, to her the old servant was holding Hanne's severed head.

"Please understand, we don't not mean for my kin's remains to be littered across the island but last night," she shook her head, "last night Hanne broke out of the barrow and scattered the bones of her husband and followers. Alof and the others have been gathering them all day."

"This is the last one." Alof reported.

"Let us put her to rest." Said Hanne. The four, with the small crowd of servants, walked to the back of the hall. They followed a narrow path along the rocky ground and through a small copse of pines. In the centre they was a large barrow, a man-made hill of earth. A door lead into its pitch interior. Before the door was a pile of rocks, it looked as if it had filled the entrance but was kicked down from the inside.

Mjoll reached out and a thrall handed her a lit lantern. Alof handed her the skull. She turned to look at the siblings and asked, "Do you wish to pay your respects?"

Vanadis stared into the dark entrance way, she saw shapes moving inside and froze.

Mjoll noted this and said gently to her niece, "It's alright, Vanadis. You've seen enough of Hanne already. You don't have to come in. Gamli? Do you wish to pay your respects?"

Gamli looked torn between his sister's terror and the barrow.

"I swear he'll be safe." Mjoll said to Vanadis.

Vanadis pushed Gamli forward. "Then, go, you want to, no?"

"But sister..."

"I'll be fine." Vanadis insisted. "A-as long as I don't go in there."

Gamli squeezed his sister's shoulder and nodded in thanks. With that he, Mjoll, and Vinglunr entered the barrow.

***

They took several steps down and found the interior was constructed of wood and stone. The air was old and musty. Benches were fitted on the walls, on these lay neat piles of bones with skulls placed on top. Small wooden chests sat underneath the bench underneath each pile of bone. On two altars lay two oak coffins. A dark pine table, with polished wooden bowls and cutlery, sat at the heads of the coffins. Larger, ornate chests sat at the foot of each altar.

Gamli walked, with reverence, to the coffins. "Our parents?" he asked.

"Yes." Mjoll walked towards the coffins, "This is your father Kvistr Dusk Torch." She touched the one on the right. "This is your mother and my sister, Hanne the Clever." She touched the one on the left. She handed Gamli her lantern and opened the coffin., "Here you go dear." She gently placed the skull inside.

They stayed as long as it took for Gamli to pay his respects.

***

The three exited the barrow to return to the bright noon sun. As soon as they passed the threshold servants galvanized quickly to piling up the rocks to fill in the barrow door.

"Well, how did it go?" asked Vanadis, a little more at ease now that the grave was being sealed.

Gamli considered the question for a long moment and answered, "We had parents. We have family. It couldn't go any better." He was near tears.

Vanadis dried the corner of his eyes and regarded Hanne over his shoulder. "That we do."
***

Mjoll guided everyone back to the hall. There the siblings were served a hearty stew, thankfully not venison. They were also given warm cider. Mjoll questioned them no further. Vinglunr ate quickly and picked on his lyre filling the hall with calming music. Gamli sat with Mjoll and questioned her about Kvistr and Hanne. Vanadis ate a little and drained the cider. Sleep pulled at her conciseness, but she strove to keep herself awake, the malevolently smiling visage of her mother fresh in her mind.

Mjoll approached her. "Vanadis, you're exhausted - you must rest."

"No," answered her niece, grabbing Mjoll's sleeve. "Hanne will come for me."

Mjoll took Vanadis' hand and held it comfortingly. "Worry not. This hall is warded against evil, my sister can't bother you here. Ragnhildr, please see that she rests in my chamber."

"Yes, Mistress." Ragnhildr helped Vanadis to her feet, "Please come with me." The thrall brought her through two cloth dividers to the back of the hall. She then helped Vanadis out of her clothes and dressed her in a linen gown. "There you go, dear." Ragnhildr helped the young woman into the bed.

Vanadis' hit the pillow and she immediately drifted off to sleep. She dreamed but Hanne had no part in it. She ran once more at Dorte's beck and call. Her brother once again toiled at the forge. Flosi said ridiculous thing that brought a smile to her lips. The victory festival was upon them but they were at ease, one of the hostage ransoms wasn't paid so he'd be going to the altar instead of them. Gamli danced with Petra, Sorli with Dorte. Vanadis was content to sit and play hnefatafl with Gerd. The doors to the Great Hall opened and Vanadis woke up.

***

The pillow, the fox fur underneath her, the woollen blanket over her. In Master's bed? How? If she was found out...

"Ah you're awake." Said Ragnhildr who'd been busy folding sheets. "Breakfast's finished but we saved you some. Your aunt is offering sacrifice to Sif in thanks to you and your brother's return."

Guilt stabbed at her and Vanadis blurted, "Surely not one of you?"

Ragnhildr looked stunned, and then she laughed. "Of course... you were brought up with Steinarr. No, Mjoll would never sacrifice any of us. If she did you think I'd have reached this age?"

"No, I suppose not." Vanadis said with a sigh.

"We did lose a fine lamb. At any rate, up with you. I'll draw you a bath and then get you some proper clothes."

Vanadis slid off the bed looking ill at ease. Proper clothes, someone drawing her a bath? She pinched herself. "Ow."

Ragnhildr shook her head, "It's not all that rosy. For one, you won't be sleeping there again. This'll be your place." she patted a spot on a nearby bench.

Vanadis smirked, it beat the floor by a long shot. "Oh, how shall I ever survive?" she laughed.

The bath was wonderful. Ragnhildr noticed that Vanadis' ears weren't pierced, she offered Malin's expertise in doing so. Vanadis agreed. The process was short and painful but she ended up sporting garnet studs. Her hair was braided. She was then given a fine dress of light blue, new leather shoes, and draped in a darker blue cloak. Her breakfast was the left over stew, cold but somehow that made it taste even better.

Outside the hall, she could hear cheering, music, and laughter. "What's going on?"

Ragnhildr slid a silver bracelet on Vanadis' wrist and answered "A celebration, for your return."

Vanadis smirked, "You've moved past the terror, then?"

The thrall chuckled, "We were never terrified of you; we were terrified of your mother. You look much like her but we like your manner more."

"Why thank you." Vanadis said, rather pleased.

***

They stepped outside to find a small fair grounds. Mjoll sat on a dark ornate chair. Several women attended her but also watched the proceedings with equal interest. The men had laid down some old sails in the centre of them stood Gamli. He was shirtless and his powerful body was sweat soaked. On his right arm was a gold band that curled around it like a serpent. He had just thrown out of the sail boarder, a dark haired free man. He roared with laughter and victory. The crowd cheered.

"You're not champion yet." said Vinglunr was he stepped into Gamli's domain. While Vinglunr carried himself as a Skald, his physique spoke of a warrior and even boasted a few scars.

Mjoll caught Vanadis' look at her foster son. "Every few years Curonian pirates threaten this house. Sif favours strong warriors, Vinglunr has won many battles."

Gamli and Vinglunr circled each other. They locked in struggle and the crowd surrounding them cheered. Vanadis did as well but she didn't call out to Gamli specifically, she didn't want to distract him. Gamli was bigger than Vinglunr, he also looked stronger. Before he could toss the skald, Vinglunr stepped out of his grip, to his side and heaved with his shoulder. With a cry, Gamli stumbled a few steps and Vinglunr charged, he connected hard with Gamli and he flew off the sails. The men on that side of the ring caught him. The crowd roared and applauded.

Vinglunr bowed to Mjoll, when he rose his eyes rested on Vanadis.

"By Frey." Gamli huffed, "my sister's an actual lady, who knew?"

"You've proven yourself a bore." Vanadis shot back.

"Enough you two." Mjoll giggled. "Gamli, congratulate Vinglunr on his victory."

"Aye," Gamli gripped his arm in friendship, "you won."

Vinglunr reciprocated. "Indeed, but only after you bested everyone else in our house."

The day drew on. Races and ball games were played. Vanadis lost to Mjoll soundly at hnefatafl. Vinglunr told tales of the Aesir; how Odin stole the mead of poetry, how Loki cut Sif's locks only to replace them with true golden tresses. He told of the victories of Bjorn Eriksson over Harald Fair Hair. Gamli and Vanadis asked for tales of the Vanir. Vinglunr obliged with tales of the trouble Freya and Ordr got into and out of. He ended with the story of Frey's wooing of Gerda. His deep voice, the strum of his lyre, the passion he held for these old tales drew the denizens of the hall close. Ragnhildr was forced to have the thralls work in shifts for they would not stand to miss all the stories. The sun was setting by the time he finished.

"It's time to eat." declared Mjoll. "Our small island can't offer you the grand affair of Kelifar but I hope it suffices."

"I'm certain it will." Gamli said with heartfelt honesty

"You're too good to us Mjoll." Vanadis added.

"I have every reason to be." Mjoll answered, a slight shadow of painful memories crossing her face. "Come, let's have dinner and after we can talk of more serious things."

***

The entire hall gathered and shared a delicious meal of smoked beef, fine cheese, dried honeyed apples, and mead. Mjoll cautioned the siblings not to drink too much, they had a serious talk coming.

Late that night, Mjoll, Vinglunr, Gamli, and Vanadis sat in the back of the hall. The thralls, servants were pushed out. Two shieldmaidens stood guard on the other side of the divider.

Mjoll pushed her mug aside, a serious expression on her worn face. "Before we talk, I have something weighing my heart. Gamli, Vanadis, the tale of my involvement in your parent's deaths is true. I cursed the sword Steinarr sold to your father. The one that wouldn't cut, it led to his death."

Vinglunr watched the two carefully. Both siblings glance at each other, Gamli was the first to speak. "I-I wished to believe the story was false. You seem too good."

"You are too good. Did my mother drive you to it?" Vanadis asked.

"No, no." Mjoll answered. "You mother was a very different person when she was alive. How I wish you could have met her then. I'll get to that but first, my part in Steinarr's victory...He and Kvistr hated each other so. Steinarr attacked him openly three times and was always repelled. It lead to so many deaths. Steinarr came to me and begged for help in settling a truce." Mjoll turned down her gaze, ashamed. "He was very charming. He convinced me he wanted peace but was afraid Kvistr would strike him down. He told me of his plan to get a blade into Kvistr's hand, one that wouldn't hurt him should Kvistr become enraged. It would give Steinarr time to ease his fury. So I asked for Sif's blessing and the blade was enchanted. Steinarr lied and you two know so well the results."
Then, in a determined tone, she added, "I am resolved to help you in any way I can, no matter what. But something, has plagued me, there is one thing I must know." She glanced at her nephew and niece, tears beading at the corners of her eyes. "Can you ever forgive me? For the part I played in killing your parents, and also for allowing myself to be ignorant of your survival. I know foolishness and stupidity are no excuse, I know that I'm unworthy of it but, still I must know. Is there a place in your hearts for your aunt?"

Vinglunr looked as if he would comfort her but he held back, this business wasn't his.

"Stop that." said Gamli, taking a cloth and drying her eyes. "I forgive you. I've never known my parents but I'm glad to have met you. I know my sister feels the same, don't you Vanadis?"

The young woman closed her eyes to avoid glaring. Her fist was clenched and she rested her lips against it. It was so easy for Gamli to forgive. But her? She recalled each blow that fell upon her, each humiliation in her miserable life. Then, Dorte's silent pleas suddenly rolled into her mind, and that knocked her indignation out. Vanadis opened her cool grey eyes and regarded her aunt. "What's done is done. I choose not to hate you. I-I forgive you." the words came harder than they did for Gamli but it was said.

Mjoll reached out and the three embraced. Mjoll sobbed thankfully and openly. Gamli and Vanadis held back tears.

"Thank you." Vinglunr said warmly. "You've spared my mother suffering and for that I am grateful."

"You have more than you'll ever know. Now, onto other business." Mjoll said, composing herelf. She focused her attention on Vanadis and said, "I know why Hanne haunts you."

"You have my full attention."

The priestess fell into a thoughtful demeanour and said, "We are the direct descendants of a powerful witch; every generation is cursed by spirits trapped within this world, spirits that can go to neither to Asgard nor Niflheim. The curse allows them to work their will through the she who is cursed. Your grandmother Halla Varindottir was struck by it but she mastered the curse and became a seithkona, a practitioner of seith magic. The curse fell to me but my devotion to Sif warded it off. It's now fallen on you."

"So, I simply devote myself to a Goddess?"

"Do not speak lightly of devotion. I love you, dear, but I'm afraid you lack the piety."

Vanadis glared at her. Gamli nodded at Vinglunr as if to say it is true.

"I see now why you saved this until after I forgave you."

Mjoll held up a hand for silence. "I believe you may have the will to control the curse it but you must seek training."

"So, I am to be a witch?" Vanadis asked incredulously.

Mjoll sighed, drawing upon her patience, "Yes, better a witch than an unwilling focus for wrathful ghosts."

She thought. And why are they so wrathful, auntie dearest? Could it be because you helped kill them?' Vanadis bit back those words and instead asked, "Can't we simply bring my mother peace?"

Mjoll shook her head, "I'm afraid not. Even if my sister, your mother, could be put to rest new spirits would find you. Hanne found you first because you're her daughter. Oh, she seems evil but please understand; spirits trapped in this world thrive on emotion that keeps them here. For Hanne, it is hate and loss. Revenge never quenches these, even with Steinarr dead, it continues to sustain her. However, if you learn seith magic you'll be able to ease her suffering and all she holds here. You'll also be able call upon them in times of need."

Vanadis took this in and rolled its meanings inside her head. A witch. To her surprise, she didn't mind the idea. ... "Is my grandmother still alive, can I learn from her?"

"Your grandmother... I know not if she's alive. I haven't seen her for years." Mjoll admitted sheepishly.

Vanadis glanced away so as not to scowl. You excel at forgetting which relatives are alive,, don't you Mjoll?

"I have a plan," Mjoll stated, "I've been thinking about it all day and I'm sure it will work. However, first I have a...revelation." She laid a black velvet cloth on the table and unwrapped it. From it she pulled an arm ring. It was actually three thin silver rings intertwined, on one side all the rings were twisted expertly to resemble an oak. "Barnstokkr," Mjoll tapped the tree, "our ancestral home. We three are Volsungs."

A silence followed, all were familiar with the stories. Volsung was the great grandson of Odin, the true ruler of Hunaland, which was the name of their Alands before the Nibelung conquered it. He built his hall around the great tree Barnstokkr. He and queen Hiljod had 10 sons and one daughter. On night of his Signy's wedding to King Siggeir, Odin, in the guise of a wanderer, visited the hall and thrust the majestic sword Garm into the tree. He told the revellers that the sword could only be removed by he who it was meant for. All tried to draw the sword, especially king Siggeir, all failed except Volsung's son Sigmund. Envy for the sword filled Siggeir, so much so that he cut off the wedding festivities and returned to Gotland to fume over his loss. In the spring he sent words of reconciliation and invited his father in-law and his sons to a great feast to make up for the snub. His wife Signy, daughter of Volsung, sister of Sigmund, knew this to be a trap. Despite her warnings

Volsung and his kin arrived. Siggeir slaughtered Volsung and his men. He captured his sons and, one by one, fed them to his mother who wore a form of a wolf. Only Sigmund escaped and that was only thanks to the cunning and magic of his sister. The two made a pact and together, with their son Sinfjötli, eventually killed Siggeir, avenging their kin's deaths. Signy died with Siggeir.

Years later, Sigmund married Hjördís daughter of king Eylimi. Soon after, Odin slew Sigmund for Valhalla but only after Hjördís was pregnant with their son Sigurd. Sigurd grew to be the famed slayer of the dragon Fanfir and claimer of his great riches. His fame, strength and wealth enabled him to reclaim his family home of Alands and win the admiration of the powerful Nibelung family. He was soon married to the king Gjuki's daughter Gudrun.

However, Sigurd's treasure was cursed. It had twisted his heart and the hearts of those he loved. The Valkyrie Brynhild, Sigurd's true love turned furious at him. She scolded the Nibelung heroes Gunnar and Hogni to slay him. They set up a trap and their brother Guttom slew him. Soon after the Nibelungs claimed Sigurd's treasure and his kingdom for themselves. In time, Gunnar and Hogni would hide the treasure and in turn be slain, but that is another story.

Jonakar and Hogi's sister, Gudrun the Blood Queen, renamed Hunaland to Alands to put an end to the tragic tale. A tale that now echoed ghost like in the room.

"How?" asked Vanadis. "Sigurd's line moved west with princess Aslaug. Surely, we're not related to her."

"We are not." Admitted Mjoll. "Before Signy bore Sinfjötli, she bore many sons. She did so as to have an avenger for her father. She found all but Sinfjötli lacking, so she killed rest, or had Sigurd do so." Hanne looked disgusted at the mere thought. "One of Sinfjötli's brothers survived, his father was a clever stranger who spirited him away.

Hanne, I, and the two of you are from that line. Hanne and I grew up Avaldsnes, our parents were advisers to King Harald Fair Hair himself. Hanne was unhappy. She loved the stories of the Volsungs and saw Alands as her birthright. We heard tell of Kvistr Dusk Torch, the Pohjalander who conquered Kelifar and held it. This was irresistible to Hanne, if she could marry him she could rule a piece of our ancient home. I went along with the plot for Sif had shown me this very hall in my dreams. With Hanne's beauty," she gestured to Vanadis, who looked surprised and blushed slightly, "and her cunning it was easy to get Kvistr to propose." With a guilty look she added, "I suspect Hanne had planned to kill your father and become sole ruler of Kelifar. I planned to stop her but, fortunately, Kvistr turned to be loyal and loving. Hanne fell for him and so falsehood became truth."

Gamli looked absolutely taken aback. Vinglunr offered him mead, which he took gratefully.

"You say my mother wasn't evil?" Vanadis commented dryly.

"No dear, she had evil thoughts but in the end did not act on them." Mjoll explained.

"So," said Gamli grimly, "Should we sitll hate the Nibelung, for killing Sigurd?"

"No." scoffed Vanadis, "That feud is long over. Besides, aren't we more Pohjalander than Volsung?"

Mjoll chuckled, "That's not how Hanne would see it,", then in a more serious tone, "and that's not how Alands would see it. You have Volsung blood, as such, here you're a deadly danger to any Nibelung, or so they believe. Even to this day they fear our vengeance and, with my sister's actions, I'm afraid this vengeance has been taken."

"Then we keep it secret. It's worked so far." reasoned Vanadis

Mjoll shook her head. "This is a half of a pair", she tapped the arm ring, "Hanne had the second half. When Kelifar fell Steinarr sent it to his brother jarl Truvor, to prove that his action was wise. The Truvor confronted me and, I'm sorry to say, I'm not a very good liar. Truvor swore to keep the secret and stay his hand if I swore to always heal his men when they came to my door. As a one devoted to Sif, Goddess of hearth and home, this was an easy vow to take." Mjoll held her cup of mead and stared into the dark liquid, "Now, though... Once Truvor's learned what's befallen his brother, I'm not sure he will honor his word."

"Why hasn't Steinarr attacked your hall?" prodded Vanadis. "Surely he expected you to take revenge on him?"

"I," Mjoll was at a loss for words.

Vinglunr cut in, "At ease, Mother." To Vanadis, he addressed, "He did not because he was no fool. Mjoll is beloved, many owe their lives to her healing magic. Steinarr knew that to harm or perjure her would be to court scorn and disfavour." He ended with a glare, one which Vanadis returned.

"However, in death," Mjoll added, "Steinarr is beyond reproach. If Truvor lets loose our secret then all of Alands will turn against us."

"You have a plan, right?" Gamli asked.

"I do.", she took a sip to steady herself before continuing. "You are welcome here but it is not safe. Therefore, I recommend we secure a fast ship and send you to your father's homeland in Pohjola."

"Our Pohjalander family is there?" asked Vanadis.

Mjoll smiled craftily, "Perhaps, but there's also Queen Louhi."

"Why would a foreign queen help us?"

"Because, she was once like you. She was a maid in Kalevala when the seith curse took hold. It caused trouble and she was forced to flee, just as you are fleeing now. That's why I'm certain she will find sympathy with your plight. Also, long ago, one of her daughters grew gravely ill. To ease relations between Kvistr and his homeland I fashioned a cure and Hanne delivered it. The child was saved and our Kelifar became Pohjola's sister city up until Steinarr conquered it. Louhi's a powerful and feared seithkona and Pohjola's position in the mountains makes it unassailable. If you get sanctuary there not even the full might of the Nibelung can reach you."

"You'll come with us." Gamli stated.

Mjoll shook her head, "I can't dear. Sif has chosen this hall for me to tend. I will die here, whether peacefully or no."

"Mother," Vinglunr pressed, "you must go. Surely there's someone else who's a worthy patroness?"

Mjoll smiled at her ward. "I know you mean well Vinglunr but not just anyone can be hostess here, it must be me."

"I insist you come with us." growled Gamli.

"It's best she stay here." judged Vanadis.

Her brother and Vinglunr glanced at her with sudden shock and disgust.

"Hear me out. The Nibelung will blame what happened on Gamli and I. The first place they'll search is here. Aunt, when they do, simply tell them that we stayed and moved on quickly. Yes, you knew who we were when you saw us, but we seemed in a hurry and, knowing nothing of our crimes, you saw no reason to stop us from leaving. When they tell you what happened act mortified. True, you're not a skilled liar but your reputation will make up for it. If they know you're a Volsung simply point out you've done nothing but heal the Nibelung since you've lived here. Further you're blessed by Sif, do they really wish to incur her wrath?" Vanadis dusted her hands as if ending the matter, "Of course not."

"I'm not so sure." Gamli said stroking his beard.

Vinglunr tapped the table in thought, puzzling out the merits of Vanadis' words.

"Is it really so farfetched?" Vanadis asked, "Siggeir spared Signy for warning her father. Atli spared Gudrun after she had killed dozens of his warriors. Surly a gentleman such as Truvor will spare Mjoll?"

"She's not his wife." grumbled Gamli.

Vinglunr seemed torn.

Mjoll touched Gamli's shoulder and said, "I'm not but your sister is wise. I'm sure if I heed her advice I'll be safe." She turned to Vanadis, "Though, feels wrong, blackening your name further."

Vanadis reached across the table to squeeze her hand, "You do so with our permission. We've forgiven you Mjoll. Besides, if your reputation remains unsullied then one day you'll be able to help us lift the charges. Perhaps, we can gather a blood price, pay it and be all be together once more?" Vanadis' voice trembled but her aunt's smile warmed her heart.

***

A few hours later Vanadis woke from a fretful slumber stepped out of the hall to find Gamli standing at the head of the dock stairs, staring up at the silver shining stars in the clear, black sky. In his hand he played with the Volsung armband. She joined him.

"How are you holding up?"

"Not well." she answered in full honesty.

He glanced at her questioningly.

"My curse called mother's ghost. My curse killed everyone we knew. It was my choice not to warn anyone. Yet you've stayed with me through all of it." her voice cracked with bitterness, her gaze fell to the waters. "I've wrapped you up in this Gamli, I'm a murderess."

Gamli snorted and wrapped his arm around her in a brotherly fashion. "Did you have intent? Did you mean to kill everyone?" His tone was gentle, as if he already determined the answer.

Vanadis sniffed and rubbed a tear from the corner of her eye. "By all the gods, no. I-I hate Steinarr, especially for what he did. Dorte, her favour saved me from torment. She was a haughty, demanding mistress but she protected me. She didn't deserve to die. Nor did Asvard, or Petra, or Gerd, nor most of them."

Gamli hugged Vanadis close as she cried "You hear me, you're no murderess. I know you, this wasn't your fault. I'll never leave you, I swear it." When they were young she had always protected him. Now he would protect her.

CHAPTER 5

Your life is happy. | You are rich and stable.
Be not a fool, the fates will rob thee.
Misfortune will kill thy loves. | Darken your pleasant days.
Be not more foolish, you can't handle it alone.

A week later, Skili's ship rowed at good pace southward along the seas of Alands. The crew were boisterous and sang songs of wine and women as they pulled the oars. Hardegon sat with Skili at the head of the ship. Starkad was not among them.

"It's said better to live in filth in one's home than in splendour in a foreign land." Skili mused.

"I say it's better to have a sound mind no matter where you are." Hardegon retorted. "Tell me something useful Skili, what is your take on old Väinämöinen?"

Skili considered his whittling for a moment and answered, "I can't fault his hospitality, and he seems honest," he pointed his knife in emphasis, "but his ways are strange. He may heal your brother's head but he'll also fill it with foreign ideas. Mark my words, Hardegon, Starkad will return changed."

"He's already been changed; if he returns with less anguish and if he's is able to live a good life, it'll be worth the price paid for his healing."

Skili nodded ruefully, conceding to Hardegon's wisdom, only if just barely.

The sky above them was grey. Flecks of white snow fell down. It was cold enough that, even with their rowing, the men wore furs and mitts. The wind pushed against them but their sleek longship cut through thanks to the strength of Hardegon's warriors.

Ahead of them sped a merchant ship, a knarr, its square sail taught. She was manned by a small crew.

Hardegon signalled the warriors to cease rowing and called out to the ship, "Hail, what brings merchants sailing this close to winter?"

He grinned at the crew's sudden scramble, understandable since they were in the path of a warship. Skili's warriors took a rest an eyed the vessel hungrily.

The headman stepped to the bow of his vessel. He had hair and beard that were pitch as night. He was fine featured with deep brown eyes. He wore brilliant green garb. He also sported a thick knotted leather belt and a worn brown cloak with gold trim. A short sword hung at his side.

"Not a merchant but entertainers." answered the man in a rich baritone. "We make for home in Joksula in Norrland."

Hardegon spied two of his troop who sat in the middle of the ship. They wore fine cloaks, one brown, and the other green. Their hoods were pulled deep over their heads and they had their backs turned. The other crew members watched Hardegon's vessel with trepidation, though still, the headman seemed at ease.

"Who are they?" Hardegon asked pointing to the cowled passengers. "Why don't they turn to see us?"

"Ah." said the Skald, he walked over and put his arms around them. "This is my brother and sister, Grimkell and Velaug. They caught a most deadly illness and are ashamed of their pot marked faces." the two waved without removing their cloaks.

Hardegon's entire crew recoiled. Even the hero's heart skipped a beat. "Then why do you draw near? Keep back and move along. I thank you for leaving our Alands."

Skili signalled the men to pull quickly on their oars. The man at the rudder turned the ship swiftly to port to widen the gap between the vessels. The dastardly Skald laughed and ordered full sail. Hardegon's men rowed for all their worth until the plague ship was far away.

"My lord, we must make haste to Neshraun." Skili insisted.

Hardegon frowned and eyed the anxious sailors. "We should pick up Mjoll the Gentle first?"

"No my lord, she is bound by Sif never to leave her island. If this sickness has struck Neshraun we'll take as many to her as we can."

Hardegon looked ill at ease at that, his thoughts drifting to his own kin in Kelifar and Öland. "Fine, we go to Neshraun but I'll need to borrow your ship and men to take me to Kelifar as soon as we can."

"Aye my lord, and I'll bring my daughter Asta, she's our best healer."

***

They arrived at Neshraun at midday. There was a small awaiting crowd, everyone else was missing. To Skili's great relief he found this was because most were in toiling in the mines. Word about the plague spread among them but as of yet, none were afflicted.

Skili's daughter Asta was brought before them. She was full grown woman, dressed in blue and bundled for the chill fall air.

When the oarsmen quailed at journeying to Kelifar Hardegon addressed them, "You would forsake your duty to the jarl's son? Look at Asta here. A fine woman who fears not Hel's curse. Can none of you match her courage?"

Ashamed they retook their seats, much to the chagrin of their kin. Skili too took his place beside Hardegon. "We shall soon return."

***

With that the longship made good speed towards Kelifar. They reached her before sunset. Her beach and harbour were empty. The town was silent aside from the rolling sea and the call of migrating birds. No fires rose from the town, not even from the Great Hall at the top of the hill. Strangely, her great doors were open but they could see none inside.

"Pull ashore, immediately." cried Hardegon. The warriors heeded the edge of command in his tone and beached their ship. Hardegon leaped off the boat and called up. "Hail, Uncle Steinarr! Hail, Aunt Halldora! Hail, cousin Dorte! It is I, Hardegon!"

A few of the island cats emerged from the halls and ran down the hill. They watched him warily.

"Hail! Can anyone answer me?"

There was no answer.

He felt a gentle squeeze on his shoulder, Asta was at his side, with her Skili.

"We'll go check, my lord. Please wait here."

Hardegon was about to refuse but Skili interrupted. "Asta's fought off every illness that's come at her, she won't fall to any plague. As for myself, just remember this service when it comes to my sons."

"I will." Hardegon said gratefully.

"You lot stay with the jarl's son. Don't do anything until we return." Skili's men muttered their assent.

With that, the father and daughter walked up the hill, towards the Great Hall. A few of the town cats followed, crying for a meal.

Hardegon paced the beach, lost in worry and thought. The laughter of the Skald rang in his ear and the swordsman's expression turned seething. Hardegon's small troop sat away from Skili's men and marked their lord's demeanour with concern. Skili's men dared not approach him.

Eventually one of Hardegon's own shouted, "Sire, Skili returns." Hardegon glanced up to see the Lord of Neshraun quickly descending the hill, a troubled look on his face.

Hardegon quickly marched up to him. "Where's Asta? What's the word?"

Skili shook his head, "It's not sickness, you can go on up. How she stands the sight... she takes after her grandfather, he was hard one."

Hardegon nodded to his men, they joined him and quickly they rushed up the hill. As they did so Skili organized his men. "Alright, you lot, the danger's passed, would that we had been here to stop it. Beach her, we've got long night of grim work ahead of us."

Hardegon and his group crested the hill and they all paused at the sight of the Hall. The residents of Kelifar were scattered at the entrance and inside, reduced to rotting corpses. At the top of the Hall the stench wafted passed them. Walking among them, her kerchief tied over her nose and mouth was Asta. She was in the back, beside what remained of Steinarr.

Heeding neither horror nor stench Hardegon stormed inside. The bodies lay scattered about, none wore armour, none held weapons but their splayed limbs, the knocked over chairs, the shattered dishes indicated there was a struggle. As brave as he was Hardegon could not look long at the dead children whom he had to step over.

He reached Asta who had flipped the corpse of Steinarr on his back. What was left of his face was a mask of rage. In his chest was buried a dinner knife.

Asta said no word, she merely pointed to another corpse. It lay in a dress Hardegon recognized. Her head was missing, a thick dried stain of blood pooled beyond her end ended in bloody footprints that led outside the hall.

Hardegon's being was swept up in revulsion, shock and grief. His mind caught up with the meaning of Asta's signs and rage soon followed.

"Who?" he whispered in deathly seriousness.

His men, who had joined him in the Hall, who were equally shocked, had no answer.

"My lord." addressed Asta with the utmost politeness.

Hardegon turned to her but said nothing.

"No one else has wounds, they were all poisoned. Before he succumbed your Uncle must have confronted the murderers." She considered the corpse with pity, "But he couldn't fight, I'm sorry my lord but this was no battle, it was murder."

Hardegon spun on his men. "Search this Island, every nook and cranny of it. Find any survivor and bring them to me!"

"Aye." They cried and rushed to work.

"Half of you help." said Skili who had reached the entrance hall. "The rest, we're going to move these poor souls. They shouldn't rest like this."

Hardegon nodded in thanks to Skili and rushed out the Hall to search with his men. They searched till sunset and found nothing. The halls and shops were empty. The altar held only a few flowers that were not blown away on the wind and the old bloodstain from the blot's sacrifice. Aside from the Great Hall everything was peaceful.

Skili, Asta and a group of luckless warriors gathered the dead. They were wrapped in furs, linen and canvas and placed in an orderly fashion in the hall. The tables were stored. The rubble cleared. The cats shooed out.

The warriors eventually left the Great Hall to the dead and chose the largest of the fishermen dwellings rest during this cloudy night. The crackling fire pit was welcome. They supped from the dried provisions from their ship, not wanting to risk any of Kelifar's food.

Hardegon sat apart, wrapped in his cloak, glaring off at the darkened wall. Skili walked over and sat beside him, offering a drink from his wineskin.

The jarl's son refused but asked, "Tell me, Skili, what's your take on that, Skald, and his performers, the ones we ran into this morning?"

"I'll tell you that and more but first you must swear not to rush after them in this darkness."

Hardegon scowled. "What do you know, Skili?"

"A fair amount, I'd wager. I know it's folly to sail Alands in the middle of the night, and that it's wrong to leave your dead untended, even if you're chasing their murderers."

Hardegon stood in anger. "I'll take whatever risks I like. My uncle has been robbed of both life and Valhalla! He needs no funeral, he awaits vengeance!"

A silence descended and all eyes turned to him and Skili

"Surely, my lord, you don't mean that, right?" asked the chieftain. "I'm certain, if we perform the proper rights, your uncle and all the people of Kelifar will find their place with the gods. They would not forsake them so."

"What good was Freya's protection?" hissed Hardegon.

"Well enough, Kelifar's always been hale, hearty and bountiful. Freya will grant luck but she will not slay your foes for you."

"Odin's beard." Hardegon snarled.

Skili said, with soothing words, "We tend dead as is right, then, there will be time enough for vengeance. If winter strikes before we can find our quarry they'll be as snowed in as we are. Midgard's not so vast as to hide anyone from the likes of us."

He turned to his men, "Who here will pledge themselves for justice for the jarl's son? Who will hunt these cowardly curs with us?"

All his men stood and cheered, has did Hardegon's.

"As you see, my lord, we are with you but first you must tend to your kin."

Hardegon sighed and dropped to his seat. "Of course, you're right. Forgive me, my blood runs hot at my uncle's murder."

Skili laughed and patted him on the back. "Lord Hardegon, we'd lose respect for any man who took the death of his kin easily. Everyone, raise your glasses in toast to the memory of our dear Steinarr, in memory of his lovely family and in anticipation for our ensuring justice."

The entire hall cheered.

***

Three days passed. Skili summoned his priestess of Freya, a golden haired woman of regal stature and his angel of death, a dour woman who knew the rights to ferry souls to their rightful destination. An entire boatful of Neshraun's citizens followed, they were warriors and miners and their families, come to pay respect to the city that had dealt well with them in honest trade. So too came Skili's sons, the twins Radur and Nafi. They swore themselves to Hardegon's quest.

Hardegon, Skili, the priestess and the crone organized the crowd. They moved the corpses from the Great Hall. The priestess purified the altar and offered a blot, a willing slave who gave herself in sacrifice. At this the weather turned warm. The cats of the village came out of hiding and wove among the people, a sign of favor from Freya. The angel of death and her attendants worked tirelessly to prepare every corpse, when they had finished they were wrapped up and no longer gruesome, merely solemn. Hardegon watched it all with a careful eye. He noted well that the mourners were true; they seemed to hold no interest in looting his uncle's town. Many came to express their concordances; Hardegon was polite yet terse with them. He did go out back and spar with Skili's sons. He found them skilled but trounced them non-the-less.

On the third evening, the pyres were set all along the beach. Steinarr, Halldora and Dorte were placed on Steinarr's own longship. Hardegon walked on its treasure laden deck, running his hand on the gunwale, remembering a younger him sailing on board. Remembering Steinarr's jovial laugh. Remembering Dorte's charming smile. The bodies before him were wrapped thickly in expensive purple linen. He found himself turning away when his eyes came upon Dorte's remains, a head too short.

Hardegon leaped off the boat and gave the signal. His men pushed the longship where it drifted out to sea. He reached his hand out and was handed a bow and a flaming arrow. To the crowd before him he said, "Let it be known that before you lies the remains of a great man, one greater than even my father. Steinarr was a proud as Gunnar, strong has Hogni and fearsome as Gudrun. He taught me everything I needed to bring glory back to our Nibelung family. However he was robbed, poisoned, murdered in cold blood. He. . ." the words caught in Hardegon's throat. His heart was caught between the expectant eyes of the mourners and his firm belief that Valhalla had been denied Steinarr. Finally he managed to say, "Those who know me know my heart. I hope my Uncle finds a place at Odin's side." With that Hardegon spun and fired his arrow. It struck true and Steinarr's ship ignited. The crowd cheered and the pyres on the beach, each with a body of a citizen of Kelifar, including Asvard and Petra, were lit as one. Then, the mourners backed away to watch the deceaced's final journey.

***

In the Great Hall, the mourners of Neshraun celebrated Steinarr's life. Radur and Nafi told tales of Steinarr's many victories and the honour he gave to the Goddess Freya. The music was lively. Mead and meat, from Neshraun, flowed. Hardegon sat on the high seat and oversaw it all, his grim countenance lightened a little.

As the celebration died down Hardegon held up his hand. The Hall grew silent, all eyes turned to him. "Tomorrow I make haste northwards, I have a good idea of the shape of my quarry and will not let them slip. This means I will need Kelifar tended. I see before me her wardens." He swept his hand across the hall. "You of the generous hearts, you, who have left your own halls to mourn another man's kin. Kelifar is yours, treat her well."

The crowd, even Skili was taken aback.

Hardegon grinned, "What's this silence? I jest not. Skili do you not wish to own both a mining and trading town?"

"You're too kind my lord." Skili gasped with a bow. The rest of the crowd followed with murmurs of wonder and thanks. Then there were a great many cheers.

Hardegon then gestured, "Asta Skilidottr, step forward." The woman stepped forward and bowed. "I have asked your kin and have come to understand your valiant husband Bodmodr was slain in this year's raid."

"It is true my lord."

"If you're willing I will speak highly of you among my family, I suspect you'll have your pick of wealthy suitors."

"My lord?" she gasped.

Hardegon chuckled, "I'd marry you myself but my Thora would kill me. Still, I would have you in my family. If that does not work out, trust that you'll still be richly rewarded."

"Thank you my lord." she said gathering her senses. Skili looked proud.

"With that I bid you all a good night. Warriors, we'll be up early tomorrow. We must catch the scoundrels before winter catches us. It'll be a hard hunt but we'll be rewarded with glory and honor."

Hardegon left the cheering revelers to walk past the cloth divider to find a place on the benches. To sleep in his Uncle's bed, that would be too strange. As he sat, Skili entered.

"My lord, you have been too generous."

"No, I have been overwhelmed by your generosity. I truly hope Asta will marry one of my cousins, I would unite us further."

"As would I." Skili sat down beside him. "Before you sleep my lord I would tell you of our prime suspects and where they're most likely hiding."

"You know of the Skald on the plague ship?" Hardegon asked with sudden interest.

"He seems familiar," answered Skili, "but I have more pertinent information. Do you remember the thrall girl whom you gave Dorte's present to?"

Hardegon nodded gravely. "She was striking."

"She and her brother were not among the dead. Let me tell you about their parents, Kvistr Dusk Torch and Hanne the Clever."

CHAPTER 6

Make no mistake, you are blood. | Your body and mind is formed from it.
In your blood is the spiral map of fate.
It blesses you with all your strengths. | It curses you with all your weaknesses.
Blood is simply your fate, out of your control, it is neither your fault nor is it your victory.

A few days earlier, Vanadis watched Hardegon's ship row swiftly way from their knarr as Vinglunr laughed. They made such speed the knarr rocked in the longship's wake. A weight of fear lifted from her and she covered her mouth and giggled.

"Well done." she whispered, "Never thought I'd be pleased at being called pot marked."

Vinglunr flashed her a cunning grin. "It was inspired wasn't it? Still, I'll only rest easy when they're out of sight." To his men, he called, "Keep the sail taught, we need to make the most of this wind."

They had been travelling for a few days, and travelled for a few more. They sailed northwards keeping close to the rocky shore of Helsingland. At night they camped on rocky beaches, near thick forests, keeping well away from town and hall. Vinglunr said this was to keep witnesses low and hide their true destination. Seven others sailed with them. Two of Mjoll's shieldmaidens and five defenders of her hall. There was a tension about the trip but no grumblings or gripes.

"I entrust to you my dearest nephew and niece. Guard them as you would me." Mjoll had entreated.

As such, these few warriors had treated the siblings as a highborn lord and lady, only giving deference to Vinglunr who was leader of their troop. They were well equipped with weapons, supplies, and treasure. Vanadis had never owned some many clothes in her life, especially of such fine quality.

***

Before they left, Mjoll had embraced Gamli and said, "Watch and learn from Vinglunr, he'll teach you how to be a noble and strong free man. Look after your sister and know that I will always care for you."

Gamli fought back tears but barely. "Thank you, Aunt. We'll make you proud."

Then Mjoll embraced Vanadis, but the young woman noted her aunt's trembling touch. Vanadis looked questioningly in her grey eyes and found resignation. "Aunt, surely we'll meet again?"

"O-of course." she said swallowing back tears. Vanadis easily caught the lie.

"Stick with my plan and we will." Vanadis urged.

Mjoll regarded her and suddenly gained strength. "Vanadis, you're like your mother in more ways than one, this is good. Keep your wits about you, urge your brother and my Vinglunr to the wisest actions, even if they are distasteful or wrong. Then, when you become a seithkona, protect my boys." there was a rumble in her tone, like a mother bear.

Sudden respect for her aunt rose in Vanadis, it cut a little though since this was the time of their parting. She wiped away tears but smiled fiercely. "Trust me, when I learn to master this curse all who threaten us will despair."

Mjoll embraced her again, "I'm glad. Go with the blessings of Sif."

***

In the days that followed, Gamli heeded Mjoll's advice and questioned Vinglunr on many different things. The skald turned out to be an earnest teacher. On the journey, they discussed law, customs, and trade. At camp they sparred, Vinglunr's speed and skill always outmatching Gamli's brute strength. However, Gamli was a swift learner, he fought a few of the warriors and one of the shieldmaidens to a stand-still. The maiden he fought, Bera Wolf Heart, also had long talks with him, more than once Vanadis caught her admiring Gamli's powerful physique.

Most of the crew stayed apart from Vanadis. At times, she spied them making small offerings to Freya, praying for protection against evil magic. The shieldmaidens however, stuck close. Their demeanour started formal but Vanadis knocked down their barriers. Bera talked about the world, she had never travelled but heard tales of the verdant west and even far off Islandia, which Vanadis listened to eagerly. Asny Iron Hair was the stricter of the two and harshly corrected all of Vanadis' manners. For her part Vanadis shared what her former life was like and even a little about her experiences with the curse.

***

On the fifth night, Vanadis had a dream.

She sat outside the storehouse of Kelifar grinding corn to flower. Her fellow thrall Janne sat across from her. They'd been taking turns. It was gruelling work. The top and bottom stone were heavy, the both had to lift it to carry it into the shade outside. To grind the flower the handle had to be gripped and the heavy stone turned swiftly, after a few goodly turns one would rest and the other would turn in the other way. Thus, the tray filled with raw flower. There was no time or energy for talking. Those who passed occasionally mocked that they needed to work harder. Vanadis finished the last few turns, her arm felt as if they would fall off and she was drenched in sweat. They split the flower between their two sacks.

Janne stood and hefted her bounty. She frowned at Vanadis', "What this? Why is yours so much bigger."

Vanadis was about to argue but, looking at her sack, she saw that it did seem rounder. "That's funny," she said lifting it, "Did we even make this much?"

Suddenly Janne staggered back "N-never mind, you can keep it." she ran.

Vanadis watched her go, a puzzled expression on her face. She felt drops of rain on her foot. She glanced down to see it wasn't clear, light liquid, but heavy and red. Her grey eyes widened as she noticed her sack was blood-soaked. With a shriek she dropped it. Out rolled Dorte's head, it knocked against the wall, her glassy eyes staring at Vanadis.

***

She awoke with a cry.

A shadow sputtered awake and reached for her axe, "By Freya!"

Vanadis shirked back against the tent wall watching the figure frightfully.

"What's wrong?" asked Asny.

Recollection rolled back onto Vanadis, she sighed and caught her breath. "I'm fine, just a nightmare."

"I'm going back to sleep."

Vanadis noticed the tent was a third empty. "Where's Bera?"

"She took watch with that brother of yours." Ansy snorted, rolling, her back to Vanadis. "If it's after watch, they'll be doing more than that."

Vanadis recalled Gamli at the fire last night, brooding back at Kelifar. "I think they'll just talk. He's still mourning she who died at home." She quickly pulled on a dress, sandals and cloak. "I'm going out."

"Don't go far."

***

Vanadis stepped outside of her striped tent and into the camp. Vinglunr sat by the fire stirring the coals, staring off across the waters. He looked concerned, thoughtful. Vanadis sat across from him, warmed her hands and asked, "Worried about Mjoll?"

"Aye," he handed her his wineskin, from which she took a drought, "I fear winter will hit when we reach Pohjola and I won't be able to return to her."

Vanadis tucked her own fears for Mjoll aside and said, "She'll be safe this winter, less mouths to feed will make it a comfortable one. When spring comes we'll find you a faster ship home."

"We still have to return this fine vessel." he said, pointing at the beached Knarr.

Vanadis snorted and took another measure of his wine. "Mjoll's safety comes first. Besides, the rest of the crew can return her."

"I see... I hadn't thought of that." Vinglunr said stroking his neatly trimmed midnight beard.

Vanadis took that moment to admire his handsome face in the firelight. She caught herself and shook those desires away. "Where's Gamli?"

"On a walk with Brea," he gestured to the footpath into the woods, "she's a fine companion."

Vanadis glanced in that direction with a surprised expression. "I didn't think he'd be ready."

"Brea thinks he is." Vinglunr chuckled, "Though, you might be right. Gamli's still reserved from what happened in Kelifar."

Vanadis glanced up at him to share her thoughts on the matter when something caught her eye and she froze. In the clear, cold moonlight, in the distance she spied a woman. Though far away, Vanadis' vision focused and she could see her clearly. She was in a silk dress of white. A long cloth of clean pearl linen was draped over her head and face like a burial veil, it was held in place by a gleaming golden circlet. Her shoulders and forearms were bare, they were a corpse pale. Her fingers tapered into claw like nails. She stood on a rocky shore, though her features were obscured Vanadis was sure she was looking back at her. Vanadis refocused on the circlet and noted its tiny rubies. She stifled a frightened gasp, she had held that very crown.

Vinglunr caught Vanadis' sudden look of terror and spun around, hand on the hilt of his sword. The woman in white drifted gracefully back into the forest.

"Wake Asny and have her arm herself. I'll find Gamli and Bera." Vinglunr said, in a commanding tone, he then lit a torch in the fire and darted off. Vanadis hesitated, torn between going with him and staying, her delay was long enough for Vinglunr to enter the woods with no objection.

Vanadis rushed to the tent and at her urging the shieldmaiden was up, armed and alert. Thanks to the ruckus a few of the warriors joined them, annoyed but concerned. Choosing her words carefully Vanadis addressed them and said, "Vinglunr and I saw someone over there. We didn't catch a good look at him because he dashed into the woods. It's most likely nothing but Vinglunr's gathering Gamli and Bera just to be safe."

Moments later, Vinglunr returned with the two. Bera looked flustered, she rushed into the tent for her weapons. Gamli stormed over to his sister. "Are you alright?"

She nodded, "I am, just nervous."

"Is it her curse?" One of the warrior's asked. The others murmured.

"We cannot jump to that conclusion." Vinglunr said, his voice cutting across the crew. "There are many dark things in Norrland, this is likely unrelated."

"What did you see?" asked Asny.

Vinglunr stroked his beard thoughtfully. "A woman but she looked wrong. Perhaps a dark elf, or mayhap a haugbui?"

"The undead? This does not put me at ease." one of the warriors hissed.

Bera emerged from the tent armed.

Vinglunr laughed. "Oh ye of little faith. You forget my magic." He drew a deep breath and began to sing. The song's language was in a strange tongue, the tone was long, deep and dark. His voice echoed clear around the camp and after each verse ended with a stomp from Vinglunr, each stomp reverberated as if he were a Giant. He finished his verse and raised his hands, everyone's breath frosted in the air. The air shimmered in a half-moon around the camp, then there was a tremendous crack, suddenly they were cut off from the forest by a wall of blue ice, a full twenty feet tall. The warriors and shieldmaidens cheered. Vinglunr grinned proudly. Vanadis and Gamli were gobsmacked.

"That," said Vinglunr pointing at the wall, "will keep elves and ghouls away from us tonight, so sleep in peace. If it doesn't then I'll sing whatever threatens us into submission. Just bundle up, it'll be cold."

The crew, who was satisfied with this, returned to their tents.

"Excellent casting Vinglunr but it's still your watch." remarked Asny as she and Brea went back to the tent.

"What in Hel's Hall was that?" asked Vanadis.

"Distasteful, but useful, music from Jotunheim." Vinglunr said with a look of mild repugnance. Then he brightened, "Have I not told you? I have Kvasir's Mead, the Mead of Poetry, in my veins."

"So you know magic. Is it something you can teach?" inquired the young woman.

Vinglunr shook his head, "I know only a few spell songs, they come unbidden and only in moments of great inspiration. I have tried teaching the words, the tune, and gestures to others but, none have been able to master it aside myself. It's in my blood, as sieth is in yours."

"I'll trade you, my blood for yours." Vanadis said dryly.

Gamli nudged her, "Pay more respect, we come from a proud line..."

"You're not the one our line is tormenting." Vanadis hissed back.

Vinglunr considered Vanadis and then cut in, "While I would revel at being a Volsung, seith magic is too womanly for my taste." He chuckled

"Then you prefer the taste of men?" Vanadis shot back. "Gamli, keep him company." with that she walked back to her tent.

"My deepest apologies." groaned Gamli, "I'm sorry to say but if you have to kill her, I'll have to stand in your way."

Vinglunr watched her go with no hint of outrage. "I'd be a poor skald if I couldn't take barbs." Suddenly an idea struck him, "That reminds me, I'll need to teach you how to insult properly, every free man does it, especially when the mead flows." He gestured to the fire, "Come, let us trade insults."

CHAPTER 7

In the towns, there is law. | In the wilds men are beasts.
One wrong turn and you must stave off death with sword and axe.
We are quick to violence. | It is because we are Odin's dogs.
When your friends lay cold upon the ground, your foe's blameless, the nature of man is the true culprit.

They sailed onward for a few more days. Every night Vinglunr would summon his wall of ice which put the crew at ease. During this time Vanadis did not see the return of spectre from before. Asny and Bera grilled Vanadis on what she saw, the young woman answered evasively and, given there were no further disturbances, the two shieldmaidens let it be.

Gamli had watched her closely and one night he took watch with her. "I'm concerned." he started.

Vanadis eyed him, "You bring this up now, when there's been no trouble?"

Gamli crossed his arms and gave her a judgmental glance, "I know you sister. I also know you'll tell me what's wrong."

Vanadis sighed and glanced around, everyone was in their tents, the fire illuminated only empty shadow, still she whispered, "The circlet the haugbui wore, I thought it was Dorte's."

"Dorte?" Gamli stuttered. "Are you sure?"

Vanadis sighed, "I don't know. She wore a veil that hid her face. I had a nightmare about her just before that creature showed up."

Gamli frowned, "You didn't tell us?"

"I thought it was just a dream." his sister pleaded.

Gamli glared at her, "Remember the Kelifar nightmare."

His words stung. "It didn't feel the same, it wasn't as intense."

"Tell me about it, now."

Vanadis did, the entire dream up to when Dorte's head rolled from the flower sack.

Gamli stroked his moustache in thought. The week had been kind to him, Vanadis could no longer see the faithful thrall that her brother was. He was now Gamli Kvistrson, proud inheritor of his father's legacy.

Gamli noticed her look. "Why are you smiling?"

Vanadis giggled, "It's nothing. So, do you think my nightmare is a portent?"

"What do you think?"

"It's not. I had the nightmare because of everything that's happened. The creature Vinglunr and I saw must have been unrelated."

Gamli nodded, "Good. Now swear you'll tell me all your nightmares."

Vanadis cocked an eyebrow, "Truly? I didn't know you were sensitive to womanly terrors."

"This is no jest."

"I won't share with you every private dream brother."

Gamli sighed with frustration.

Vanadis lightly touched his arm and offered, "How about this? If I ever have a dream that I suspect is a prophecy, I swear I'll tell you. Will that do?"

"Well, enough, I suppose." Gamli said, clearly more at ease.

***

The next day was dismal as the previous night was clear. The wind picked up which made for good speed but the clouds were heavy in the sky. The crew were bundled up tight. The choppy waves spilled water into the deck and all free hands bailed. The dark, cloudy sky threatened rain, in midday it was as dark as twilight.

"We'll make land at the next beach!" cried Vinglunr.

The shore to their port was cliff laden. The crew kept a keen eye on the rocks to ensure they didn't miss a break or get too close. Then the sky opened up and freezing rain fell down.

"Oh, this is wonderful." Vinglunr cursed.

"There, I see a landing!" cried Gamli.

They passed the edge of a cliff face and beyond it was a rocky shore. A ship was already occupied it, a longship painted ice blue. It was flipped and rested inland. Beyond it lantern light shone under a large, red canopy.

Vinglunr squinted through the rain and frowned. "Make for it," he called, "and keep your arms at hand. We don't want trouble but neither should we be unprepared for it."

"Aye!" cried the man at the rudder. Their knarr turned swiftly and skillfully and they sailed for the beach. Once they were close a few of the crew, including Gamli, leapt out, as the sail was furled and the mast lowered, they pulled the ship onto the rocks. Then the rest disembarked.

"Grab the supplies. You lot form near me." called Vinglunr. Vanadis and a third of the crew seized the provisions, the warriors, including Gamli gathered around Vinglunr. The shieldmaidens stuck close to Vanadis.

"Come, let us greet our hosts." suggested the skald and they marched towards the pavilion.

Seated at a small wooden table were two women. One was had sharp features, blue eyes and long red hair tied in braids that lay over her shoulders. She warded off the chill with a black raven feather cloak, she looked young but had the demeanour of a matriarch. Her companion had silky black hair loosely tied in a long braid that fell behind her back. Her eyes were blue, her full lips drawn up in a playful smile. She wore a blood red dress of silk and gold. They were in the middle of a dice game, playing for biscuits. The red haired one currently had the largest hoard.

She glanced up at Vinglunr's party and smiled at him.

The Skald was taken aback. "My ladies, would you mind if this humble Skald and his troop takes shelter?"

The one with raven tresses nodded and said in a sweet voice, "Of course you may. Our table is yours."

The red haired one bowed graciously in her seat.

"Fool! Behind you!" cried Vanadis.

Swiftly two small groups rushed them from either side of the bay. They were armed and armoured vagabonds. When Vanadis shouted they left all pretense of sneaking and charged with battle cries.

Vinglunr reacted immediately. He called out a song in clear, even tones, his powerful voice cutting through the rain, cutting through even the war cries. The words were soft, wind like, the tone was deep, the notes long, oozing through the air like honey mead. The bandits, who were charging at him, slowed has if hit with sudden waking dreams. The women in the tent were also thus affected.

This didn't stop the group charging for Vanadis. Immediately, Asny and Bera stepped against them. Bera hacked one of the assailants aside with her axe and blocked his companion's strike with her shield. Asny stood before their leader. He was tall, broad, with wild dark brown hair and a bushy beard, he wielded a massive club. He swung, Ansy dodged and her axe sliced through his hide armour, cutting him deep.

While singing, Vinglunr drew his blade. His warriors crashed into the stunned assailants, cutting the first few down. Gamli drew his sword but hesitated at this ruthlessness. The red haired hostess managed to shake off Vinglunr's spell and clawed the air before her spitting out something hateful in a foreign tongue. Vinglunr's song was suddenly cut shot with his cry of pain, his shield arm suddenly twisted and strained by an invisible force. A tall, lanky man with a stubble for a beard and hair of moulted black and white, snarled and smashed his helmeted head into the Skald, Vinglunr reeled to the ground. Gamli, with a shout, swung is sword up and cut into the strange man's ribs.

The leader of the beach vanguard roared with rage. Suddenly, he grew to twice his already huge size and towered like an ogre before Asny. She was not shaken and swung her axe again cutting deep into his leg. The mountainous man bellowed and struck her full on with his maul, knocking her flying, she twisted in the air, broken. At this Bera screamed with fury and struck with her axe. Her opponent knocked it aside with his forearm. Bera drove a dagger deep into him. Relatively deep, given his size, he swiped at her and she ducked under it, withdrawing her blade which slick and red. The rest of Vanadis' troop dropped to the clubs and axes of the bandits leaving Brea's flank was open. Vanadis, grabbed a spear form a fallen ally and stepped between them. One of the assailant's jumped forward, Vanadis stabbed but the bandit grabbed her spear and his ally cuffed her on the side of the head. She saw stars and fell to the muddy earth.

Meanwhile, the man Gamli sliced grinned at him. His grin stretched impossibly wide, his limbs stretched, he howled and suddenly Gamli was knocked to the ground, a red wolf's jaws bearing down at him. He blocked with his sword and the beast chomped down without a care. A fog like haze shifted around the hostess of raven tresses, she reached out, spat words that could only be a vile curse, ethereal shadows, bone like in shape, lanced through one of the warriors; he fell with a look of supreme terror on his face.

The red haired maiden drew a shining sword from under her cloak; it fell back revealing fine scale mail. Vinglunr rose out of the mire his own sword in hand.

The woman lowered her blade slightly and smiled chillingly at him. "This is costing more than expected."

With a heave Gamli threw the wolf off him. It rolled to its feet and snarled, Gamli took a step back; the wolf was quite large.

Vinglunr lowered his own blade but kept a keen eye on her. "I'm pleased our price proves high." he said tightly.

Beyond him Bera stepped to Vanadis' defence. Her large foe swung, she ducked, and he leveled several of his allies.

"Still", she nodded at the prone Vanadis and the still Asny, "you have lost more. How about a truce?"

Vinglunr glared at her.

"We have healing magic, I swear if you agree, we'll share in its power."

Vinglunr considered in judgmental silence.

"Another promise, if we continue this we'll both lose dear friends." the woman urged, a slight tremor in her tone.

Vinglunr raised his hand. "All halt, we have a truce." Again, his voice cut through the chaos.

The woman raised her hand as well. "He speaks truth, cease this at once." Her voice held the strength of command.

The wolf backed away from Gamli and the young man lowered his sword. The towering man returned to his former size holding his many wounds. The warriors on both sides lowered their weapons.

"Katla?" the red haired warrior called back to her companion.

The illusion around the woman at the table faded. She was wrapped in a red cloak with black trim, hood pulled over her face to hide everything but her pale chin and red lips. She took her cup and knocked it on the table once.

"Have Moldan tend the wounded please."

The witch at the table gestured and a white cat darted from the sleeve of her robe. It grew until it was a large as a medium sized dog, and hairy as a lion. When he touched the mire, he was not mired himself, his fur remained spotless. Furthermore, a shimmer soft light, like tiny willow wisps, floated around him. He leaped over a fallen warrior and he groaned, feeling his neck where it was no longer slashed. The cat then rubbed on the next and his bleeding, broken leg was whole. Moldan continued from warrior to warrior, at each touch they were healed. Even the grizzly wound Gamli gave the wolf. Even the many cuts the mountainous man suffered. Even Vinglunr's bleeding scalp. The bandits took this as matter per course, holding their own wounds until the feline got to them. Vinglunr and his crew watched with wonder.

"You don't have any songs like that?" Gamli asked.

Vinglunr shook his head, "Till now I thought only Mjoll had this kind of healing spell."

Finally Moldan rubbed his head on Vanadis' side, slowly she sat up.

"Oh Gods." Gamli stammered and ran to her side. "Sister, are you well?"

"What about Asny?" cried Brea over the shattered, still form of her fiend.

"Moldan cannot bring back the dead I'm afraid." said the leader with the red braids.

Vinglunr took assessment, three of his ten were gone, Asny the sorest loss. Five of Red Hair's warriors lay still. He scratched his beard and considered the numbers, they were still outnumbered by three.

Leader Red Braid seemed to make the same assessment. "Let us wrap our fallen, then you can bring your goods under my tent and we can talk."

Both sides sheathed their arms and quickly wrapped their dead and placed them respectfully under the sails. Gamli worked beside the wolf-man, the ogre and Red Braid but at obvious ill humour.

"We're just going to let them get away with this, with killing Ansy?" whispered Vanadis to Vinglunr, clearly outraged.

Vinglunr frowned at her for a moment and asked, "Have you never been to battle?"

"Steinarr did not have an army of thralls."

His expression softened. "I see. That explains Gamli's sourness as well. Do not mourn them, they go to Valhalla and Asny goes to Fólkvangar, tonight they dine with no less than Odin and Freya."

Vanadis pulled her hood up and turned away to hide her tears. Skepticism caught her grief and held it tight.

Vinglunr put a gentle arm around her. "When we cremate them pay close attention, you will see them rise."

All Vanadis currently saw were bodies under a tarp. No, that wasn't true. She also saw her brother glaring at the fallen, wrapped in his own internal struggle. She also saw leader Red Braids, who stoically swallowed her own sorrow. She also saw Brea speaking cordially with the mountainous man who shook his head sadly at his lost companions. Madness, madness they were killing each other moments before. Now? "You're saying I must choose hope."

"Think of Asny, do you deny she is worthy?"

Vanadis smiled sadly, "If anyone was. Hope it is then."

"You show wisdom." Vinglunr said kindly. "Now, let's get out of this rain and meet our new friends."

Larger tables were brought out, as well as mead and a large supply of salted meat and fish. The warriors of Mjoll and the warriors of leader Red Braids sat together and shared a meal.

The red haired woman took a healthy swig from her silver cup, then donned a pointed circlet of iron. She turned to the Skald and his crew, "I am Vargeisa Fire Wolf. The shrouded woman is Katla the Hidden. My other companions are Wolf and Bear" the scraggly man with the white and black hair, and the mountainous man bowed in turn, "You've met Moldan." she stroked the cat who leaped on the table and meandered over to rest in Katla's lap, "The rest can introduce themselves in good time."

"I am Vinglunr Spell Call, ward of Mjoll the Gentle. These are my crew and trusted companions."

Vanadis sighed, grateful he didn't introduce them by true names.

Her brother nodded in a guarded manner.

Vanadis pulled off her hood.

Vargeisa drew back, "No," she said with shocked disbelief.

Wolf and Bear noticed and reached for their weapons. Vinglunr and Gamli did the same.

"Hold." said the Fire Wolf, leaning closer to get a better look at Vanadis.

"Pardon, but I don't think we've met." Vanadis said uneasily.

Vargeisa's keen blue eyes took in Vanadis' every feature.

Katla lifted her own hood and also took a closer look. Her skin was as white as the snow, making her deep brown eyes stand out. Her raven locks were gone, leaving auburn hair fall off her shoulders. Keeping her gaze on Vanadis she leaned over and whispered something to the Fire Wolf in words so soft that none but Vargeisa could make them out.

"This is my charge." Vinglunr explained. "If you have business with her I would hear of it."

"As would I." added Vanadis.

Vargeisa's attention then went to Gamli and a thoughtful smile alighted her face. "Back home in Pohjola there was a man named Kvistr Dusk Torch." Her voice melted into a soft accent. Gesturing to Gamli and Vanadis she asked, "Are you two by chance related?"

Before Vinglunr could give a measured response. Before Vanadis could think up a pleasant lie, Gamli answered "Yes, we're his son and daughter."

Vanadis glared at him. Vinglunr rested his forehead in the palm of his hand.

"Did I misspeak? It's the simple truth." Gamli stated.

Vargeisa laughed, and then said to a flushed Gamli, "Not at all. The truth's rather refreshing and I' will tell you a truth in kind." Regarding Vanadis she said, "Long ago your mother did me a great service, I'll never forget her face, the one you share."

Vanadis pondered the best response and answered, "Your memory's astounding. Hanne died long ago, you must have been very young when you met her."

"She left an impression." Vargeisa said simply.

"I would know more of this service."

Vargeisa considered this and then answered, "As is your right, both yours and your brother's. I was a sickly child, every day of my short life was a struggle against the deathly river of Tuonela. I was a wilful, this struggle lasted for years. My mother sought aid but no healer could ease my suffering. That is until Hanne the Clever journeyed from Kelifar and bestowed upon me a healing broth. I remember well her face, for the day I met her was the day that breathing no longer caused torment."

"I see" Vanadis said, taken off guard by this tender description of her mother. "I'm pleased she saved you."

Recognition lit Gamli's face, "She must be..."

Vanadis nudged him. "We'll discuss that later."

"Tell me, what brings you to these dismal shores?" Vargeisa inquired.

"I would ask the same of you." stated Vinglunr.

"We are on a quest. It involves some danger and there are some who would stop us." the Fire Wolf replied.

"You assumed bounty hunters would chase you in a merchant ship?" Vinglunr asked skeptically.

Vargeisa favoured him a playful smile, "We were unwilling to take the chance they wouldn't. Had we known you guarded Hanne's family we would not have attacked." A sly expression crossed her face and she added, "Didn't Steinarr the Rouge slay poor Kvistr? Take his city of Kelifar? He wouldn't be very happy that his foe's heirs run free."

Despite Vinglunr and Vanadis' stony expressions, Gamli looked ill at ease.

Vargeisa focused on him. "Perhaps, you'd like to join us? We can't return your birthright but we can offer strength and companionship."

"He's bound to our own quest." said Vanadis.

"I can answer for myself." rumbled Gamli, then to Vargeisa, "We hope to find sanctuary in Pohjola, for my sister." Vinglunr and Vanadis both shot him a glance, he ignored them. "Can you help?"

"I can and will offer council." answered Vargeisa. To Vinglunr she asked "Skald, have you heard tell of the Hounds of Louhi?"

Vinglunr thought and then nodded, "I have, songs tell of how heroes must by pass them to reach Pohjola."

"They lie not. The hounds are indeed real. Consider Moldan here," Vargeisa reached for him and Katla put the feline in her arms, "this fine boy," she scratched his head and he purred, "is larger than most of his species and is blessed with potent magic properties. The Hounds of Louhi are the same except where our Prince of Cat's magic heals, their magic tears apart. Skald, have you ever heard a song where the Hounds were brought to submission by spear and axe?"

Vinglunr thought again and answered, "No, the heroes of Kalevala have always snuck past."

"Have you such magic?"

"Only the song I enchanted your party with, that is until you threw your hex."

"It is a potent spell, it's not every day I could shake something like that off. However, the Hounds can, and after they do you'll all die."

"We can't simply announce ourselves?" asked Vanadis incredulously. "We're not coming to Louhi's halls as thieves."

"Louhi is at ill terms with the old and cunning Väinämöinen, his magic rivals her own. She does not take visitors for fear they are his agents."

"Kelifar has traded with both for years." insisted Vanadis, "Her gates cannot be barred to all."

"Louhi has built the town of Tornio which sends and receives all Pohjalander goods. The residents though, cannot enter Pohjola itself. Väinämöinen's Kalevala on the other hand is open to all who bring no ill intent."

Vanadis regarded her closely, she could find no chink in Vargeisa's logic.

"Then we've come all this way for nothing." Gamli grumbled.

"I did not say that." Vargeisa replied, signalling coyly for patience. "I have a charm that will get you past the Hounds, it will also prove you are not one of Väinämöinen's spies. You will be brought to Louhi, but the rest will be up to you."

Gamli grinned, "This is good news."

"Good news with a price." Vinglunr stated.

"Of course there is a price, the charm is dear to me; you would have to aid in my quest for me to even consider parting from it."

Vanadis shared a glance at Vinglunr, he seemed to share her trepidation. "Tell us how we can aid you, and then we'll consider it."

Vargeisa paused her and stewed over what she was going to say, she glanced guardedly at her allies. Wolf shrugged. Bear shook his head as if these things were beyond him. Katla nodded. Finally Vargeisa replied, "Katla is an oracle. It was she who led us to this cove. She foretold that if we waited here for a day I would find a means to my quest, I would recognize it on sight. There is one among you that I very much do recognize."

"Her?" questioned Gamli.

"Me?" stuttered Vanadis.

"So it would seem. What I would need is for us to sail south for a few days and then up the river Indalsälven. This shall take us to the forest of Myrkvid, in that forest is a hidden settlement. You, Vanadis, will lead one of its residents to me, she will answer my questions. Afterwards, you'll get your charm and I'll take you to the shores of Torino"

"Myrkvid?" Vinglunr laughed, "Do you think us mad?"

Vargeisa scowled "I make no jest. If I were playing a game my voice would be jolly. If I were lying I'd tell a far more feasible tale."

"You wouldn't perhaps, tell us the ultimate goal of this quest?" asked the skald.

"No, I shall not." Vargeisa said curtly. Then, back to her casual manner, "Of course you can always risk sailing the rainy Pohjanlahti and then face Louhi's Hounds."

"A moment, I must confer with my charges."

"Of course."

Vinglunr signalled the siblings and, after pulling up their hoods, they stepped out in the rain and walked to the sea shore.

"Myrkvid..."mused Vanadis.

"Where Sigurd slew Fafnir." Gamli added.

"Myrkvid's more than even that." stated Vinglunr. "It's full of stories and rumours, most of which lead to blood. Mjoll once healed a poor soul who'd wandered there, lost for days. His family brought him in, he had terrible wounds, his mind wasn't quite right. The only way to make him whole was to knit his body with magic and have him drink him a potion that would make him forget."

"I'm against my sister going." Gamli stated flatly.

"On moment Gamli. Vinglunr, do you think this Fire Wolf is telling the truth?"

Vinglunr stared at the sea and gathered is thoughts before answering, "She's a Pohjalander, of that I'm certain. Her accent's perfect. The style of her arms, clothing, they're foreign, very similar to the garb of the Pohjalanders I've met. The others, they're of our race and creed yet, from their manner, I'd wager they are close allies. As for her request, she's too canny and it too fantastic for it to be false. Also, she let her manner slip in merely mentioning it. As for the Hounds of Louhi," he mused, "I'm not certain... If she's truthful and we refuse our aid you'll have nowhere in the East to hide from the jarl and winter will prevent us from going West."

"Your counsel then?" Vanadis urged.

Vinglunr struggled with this thoughts and answered, "None. We're in a mire of trouble."

"Gamli, now that you've heard Vinglunr's take, what do you think?"

"Vargeisa's Louhi's daughter isn't she? The child Mjoll brewed the potion for, the one mother saved? "

"From her reaction, it seems likely." Vanadis answered.

"Agreed, which lends credence to her knowledge of the Hounds." Vinglunr added.

"That would mean mother would know a way around the hounds, perhaps if I contact her..." Vanadis mused.

Vinglunr pondered this and shook his head, "Unlikely, if Louhi was looking for a healer, she would have leashed her hounds but only as long as she needed to."

"Hel!" Vanadis cursed, "I suppose going with her the best of bad options."

"I agree," stated Gamli, "but know I'll be with you all the way."

"As will I." Vinglunr agreed.

Vanadis regarded the two of them, her brother broad and strong, Vinglunr wise and skilled. Both courageous. She smiled warmly. "Then to Myrkvid it is."

Once under the pavilion Vanadis said, "We accept."

Well pleased Vargeisa answered, "I am grateful."

CHAPTER 8

There are many songs for battle. | Many tales for those who've died by the sword.
Glory is for those who trade in Odin's bloody business.
Oh we are quick to forget. | Quick to dismiss courage that does not result in Valhalla.
That those who die standing against sickness and disaster, they have no tales, is true injustice.

The parties joined and dried themselves by a fire under the pavilion. Wolf left but he soon returned dragging a doe in his massive jaws. The group worked swiftly and cooked fresh venison for their supper. Paired with warm tea and a little wine, it made the camping in the frozen torrent almost pleasant.

Vargeisa's men turned out to be less brutish than they acted in battle. They traded jokes with their new friends. Vinglunr sang the tale of Wayland Smith, who had famously hid in Myrkvid, his rich voice, paired with the thrum of his lute and his veteran charm put all at ease. Gamli sat with his arm around Brea whoe mourned Asny's passing. Wolf pulled off some skilled juggling of dried fish, snapping them down whole for the amusement of the crowd. Bear sat and drank in silence. Vanadis, Vargeisa and Katla had a spirited game of dice, Vanadis losing a fair amount of skatt.

When the rain let up that evening the whole camp pitched in to build pyres. Vanadis was concerned they wouldn't burn, Vargeisa insisted they would. The possessions were lain with the corpses as well as provisions and a little wine. Once all was set tears were shed and sour looks shot across both sides.

"Skald, you have words I trust?" asked Vargeisa.

"Aye," Vinglunr stepped forward and said, "Let no one here hold umbrage for the battle we fought was fated long ago. Furthermore, let none be ashamed for no shame was found in this fight. There were no cowards, no weaklings. Those who lay before us are the fortunate for tonight they will be welcomed in Valhalla as Ansy Iron Hair will be welcomed in Fólkvangar. Come, let us tell tales of their valour."

They did, each one in turn. Wolf's stories made everyone smile in remembrance. Bear rumbled a few words before tears overtook him. Katla whispered her piece into Vargeisa's ear. Gamli talked plainly of the valour he had seen this in battle and the honour he felt at having known the fallen. Vanadis said little but chose her words well ending with, "Ansy died to protect me. I won't forget her." Her voice cracked. Bera had more to say on her brothers and sister and she said it with heart. Vargeisa told simple stories but with an authority of command. When the torch was passed back to Vinglunr he gave each of his comrades a proud farewell. He finished with, "Odin! Master of Asgard send your Valkyries to carry these souls off to their just reward." The crowd roared in agreement, while Vargeisa whispered a prayer. Then Katla took the torch and stepped before the pyres. As the flame licked the wet wood she whispered a hex and it lit regardless. In such a matter the all the fallen were conducted to their fiery way to the next life.

Everyone was exhausted and slept deeply, there was a late start the next morning. After a brief discussion, it was decided that Vargeisa's longship, the Sapphire Haunt, would be their vessel. The trusty knarr was emptied and the ship hidden in a nearby wood. The valuables were stored on the longship as well as needed supplies, of which the Haunt had been short. Vargeisa's crew jested about thanking Vinglunr's for the treasure and they'd put it to good use it. The Fire Wolf got them to cease before Vinglunr was forced to utter some choice words.

Then they were off. With a full complement at oars the Haunt sped southwest across the sea. There were enough shifts to ensure its speed was swift and constant. In the late afternoon they turned north and followed the peninsula until they reached wide mouth of the river Indalsälven. They rowed up the great, wide, dark river until evening. They camped on the sandy eastern shore.

During dinner Vanadis took her plate and walked away from the fire to stand before Katla who sat leaning against the overturned Haunt. "Excuse me, mind if I sit with you?"

Katla stared up at her guardedly and nodded.

Vanadis was taken aback at the immediate refusal. "I mean no offence. I simply have a few questions."

Katla frowned and shook her head.

Something was off about her, Vanadis peered closer, Katla's face and form seemed more like a dream, did she still wear an illusion? Katla shrank back against the ship and looked increasingly uncomfortable under Vanadis' stare.

Catching herself Vanadis said "I'm sorry. I'll leave you be."

"No need." Vargeisa called behind her. She walked around Vanadis and sat beside Katla with the familiarity of an old friend. The oracle smiled in greeting.

"Katla is shy, she'll only talk to me but she can stand company while I'm around." Vargeisa said magnanimously. Katla, looking much relieved, gestured for Vanadis to sit.

Vanadis did, "Right... Then I won't approach you again unless Vargeisa's with you."

Katla nodded pleasantly, as if to say thank you for understanding.

"All questions you have for her you can ask me. Now please, tell us what's on your mind." said Vargeisa.

Vanadis considered the Fire Wolf carefully, then finally answered "Our men say the two of you threw curses in battle. I was wondering are you..." Vanadis searched for the word.

"Witches?" Vargeisa grinned evilly.

"Seithkona." Vanadis corrected.

Katla seemed comfortable with this question and nodded.

"Yes, that is your word for it." Vargeisa added. "I am, as well as my mother." A curious thought struck her, "How about yours? Was Hanne the Clever a witch?"

"No, if she was things would have taken a different turn in Kelifar."

Vargeisa chuckled, "I imagine so. Did you know her?"

"She's had a great influence on my life." Vanadis answered enigmatically. "My grandmother was one, so I might have the talent. I thought, since we were journeying to Myrkvid, it might be useful if you taught me a spell."

Vargeisa giggled. Katla stared at Vanadis with amusement.

"I take it no." said Vanadis dryly.

"We mean no offence, but just because your grandmother had some power doesn't mean you do. True, you might have the right blood but even so you still need to be opened to the spirits." Vargeisa chided.

Vanadis fumed, "Open to the spirits? Hah! I'm open enough they used me to kill Steinaar."

Vargeisa smirked proudly as if she had just captured the king in hnefatafl. Katla shot a look of shared discovery, a secret revelation between them.

Vanadis glowered, then, she stood up to leave. Vargeisa pulled her back down. "Come, don't be like that. You have nothing to fear from us. To turn you in to the Jarl, when your mother saved my life, it would be the highest dishonour."

Katla nodded in solemn agreement.

"Well, now you know that I can be taught." pressed Vanadis.

The Fire Wolf considered this, "You know of no spells, yet Steinarr was killed with your magic?"

"I didn't mean for it to happen." Vanadis admitted with a hint of guilt.

"Then you have great potential but we still cannot help you, at least not for the moment" Vargeisa concluded.

"Why not?"

"For you to learn magic we'd need to conduct a ritual that would draw the spirits into you. If you lack control, what happened to Steinarr might happen to us."

Vanadis paled, she glanced to Gamli chatting with Bera and Wolf, to Vinglunr who was laughing with Bear, "Right, if that's the case, best not risk it."

Vargeisa reached over and squeezed her hand. "Do not give up hope. Focus on this quest, succeed and you will learn at the feet of Louhi herself, her power outshines twelve of us. Furthermore,

I see now why I need you, why the denizens of Myrkvid will follow you. I need your raw connection to the spirits to succeed in Myrkvid, you are absolutely essential. I cannot do what you will do, Katla cannot do it either. Remember this."

In spite of herself Vanadis was drawn in by Vargeisa's presence and found herself saying, "I'll do what I can."

The Fire Wolf clapped her on the shoulder. "Our victory is fated."

The rest of the night passed pleasantly.

The morning was cold and still, the sky grey. The party slid the Haunt back into Indalsälven and unfurled the sails. The wind was kind and they made good progress along the mighty river as it wound steadily further north and then northwest. Scattered woods greeted them on either side of the shore. In the evening they docked at a small hunting outpost. The hunters welcomed them and traded a small meal of fresh meat for a goodly portion of dried fish. This evening was more solemn than the first, rain pounded on the roof and the travelers were glad to be indoors.

The next morning, at breakfast, the hunters urged the party to sail back south. They were certain there would soon be a winter storm, the worst thing for Vinglunr and Vargeisa's crew would be to stuck near Myrkvid until the Spring thaw. The skald and Fire Wolf set the hunter's concerns at ease by stressing they would not be up north for long. Again, they set sail, this time on choppy waters.

Their way soon curved west and the woodland gave way to a stretch of plains. As they sailed they saw the occasional rider on the shore roads. Around midday an old man in a wagon halted and shouted at them to turn back. Vinglunr stood at the prow and answered, "I'm afraid we must journey on, even into Myrkvid. Please, offer a sacrifice for us." The old man called back, "I will, Frey protect you."

In the distance, they saw an imposing wall of dark, leafy greens. At the edge of the south and north shores were two enormous ash trees. They stood like giants, their branches reaching out as if they held the heavens up. As the Haunt sailed closer they took on more and more of the shape of a man and woman. The southern giant had thick hair and beard of deep green leaves. The northern giantess had long tresses of golden leaves. They swayed in the wind. The crew stared at them in awe.

"Frey and Freya," whispered Vinglunr reverently.

"The actual gods?" Vanadis asked with anxious fear.

"Nay. They simply borrow their shape and watch Indalsälven. It is said the Vanir first visited Midgard through Myrkvid, it is sacred to them." answered the skald.

"Let us sail with respect, no one curse as we pass." Urged Vargeisa.

The Haunt sailed between the trees and they loomed with terrifying magnificence. They made it through without issue.

The sun hung at its highest point and Vargeisa frowned at it. "We should make haste, we still must cross to the western shore of Lake Storsjön and I would not be on the water after sunset."

"To oars then." called Vinglunr.

The sail was furled, the mast lowered, and crew took to the oars and rowed swiftly up river. The trees grew thick around them. They had entered a primeval world cloaked in clammy mist, untouched by man. The wind blew, the trees rustled, ravens called, and underneath it all ran an alien calm. The woods seemed to wait, wait for men to walk their hidden paths and vanish, their footfalls silenced by the fog, their voices stilled. Those at the oars focused on the rowing. The others could only look and fret at the weird menace about them. When it was time for a switch in shifts, a few of the men, including Gamli, chose to keep to their oars rather than sit and ponder eeriness that pressed upon them.

Indalsälven turned sharply southeast for a short distance, then the way opened up west to Lake Storsjön. The white fog thickened enough that only a stone's throw lay visible before them.

"We must slow." said Vargeisa. She made her way to the prow and knelt beside Vanadis. "Row with caution, we'll guard against rock and log."

The oarsmen slackened their pace and the Haunt crawled along the misty waters. All was incredibly still, the only sound being the oars' gentle splashes. A half-hour passed in agonizing stillness, no shadow of tree or land was spotted.

"This lake is endless," whispered Vanadis.

Vargeisa glanced to see streams of light falling through the fog, she frowned, "It best not be, the day is not." she sat vexed for a moment and then called back, "The sun is setting, row for all you're worth!"

With that, the oarsmen heaved and the Haunt picked up speed. Vargeisa and Vanadis peered forward, keeping close eye on the water and mist before them. Meanwhile the great presence of the sun sank further into the west, her light cut by the unseen forest ahead of them. Suddenly the shadow of land loomed.

"Hold!" cried Vanadis in a panic.

The oars were thrust into the water, Bear held the rudder steady. A large rock suddenly pulled out of the mist.

"Turn port!" commanded the Fire Wolf.

Bear heaved on the rudder; the Haunt shifted but still hit the rock with a crunch. The ship jolted, a hole tore through the hull and dark water began to seep in.

"Hel!" Vanadis cursed.

Vinglunr's voice suddenly called out in song, the slow, dark tune he had called days before. The crew's breath suddenly frosted. Vanadis' eyes widened and she pulled Vargeisa back as the water rolling into the hull froze and the ship suddenly rose in the water. Within a moment, the Haunt was resting on an ice float. Vinglunr's crew paused and then cheered, Gamli gratefully slapping the skald in the back. It was time for Vargeisa's crew to stare in wonder.

The Fire Wolf looked upon Vinglunr with new respect, "Well done skald, you have plucked us from the Tuonela." She turned to Vanadis and bowed, "Thank you, as well, you have saved me from freezing to the deck."

Vanadis grinned and said, "Glad to be of service."

Vinglunr and Wolf stepped up to the bow to examine the damage. They were no longer in danger of sinking but the rock through the hull anchored them in place. The skald regarded the stretch of water between them and the dark shadow of land and forest before them. "I shall sing us an ice bridge so we can reach the shore with our supplies, though, I am uncertain how we'll save our vessel."

"Can you undo your enchantment?" asked Vargeisa.

"Of course."

"Bear, gather as much rope as you can, we'll tie one end to the bow. Well take the other with us and, once our fine skald banishes his ice, we'll heave her to shore." Vargeisa suggested.

Wolf stroked his stubble chin. "That'll damage her farther."

"I'll swim back and dislodge her." suggested Bear, "Then, you can pull."

"Then, we have a plan." Concluded Vargeisa with a smile, "Come, let's enact it quickly!"

Vinglunr sung them another float of ice, one that stretched all the way to the shore. The crew gathered their sea chests and supplies and crossed the ice bridge. It took several trips, the sun had set in the meantime and they were forced to use torch light. Vinglunr sang his strange chorus to keep the waters frozen. At one point Wolf nearly slipped but Gamli caught him before he could fall into the water.

Finally the Haunt was empty. Vinglunr said to Bear, "I shall sing the ice away but know the water will terribly cold. Do what you must and return quickly."

Bear nodded, he stood ready, only in his trousers. His body was as hairy as his namesake.

Vinglunr gestured and seemed to relax. With his concentration gone the ice before them quickly melted. Bear waded in following the rope the rest of the crew kept taunt. Soon he was forced to swim and vanish into the fog. Moments later they heard an animalist grunt, then a snarl. Then an ursine roar echoed across the lake.

"That's the signal!" called Vargeisa. "Heave!"

The crew pulled for all their worth, Katla in the front, Gamli anchoring the back. Together they quickly heaved until the rapidly sinking Haunt beached before them, close enough to see its shadow.

"Bring her on shore!" Vargeisa commanded. The entire crew, waded into the lake. Together they turned the ship over, got underneath her and portaged the damage vessel back onto land. When the ship was finally resting on its side on the dry forest floor the crew cheered. Wolf titled his head back and howled, it pierced the fog and rung out across the lake. There was something cheering about it, perhaps it was simply that it reminded them they had a forest denizen on their side.

Vanadis, who herself had helped in the portage, stood trembling. "This cold will be our end. Quickly build a fire."

The crew set to work at once and soon had a large crackling fire. They sat close around it and dried their bodies and clothes. Katla suddenly looked concerned and whispered in Vargeisa's ear. The Fire Wolf jumped and glanced around the crowd. She raised her hand for silence and asked "A moment, where's Bear?"

The crew muttered to each other in anxiousness and confusion. As one they raced to the shore and called out his name. Their cries resounded across Lake Storsjön, but their cries were met with dismal silence. Katla blinked away tears and shook her head. The crew fell quiet.

"Curse it!" snarled Wolf. He tossed a stone with such force that it skipped across the waters. "Bear!" he cried, "Bear, if you live you best come find us. Mark my words, if you've sunk to Niflheim after death I will find you and make you a rug!" He then spun on his heel and stormed to the fire to brood.

"Everyone, away from the lake." commanded Vargeisa with sorrow, "There is nothing we can do for him." Turning to Vinglunr she said, "Skald, I shall tell you of my friend and you will make songs for him."

"Of course." said Vinglunr cordially. "His courage will not be lost under Storsjön's waters.

CHAPTER ◊

Are the gods worthy of faith? | Are men worthy of faith?
Must a king be a slave to the divine, must we be slaves to the king?
The gods care not for faith, only for its fruit. | Tribute for Frey, Warriors for Odin, Praise for Thor.
A King cares not for faith, only its fruit. Even loyal thralls are killed if convenient.

An hour earlier and far to the south, Skili's longship docked in Mjoll's port. Hardegon, Skili, Radur, Nafi, and a score of other warriors marched to the Hall. The sun sank in the west colouring the sea orange. Servants and thralls paused in their work to watch them advance. Mjoll's doors were open wide, the tapestries of Thor and Siff fluttered in the wind.

Hardegon and his troop entered the hall to find it warm and the fire lit. Eight warriors stood at attention by their benches, a defense but seeming like an honor guard. Seated at the table in the middle of the hall was Mjoll, flanked by two shieldmaidens. A supper, enough for Hardegon's entire party, waited for them on the table.

"Welcome." Mjoll said warmly. "I am pleased to see that all of you are well. Most who visit are plagued with wounds and sickness. What brings you to Sif's Hall?"

Hardegon paused, on a small table nearby he spied a hnefatafl board. The gleam from its white and black pieces drew his attention. He noted that the king was close to escaping in the northwest corner.

Skili cleared his throat and nudged his prince. Hardegon snapped out of his ill-timed musing. "Yes, of course." He walked down the table to stand beside Mjoll, "I'm afraid I bring ill news, it is of my Uncle's murder."

Mjoll flinched, "Murder? My poor dear please sit. Eat if you're hungry. Speak and I will listen." Then turning to the rest of the warriors she added, "All of you, please, sit. You may eat and warm yourselves in this house. Ragnhildr, close the doors immediately, the night is full of frost." Her tone was hospitable, as if she failed to notice the troop's weapons and armor.

"We shall stand for now thank you." Said Hardegon, "The news I bring is grim, it bodes no casualness."

"As you wish my lord." answered Mjoll, "Please, share what's on your mind."

Hardegon did just that. He told Mjoll of how he stumbled upon Kelifar and the grisly remains of her people. He shared with her Asta's astute observations about what killed them, emphasising the knife wound in his uncle's chest. Mjoll stood and listened, Hardegon's words worked like a poison upon her, her expression dropped, she could not meet his gaze, and she brooded with sorrow.

Meanwhile Ragnhildr shut the doors tight against the evening's chill.

"After the funeral my man Skili imparted hidden knowledge of the past. Skili? Will you share this knowledge with Mjoll?"

"Aye my Lord." Skili stepped beside the jarl's son. With a hint of gentle resignation he said "I counted the dead and found two bodies missing. Thralls named..."

Mjoll suddenly glared at him. "Do not call them thralls."

"Pardon?" Skili, Hardegon and the warriors were taken back at gentle Mjoll's sudden, cold fury.

One of Mjoll's handmaidens touched her shoulder but Mjoll shook it off. She focused her furious gaze on Skili "Through the power of Sif I mended your wounds. Thanks to that you two could be born." She gestured to his sons. Then, glaring at one of Hardegon's troop, "Loftor Kolson, you brought your son to me and through Sif's power his sickness was cured. Haf Gunborjnson, you washed ashore at my hall and I nursed you until you regained your strength. I have done nothing but serve Alands' sons for years, yet when it came to my nephew and niece, none of you thought fit to tell me they were alive."

"Now Mjoll..." Skili cautioned.

"You, of all people, knew full well Skili. You and Steinarr, who slaughtered my sister; Vanadis has grown to be her twin. I know full well how Steinarr's house treats his women thralls." She paused to contain her outrage and wipe away her tears, "That my niece was treated as such. Never call Vanadis or Gamli slaves again or I shall ask Siff to strike your house barren."

Skili staggered back having lost his words.

Hardegon found himself goaded by Mjoll's anger, "Your fine relations denied my uncle's place in Valhalla."

"Steinarr did that to himself. Do you think Freya, Mistress of Seith, would have allowed him to be cursed if he was a true follower? He transgressed by keeping free folk thralls. He transgressed by defiling the laws of hospitality. The vengeance brought upon him was his own doing."

"Still thy lying tongue!" roared Hardegon. "No hex befell my uncle, he was poisoned by Gamli the Serpent, betrayed by Vanadis the Cursed."

Mjoll sneered, "What scholars you Nibelungs are, you write murder as valor, falsehoods as truth, and greed as glory."

Hardegon flinched as slapped but then retorted in full rancor, "You accuse my family of your own crimes. You defend slayers of children! Kelifar's hall was littered with child bodies. My cousin Dorte, in the early cusp of womanhood, was beheaded! Do not defend these cowards!"

It was Mjoll's turn to act as if struck. Clearly pained by such images she said, in a quieter tone, "I-I cannot defend those actions but my living kin did not commit them."

Hardegon fumed but before speaking further mastered his fury. "You are gravely mistaken." He locked a steady gaze at her; she seemed reflective, moved at least by some of the plight of Kelifar, "Given your speech to my good man Skili I believe you had no hand in this crime. If you but help me find your niece and nephew all can be forgiven."

"Please, you must understand," begged Mjoll, "Vanadis cursed Kelifar in error. Seith magic runs through her, through her Hanne wreaked her revenge. It was a killing at worst, they are no murderers. I beg you, give me time and I shall pay the jarl a fair blood price."

"She's a seithkona." remarked Skili, "That would explain much." His warriors murmured in agreement.

Hardegon frowned in deep thought, he shook his head, "Your familial loyalty is admirable but you are mistaken. Steinarr was a good man, faithful to Freya. As you have said, if this were a curse, Freya would have saved him, therefore it must have been poison."

"My lord, I'm uncertain that Mjoll is wrong. We know Steinarr kept Alanders as slaves."

"Kvistr was a Pohjalander," declared Hardegon "Steinarr won his children in a raid, he is not at fault."

"What of what they did to my poor Vanadis?" urged Mjoll.

"Detestable," answered Hardegon, "however also lawful. A slave is her owner's property as laid down by Heimdall when he wandered Midgard as Rig."

"Lord Hardegon, surely this is at least something for the lawgiver?" stressed Skili. Mjoll nodded.

"I will not delay justice for my uncle." declared Hardegon. He regarded Mjoll and said, with a sigh, "Nor will I force you to betray your kin, no matter how misguided your love is." He looked around the hall at the shieldmaidens and the warriors who protected it and the servants, "I will force one of these to tell me what I need." He drew his sword. His and Skili's warriors drew their weapons.

The protectors moved not. Mjoll calmly drew a dagger from her belt.

"No Mjoll, don't." begged Skili.

Mjoll smiled sadly, "You think I will fight? You know me better Skili." She turned and addressed Hardegon, "I was advised to lie. To claim I knew nothing of Kelifar. Now that I have your measure, I'm glad to have spoken only the truth." Turning to the hall she addressed the enemy warriors, "My nature is my Goddesses'. Yes, Frigg, eternal partner of Odin, is ruthless, and Freya, Vanir goddess, is fierce, and Skaldi, Giantess wife of Njord, is terrifying, but Siff is gentle and so I am. I cannot raise my hand in violence." Then she swiftly plunged the dagger into her heart. She coughed blood, it stained her white dress crimson. "Battle my warriors, they shall see you to Valhalla." With that she fell over the table, her life spent.

Hardegon's jaw dropped. The shieldmaiden nearest to him swiftly slashed at the jarl's son with her sword. However, Hardegon's reflexes kicked in thoughtlessly, he parried. Then, with his senses returned, he kicked her in the stomach and punched his blade through her body. The second shieldmaiden let out a cry and slashed with her axe. Hardegon ducked, her blade slicing his golden locks. He drove up, his sword cutting for her chin but she blocked expertly with her shield. They traded a quick series of strikes, neither giving ground but Hardegon proved the more skilled; he got a slash on her leg, when she stumbled his blade crashed against her temple, sending her topping to the ground.

The protectors of the hall were already engaged with Skili and Hardegon's warriors. A few of Skili's men, those who knew more about the pick axe than the battle axe, fell swiftly. However, Skili and his sons held their own, and vanquished each a foe. Hardegon's men finished the rest.

The Nibelung hero wrinkled his nose as he detected an acrid smell. He then noticed the walls were flickering and glowing from the outside. Black smoke rose from underneath the door. "Fire!" screamed Hardegon. "The Hall's been set ablaze!"

At this his and Skili's warriors, now fewer but victorious, crashed as one against the great doors, they held. Furthermore the heat ripped driving them back. Hardegon rushed past the cloth dividers to find the back entrance. He stopped before a wall flame.

"No." he said, his stomach dropping in fear, "Not like this." he said anger rising in him. "Odin, I will not die like this!" Suddenly the hnefatafl board flashed into his mind and the king escaping through the northwest corner. Without pausing Hardegon covered his face with his arms and charged in that direction, the corner was fully ablaze. He hit, the flames lit up around him biting clothing, hair and flesh. However, the wood gave way. The jarl's son broke through the corner rushing out of the hall like a living torch. With a scream he raced off the cliff, the world tumbled and he landed straight into the sea, its cold waters immediately extinguishing his fiery aura. He reached for the surface and pulled his head up into blessed air. He saw the dock nearby and fought the waves, swimming strongly for it. Soon enough was lying on top its wooden surface, watching the smoke from the hall block out the stars.

Despite his agonizing burns, he pulled himself to his feet and rushed up the stairs, his mind and heart laced with fear for his men and allies. He reached the top weaponless, for his sword had been lost in the sea, but he was ready for anything.

No foes stood to greet him, only the burning hall. The banners of Sif and Thor had been consumed. The hall was now a towering inferno, waves of heat crashed against Hardegon and he was forced to shield his eyes. If there were still screams he could not hear them over the roar of the flame. The Nibelung hero pulled his gaze away from the hall to look down at the dock. Skili's longship had been cut loose and floated far away crewless. Further in the distance he could see small boats making good speed. Hardegon clenched his fists and let out a scream of rage.

"Cowards! Worthless curs!" He sunk to his knees and struggled with the surge of fury and grief that threatened to overwhelm him. Mjoll's last words echoed in his mind "Battle my warriors, they will see you to Valhalla."

"Was this battle?" he muttered. He searched his wracked soul and could find no answer. They fought yes but would Odin find Skili and his sons worthy? Would he find his brothers in blades worthy? Perhaps, but Hardegon knew so few were chosen. He was certain most of his friends had fallen to Hel.

A sharp caw drew Hardegon's attention. Sitting in a leaf barren tree was a raven. His fine black form was perfectly visible in the hall's burning light. He titled his head and snapped up a trinket that rested in the branch with him. With a nod he tossed it and Hardegon caught it. He stared what rested in his burnt and cracked hands, the white king from the hnefatafl board. Then the raven took flight and flew off into the dark sky. Glorious purpose suddenly welled inside Hardegon, it proved a balm for the aches in his body and soul. He stared up at the dark heavens and called out, "Odin, you have pulled me from the fire! I will use all the life you have given me to peruse my foes and bring them low. The wrongful deaths of Kelifar and here shall be avenged!"

CHAPTER 10

Deception is a game of skill. | Kings and jarls ply it as a matter of survival.
It's not enough to draw up a fantastic story and hope your marks believe.
You must tell them what they wish to hear. | At times, you must allow yourself to appear weak.
Most of all, you must spin falsehood from truth, for from truth come the sweetest of lies.

Vargeisa, Wolf, and Katla sat a distance from camp by a small fire that only barely held the mist at bay. Wolf cooked three fresh fish on the fire, his attention focused solely on his task. Katla stared into the flames sullenly.

Finally, Vargeisa broke the silence, "I could not imagine that Bear would perish, this venture's cost is too high." Her soft voice sounded louder, as if the fog were keeping it in.

Wolf frowned at her over his turning spit. "We've paid it already, best see it through."

Katla nodded in agreement, she drew out one of her pouches a long iron nail. She offered it to Vargeisa. The Fire Wolf took it and was surprised at its weight, it tugged, with some force, away from shore, to the west. She ran her thumb across its rusted surface and felt the tiny runes etched along it. "To think this will hold one of them." She secured it to her belt, as if it were a small, naked dagger.

Wolf lifted the spit and cut the fish free. He dropped them each onto separate wooden plates and handed two to his comrades. "I take it you have a plan. The skald and the brother could easily make trouble for us."

Vargeisa cut into the fish and scooped up a bite with her knife. She smiled, pleased to find Myrkvid fare tasty. She flashed a conspiratorial glance at her friends. "Trust me, our little Vanadis shall wish to walk, alone into the fortress. Of that I can assure you."

Wolf's human jaw opened a little too wide. He crunched the fish whole, his lips smacking with satisfaction. After sucking the juice form his fingers he asked, "That tale you told them, about her mother saving your life, is that true?"

Vargeisa suddenly looked uncomfortable, "Yes, every single bit."

Wolf chuckled, "Perhaps you should be called Vargeisa Dragon Eyes? You're as ruthless as Fafnir."

Katla glared at him. While she did Moldan's paw snuck up and snatched away the rest of her fish.

Vargeisa squeezed Katla's hand and said "At ease, Wolf speaks the truth. In sending my saviour's child to her doom I prove myself heartless."

"Do what you must." Wolf said with a proud grin, "Angrboda would be pleased at the lengths you go to, to free her son."

Two hours later the camp awakened. A larger fire was lit, more fish was roasted and the heads party, Vargeisa, Wolf, Katla, Vinglunr, Gamli, Vanadis and Brea, gathered under the pavilion to ease their hunger and finish off the last bit of wine.

As the last mouthfuls were savoured Vargeisa rang her goblet with her knife to gather everyone's attention. "Friends, allies, we are on the cusp of completing our mission. I will win the information I need." She nodded to her crew, "you will be paid the second half of your princely sum and," she nodded to Vinglunr and his party, "you will have a means to pass the Hounds of Louhi."

"Something we look forward to." said the skald.

"Now, let us discuss our plans."

"Excellent, I am eager to hear you."

Vargeisa drew the nail and held it in the palm of her hand. It spun, of its own accord to point west. The crowd leaned in to look at it curiously.

"This nail has been laced with troll blood." Vargeisa explained. "It points to wherever they lair. This, is where Vanadis and I must go."

Aside from Vargeisa's close allies, everyone looked suddenly hesitant.

"Trolls?" Vinglunr asked incredulously.

"I have it on good authority that to the west of Lake Storsjön is a fortress of Troll women. They are seers without peer. I need but question one to gain the answers I seek." Vargeisa declared.

Vanadis regarded her skeptically, "How am I supposed to aid you with Trolls?"

"A fair question, I have thought long on Katla's prophesy, that you are the key to this, and have finally augured an answer. These Trolls hunger for human flesh."

"I am to be a feast?" Vanadis laughed nervously.

Vargeisa held up her hand for patience. "They find man flesh most delectable, though I'd wager they'll make due with haunch of woman. Vanadis, from what you've told me you're cursed with uncontrollable seith, yes?"

Vanadis glared at her. Vinglunr and Gamli turned to Vanadis in surprise. Vargeisa's crew murmured in displeasure at this sudden revelation.

"You spoke to her without our knowledge?" asked Vinglunr, holding desperately to his own patience.

"That was stupid." grumbled Gamli.

Brea nudged her harshly.

"Enough." Vargeisa commanded, "It was good she confided in me, for it sparked a plan." She crossed her arms and leveled her keen gaze on the former slave girl. "It's a daring plan, not for the weak of heart."

"Out with it." stated Vanadis.

Vargeisa took a moment to take her measure. Vanadis' appearance was striking, dignified in a way. Her grey eyes were full of skepticism, caution. The Fire Wolf remembered a similar face, a kind but satisfied smile on her lips, a gentle hand on the back of Vargeisa's head as she lifted it so the girl could drink the hot peppermint broth that cleared child's wheezing breaths.

"Are you well?" Vanadis asked.

Vargeisa snapped out of her recollection to find Vanadis eyeing her with concern and suspicion. Her brother and Vinglunr shared her scrutiny.

Vargeisa turned away, "Never mind. It is too dangerous. I won't risk Hanne's daughter." This drew surprised looks from Wolf and Katla.

"You can't leave it at that. What's your plan? I would hear it." Vanadis urged.

Vargeisa found herself torn between shame and smile. With feigned resignation, she said, "Very well, I believe you are the only one that can approach the fortress and not become a meal. Do not take this the wrong way, but the stench of the grave is upon you, the Trolls will consider you most unappetizing."

"She is rather bitter." joked Gamli.

Vanadis punched him in the arm and the crew, even Vinglunr and Brea, laughed.

"Who here would say being unappetizing to a Troll is a bad thing?" Vargeisa asked with a grin. The answer was a few more chuckles from the crowd.

"You have a point." grumbled Vanadis.

Vargeisa said with calculated warmth and certainty, "Fate has made you capable of this task. Not only will your scent protect you but you take after your mother, you are both cunning and wise. I'm certain you'll be able to draw one of the seers away to speak to me."

"Wouldn't it safer if she simply asked your questions in your stead?" suggested Vinglunr.

"It might be," admitted Vargeisa, "however," she began to count on her fingers "I have a number of questions, I am unwilling to share them with you, as mentioned Vanadis is cunning, it would be simple for her to not speak to the seers and return with falsehoods." to Vanadis she added, "I mean no offence."

Vanadis smirked, "None taken. If I were in your place, I'd worry about the same thing."

Vargeisa bowed in acknowledgement.

Vinglunr stroked his beard looking troubled. He licked his finger and raised it, testing the wind. "One ill breeze and this camp is doomed."

"The camp is safe." Wolf cut in. "My howl signals we are at one with nature, this forest considers me brother. The wind will not betray our position."

"Which is why, unfortunately, Wolf must stay here." Vargeisa added. The crew seemed to be slightly more at ease with that news.

"Furthermore, it will be dangerous for men to come with, Trolls can smell their blood far better than women's."

"Too bad, I'm going." stated Gamli, in a tone that dared anyone to disagree.

For a moment Vanadis looked uncertain, then a sudden resolve hardened her expression, "N-o brother, Vargeisa's right, it's too dangerous. You should stay here."

"How can you say that? After everything we've been through?"

Vanadis gripped Gamli's arms and stared meaningfully at him, "Please, I'm terrified, I want you and Vinglunr with me but that would be foolish. If the Trolls smell you; you, me, Brea, this entire camp would be in danger."

"V-vanadis..." Gamli struggled with his thoughts, unable to find a rebut to his sister's words.

Vinglunr put a steadying hand on her shoulder, "There is another path; you can choose not to go. If you do, I and my crew are honor bound to take you and Gamli out of these woods and find a place of safety."

Vargeisa had turned away, she did so as soon as Gamli entreated her sister, her face an unconcerned mask that hid her own turmoil. She remembered how her lungs felt they were on fire, she remembered Hanne's face, confident and wise as if she were a benevolent maid of Ukko, she remembered breathing clear for the first time in her life.

Katla nudged her and she heard Vanadis say, "You seem rather unconcerned with your quest."

The Fire Wolf forced a casual smile. "Oh, I'm quite focused. My mind is running through a number of tricks and plots to get us back safely."

Vanadis sighed with impatience and said, "If you can spare a moment, I have a question."

"Please ask."

Vanadis locked her grey eyed gaze straight on the Fire Wolf. "If I die in this service, will you give your charm to Gamli?"

"Of course." Vargeisa answered straight away. "I would not dishonor your bravery so." Then, swallowing her rising guilt she added "But, let us go into this with the intent of returning alive."

Vanadis grinned, "Then I am at your service."

"Vanadis, no." rumbled Gamli.

Vinglunr put a hand on his shoulder. "Enough.", he regarded Vanadis with a look of deep respect, "She's made her decision and proven herself a worthy lady of Mjoll's blood." Then to Vargeisa he added "Bera, of course, will journey with you."

"Of course." Vargeisa said with a forced grin. "I'm pleased to have such an honor guard."

"I am pleased to guard the worthy Vanadis." Brea answered, sitting up proudly beside her charge.

Soon after the three, Vargeisa, Vanadis and Brea, were packed and ready for their journey. Vargeisa wore her scale mail, had her sword belted at her side, and wore a rucksack with ample supplies. Bera had donned her thick leather armor, carried her axe and shield, and also had a back on her back. Vanadis carried a spear, wore thick furs to ward off the chill and wore her own pack well.

The crew stood with them at the edge of the camp. Wolf looking pleased. Gamli standing livid. Katla sat with her back against a tree, petting Moldan and watched the three with a forlorn expression. Vinglunr stood a little too at ease as if he were up to something.

"We're off." Vanadis said.

Gamli wrapped his arms around her and lifted her up pack and all.

"Brother," she oofed, "You're squeezing the breath out of me."

He dropped her to her feet. "You come back." He stared down at Vargeisa, his blue eyes focused on like a hawk on a hair, "You make sure she comes back."

The Fire Wolf was suddenly, keenly aware just how large this man was. "I'll do everything within my power to return her to you." she said with a bow, inwardly reflecting on how little control she'll have over Vanadis' end, once her plan rolled into motion.

"Fear not Gamli," Brea said, "for I watch your sister, even trolls will prove powerless to harm her."

He looked down at her, taking Bera's full measure. "Very well," he said, "I trust you with my sister's life."

Suddenly Brea grasped his shirt and pulled herself up to his lips. Gamli looked stunned, but only for moment and then fully returned her affection.

Vanadis shared a conspiratorial look with Vinglunr. The crowd cheered.

When Brea broke the kiss she sighed, "For luck."

"Of course, thank you." Gamli said, regaining his composure.

"We'll be back soon, brother." Vanadis said, giving him a quick hug of her own.

"We best be off.", said Vargeisa. To the crowd she addressed, "We'll be gone for at most three nights. When we return I expect the Haunt to be patched, then we'll make a hasty retreat before winter hits."

"We'll be ready for your return." promised Wolf.

"We'll pray to Freya." added Vinglunr.

"Please do." Said Vargeisa with a fake smile. Behind them Katla grinned surreptitiously, signalling that she'd be making her own prayers.

With that, Vargeisa waved, drew her nail and the three began to follow its pull. They journeyed many hours through the thick mist and tall trees. The going was tricky for the stones and trailing roots threatened to trip them with every step. They talked to ease the unease of the fog pressing on them. Brea told many stories of her and Asny Iron Hair's battles against the Curonian pirates. She told her tales with vigor and emphasized a certain viciousness that Vargeisa found entertaining. The Fire Wolf was, for the most part, content to listen, she noticed that Vanadis said as little as well.

They stopped to rest for the third time that day, sitting and leaning their packs against the trees.

Brea nodded at mystic nail. "Does that give you any clue how much farther we must travel?"

Vanadis peered in the direction of the streaming sunlight through the fog. "It'll be dark soon."

Vargeisa judged the direction of the light and the pull of the nail. The farther west they traveled the stronger its tug, as it stood right now Vargeisa feared that the nail would fly from her hand if she let go. "Not much farther, I have faith we'll reach fortress before sundown."

Vanadis pondered this, "When we see its wall I'll have to travel alone right?"

Bera frowned at that.

Vargeisa answered, "It is the wisest choice," to Brea she said "we are obviously warriors, if we approach Trolls may become angry."

"Then I'll leave my weapons behind." answered Bera.

Vanadis frowned, "No Bera, if the Trolls devoured you I couldn't stand it. I'll approach them alone." Her voice was hesitant, slightly fearful but her expression determined.

"I must insist..."

"Bera no. You must watch her, to ensure her honesty." She nodded at Vargeisa, with a smirk she added "I pray you take no offence."

Vargeisa smirked back, "In your place I'd take the same precautions."

Bera narrowed her eyes at Vanadis, then regarded the Fire Wolf, she then snorted. "When you make your way to the fortress we'll set up camp and keep a close company."

"It'll be like the old days with my sisters." Vargeisa said, not sounding entirely pleased.

What happened next was so sudden it seemed like a dream. Stepping out of the fog came a woman in white, her head covered entirely by a burial shawl held in place by a golden circlet. Brea spotted her and was taken aback. Vanadis suddenly turned pale. A spike of fear shot though the Fire Wolf as she instinctively knew a corpse stood before her. The woman in white pointed talon like finger at Vanadis, silver spectral chains spawned in the air and wrapped themselves tightly around her, cutting through her furs, drawing blood. Vanadis screamed in agony.

Brea rolled up and smashed her shield into the corpse sending it staggering back. Vargeisa rose and rolled back her eyes silently calling the spirits. She felt the familiar nausea of them turning in her stomach, one of her white sightless eyes turned pitch black. She opened her mouth, with a shriek she spit a wave of arcane force that slammed into the Woman in White.

The wraith still stood. She raised her left hand and slashed towards them, the screams of the dead followed her motion and hit the three women like a chilling wind. The Fire Wolf cried as her spirits were driven from her, it felt as if nails tore into her flesh. Brea did not scream though she did stagger. Vanadis writhed on the ground, against her chains, wailing in pain.

Bera glanced at Vargeisa, "Take her and run for the fortress, I'll hold the creature off."

The Fire Wolf nodded and rushed forward scooping Vanadis over her shoulder. The creature reached out and Vargeisa felt tiny invisible hands seize her arm and leg. "No." she focused her will and took off at a run, breaking the ghostly grip. Brea shouted a battle cry and swung her axe, it cut into the creature's arm but stopped as if it were made of solid oak. The creature raised its left hand, on the back of it blazed ᛉ and suddenly Bera recoiled in pain.

Vargeisa simply fled, caring not for Bera, or their supplies. She focused on the pull of the nail. The fog quickly swallowed the sound of the battle between shieldmaiden and wraith, and Vargeisa was left with her own panting, panicked breath.

Her path took her across fallen tree that spanned a wide river, she nimbly and quickly made her way across. With a few more strides she skidded to a halt on a road, before her it stretched up to a steep dark hill, the Fire Wolf squinted and could see the shadow of walls.

Vanadis moaned and Vargeisa put her gently down. The chains had vanished but the young woman seemed as pale death.

"Can you stand?" Vargeisa asked.

"What? Where are…"

"No time." hissed Vargeisa. "The wraith fights Bera, I must know if you can make it for the fortress while I return to her aid."

Her words brought Vanadis focus and she shakily stood. Vargeisa smiled with relief. "Good, you must rush there, there you will find refuge." she pointed down the road towards the looming hill and walls. "

Vanadis accepted and nodded, "Go aid Bera. I'll return with your seer." With that she spun and raced up the hill.

Vargeisa watched her flee for but only for a moment. Then she turned and raced back the way she came. At the stream she sped across the river. She ran through the woods and nearly tripped over Bera.

The shieldmaiden lay on her back, stiff as a corpse, a look of terror in her wide blue eyes.

CHAPTER II

Warriors shed blood and die for one hope. | All eyes on the battle field strain for one sight.
A woman of beauty who rides on a winged stead, Odin's choosers of the dead.
They are a light of hope in a blood soaked Midgard.| A promise to transcend mortal graves.
Do not be foolish, they are spirits of death, the wise know to fear them.

Vanadis fled up the hill until she halted at a large wooden gate. She hammered her fist against it and screamed, "Hello? Please let me in! I need help!" She turned and pressed her back against the wall, watching the road down the hill, at least as far as the fog would let her.

Her mind raced: Did Vargeisa reach Brea? Could she be trusted? What was... a sudden realization hit her. That thing, Vinglunr called it a Haugbui, the circlet that held the shroud, Dorte. Vanadis covered her mouth and gasped, it was really her. Dort come to seek vengeance like Hanne sought vengeance from Steinarr.

"Hail traveller, do you come alone?" called a commanding, feminine voice above her. Vanadis looked up and could see the shadow of a warrior peering down from the stone wall.

Vanadis frowned, the guard sounded human, not the guttural troll she expected.

"I'll ask but one more time, answer me or rot out there. Do you come alone?"

Vanadis answered, "I was separated from my party. I don't know where they are. In this a forest like this they may already be dead. Please let me in." The panic in her tone was real enough.

After a long pause the woman replied, "Hold, we'll open the door a crack."

"Freya's blessing upon you." Vanadis called back. She then waited, keeping a close eye on the rolling fog, expecting at any moment to see the specter Dorte walk out of it. Moments later she heard a rumble and felt a great set of bars lift from the other side of the gate. She turned and stepped back. They opened before her, from behind she heard, "Quick, step inside."

***

Vanadis squeezed through the narrow gap and stopped gobsmacked at those who stood before her. There were three women dressed in gleaming chain mail. Each was a head taller than Vanadis, each built sleek and powerful. Their silky long hair hung loose from under their steel helms. Each carried a spear with a silver tip. They held an awe inspiring beauty that stole Vanadis' breath away. These were not human, but Vanadis doubted they were trolls.

One of the guardians chuckled at Vanadis' expression and gently pulled her further in and away from the entrance. She pushed the great oaken gate closed with her booted foot, and slid the huge beam she carried into its brackets to lock the gates. Her sister, who held another beam, did the same.

The third removed her helmet and rested it at her hip. Her eyes were as green as the forest, her hair blacker than night. She regarded Vanadis with suspicion and asked, "Necessity brings you to our home but I would know what insanity brought you to these woods?

The need for an answer snapped Vanadis' mind to the present. She regarded this goddess with an expression of caution as her mind grasped for words.

"Answer, now." the guardian snapped.

"We were looking for treasure." stammered Vanadis.

"What treasure?" the guardian probed.

An idea struck and she answered fearlessly. "Maybe yours?" The three towering ones glared at her and Vanadis added, without skipping a beat, "Obviously, we failed." She spread her arms to show the cuts through her furs and bleeding wounds.

The three grinned and laughed.

Inwardly Vanadis sighed, being bold was a gamble, thankfully the right one.

"Fafnir's treasure is long gone." said her hostess, her manner now casual. "Have any of your party survived? We may be able to lend them aid."

Vanadis summoned the sickening guilt and worry she felt about Brea and used it as a mask of grief. "I don't think so, there was so much blood... no one survived, I'm sure of it."

"I am Haldis the All Wise. These are my sisters Helen White Swan and Fastny. Who would you be?"

"Vargeisa the Fire Wolf." Vanadis lied with a bow. Her 'ally' was obviously playing a game, best these creatures know of her.

"Interesting name and you have a noble bearing, of what tribe are you?"

This caused Vanadis to pause, "It's of little importance, let's just say I'm a free woman who hopes to improve her fortune."

Haldis glanced to both of her sisters, each nodded in turn. "Consider you fortunes improved for you stay with us tonight." She gestured to the hall.

Again, Vanadis was stunned. The road ended in a copse of apple trees that were twisted and growing together. There were dozens of them clustered in a large circle, their leafy branches rising high, sporting white flowers, even in this late fall, and seemingly holding the fog at bay. Even at the edge of the wall Vanadis was nearly under their branches. Windows glowed out of their trunks, an open gate stood wide in the center of the cluster, the torchlight inside revealed the interior of a vast hall.

"Helen will tend to your wounds and prepare you for dinner. Fastny will announce your presence to our Queen Alruna, I am certain she'll be pleased to meet you. I must stay here and keep watch."

Haldis' sisters bowed to her, as if she had done them a great service by offering to let them tend their guest.

Vanadis bowed, as well, "I thank you for your hospitality."

"You will not find it wanting." Haldis assured.

"Please," Helen's voice was lighter and sweeter than her sister's, "come with me and we'll see that you are properly attired."

***

Vanadis followed the two fair folk towards the great apple trunk walls of the hall. Above her she heard an equine snort. Glancing up she saw a great black horse, with red tipped wings, walk casually across a huge branch. The sight was so magnificent that forced Vanadis to halt in her tracks.

Helen's giggle was like a bubbling stream, "You think you are in Valhalla perhaps?"

Vanadis regarded her with wonder, "You're Valkyries, and where else would I be?"

"Simply a wondrous place in Midgard." Helen assured. She touched the small of Vanadis' back and guided her into the hall, "I advise you not to call us Odin's Maidens, heavenly cup bearers, or 'the reward of heroes'. Long ago we few chose freedom in Myrkvid over servitude in Asgard."

The hall was like nothing Vanadis had ever seen. The floor was polished wood, its pattern smoothed roots that were pressed together. Small orbs of light floated about, giving soft, white illumination but they were not enough, the hall continued on into darkness. A warm darkness, the darkness of well-deserved sleep. Fastny nodded in farewell and walked beyond their sight, her boots clacking on the wooden floor. Helen guided Vanadis to the left. They passed several dividers of shimmering silver cloth. Finally they entered a small chamber with a smooth bench grown out of the living wall, across from it were hooks on which hung several dresses. The roof of the room was leafy and flowery, red apples hung from it in full luster.

Helen removed her helm, her hair was a downy white. Her eyes were a perfect blue. Her features delicate despite her shieldmaiden's build. She set the helmet on a hook and began doffing her chainmail. To Vanadis she said, "Undress and I'll tend you."

Vanadis obliged, pulling off her furs, boots, gloves, and clothes. She winced as she peeled off her dress, the fabric had clotted to some of her wounds. When she was done she examined herself closely. Her body was nicked by dozens of bloody welts, she touched them and hissed in pain.

Helen was out of her armor and wore a simple tunic and breeches. Noting Vanadis' panicked expression she smiled and said, "At ease. In this room we can heal all wounds." She plucked and apple from the roof and offered it to her, "Eat and you will be well."

Vanadis crunched into the apple and found it to be the sweetest she'd ever tasted. She mmmed with delight and quickly devoured the treat. With every bite a welt vanished, leaving clean, unmarred skin. More than that it refreshed her, all exhaustion and aches vanished. She ate the entire apple, including the core.

"There, much better." Helen gushed. "Now, sit, I must make certain there are no ills the apple has missed."

Vanadis obliged finding the bench perfectly smooth and comfortable, despite her nakedness. "I have a request, when I leave, may I take one of these with me?" she asked, glancing at another apple.

Helen giggled and answered simply, "No, you may not."

The Valkyrie then gave Vanadis a thorough examination. She looked her over carefully. Her strong but gentile hands slid over shoulder, breast, and thigh. It felt rather personal but Helen's expression was inquiring, not amorous.

"You have a strange way of healing." Vanadis ventured, her tone not entirely comfortable.

Helen seized her hand and felt along her calluses. "Hmmm," she said with a frown, "you've done much hard labour."

"My life's far from easy. I've had to learn to fend for myself."

Helen lifted Vanadis arm and looked at it carefully, "You've been broken and mended a few times." She sniffed, "Not a shieldmaiden though, you've never killed." She wrinkled her nose, "Yet death does follow you...."

"I was attacked by a wraith, perhaps it's that you smell?"

Helen pressed her hand against her patient's belly. "You're not a virgin."

"I'm well aware that thank you very much." Vanadis snapped. "What has this to do with the wounds I suffered in Myrkvid?"

Helen smirked, "Nothing, you're perfectly healthy, I apologize." The Valkyrie stood and walked to where the dresses hung. "Perhaps you'd be more comfortable clothed?"

Vanadis bit back a sharp retort, knowing well the difference between bold and foolish. "Y-yes, I would. Thank you."

Helen eyed Vanadis and carefully lifted items off the hooks. She handed her a tightly woven chestnut brown woolen dress with white silk sleeves. Vanadis carefully donned it, the clasps were made of gold. It rested well on her, even better when Helen took needle and thread and made a few quick adjustments.

"T-this is unexpected."

"I am forgiven for my former forwardness then?" Helen laughed.

"Yes, yes you are. Fully so." Vanadis said breathlessly.

The Valkyrie then sorted through some jewelry, she picked out a gold necklace with a ruby pendant and clasped it around Vanadis' neck. The dress was a little low cut for Vanadis' taste but the broach complemented it perfectly. She was then given bronze bracelets and two silver rings to wear.

"This is far too much." Vanadis stated.

"Nonsense," Helen chided, "would you visit our Queen in shabby attire? Besides, I'm certain all will be pleased at how you look." She bound Vanadis' hair in a braid using golden thread, then turned her around to get a good look at her. Helen looked pleased at her handiwork. "There, with you looking like that, even we shall be envious."

"Surely you jest, my beauty's nothing compared to yours."

Helen snorted in humor at that. "You mortals sell yourselves short." She reached over to brush the human's cheek "Your kind is so warm and vibrant," her fingers trailed through Vanadis' hair wistfully, her blue eyes became distant, alien, "you breathe, feel, taste." She took in a deep sniff and sighed, "Even under the seith I can smell your precious vital force."

Vanadis found her heart pounding as a deer in the gaze of the wolf. Then Helen laughed and the terror was gone, she was once again a hostess of ethereal grace. "I digress. Please, wait here. I must inform the queen you are ready. When she is ready, you will be summoned."

"O-of course." Vanadis answered, gathering her thoughts.

"Have another apple if you wish. Just be certain to finish it before leaving this room." Helen said with a wink. Then, she stepped out and Vanadis was alone.

Vanadis reached for another apple but paused. This fruit would be distracting, she needed to think. She sat down and mulled her situation and Helen's words. She came to unpleasant conclusions. First, Vargeisa lied. Secondly, no one is this hospitable without cost. Thirdly, Helen's words brought to mind scattered sensations of rushing down Kelifar hill in the sleet and sloshing through the frigid sea with no control of her own.

"Mother?" she called in a whisper. Vanadis was met by only silence. Deep in the back of her mind she sensed many eyes watching her, but these denizen's stayed hidden, silent and out of sight. Vanadis cursed herself for a fool, of course they did; Valkyries, Odin's fetchers of the slain, would have ultimate power over them.

Vanadis glanced at the silver cloth that sectioned off this dressing room. She pondered and determined that it was unlikely she'd be able to sneak out of the fortress.

What did she have then? Only words, but words had served her well her entire life. She thought carefully over the story she would tell, the lie that would either doom her or...she smirked, or give Vargeisa the Fire Wolf that which she richly deserved.

The divider ruffled and Helen stepped back into the room. She was now attired in a dress of deep green and black. Her white hair fell over it like snow on forest. Though Vanadis held no fancy for women her heart still skipped a beat at Helen's simple, potent, beauty.

"Ah, you haven't wandered off. Excellent, a few try and thus, spurn our hospitality. It never turns out well." She winked. "Come, Queen Alruna will see you now."

Vanadis stood, "Please, lead on."

***

Helen White Swan guided Vanadis through the dark hall and numerous hallways and rooms. They turned many corners and the young woman realized that, without guidance, she'd be thoroughly lost. After a good jaunt they entered the throne room.

It was smaller than Vanadis expected but none the less impressive. The apple tree grove grew tall and straight around, the branches criss-crossing above to make an effective roof. The throne was grown out of the wall from intricately twisted branches, white blossoms sprouted all around it. The wisps floated in the room giving it just enough light. Seated on the throne was a Valkyrie of staggering beauty, she had regal features, long golden locks, and wore a dress that seemed spun out of finest silver. She wore a tall crown of gold. She wore gold bracelets that were studded with emeralds. A golden torque was around her neck, its clasp an emerald falcon with a deep opal eye.

"Vargeisa the Fire Wolf." Helen announced with a deep bow, one which Vanadis mimicked. The Valkyrie then left her side to join her eight sisters who stood flanking their Queen in a semi-circle. Vanadis recognized Fastny among them, Haldis was absent. Each were attired in splendor, each held a loveliness that made Vanadis feel like a beast in comparison. They regarded her with appraising looks of disgust, as if Vanadis were an unsavory dish, yet they were hungry. The only exceptions were Helen, who stood with no look of judgment on her face and the Queen. She suddenly smiled in recognition.

"My Queen." Vanadis said bowing her head swallowing a sickening apprehension. If Alruna knew of Hanne the Clever, Vanadis' story would be undone and she'd have no time to spin another.

"Helen," Alruna admonished, her voice magnificent, "you said she was a thrall."

"Isn't it obvious my Queen?" Helen said gesturing to her, "her hands are calloused, she has a sturdiness that only grinding corn and enduring scorn can bring."

"Come closer." the Queen ordered, Vanadis found herself obeying without thought. The Queen examined Vanadis' hands for herself but she also glanced up and stared long at the false Fire Wolf's features. She seized her chin and turned her face from side to side. In the Valkyrie's powerful grip Vanadis chose not to complain. Then Alruna laughed in a lilting fashion and gently pushed Vanadis back a step.

"My Queen. I am told I have a familiar face." The false Fire Wolf stammered.

"You do." Alruna said with a warm smile, "you are Signy reborn. That you've gone through troubles is only further proof, Volsungs are always worthy but rarely happy"

There was a collective gasp among the Valkyries and all regarded Vanadis with a sudden, keen interest.

"Since no one else wants her, I'll have her." said Fastny.

"No, you will not, it's my turn." said a sister with numerous freckles.

"You forsook your turn when you refused that washerwoman!" stormed another with fierce brown eyes.

"Enough." snapped Alruna and all were silent. Turning to Vanadis she said congenially. "My apologies for their outbursts." She paused, thought and added "We prefer the company of women, human women are much desired here, so you have stirred an interest."

Vanadis nearly humphed, for an immortal she was a terrible liar. The false Vargeisa put an expression of mild discomfort and answered, "I-I see. I'm flattered."

"Of course you are." Alruna said haughtily. "Vargeisa, my sisters and I would know you better, Fastny informed us that you sought a treasure, what treasure was this?"

"I am hesitant to say my Queen." Vanadis lied. "I afraid you would grow furious."

"I'll only grow furious if you remain silent."

So Vanadis spun a tale. She told them how she grew up the ward of a witch named Gerd Laughing Crow. How Gerd was obsessed with the trinkets of the great Wayland Smith, who, in legend, hid in Myrkvid. How, after finally securing the wealth she needed for the excursion, the seithkona, herself, and a host of hired mercenaries entered Myrkvid to search for them. However, their ship hit a rock in the Indalsälven and the party was scattered. She, Gerd and their body guards were separated and she was attacked by a wraith.

The Valkyries listened to the story with rapt attention and Vanadis lead them along its path, throwing up masks of grief, fear and pain as needed. When she recalled the wraith's attack she said she could go no longer, Helen gave her some mead and Vanadis 'found the strength to continue'. Vanadis made certain not to embellish her own part. She wasn't bragging, simply telling a tale of sorrow.

"I fled and found your doors. Helen and Fastny know the rest."

Alruna had listened without interruption and regarded the false Fire Wolf in a painfully long silence. Then she said, "So you would steal Wayland's treasures?" Her tone suddenly icy.

Vanadis chuckled bitterly, "My mistress would. As her bound servant I was forced to aid her. It's lead me only to misfortune." Gathering up her courage Vanadis leveled her gaze on Alruna and made her boldest move yet. "Of course I've heard of you, Alruna famous lover of Wayland. The torque you wear must have been fashioned by him." She bowed her head, "I'm a fool for telling you the truth, but you have been so kind to me, I felt honor bound. I only request that you kill me quickly, do not to let me suffer the fate Gerd has laid out."

"What fate has she laid out?" Alruna asked, her tone was slightly less harsh.

Vanadis swallowed and gathered her courage, "If I am not in my mistresses' presence before the next sun up, she will scream and I will be torn apart." She snorted in mock fear, "It sounds ridiculous, I know, but I have seen the curse's work with my own eyes. Just the thought keeps me up at night."

"Helen?" asked the Queen.

"We can all see the spirits inside her. I thought, at first, that she is seithkona, however, they could be there to devour her."

"I see... Can we rip them out without making her useless to us?" asked the Queen with chilling casualness.

Vanadis turned away swallowing her anxiousness. Yes, Hanne being removed from her would be good but 'rip' sounded lethal.

"No, such an act would tear her asunder." Helen answered.

"I see..." mused Alruna. "Vargeisa, that the curse is still active indicates your mistress is still alive. You have proven truthful and, I'd wager, would make a useful friend of this hall. Know that being a servant for us is as being a Queen in other lands. I would force this Gerd Laughing Crow to lift this curse from you. Tell us about your mistress."

"Thank you." The false Fire Wolf answered gratefully. She then told the Valkyries all about 'Gerd.' That she is a Pohjalander witch and claims to be one of Lohi's daughters. That she commands both spirits and wolves. That she's a cunning spinner of lies. That she's powerful, able to break bones with a gesture or summon ghosts that cause direct harm.

"I hear Louhi's daughters are beautiful. Didn't both the wizard Väinämöinen and the wondersmith Ilmarinen once clash over her eldest? She who was known as the Rainbow Maiden?" said Fastny.

"Vargeisa, tell us if this witch is like her sisters in form and beauty." ordered Alruna.

The hungry eyes of the Valkyries focused on her, it was all Vanadis could do not to smile. With a huff she crossed her arms and said "I am most envious of my mistress. Looking at her," Vanadis gestured measurements with her hands, ones that put hers to shame, "you'd think she was my age. She has red hair comparable to the beautiful one over there," she pointed at the freckled Valkyrie, "and carries herself like a queen."

"Louhi is ancient; those of her blood live a long time." said Helen. "This Gerd will keep her beauty for many years to come."

"Surely, then, you will wish to confront her yourself." said Fastny to the Queen.

Alruna mused on this for a moment, then answered, "No, I am done with the mortal world and its conflicts. The honor of seizing this witch will go to you Fastny."

"May I go with her, then?" Vanadis asked.

All eyes turned to her.

"I have a right to see Gerd brought low, for all the threats and curses she's showered upon me..." Vanadis stressed.

Alruna thought it over and answered, "Yes, I will allow it. Best to see the curse die in person." She gestured to the cloth divider, "Now kindly wait in the hall, I have instructions for Fastny in how to enact this justice.

"Thank you my Queen." Vanadis said with a bow, and then promptly stepped outside the throne room.

Alruna gestured for the sisters to gather close. They did and she whispered "Fastny, you will force Gerd to end Vargeisa's curse. Once this happens you will choose one of their lives for yourself. The second will be for Haldis, she who chose watch over reward."

"Yes, my Queen, you're most gracious." Fastny said with a bow, with that she too left the throne room.

CHAPTER 12

Before you are born your fate is set. / It'll pull through both gain and loss.
Rare is the truly fortunate or truly miserable soul, most of us fall in between.
We'll stumble upon substantial gain./ Only to be cursed with wretched loss.
Plan, plot, struggle all you want, the current of fate is too strong for the rudder of your will.

Vanadis walked carefully along the crooked branch. Yes, it was thick and strong, yes it was wide but still they were very high up, one slip and she'd break her neck.

"Will you hurry?" Fastny asked with good humor. She stood at a platform on the edge of the branch. Two railings hung on it, one held a trough of clear water. There was no need for feed, plump apples hung in the leafy branches above and around. The Valkyrie stood beside a black, winged stallion. He was a sleek, strong, magnificent creature. He wore a saddle and bridle of the finest leather.

'Yes, focus on him.' Vanadis thought. She did and was able to walk the rest of the branch without problem. She reached out and the steed nuzzled her hand, Vanadis heart melted. "Oh, he's so wonderful." She said stroking his mane.

"This is handsome Arnkel." Fastny said with affection. She joined in the petting. "Best of all, after this business with Gerd, you'll have your own winged steed."

"No." Vanadis exclaimed in full disbelief.

"You will be as one of us."

Vanadis spied the knives behind her smile and knew full well their meaning. Still, best keep up appearances. "I would like that very much."

"The first step," Fastny said mounting her steed, "is to fly with me." She held out her gauntleted hand.

Vanadis took it and Fastny effortlessly swung her in front half of the saddle. Vanadis had never ridden like this before. The Valkyrie's arms reached around her to hold the reins, pressing the young woman in a hug of sorts, Valkyrie's arms felt as powerful as any man's. Her chainmail clad chest, pressed against Vanadis' back, strong and secure. All fear of heights left the young woman.

Fastny leaned close to whisper in Vanadis' ear. "When we fly I will pull us up, spend your screams then but fear not, I will not allow you to fall."

Vanadis nodded, and banished the foolish fantasies that rose in her mind. This was no noble hero who held her, she was rebellious spirit of death.

Fastny snapped the reins and kicked. Vanadis' stomach lurched as the steed dove down through the branches.

"By Freeeey eeeee!" The false Fire Wolf let out a full shriek as they fell. Arnkel snapped his wings and they rushed across the clearing and pulled up before hitting the tree line. Then all was dark. Fastny clicked her tongue and a nimbus of light surrounded them, illuminating the rolling fog, Vanadis could see the shadows of the trees rolling underneath them. Vanadis giggled, then laughed and then let out a cry of exhalation as the wind rushed past her face.

"Yes," Fastny yelled above the rushing gale, "yours is the correct response to my Handsome Arnkel's flight!" She reached over to ruffle his mane.

"Thank you for this." Vanadis yelled with glee.

"This is but one of this night's delights." said Fastny, "Next you will see your witch broken and defeated. Do you know where she would be?"

Vanadis frowned and mused, she had guessed Vargeisa's plan to the point of her being an offering, but then what? After further thought she answered, "She might be hidden, watching your fortress."

"Whatever for?"

"She knows the tale of Wayland and suspects you're here. She'll watch and plot, best reach her before she enacts her plan."

"Very well. Prepare yourself and do not scream." With that Fastny kicked Arnkel and he dove, straight towards Myrkvid. They flew so swiftly towards the thick trees that Vanadis let out a strangled cry that Fastny muffled with her palm. Arnkel, Fastny and even Vanadis passed swiftly through the trees like ghosts. They sped through the woods and even darted straight through Vanadis' camp, ghosting through the pavilion and the Haunt as they went. Arnkle ran across the lake, Fastny pulled on the reigns and walked him back towards shore. Soon they stood on the beach.

"Not a sound." Fastny threatened in a whisper. "With this aura we can see them but they cannot see us. "Vanadis nodded and the Valkyrie removed her hand from her mouth. "Now, tell me Vargeisa, is this thing your Gerd?"

Katla sat across from the haunt, staring up at them in terror.

"No." whispered Vanadis "I've never seen her before. She must be from a separate party, most likely here to hunt us. My mistress has made many enemies." The young woman glanced around. Other than Katla's silent dread the camp was peaceful. A large fire crackled at its center, Vinglunr sat with a mix of Vargeisa's and his men' he had them wrapped in one of Ragnar Lothbrok's tales. Wolf sat under the pavilion playing dice games with the rest of the crew. Gamli knelt at the Haunt, he carefully smoothed the replacement planks. A wood bowl with blue paint sat beside him.

"Good." Said a pleased Fastny, "I had feared you lied about her...form, and beauty." She then turned her harsh gaze on Katla, "As for you, keep silent about what you've seen and I promise not to sully my blade with your blood."

Katla's fear turned to hate, she fumed enough to let out a short cry. Moldan hopped off her lap and hissed at them. Gamli noticed and walked over to her.

In a concerned tone he asked "Katla, what's wrong? Is there something in the lake?"

"Let's find your Gerd." said an amused Fastny. She kicked, the stallion took flight, and rushed through the woods. The Valkyrie leaned forward so her green eyes could take in more, Vanadis found herself pressed against Arnkel's neck. After a few mere moments they rushed past a camp fire. The Valkyrie pulled Arnkel to a halt and stared back at the dimly glowing piece of orange fog. "We've found her." she nudged Vanadis and helped her off her horse. She then slid off herself but made no move to tie her steed to anything. Ankle snuffled Fastny's chestnut hair and kept his place. The Valkyrie smiled at Vanadis, "Your description was most accurate." She stared down keenly at Vanadis, "You present me with a hard choice."

Vanadis swallowed her apprehension and asked, "What choice is that my Lady?"

The Valkyrie caught herself and answered "Only how best to protect you when we confront the witch."

Vanadis smirked, "I have an idea."

***

A few minutes later, Vanadis walked confidently through the fog, the hem of her expensive dress swaying as she walked. Soon, she stepped within the firelight to find an alert Vargeisa standing with her nail clenched in one hand.

"Hello 'Gerd'." Vanadis greeted pleasantly. She stood there in full confidence with her arms crossed.

Vargeisa peered at her for a long moment then cracked a smile. "Vanadis? You live?" She laughed, "This is good news."

"Not necciarily for you." Vanadis huffed. Behind Vargeisa loomed the shadow of Fastny.

The Fire Wolf spied Vanadis' look. "You've brought my 'Troll'." Vargeisa said in gratefulness and suddenly threw her nail to the ground. It sunk immediately. A hallow boom echoed from around it. A blast of air rushed passed Vanadis. The shadow of Fastny immediately toppled.

Vanadis was still processing this when the Fire Wolf rushed and punched her, with a gauntleted fist, in the gut. Vanadis crumpled and somehow managed to hold in her lunch.

"I'm sorry that you've escaped with your life only to become barter, but that's just your fate." Vargeisa shoved Vanadis hard and she fell back, cracking her head sharply against a tree behind her.

***

When her vision cleared, she found her wrists bound behind the tree and her body tightly lashed to the trunk. The true Fire Wolf had just finished binding her ankles, the ropes so tight they pressed through the leather of her boots.

"Hel take you." Vanadis hissed.

Vargeisa grinned up at her. "Oh I'll never belong to her. When Pohjalanders die we sleep peacefully in the river of Tuonela."

"Then drown in it." Vanadis snarled, tugging at her strict bonds.

Vargeisa considered her for a moment, pondering how best to reply. Behind her Fastny groaned. The Fire Wolf smiled, "Ah, our buyer awakens." She swiftly stuffed a linen cloth in Vanadis' mouth. As Vargeisa bound another cloth between her lips she explained, "I can't have your sharp tongue spoiling the barter." She then smoothed out the outraged Vanadis' dress and pulled her locks out of her eyes. "You look perfectly fetching." She kissed her on the forehead and Vanadis let out a string of muffled obscenities.

"Gerd." cried Fastny. "You know not who you deal with. Release me at once or you'll be driven to sore lament." The Valkyries helmet had rolled off, revealing her dark, chestnut locks. Her green eyes glared at Vargeisa with an ursine ferociousness. She lay flat on her chest. She tried to push herself up but seemed stuck to the ground.

"Gerd? Is that what she named me?" Vargeisa asked, as she stood and walked up to the prone Fastny. "As for my knowledge, I know perfectly well who I treat with, otherwise I wouldn't have brought my wonderful nail. It's useless to struggle; the prize was stolen from the most sacred temple of Odin. It's crafted to hold a whole troop of you, you won't escape unless I chant the appropriate spell."

Fastny glared at the bound Vanadis, "Vargeisa, did you know of this?"

The false Fire Wolf shook her head, quailing under the glare of the Valkyrie.

The true Fire Wolf laughed, "Ah, so she's Vargeisa? What wonderful tales she must have shared." The true Vargeisa winked at Vanadis, who now returned to fuming.

"You dare lie to me, to our Queen? I'll shred you to pieces!" Fastny growled and pushed against the ground with all her might. She didn't move an inch. Vanadis grumbled something behind her gag.

The Fire Wolf sat down beside the prone Fastny and ruffled her hair. "She's right. Who can blame the mouse for lying to the cat?"

"I'll will grind her bones to dust and use her hide as a standard."

"You're thinking about this wrong." Vargeisa said, gently rubbing the Valkyrie's back. "Much better to wear her as a costume and dance among us mortals, yes?"

"You have no say in what I do to her." Fastny spat back.

Vargeisa giggled, stood and walked behind the young tree that held Vanadis. She wrapped her arms around it and rested her chin on Vanadis' shoulder. "Oh, I do, she's mine, but she'll be yours if you answer my questions."

Vanadis' brown eyes widened and she muttered something foul under her gag. Vargeisa patted her cheek and stood. "Think about it, she's young, hale, I'd even say beautiful in a regal sort of way."

"She has the hands of a slave."

"Ah, I have it on good authority that your young Vanadis is the child of Kvistr Dusk Torch, a hero among my people, one who held the Nibelung town of Kelifar for over a decade."

"You say 'held' which means she has no claim to these lands."

"No." said Vanadis, "However, she travels with us with a great inheritance. With this, her looks and your bearing I'm certain you could secure a powerful husband."
Fastny fell to silent brooding. Vargeisa sat beside Vanadis again, and gestured to Vanadis, "If marriage isn't your desire then Vanadis is an even greater prize. Look at her, she houses an army of spirits. I'd wager that, through her blood, you could exert your full power." Fastny looked up and considered Vanadis who was, more and more, seething with rage. "As seithkona I know well how possession works. Even a powerful spirit can do little through a weakling host. This host, however, is very strong. Through her you'll have all of your strength and speed. You'll walk among us lesser warriors like a dragon in sheep's wool. Through her you can win glory and experience every single human delight. You need simply answer my questions and she's yours."

"You'll free me and give me her life?"

"Yes, if you answer my questions."

Fastny pondered this. Vanadis grunted loudly but failed to get the Valkyrie's attention. Vargeisa waited as if she had all the time in the world.

"Fine but fulfill your end of the bargain first." The Valkyrie ordered.

"No, no, no," Vanadis tapped Fastny's nose, "I get my answers, I leave and, after I'm far away, I chant the spell to release you."

"You are a coward." Fastny snarled.

"This from one who won't travel under open sky?" Vargeisa shot back, "One more insult like that and I leave you here till Ragnarok. Whether you like or dislike this fate is of little consequence. I hold your freedom and Vanadis in my hands, it will be by my will alone that you will receive either."

"Fine," sighed Fastny, "I would hear your question."

Vargeisa smiled in anticipation and asked, "Then tell me Valkyrie, how may I enter and return safely from the realm of the Dragon Nidhogg?"

"Hvergelmir?" Fastny laughed, "There is no safe return from that wold of serpents. You ask how to meet ultimate destruction."

Vargeisa swiftly knocked Fastny's face into the dirt. "Do not mock me. Your kind travels in and out of all the worlds."

The Valkyrie pulled her bloodied face up and snarled, "You dare..."

"Another unhelpful word out of you and I'll leave, with your prize. You'll never be free from this circle, your sisters won't dare approach it, no force save my spell will remove it. Are we clear?" Vargeisa stormed, her blue eyes flashing with fury.

It was enough to subdue Fastny's outrage. "Y-yes. Fine, I relish sending you to Hvergelmir."

"Then answer my question." Vargeisa said, instantly switching to pleasant. "How can I get in and out?"

Fastny was silent in a moment, her expression one of careful thought. Finally she said, "We Valkyries go to all worlds except Hvergelmir, the way there is barred. I've never desired to go there, nor have any of my sisters, we know of no way. However, I do know how you might contact one who does."

Vargeisa scowled, brooded and finally answered, "Very well, then, tell me."

"Will our deal still remain with this answer?"

"If it is something of use to me, then, yes." answered the Fire Wolf.

Vanadis had been quietly working on her bonds, but this conversation drew her in. In spite of her dire predicament she found herself listening intently.

Fastny closed her eyes, drawing upon ancient memories. Finding what she sought she said, with a distant reverence, "As you may already know, long ago Odin consulted the wisest Jotun seer on the fate of his people. It was through her he learned the Fate of the Norns, through her he divined the end of the world, Ragnarok. It is this volva you must seek."

"I see. You know how to contact her?" asked Vargeisa.

Fastny nodded sagely, "I do, but it will be a difficult task.

When the seer was alive Odin saw her as a threat, her wisdom could lead the Jotun to victory. When Odin received his mystic spear Gungnir, she was its first victim. When she died Odin uttered a curse that destroyed her name. In this way he was able to ensure that no Jotun seithkona could call upon her spirit to advise them. However, the Aesir king had questions of his own. He mixed her blood with clay and formed a bowl which he called Barrow Bowl. He then traveled to Midgard, to the mounds of Skane, which have always had a strong connection to the realm of the dead. He used the bowl to contact the volva and, by deceit, won her knowledge of Ragnarok."

Vargeisa looked ill pleased at that, "This is of no use to me. I cannot steal from Odin."

The Valkyrie grinned, "I promised to send you to Hvergelmir didn't I? You will not have to steal it...from Odin. When Odin's task was done he shattered the bowl and scattered it across the mounds. It was lost for centuries, that is, until certain Midgard sorcerers contacted our Queen Alruna. She bartered secrets with them, they taught her how to permanently take a Human life for her own, and she told them of the bowl. These sorcerers scoured the Skane mounds and found every piece. Through powerful magic they repaired the bowl. What they asked the volva for I know not. What I do know is that the Barrow Bowl can only be used in Skane. If one such as yourself were to search there, I'm certain you'd find it."

The Fire Wolf mused on these words, she glanced up at Vanadis as if to ask 'what do you think?'

Vanadis glared back at her in forced silence.

"Well?" Asked Fastny, "Dose my wisdom suffice?"

Vargeisa patted her on the back. "It does." She stood and walked over to her captive. Vanadis watched her approach with hate fueled courage. Vargeisa croutched down before her and drew her knife. Vanadis did not wail, she did not cower, her fists were clenched behind her back, and her grey eyes expressed only determination for vengeance, even if it must come from beyond the grave. Vanadis did shed tears but only out of despair at never seeing her brother, Vinglunr and Mjoll again.

"Don't kill her." called Fastny, "I'll need to do it if I am to steal her life."

Vargeisa regarded Vanadis with the dull stare of an executioner. Then she cracked a smile. Then she snickered, then she giggled. Then she outright laughed with enough force that she nearly fell over.

"I'm glad you find this mirthful, leave my body alone, I'll claim it after you free me." snarled the Valkyrie.

Vanadis glared at her in indignation.

Vargeisa managed to control herself and addressed Vanadis "Understand, I have no wish to stab you but, if you strike me after I free you, I will."

Vanadis raised an eyebrow and froze in utter confusion. The Fire Wolf took that moment to cut her bonds.

"What are you doing?" Fastny asked dryly.

"Returning to my camp with my ally." Vargeisa answered innocently.

Vanadis tore off her gag. "What are you playing at?"

The Fire Wolf stood and drew her sword to keep it between Vanadis and herself. To the Valkyrie she explained, "I said I would give you her life but I didn't say when."

Fastny's jaw dropped.

"You can have Vanadis' body after she's done with it." Vargeisa added with a grin.

"That makes it useless to me!" Fastny fumed.

Vargeisa shrugged "That is none of my concern, though I thank you for your council. Vanadis, we're leaving." She jabbed her blade in her 'companion's' direction for emphasis.

Vanadis wiped away her tears, still looking both angry and flabbergasted, and then walked in the direction Vargeisa was pointing.

"No, this is not how this works. You bring her back now traitor! Liar! Deceiver!"

The Fire Wolf ignored the Valkyrie as she and Vanadis vanished through the fog.

CHAPTER 13

Home, a place that has banished fear. | A fireside bench shared by your loved ones.
For most of my childhood, I never knew home.
Aside from my brother, I feared my loved ones.| Benches were for others, it was the floor for me.
Strange then, my first real home, my resting place of the heart, would be in 'Dismal Sariola'.

They walked for some time, when Fastny's ravings were finally dimmed to nothing Vanadis asked, "Where's Bera?" Her voice shook from the storm of emotions inside her.

The Fire Wolf lowered her sword, grimly, she said, "We are near her resting spot, come"

They walked a short distance further and came to a small mound of earth which had an oak for a marker.

"Please understand, I had intended to save her but the wraith had done its work before I could lend aid." Vargeisa said, keeping a close eye on Vanadis.

"Is this true?"

"Of course I..." The Fire Wolf paused when she noticed who Vanadis was talking too. Standing over the grave, the fog rolling through her, was Bera.

The phantom turned her gaze on Vargeisa and answered, "The wraith made quick work of me and vanished. She could not have helped." Her voice was hallow, she sounded lost.

"I swear on the spirit of my sister Vanadis, I did not conjure that creature."

"I know." answered Vanadis. "She was my mistress, Dorte, she was after me. My curse brought this about." Vanadis voice trembled, seemed close to tears but did not shed them. "I-I killed you Bera, just as I killed Steinarr."

The phantom turned to Vanadis and shook her head, "Do not mock my sacrifice. I chose to fight the wraith, this death is mine."

"Why are you here Bera?" Vanadis choked, "You should be in Fólkvangr."

Bera looked up forlornly, "I would have to burn first but even then the Valkyries cannot see me," She looked to her feet, "and I see no path to Niflheim. I would accept either." Her voice cracked with sudden despair, "In Fólkvangr would I would drink with Asny, in Niflheim I'd see my grandfather, he was a fisherman, not a fighter. Here," she sniffed, "here I will be alone."

Vargeisa touched Vanadis lightly on the shoulder, she shook her off. Never the less Vargeisa persisted, "It doesn't have to be this way. Invite her to you." The Fire Wolf said gently.

"What? So she can be like Dorte?"

The Fire Wolf shook her head, "No, we are seithkona, our souls are like unto homes for spirits. Taking Bera with you would be a kinder fate than leaving her here."

"How? How can I do this?"

"Simply say the words." Vargeisa urged.

Vanadis turned her attention back to the phantom, mustering her courage she said "Bera, if you don't hate me, I will gladly take you with me. We'll journey together, I'll live a glorious life so we can attain Fólkvangr."

Suddenly Bera smiled and she shone with a silver, ethereal light. "Yes my mistress. I would like that very much. I will stay by your side and be a guardian, simply call on me and I shall bring steel and fury." The phantom flew like a rushing wind at Vanadis and embraced her. The young woman was lost in Bera's glow for a moment and then it faded. Vanadis cried in both grief and joy, she was so overcome that she was forced to sit until she until she had finished weeping.

Vargeisa sat beside her and put a comforting arm around her. "There, there, I was the same way when I accepted my sister who had been killed in ever vile Kalevala."

When Vanadis had stilled Vargeisa asked, "Are you well enough to walk?"

Vanadis nodded, she looked drained but also and suddenly more confident, "Before I do, explain your plot."

"My plot?" Vargeisa asked innocently.

"What this was all about. If you don't I swear I'll figure out how to summon Bera and she will thrash you."

The Fire Wolf laughed, "Very well, but I would do this by a warm fire and with some food, will you agree to that?"

"Will it be poisoned?"

Vargeisa chuckled and shook her head, "No, if I wished you dead I would have completed my deal with the Valkyrie." She stepped around the grave oak and pulled out her pack from its hiding place. She glanced at Vanadis thoughtfully and undid her raven feather and cloak and held it out to her. "That dress looks stunning but I think it's ill-suited for this weather. Wear this until we get back to camp."

Vanadis nodded and wrapped the cloak around her.

***

Then the two marched off, Vargeisa pausing occasionally to hold up her fist and judge their path by that. When Vanadis eyed her for this the Fire Wolf smiled and answered, "The nail cost us a fortune. This ring," she tapped a copper ring she wore, "is a much gentler magic and far less pricey. It'll guide us to Katla who wears its partner."

"I should steal that and leave you here." Vanadis huffed.

Vargeisa snickered." You might succeed but then you'll have to deal with Katla and Wolf.

They continued on in silence, not stopping for rests, until the glimmer of the sun danced through the western fog. Then Vargeisa found a sheltered clef in forest rock and made camp. As soon as the fire was started and after Vanadis had drank from her wineskin and ate half her remaining rations, only then did Vargeisa tell her tale.

"Vanadis, I have someone I care deeply about, I care about him as much as you care about your brother. The only way I can save him is to descend to Hvergelmir and return. Getting to Hvergelmir isn't easy, some would say impossible, but I'm determined. Thankfully, I have good friends, Bear, Wolf, and Katla. I told truth when I said Katla is a seer, her predictions are always trustworthy. She once told me "Three years from now, on the third Moon Day of Haust-Mandur, in Traitor Bay in Helsingland, you will find a key. You must secure Hel's nail. If you take the key and the nail to the Valkyries of Myrkvid the path to Hvergelmir will be open to you." It took some doing to get nail. In fact, we barely had time to make it to Traitor Bay. However, we did and you know the rest of the story."

Vanadis stared into the fire, her brows creased in thought. "Why Myrkvid? Why not throw your nail during a funeral?"

"We would have secured a Valkyrie yes, but she would have been one of Odin's. The Aesir would notice and swift punishment would follow. The Myrkvid Valkyries are rebels. They cannot leave the cover Myrkvid as they fear the unblinking eye of Heimdall. Yes, they could hide in human skins and chase me but then they'd be much easier to deal with."

"Why use me? Why not walk into the fortress and throw the nail there?"

Vargeisa shook her head, "Too risky. I bluffed when I mentioned the power of the nail. Yes, it might hold a few of them, but it would not have held the entire fortress." Vargeisa poked at the fire and paused, sifting her words carefully. Finally she added "When I sent you I expected a Valkyrie to take your life. She would then have your memories and looked for me. I would have then bound her and wrung my questions from her. I did not expect you to return with you spirit intact."

"If you expected me dead, then, why did you save me?"

Vargeisa regarded her thoughtfully and answered, "In everything I've told you I've mixed truth with lies. Your mother did indeed cure me when I was a child."

"Then how could you send me to my death?"

"I owe your mother, not you." She stirred the fire, sparks flew up into the fog. "Still, enacting this plan wasn't easy. You didn't deserve the doom I was sending you to." She glanced up at her camp partner again, "Tell me truthfully Vanadis. If you had to sacrifice me, a woman you just met, in order to save your brother, would you do so?"

Vanadis turned away, which was answer enough.

In a warmer tone Vargeisa added, "I saved you because I admire you."

Vanadis snorted.

"It's true," the Fire Wolf laughed, "I expected your life to be taken. Clearly it was not. For all my tricks and cunning I couldn't have pulled off that ruse. You must tell me how you managed it."

Vanadis' expression softened, slightly.

"I admire talent Vanadis. I surround myself with capable friends. Bear sacrificed himself to save us all. Wolf keeps our camp safe from Myrkvid itself. I don't know what I'd do without Katla. If you secure training with my mother you will be a force to be reckoned with. I'd like to end the bad blood between us. I hope we can be allies."

"How will I get past your mother's hounds?" Vanadis asked snidely.

Vargeisa grinned and pulled, from a pouch on her belt, a smooth flute made of birch wood that was carved to resemble a howling dog. She offered it to Vanadis, "Another truth I told. I indeed have a charm against my mother's hounds and, as per our agreement, it is now yours."

Vanadis scooted around the fire and took it, it was beautifully constructed; she couldn't help but admire it.

"I had planned to give this to your brother but am happy you are alive to use it."

Vanadis closed her hand around the flute and kissed her fist, offering a silent prayer to Freya in thanks. She then hung it around her neck by its leather cord.

"I apologize for putting you in peril. Can we at least not be foes?" prodded the Fire Wolf.

Vanadis considered her for a moment and then, she answered "We're not foes but only because I still need your ship."

Vargeisa chuckled, "That will have to do."

Vanadis smirked, "Now, let me tell you how deceit really works." With that, she told Vargeisa exactly how she saved herself from the Valkyries. The Fire Wolf found the tale most amusing.

***

They reached camp the next morning. Vinglunr, who was running combat drills with both sets of troops, spied them first. "Halt!" he called, singling the end of practice. "Our sisters return to us." His smile dropped, "Minus one." He rushed up to them, Gamli following close behind.

"Bera?" the Volsung brother asked for both of them.

Vargeisa shook her head sadly.

"It was my curse." Vanadis said, her voice unsteady. "Bera, like Ansy Iron Hair, sacrificed herself to save me."

This hit Vinglunr like a blow to the gut.

Gamli looked even more wounded. Still he reached out to his sister, "It's not your fault."

Vanadis allowed herself to fall into his hug. "I know." She said, struggling with her grief, "that's what Bera keeps telling me. She's with me now."

"She was not taken to Fólkvangr?" Vinglunr asked with deep concern.

"We've discovered that souls of those killed here stay here," The Fire Wolf explained. "Unless a seithkona take them unto herself. If you'll excuse me I must fetch Katla, we must pull Bear's ghost out of that lake immediately."

"Of course." Vinglunr made way for her.

Vargeisa squeezed Vanadis' shoulder and marched off towards the boat, towards a joyful looking Katla. Wolf, who had just returned from fishing eyed Vanadis in surprise and rushed to the Fire Wolf. They could hear her say "Explanations will come later, we need to save Bear, now."

The skald, with a heavy look at Vanadis said, "While I mourn for our fallen sister, I am glad you've returned to us."

"Not your fault." stressed Gamli.

Vanadis leaned on her brother for support and pulled the hound whistle from under the top of her dress, "At least our quest was successful."

Vinglunr gently took the charm in hand and observed it closely. "Yes, this has some magic to it. It's good to see the Fire Wolf was true. I won't have to spring my surprise on her."

Vanadis titled her head inquiringly.

Vinglunr chuckled and whispered, "Wolf knows nature, Katla knows spirits but they're both fools when it comes to money and politics. If I say the word, Vargeisa's warriors are mine."

Gamli looked stunned, "Really? How did I not know this?"

"Because I never told you Gamli. You're a great warrior, an excellent shipwright, but a lousy liar." the skald teased.

"Ship wright?" Vanadis asked.

Vinglunr gestured to the Haunt. It lay inshore, upside down, as expected but the hole in her bow was gone. Vanadis glanced at Gamli in disbelief. "He's never repaired a ship in his life."

Gamli shrugged, "At first I was only helping, then Wolf just left me to it. It was easy."

Vinglunr clapped him on the shoulder. "I've seen many ship repairs, what you've done was far from easy. You must have the blood of Wayland in you."

"Speaking of Wayland." Vanadis nodded towards a tree at the far end of camp. "I have much to tell." The three retreated there and under its branches Vanadis told her tale. First, she related Dorte's attack and Brea's final act of valor. The telling was hard on Vanadis but it seemed to put Vinglunr more at ease. When she reached the part of the Fire Wolf's betrayal the skald was forced to seize Gamli to prevent him from charging her. When Vanadis reached the part where Vargeisa spared her life, Gamli's anger was mollified but he was still in a foul mood. When it came to Vargeisa's questions Vanadis lied, "She whispered them to Fastny, I couldn't hear a word." She felt no guilt at this, Vargeisa's further quest was none of their concern.

Meanwhile Vargeisa and Katla stood at the edge of Lake Storsjön. Wolf drove curious on lookers away. Vargeisa's men returned to a dice game under the pavilion. Vinglunr's went back to arms practice. The witches strode into the lake until they were but shadows in the fog. They swayed, those who listened heard a crowd of strange voices rising and wailing from the waters around them. The swaying and the murmurs continued even after Vanadis had finished her story. When she and Vinglunr approached, Wolf kindly asked them to stay out of it. So Vinglunr sat under the pavilion and played on his lyre, a soothing song that stretched along the camp and drew all ears. Even Moldan sauntered by to listen from Vanadis' lap. None but Vanadis saw the shadow of a bear rise up before the two witches and then dive upon them, the wake of its force causing a wave to roll up on shore. Then Vargeisa could be seen carrying Katla out of the lake. Wolf rushed up to them, Vargeisa handed her to him and they sat by the fire, conversing while Vinglunr finished his songs and stories. By then, it was dark.

"These songs were in honor of Bear who saved our lives and Bera who gave hers to protect my charge. No matter where the fates have taken them, they have gone in honor." His audience, including Vanadis and Gamli cheered.

By this point, Vargeisa and Wolf had made their way to the pavilion. Moldan returned to her mistress Katla, who stayed by the fire.

"Thank you Vinglunr, your songs have lightened our hearts and calmed the dead." said the Fire Wolf. Then she addressed the crowd, "I have good news, our quest has been successful. Early tomorrow we row down the Indalsälven and out of Myrkvid. From there we'll take our guests to the shores of Tornio, and they will be free make their way to Pohjola. Beyond that is a short sail to our home port and you, my hardy troop, will receive your full payment. Just in time for a long, restful winter." All cheered at this news.

***

The next morning caught the troop with a chill in the air. Vanadis packed away her fine dress and replaced it with warm furs. The rest of the crew were likewise bundled up. She returned to Vargeisa her raven feathered cloak. The Blue Haunt was pushed into Lake Storsjön and the rowers made haste, yet were very careful to avoid the ill-fated rock that greeted them the first time they landed on its shores.

The trip across lake and up river was still eerie but also more pleasant than before. The crew felt as one. Lead by Vinglunr they sang songs. Thanks to Wolf's, Vargeisa's and Vanadis' keen vigils they avoided all trouble. Time rolled past swiftly and soon the shadows of the Frey and Freya ash trees rose. The Haunt passed respectfully between them and finally the fog lifted.

The sun was hidden behind gray rolling clouds. Snow drifted down from the heavens, a thin layer already coating the trees. Frey and Freya had exchanged their leafy hair for snowy locks. A chill wind howled past, it bit the crew's skin and tugged their cloaks.

"Winter is here." Vargeisa said through frosted breath.

"Then we best hurry." added Vinglunr.

"Raise the sail." cried the Fire Wolf.

They did and their ship sped down the rest of the Indalsälven for a few days. They made great speed when they hit the sea, but the bite of the wind was worse. Every crew member pulled down hats and pulled up hoods.

The next few days were hard as the sailors fought through choppy waters, wind and snow. The nightly camps involved fewer tents packed with many occupants, the women sleeping under the same roof as the men, survival trumping propriety.

***

Then, one day, Vargeisa and Vinglunr glared across the ice. They had lowered the sails and the Haunt bobbed on the waves. The sky was cloudy but it was too cold for snow. Even wrapped up in their warmest wools the crew rubbed warmth back into their arms. The men's beards were decked in ice. Vargeisa scowled at the ice field before them, this northern tip of the Baltic having frozen.

"There", she said, pointing to a cluster of tiny dark buildings that sat at the foot of the distant, northern mountains, "is Tornio. There," she pointed a fair distance northwest towards, to another tiny town," is Fura, our destination. It looks as if we must disembark and walk." She gestured to the western shore.

"Your walk would be easier if we docked in Tornio." said Vinglunr.

Vargeisa laughed, "Surely you're not suggesting we portage through that?" she gestured ahead, the ice field was jagged and uneven, with open pools of water scattered about.

Vinglunr smirked. "Not at all, observe." He started to sing. His tune was deep and ominous, the lyrics an incomprehensible rumbling and hissing but not unpleasant to listen to. A stone's throw away from the ship the air shimmered and the ice melted.

The crew, even Vinglunr's men, regarded the magic with awe.

"I thank you for not singing that when you fought us." commented Vargeisa.

Vinglunr frowned with distaste, "Muspeli Nightmares, a traitorous song that can burn both friend and foe. However, it should serve our purpose but take to the oars, it won't do to set our sail ablaze."

Vargeisa nodded and turned to the crew, "You heard the skald, ready the oars. As he clears the ice we row."

Vinglunr sung the ice to melting and the crew rowed carefully into the newly opened waters. The going was slow but the journey far more pleasant. Waves of heat shimmered around the ship, so much so the crew stripped to their bare chests. Three times Vinglunr had to pause. When this happened the cold returned though not with enough force to refreeze the ice. Vinglunr was given some water, some rest and when he started again those at the oars rowed. Meanwhile, Torino and the mountains grew larger. Torino became a vibrant town, whose citizens rushed out to the docs to watch, in wonder, at the ship with the singer who melted the ice. A few of them carried axes and shields. The mountains became ominous, a dark one loomed over the town, in the receding light of day orange, glowing wounds appeared on its hide.

"That is the Sariola," whispered Vargeisa to Vanadis, "the seat of my mother's power and fortress of the Sampo, a wondrous mill that drives the fortune of my people." Her tone was proud but also wistful.

The Haut came into full view of those on the docks. The watchers were a hardy people. Those with armor and weapons stood clustered near the docs, keeping a wary eye on the ship. Women, the elderly and children sat farther back, watching the ship with deep fascination. Vargeisa walked to the bow and waved. The warriors of the dock lowered their weapons, a few hailed her in welcome. Others eyed her suspiciously.

The ice near the docks melted just as Vinglunr's voice gave out. The heat shimmers vanished and he collapsed where he stood. Vanadis and Gamli shot to his side.

"You are amazing, Vinglunr." Vanadis said in full honesty, handing him her water skin.

The skald accepted her offering with a look of thanks.

Gamli clapped him on the shoulder. "Rest easy, you've done enough."

The Haunt drifted to the dock and some of the warriors pulled her to the moorings. An old veteran greeted Vargeisa in a fluid, soft language. He seemed concerned. Vargeisa smiled and replied courteously. She gestured to Vinglunr, Gamli and Vanadis and gestured up the road that led to the mountains. She then pointed westward and said something to him in reassuring tones.

The old warrior eyed the three as if to say they were in for trouble but it's none of his business. He turned to his people and called out. Reluctantly, they broke apart and returned to their homes, even the warriors.

Vinglunr tried to ask the Fire Wolf something but could only wheeze.

"Easy now." comforted Vanadis.

Gamli stepped to the forefront and asked, "Is something wrong? The old one looked at us oddly."

Vinglunr patted Gamli on the back and nodded as if to say that was his question as well.

"He's merely surprised." assured Vargeisa, "So few risk the hounds to see my mother."

"Will you come with us?" Vargeisa asked.

Vargeisa turned to look at the road and then the dismal Sariola with a pained, sorrowful expression. She hung her head, "I would love mothing more, but I cannot."

"Why not?"

Vargeisa looked at her helplessly. "Because I'll be killed. My mother holds no love for me."

Wolf patted her on the shoulder and went to shore. Katla followed but not before giving Vanadis a sour look.

"I'm sorry, my sister doesn't feel like normal people but she didn't mean to cause you pain." stated Gamli.

Vanadis nudged him harshly.

Vargeisa broke into a smile and giggled, "Given our adventure in Myrkvid I wouldn't blame her if she did."

"I did not." Vanadis said stepping forward. "Thank you so much for getting us this far."

Vargeisa grabbed her hands and squeezed them in friendship. "Be cautious with my mother Vanadis. She's harsh, unforgiving and powerful."

"Reminds me of our mother." the young Volsung said dryly. "We'll prevail. Thank you." She gave her a parting hug.

Then, Vargeisa turned to Gamli. "Mark me well, if you survive Louhi, and if he is still alive, find Ransu the Fisherman. When I was a child I saw him often with your father, I suspect he can tell you much about him."

Gamli's eyes lit up at that. He hugged Vargeisa "Thank you, I will."

After Vargeisa detached herself from the large man and stepped before Vinglunr. "Thank you for getting the Haunt to Tornio." She stroked the gunwale lovingly. "Here she can safely stay until I have need of her again."

Vinglunr smiled and bowed in a courtly manner.

The four climbed up on the dock together. As Vinglunr, his men, Gamli and Vanadis started up the road to Pohjola the Fire Wolf waved "Farewell! I pray we meet again."

CHAPTER 14

Väinämöinen, old and trusty. | The eternal wisdom singer.
It is what he is called but I do not know him as such.
In Pohjola he is the eternal ever virgin.| Ungrateful brother of the maiden slayer.
I do not know him as such. I only know he has great power and is beloved of his people.

For many hours, Hardegon sat a safe distance from the burning hall, his head bobbed in exhaustion. He couldn't sleep, his grief was too great. The sting of his burns were too painful. The heat of the dying fire still too fierce, it was a miracle the grove behind the hall didn't catch alight. No, he couldn't sleep, just rest his eyes and remember. Remember the sharp vibration of his practice sword as he blocked one of Steinarr's clever strikes, the sound of his jovial laughter. The feel of Dorte's soft embrace as she welcomed him from another successful Curonian Raid, the twist of her lip as she asked what he'd brought her. Behind her stood a sharp featured thrall, her grey eyes stared into his. Suddenly Mjoll had fallen before him, blood pooling on her table, the heat of the burning walls surrounded him. In the distance someone hailed.

Hardegon snapped awake. He rubbed his blue eyes, they did not deceive him; sailing the darkened waters was a great longship, one he recognized. A figurehead of proud Frey, the green sails and green hull, it was the Fortune Gale, the flagship of Jarl Truvor. Hardegon rose and staggered for the dock, a torn look on his face. Hardegon made his way slowly down the steps, determined not to let those on the Fortune Gale see him stagger. The ship reached the dock before him. A large warrior with a thick black beard that sported ornate with gold beads hailed him. "Hold there! Not a step forward nor a step back until we know your name and how you come to stand before the burning hall of Mjoll the Gentle."

Hardegon let out a derisive laugh and continued down the steps undaunted "Gautrek, do you not recognize me?"

"My lord!" the guard captain gasped.

"Son." said a stern voice. Truvor stepped to the bow. His long hair was grey, his face wrinkled and wizened, yet he walked with the ease of someone much younger. His blue eyes were sharp, his eyebrows heavy. He wore dark leather armor with gold filigree depicting a dragon. He was draped in a green cloak of wool, with a golden trim. At his side hung a steel longsword in a soft leather sheath. He turned is gaze to the burning hall. "Njord's beard, what have you done?"

Hardegon let out a more derisive laugh. "Oh this?" he spun and gestured to burning hall, "This wasn't me. Mjoll, aunt of murderers, mother of hall burners, bitch of Loki set her own home ablaze."

Asta Skilidottr burst forward from the back of the boat to stand beside jarl, and asked, "My lord, what of my father?"

Hardegon's irreverent look dropped, he turned his gaze and said, with great solemnity. "Your father, your brothers and all of the worthies who journeyed with me burn in that hall. Odin saw fit to spare only myself. I am humbled and shaken by their deaths."

"No," pleaded Asta, with a desprite laugh, "surely, you jest, right? They would not die in such a fashion."

"You have my apology and deepest condolences." Hardegon answered, holding in his own grief as best he could. "I was unable to save them."

Asta covered her mouth and trembled tearfully. She attempted to dart out of the ship but the Jarl held her back. "Easy child, there is nothing you can do for them now." His tone was gentle, his visage lined with pity.

She collapsed in his arms and he stroked her hair like a father. While doing so the he gave a scolding look to his son. "Get onboard, you've done enough."

Hardegon complied.

***

The next morning Hardegon awoke on a bench in Skili's hall. This section was cordoned off with wool dividers. A small fire kept the chill at bay. He lay naked, a blanket covering his lower half. He heard the snip of scissors, Asta sat beside him, she had just finished trimming his beard. Hardegon looked up at her questioningly.

She pushed her chair back and gestured over him, "Have a look my lord, behold my handwork."

Standing just behind her was a little dark haired girl with a strong resemblance to Asta, clearly her daughter. She smiled and waved.

Hardegon pushed himself up and regard his hands and muscular body. He peeked under the blanket and shifted his legs. The child giggled. Hardegon found his skin smooth, unblemished, no mark of the hideous burns he suffered. When he moved and felt no pain. He touched his face to find the only harm was much shorter hair and beard.

"Mjoll may be legendary in our craft but we in Neshraun have no small talent." Asta stated. She reached up and touched his now short cropped hair. "I could not save your beard and hair. Still, you look no less handsome than you did before."

"Why?" Hardegon asked softly, clearly moved. "Why, go to this trouble when..." he eyed her child, "Why help me after last night?"

"Run along Dagrun, help your aunt with her weaving." Dagrun favored Hardegon with a small wave, which he returned, and ran off. Asta turned to the jarl's son, "Why help you? Because you burned with my father and brothers, and because you'll bring Mjoll's wretched family to justice."

Hardegon shared a fiery look with her, he clasped her arm, smiled, and said, "That I will. By Odin I swear it."

Asta searched Hardegon's confident blue eyes and grinned in satisfaction at the steel she saw. She then gestured to folded clothes of purple on the opposite bench. "It is requested you speak to the jarl as soon as you are well."

"Wonderful," Hardegon said dryly, "I imagine my father wants to offer a fattened calf to the criminals and sue for peace."

Asta smirked but simply said, "I can't say my lord." She handed him his pants, "I simply trust you'll do what's needed."

Hardegon nodded conspiratorially, "Your trust is well founded."

***

After dressing in a rich purple tunic and breeches lined with gold. After securing his belt and pulling on boots of finest leather. After draping a red cloak around his shoulders Hardegon walked passed the divider and further down the hall. When he stepped into the common area Gautrek raised a mug of mead to him. "My lord, it's good to see you well."

"Asta has Frigg's own touch." Hardegon responded, seizing a goblet for himself and pulling a draught from the barrel beside Gautrek. To the rest of those gathered, those who were adorned in finery, who all looked equally pleased to see him well, Hardegon said, "Know that Asta has my favor. I will look favorably to any here who treats her, and her children well."

The men cheered and as one they drank.

After draining his cup Gautrek nodded to a divder further down and said, "Your father waits beyond."

Hardegon clapped him on the shoulder than then stepped within the next chamber. There sat Truvor on the edge of Skili's bed. He wore robes whose colour and lining were similar to his son's garb. A jug of rich mead sat on a table before him. He gestured for Hardegon to sit on the other side. "I'd pour you a drink but it seems you've already helped yourself."

"The bold do that father." replied Hardegon, taking his seat.

"How's your brother?" Truvor asked.

Hardegon sipped and pondered before answering. "The wizard Väinämöinen tends him in Kalevala."

"Tends him?"

Hardegon sighed, "Starkad reached too far and found magic in Danevirke that addled his mind. The magic in Kalevala will heal him."

"Foreign magic?" Truvor chuckled, "Skili would not have liked that."

"We took him to Mjoll but I found later that her true power lay only in killing good men." Hardegon stated harshly.

Truvor raised his hand for patience, "A moment. First there is the matter of your brother."

"Allow me to gather a price for his crime, Father..."

"Unnecessary." cut in Truvor, "I have already forgiven him." This caused his son to take a double-take.

The old man chuckled ruefully, "What is this? You find it difficult to believe that I, a 'spineless-coward', would choose not to resolve his problems with a blade?"

"In this one case, I am glad you have failed in your convictions." Hardegon huffed.

"I have always stuck to my convictions son. Just because they are not the same as yours doesn't make them unworthy. Unlike you I can see the error of my ways. Our runic tablet was useless in my hands, if Starkad unlocked some power form them and, if he can return with a sound mind, he will find a grateful father."

"Oh he has." Hardegon said, filling his goblet. He then smiled at Truvor, "Like Odin he has unlocked the secrets of the runes. He merely traces them in the air and sky and fire heed his command."

At this the Jarl nodded sagely, "Then I am immensely proud of him."

"Could Ragnarok be upon us? For once we agree." Hardegon answered, not unpleasantly.

"Not quite yet son. I'm afraid we are about to have another disagreement."

Hardegon regarded him warily, "About Mjoll? When have I ever told you a falsehood? She set her own hall ablaze."

A pained expression crossed the Jarl's face, "Aye, I believe you. A shame she went to such measures and a greater shame at what happened to Skili and his sons." He lifted his mug, "To their new life in Valhalla."

Hardegon shook his head, "That is the rub. Their death was not glorious. At best we can wish them solace in Hel's hall."

"If your standards are Odin's then Valhalla must surely be empty."

"They are the true standards." Hardegon shot back. "That every death is treated like a journey to Asgard is a farce! Of those who die in battle only the best are chosen. Am I the only one who understands?"

The Jarl sighed and answered ,"Yes, the only one who understands madness."

Hardegon fumed.

Truvor raised his goblet again, "Can we not at least toast in honor to a dear friend?"

"Though his death was not, he was honorable." Hardegon said with conviction, he toasted and both father and son drained their cups.

"Now, I'd like you to look at this." Truvor then reached into his pocket and tossed a silver armband on the table. Hardegon picked it up and looked at it closely, it was actually three thin silver rings intertwined, on one side all the rings were twisted expertly to resemble an oak.

"Barnstokkr?" Hardegon asked.

The Jarl nodded. "After your uncle seized Kelifar he sent me this as his justification."

His son looked puzzled.

"It belonged to Hanne the Clever, the mother of those whom you pursue."

"Volungs." A sudden fire lit within the Nibelung hero. The murder, Mjoll's treachery, it all made sense. "This is their revenge." He whispered. "That this has come about in my time... This must be why Odin preserved me."

"Be at ease." Truvor growled.

Hardegon glanced at him as if he were insane.

Truvor continued grimly, "Our ancestors murdered Sigurd theVolsung for cursed treasure. Our heroes Gunnar and were Hogni were slain protecting us from it. My grandfather related the cost as it was related to him, enough bodies to bridge the Indalsälven and enough blood to fill it. After that decades of woe and poverty, it was only through his and my careful efforts that we've returned to greatness."

Hardegon snorted, "Greatness?" he gestured around the Hall, "This? We viking at the behest of Bjorn Eriksson rather than doing so for ourselves. Our people grow fat and lazy while others drive for further glory. We are being left behind father."

"Do not go after the Volsungs." snapped Truvor. "I will not reignite this curse, it will doom us all!"

"What of your brother?" roared Hardegon. "You'll let Steinarr's murder go unavenged?"

"If vengeance costs the welfare of our tribe then yes. That is the cost of being a Jarl, and a jarl's son."

"No." said Hardegon, shaking his head in barely contained rage. He stood, "The cost is paying blood. Ours, or our foes', it's as simple as that."

Truvor jabbed his finger at his son and warned, "If you leave on this quest do not come back. Starkad I can forgive, for he risked only himself. You hope to catch a plague and spread it among us all."

"I seek not the advice nor the forgiveness of cowards." snarled Hardegon. "I will slay Gamli the Serpent and will only return to Öland after Hel has slain you in your bed." With that Hardegon spun on his heel and marched out of the hall.

***

Moments later he stood outside in the brisk, late fall air, wrapped in a warmer cloak, a new, fine sword buckled on his belt. He glanced at the ships at dock thoughtfully.

"You dealt with your father as expected." Ssid Asta. She leaned on the sail of a small craft. Inside was Hardegon's sea chest as well as a full pack and snow shoes. She stepped out of the boat and motioned him forward.

Hardegon regarded her quizzically and walked over to her.

"She's small, slow but she'll get you to Kalevala."

"Kalevala?" Hardegon asked.

"I am told that Gamli is the son of Kvistr Dusk Torch who was a Pohjalander. Is this correct?"

"Aye."

"Then the only place he could run would be Pohjola. Their Queen is the witch Louhi. Who is her eternal foe?"

Hardegon grinned, "Of course, Väinämöinen."

"Whom you know already, whom might be willing to give you aid." Asta concluded.

Hardegon shook his head in admiration, "You have the wisdom of Frigg as well."

"Thank you my lord."

Hardegon was about to step onboard but hesitated. "My father will be displeased that you aid me."

Asta snorted, "In his court in Öland, in the greater matters of our tribe, I will heed his rule. Here though? Here I am Queen, and he has no say in whom I give one of my boats and whom I feed out of my larder."

Hardegon smirked, "Mistress of Neshraun and Kelifar, many will ask for your hand. I pray you hold off for a year. I will speak of you with to my brother. When he returns triumphant, he may woo you."

"I would be happy to be your sister." Asta said with pleasure.

"I already consider you one." answered Hardegon warmly. Then, matters of family weighing on him, he added, "In spring, if you attend the festivities in Gotland, look for my Thora. Tell her and my little son Helgi, that I send my love. That I go to avenge his great uncle and bring honor to our family name."

"I'll do everything in my power to relay the message personally." answered Asta.

Hardegon then leaned close and kissed her on the cheek. She returned the gesture. He undid the moorings, unfurled his sail and waved Asta a fond farewell.

***

Hardegon sailed north for two weeks, relying on sails for most of the journey. The winds and weather were not always kind. At times he had to dock and soak in the heavy rain. On other days, the wind did not obey his will and he was forced to row or sit idle. His nights were spent in friendly halls. At every door he was welcomed with a warm bench and a fine meal. The only payment required were tales of the Curonian raids. Hardegon told these gladly. When asked about his family, he grew quite. He somberly related the news of his uncle. He asked about Gamli the Serpent. Most had no information to give. Though, at some benches, he heard of a great blue longship that made camp rather than dock in any respectable place. On his fourth day sailing he even spied the ship, but it was rowing south. Trusting Asta's wisdom, and not wanting to alert a warship, he let it pass unchallenged. On the eighth day there was a cold snap and snow began to fall. Hardegon bundled up and sailed onwards, the wind filling his sails but also biting his flesh. He was fortunate though, for while the snow did cover land and tree it fell lightly, it did not yet come in blowing torrent.

***

On the 14th day, Hardegon had sailed well past sunset, eager make Kalevala his port. The air was cold, the sky was clear, the stars and moon shining sliver down upon the calm, dark sea. In the distance the jarl's son spied the lights of a great city. As if it waited for him to notice a voice rang out across the water in melodious Soumi. The voice was old but also rich and powerful. The song he sung held a graceful tune that echoed perfectly across the water. The mystic sound of a kantele, a five stringed Kalevalen instrument played on one's lap, rang like heavenly bells and complemented the singer's music perfectly. Hardegon knew a little Soumi, he picked out words of love and loneliness across the water. Its beauty was such that tears fell down his cheeks unbidden, and his chest heaved with the song's heavy emotion. He wiped his eyes and held his sail taught so his boat drifted stately towards the docks. When he reached the docks he found well attired guards with spears, watching him progress. Unwilling to break the sacredness of the song, they said nothing. Hardegon also kept in silence, he raised his hands in peace, the guards nodded in understanding, and then Hardegon bound his ship to the moorings. He then followed the music into Kalevala.

Kalevala's halls were constructed of wood logs. Each was a tall, stately affair. The grandest, which was Väinämöinen's home, stood in the center of the city, towering above all of the others. Its roof was painted blue. Its walls painted a warm red. The main archway was open, white carvings of birch were on either side, the branches intertwining at the top of the arch. Two powerful looking guards, dressed in mail of copper and carrying sturdy looking spears, flanked the entrance. They regarded Hardegon, who was illuminated but the light coming from the doors. They smiled in recognition and nodded him in. Now the singer played a different tune, a lively one, his voice tinted with mischief and humor. Inside the hall many voices laughed.

Hardegon stepped inside to find the hall packed. The benches were full. Chairs were scattered throughout the floor, though well away from the fire pits. The audience were all healthy, hale Kalevalens. Men, women, and children, dressed in their finest wool, linen, and silk, sat, listened, and laughed. At the very back of the hall sat a long table. An ancient man played a kantele which laid across it. His skin was dark and weathered, his hair bright white. His beard so long that it fell behind the table. He wore simple green clothes, lined with gold and silver. His face and expression were pleasant, as he shared his wondrous song with his people. Hardegon knew him, the ancient magician and minstrel Väinämöinen.

Seated beside him was Starkad. His black hair was trim and neat. His black beard was cut short. He was decked in fine blue and gold. His brown eyes twinkled with Väinämöinen's shared merriment. He laughed with the rest. All traces of madness gone.

That his brother had been healed. That he was among worthy and kind people. That he stood before the master minstrel whose music commanded joy. Hardegon smiled, chuckled and laughed with the rest, laughed as if he had finally come home from a long journey. Many noticed and nodded and waved in welcome.

Väinämöinen's song faded, leaving the hall with a warmth, which was more pleasant than even its hearth fires. The wizard minstrel regarded the jarl's son with welcome and greeted, "Ah, Hardegon the Trusted. I did not expect you back so soon, never the less welcome to my hall."

"Brother!" cried Starkad, "Join us."

Hardegon obliged, the crowd calling and applauding in welcome. As soon as he sat, beautiful serving maids brought him a flagon of mead, biscuits slathered with butter, and savory pork. Hardegon eyed it hungrily but forced his attention on the wizard, "Many thanks old and trusted Väinämöinen. I have new business with you."

The minstrel chuckled, "Surely, it can wait till you've eaten and greeted your brother?"

"You're right," Hardegon conceded, "family and festivities first."

The minstrel nodded as if Hardegon had just passed a lesson and started to sing once more.

The brothers fought the hypnotic spell of the minstrel's music and conversed.

"You're looking well brother, this pleases me." Hardegon said in full truth.

"Aye, this music can fix anything and anyone." replied Starkad. Then, grabbing his brother's arm in friendship he added, "I owe you more than I can ever repay."

Hardegon smirked, "Simply continue to live in glory brother. That is payment enough. Even father is proud of you."

Starkad did a double-take.

Hardegon laughed, "Let me explain..." he discussed with his brother his conversation about him with their father. That he could now return home. While Starkad sat and came to terms with the good news, Hardegon took this chance to devour his meal. It was gone quickly enough and a maid replaced his dish with one laden with tart cheese, butter and bread.

"It will pain me to leave this place." Starkad admitted, but then, after a thought, "Though I cannot stay here, if I am to make full use of what I've learned."

"Rune magic yes?" Hardegon asked between bites of bread.

Starkad nodded.

"Tis Odin's magic, a worthy art."

"The price I paid for in it in Danevirke," Starkad took a deep pull from his flagon, "I could not pay such a price again."

"All is mended." said Hardegon after tearing into the fluffy bread, dipped in butter. With a smirk he added, "Now you can return and force Gorm the Old to pay for the harm he's caused."

His brother seemed to consider that, but then shook his head, "No, the dark things in Danevirke are cost enough for them. It's best never to return there. Instead, I shall return to Öland, use my spells in service to our people." He chuckled, "The Curonians won't know what hit them."

Hardegon slapped him on the back, "Yes that is what I like to hear. Show our father that true power only comes to those who will seize it."

Meanwhile Väinämöinen had finished his song. He spread his arms wide and announced in Soumi that the festivities had ended for the night. Some in the crowd begged him for more merriment, but it was late and most were eager to return to their benches in their own halls. Those of Väinämöinen's house cleaned up the chairs and tables. The rest filed out the door.

Then the wizard turned to Hardegon, "Now is the correct time to talk of your business. Speak your mind Hardegon, if I can aid you, I will."

The jarl's son's expression soured. Glancing at both brother and wizard he said "I bring ill news..." He told the story: Of the horror he found in Kelifar. Of his Uncle's funeral and Skili's council. Of the ill-fated visit to Mjoll the Gentle. Of his father's revelation and warning of the Volsung revenge. He ended with, "Our father is a coward, so I must enact justice on Kvistr's son."

Starkad reacted to the story with shock and then anger.

Väinämöinen stroked his long beard and listened, a look of sympathy on his aged face.

"We will find them brother. My spells are yours to command." stressed Starkad.

"It may be best you return to Öland." judged Hardegon.

"Steinarr was my uncle, too." fumed the sorcerer.

"Our father has let Nibelung glory sleep for too long. You must return to Öland and wake it, for I cannot." urged Hardegon.

Starkad was about to answer when Väinämöinen held his hand up to seize both brothers attention. "Please, the night is late and I have no part in this quarrel. If you do not have business for me after all, I will retire and let the two of you sort matters out."

"My apologise Väinämöinen," Hardegon said with a bow "brother, let us discuss our plans in the morning, there is something I must tell our trusted minstrel."

"Of course," said Starkad, "Väinämöinen you also have my apology, I did not mean to try your patience."

The old wizard smiled patiently, "Your business then Hardegon?"

"Asta, the wise hostess of Neshraun, now also the hostess of Kelifar, reminded me that Kvistr Dusk Torch was a Pohjalander, therefore Pohjola would be the Serpent's first place of refuge."

This seemed to intrigue the wizard and he said, "Yes, I had heard of Kvistr, his wife was Hanne the Clever, she did a great service for Louhi long ago. If this Gamli can get past her hounds he may stand a chance of gaining sanctuary." After a thought, he added, "He could also be killed. Louhi is harsher than she used to be."

"He wormed his way under Steinarr's watch, I'm certain the Serpent will find a way to coil at Louhi's feet." answered Hardegon with disgust.

"Perhaps..."mused Väinämöinen, "You presume then that we shall set up a raid against the never pleasant Northland?"

"That is beyond what I hoped, but I would gladly welcome it." answered Hardegon with a fierce, expectant look in his eye.

"What did you hope?" asked the wizard keenly.

"That you are old enemies with Louhi is common knowledge. I hoped to have your council, and perhaps a loan of a charm that's proof against the witch's magic. With these I can sneak into the ever dismal city, slay the Serpent and perhaps rid you of Louhi."

Väinämöinen, snorted, then chuckled, then laughed. "Oh you are bold." He signalled the indignant Hardegon to be at ease. "I shall advise you Nibelung hero. Know that I cannot fashion a charm that's proof against Louhi's magic, if it were that simple I would have done so ages ago. Know also that it is suicide to enter the city without Louhi's bidding, her hounds would rip you apart. I do have council, if you will have it, but following it will require patience."

Before Hardegon could say that Väinämöinen sounded like his coward father, Starkad cut him off. "We could be grateful for the council of the wise Väinämöinen."

"Then, he is pleased to give it." answered the minstrel pleasantly. "Know that I have spies in Pohjola, I will have them watch for Gamli the Serpent. They will verify if he is truly there. If he is not then it would be wise take your search elsewhere. However, if he truly resides in Louhi's court then I suggest you stay here. I have many tasks for you Hardegon, ones that will surely please your god Odin. Tasks for which I will reward you richly. Prove yourself and in spring, summer, fall and winter my spies will watch your prey. When he leaves Pohjola to work further evil, I will grant you a host of my warriors and a fast ship with which to chase him down and deliver justice for your uncle."

Hardegon's sour look turned thoughtful. "What if this coward decides to hide forever in Louhi's domain?"

Väinämöinen chuckled, "Your people prize battle above all things, yes? It's how you please your gods, correct?"

"Aye, I cannot stay here and risk my place in Valhalla." mused Hardegon further.

"Oh the tasks I give you will be worthy. You shall work with our hero Lemminkäinen, he is very fond of raids, battle and glory. This very winter he hopes to hunt one of the children of Otso, our bear god, I would be most obliged if you aided him. As for your prey staying with Louhi, if he hides forever under her skirt, would he truly be a worthy adversary?"

"Väinämöinen speaks truth brother." Starkad urged. "A coward who hides all year is certainly no man, certainly no true Volsung."

"Very well." replied Hardegon. "I shall work great deeds for Kalevala. For now, I am at your service Väinämöinen."

CHAPTER 15

Louhi hostess of Pohjola. | Northland's old and toothless wizard.
It is what she is called but never in her presence.
Armies of spirits await her mere gesture.| Even the reckless immortal Lemminkäinen fears her.
When we first met, I thought she would be my death.

Many days later, just after Vargeisa bid farewell to Vanadis, Gamli, and Vinglunr, they, along with Vinglunr's men walked beside the wide strong, river Tornio. Everyone in the troop had strapped on snow shoes and carried a pack and a sea chest. The going through the snow choked road was slow, the air's chill bit all exposed skin, and none had breath to spare to complain. The sun had set by the time they reached a small dock. Beside it was a small shack, beside it was tall pole on which rested a large, bronze bell. Across from the dock was a large island that rested in the middle of the river. An enormous, dark hall rested on a hill at its center. Numerous smaller halls were clustered around and beneath it, it was all surrounded by a palisade. On the island beach rested another dock and a small hall. Beyond the island loomed the ominous mount Sariola, eerie orange light shining form her many openings.

Gamli stepped forward and pulled the cord on the bell. It rang out across the water. For a moment there was silence and then a cacophonic barking rose and echoed across the waters. Dozens of shadows of black dogs rushed from the far side of the island, across the Tornio the troop could see their glowing red pinprick eyes.

Gamli turned to her sister and Vinglunr, "Not much of a danger over there are they?"

"Look." Vanadis answered, pointing in disbelief across the water.

The hounds charged across the swiftly flowing river as if it were solid ground. As they rushed forward they grew larger and could be clearly seen. Each was a black lapphund who were, impossibly, the size of horses. Their faces and pointed ears were wolf like, their fur was long and voluminous, and their white teeth gleamed in the moonlight.

Gamli drew his sword and stepped in front of Vanadis.

Vinglunr nudged her, "The whistle." he wheezed, his voice still weak from melting the northern Baltic ice.

Vanadis put the whistle to her lips and blew, it made no sound and her grey eyes went wide with outrage. Yet, the barking ceased. The lapphunds, as one, sat on the running river, watching them with tilted heads and wagging tail.

Vanadis blew her whistle again, the pack rose to barking, turned and then raced back the way they had came, their manner playful. Within but a few moments they had rushed around the city and out of sight.

A light shone from the hall by the dock and a figure stepped out. She peered at Vinglunr and his troop and called back inside the hall. Within moments she and six other rolled a boat out onto the waters of the Tornio and rowed towards them. A few held aloft lanterns which lit their way but kept them in shadow.

Gamli considered them and sheathed his blade. To the others he said, "At ease." Vinglunr showed the troop that he too sheathed is weapon and the troop followed suit.

Within moments the boat was on their shore. Most of those onboard stepped out and marched towards them. Once they shared the lantern light the rowers were revealed to be Pohjalander warriors dressed in heavy woolen clothes and carrying spears. At their head was a maiden with wild copper hair, bundled in a blue dress with intricate copper colored highlights. She looked over Gamli and the troop and said, "Strange that you were able to banish the hounds. Who are you? What's your business?" Her Soumi accent was thick and beautiful.

"I am Gamli Kvistrson," he gestured to his sister "this is my sister Vanadis. We're hoping to gain sanctuary here."

"Kvistr Dusk Torch?" asked the woman.

"The same."

"He no longer has family here I'm afraid. They were slain by that villain Lemminkäinen long ago." Noting Gamli's thwarted expression she added, "Still, his father and brothers died protecting Pohjola, the least we can do is house and feed you for the winter. You are welcome here."

"Thank you." answered Gamli warmly.

"Now the hounds," stressed the woman, "how did you drive them back?"

"With this," Vanadis held out the whistle. The Pohjalander troop and the woman stared at in surprise, "we helped Vargeisa the Fire Wolf, and, in return, she gave this to us."

The woman turned to the troop and said something urgent in Soumi. The warriors nodded and muttered amongst themselves.

Vinglunr whispered in Vanadis' ear, "Mentioning her might have been unwise."

"This will force the Queen to see us." Vanadis whispered back. "We won't have true hearth and safety if my curse slays us."

Vinglunr nodded, conceding the point.

"Come with us." said the woman curtly. Gesturing to the ship. Her warriors marched onto the vessel, they seemed agitated but did not raise their weapons.

The troop looked to Vinglunr, Vinglunr looked to the Volsung siblings.

"This is what we're here for." Gamli made his way for the ship.

"It's either this or the long march back to Torino." added Vanadis, who followed.

Vinglunr nodded towards the ship, he and his men boarded. The boat was filled to capacity, the passengers were forced to stand. The oarsmen pulled at the water and the ship slowly crawled along the river.

Beside Vanadis stood the copper haired girl. "Vanadis, I'm Salli." she greeted. "I would know, is my sister well?"

Vanadis considered Salli's guarded expression in the lantern light and detected true concern behind her stoic mask. "She causes much trouble but none of it has caught her. She's well." Vanadis answered.

Salli's expression softened in relief. "Thank Ukko." Then, in a guarded tone she addedm "Be cautious, not all of my sisters would think this good news."

Vanadis raised an eyebrow, sisters? How many daughters did Louhi have? A more urgent question reasserted itself and she asked, "Vargeisa mentioned trouble with your mother. When I meet Louhi is it safe to mention Vargeisa as a friend?"

Salli frowned and shook her head, "I have no answer to that question. Mother will not speak of Vargeisa, nor her quest."

"What about Louhi? Vargeisa says she's impatient and dangerous. Is this true or was Vargeisa playing another trick?"

Salli giggled at old memories. Then, darker memories clouded her visage and she answered, "You are wise to suspect a prank. However, this time Vargeisa tells the truth. Ever since the death of our eldest in the vile Kalevala, mother has grown dark. If she suspects treachery she'll summon howling ghosts to slay you."

Vanadis paled but steadied herself.

In consolatory tones Salli added, "However, if you gain mother's trust she will be your staunchest ally and friend. She is the matron and the hope of Pohjola."

The boat docked on the island. Salli ordered one of the warriors to run ahead. To her guests she said, "Please, follow me. Late as it is, I am certain my mother will wish to see you."

"Thank you." said Gamli with a bow. Then, with a steadying arm around his sister he followed Salli. Vinglunr and his troop formed up behind them. They walked up the road, the palisade gates were opened and they entered the city. The streets were dark but light shone from every hall and smoke rose through every chimney. Those Pohjalanders who stepped out paused to watch the procession march up the road. The hill was steep, but far less rocky that the great hill in Kelifar. At the top of the hill lay Louhi's massive hall. It was painted red with a black roof. The door was shut. A carving of a black eagle perched at the top of the doorway, its copper talons looking exceedingly sharp. Meanwhile, at the bottom of the hill, the pavilion gates were again shut tight.

Salli turned to her guests, "I shall go inside and announce your presence. When you enter please do so respectfully and leave your weapons at the door."

Vinglunr stepped forward, he took a deep drink from his wineskin, to sooth his voice, and asked, "If it is permissible, us three will enter unarmed while my men stay out here."

Salli considered and nodded, "That is acceptable. A moment please." She opened the door, stepped inside and closed it. The guests were left with the Pohjalander guards and entourage, waiting in awkward silence.

After few long moments Salli again opened the door. "My mother will see Gamli and Vanadis alone."

Vinglunr regarded the siblings questioningly.

"It's alright." Gamli answered.

"We'll be fine." Vanadis stressed.

Vinglunr nodded and stepped back with his troop. Gamli handed a Pohjalander guard his sword. Then Salli guided the siblings inside.

***

Louhi's hall was dark but warm. It was richly attired, with a wall hanging depicted the black eagle, and the Sariola. The fire pits were hemmed in with copper, not stone. Golden shields and swords hung on the walls. Many fine rugs stretched on the floor. The ceiling was decked with the bones of giant fish, serpents and other monsters. Men carrying spears and axes sat on the benches, paying close attention to the visitors. A few studied Gamli carefully and whispered to their brothers. At the end of the entrance hall sat a throne of dark pine, embedded in it were plates of solid gold. On it sat an old woman in a red and brown dress. Strange, silver symbols were stitched at the cuffs of her long sleeves and the skirt of the dress. She wore a necklace of human knucklebones that shone like ivory. She sat straight and though her face was long and wrinkled, it held a visage of command. Her eyes were a piercing blue. Her hair long and white. Beside her throne stood three women, two on Louhi's left and one at Louhi's right. They were tall, the two on the left had long red hair; one the one on the right had brown. They were decked in silken dresses with gold and silver jewelry. The stood with the posture of royalty and stared haughtily at the siblings. Salli joined them, she had a like manner, just slightly kinder.

"Louhi." Gamli greeted.

Vanadis took a knee and pulled her brother down with her.

"You, the girl, lift your head." Louhi commanded. Her voice was like old oak, corded and strong.

"Yes, my Queen." Vanadis looked up at her with utmost respect.

Louhi leaned forward and stared at her. Her eyes widened in recognition. "You..." then, after a thought, she smiled and sat back on her throne, "No, you're younger but more care worn. Both of you stand."

The siblings stood.

Louhi chuckled as if she had just solved a riddle, she addressed her hall, "See the works of Väinämöinen, he offers me the memory of happier times but behind it are spies and daggers. His sweet songs are full of poison." She leveled a baleful glare at Gamli and Vanadis, "Your ruse is over." Three of her daughters turned away, shutting their eyes tight, even some of the warriors did likewise. A spike of fear struck Vanadis as she saw a swarm of rippling spirits begin to roll from the back of the hall like a storm cloud of skulls and bones.

Before Vanadis could speak Salli cut in, "Mother no!"

Louhi raised her hand and eyed her child ruefully. The spirits halted but the cloud was not still, it bubbled and churned like a boiling stew.

"I do not think they are spies," she stated simply.

Louhi frowned.

"Mother," Salli stressed, "you set me on the shore of the Torino to ferry over only the worthy. Do you think so little of me that you'd kill my guests without at least questioning them?"

Louhi considered this and then patted Salli on the hand. "Very well, dear." She turned to the siblings and Gamli stood seemingly ready to fight. Vanadis stared fearfully behind the throne.

"Listen well," Louhi hissed, both siblings turned their attention solely to her. "I know full well that Steinarr the Rogue slew Kvistr Dusk Torch and Hanne the Clever, he would not leave their children alive. Explain then, how are you two standing before me?"

"Best tell her." said Gamli.

Vanadis opened her mouth but an idea struck her before she could start, "No Gamli," she said, "you explain."

"You're better with words." he whispered.

"I'm waiting." said Louhi with growing impatience.

Vanadis said nothing. Gamli shot her an incredulous glance, sighed and addressed the Queen, "My mother hid us with the thralls."

"You think me a fool?" asked the Queen. She pointed at Vanadis "She's the spitting image of Hanne. Steinarr would have spotted this, he would have had you both killed."

"You're wrong." Gamli said with sudden fierceness. Salli shook her head, some of the warriors flinched. Vanadis, watched and held her breath.

Louhi cackled, "Oh? How am I wrong?"

"Steinarr hated my father and loved keeping his children as slaves." Gamli answered simply.

"He just let you slip through his fingers?"

"No." Gamli said shaking his head. "My sister's..." he paused, seeing Vanadis flinch, "My mother's ghost killed him."

Louhi leaned on her hand, seeming amused, "Really? Please, tell me how this came to pass."

Gamli did, bluntly and in unapologetic tones. Louhi questioned him on the details, and hounded him until his story was driven to their departure from Mjoll's. Once or twice Gamli stammered, he even glared at the Queen when she questioned how Mjoll could be so stupid as to not know her nephew and niece were alive. Finally she said, "Enough," and turned her attention to Vanadis. "You've been awfully quiet? Why?"

"Because I am a liar." Vanadis answered sweetly.

Louhi's daughters bristled at her tone. A few of the warriors looked puzzled as to why the she would admit that.

Louhi chuckled, "You admit such?" she asked.

"If you'll allow me, I'll tell a story of my deceptive powers." Vanadis answered.

Louhi singled her servants, "Fetch beer and serve the hall." Then, she said to Vanadis, "Proceed."

Vanadis told the story of what happened after leaving Mjoll's. How they met Vargeisa the Fire Wolf and their adventure in Myrkvid. She admitted her part in lying to the Valkyries and how she planned to turn the tables on Louhi's daughter. She swiftly added how Vargeisa, in turn, won out. The hall paid close attention to her story, frothing beer was served halfway through, even to Gamli. Vanadis' crafty words elicited a few chuckles. The hall murmured in sympathy when Vanadis stressed how she'd been deceived by the Fire Wolf. For her part Louhi listened closely but her expression betrayed neither displeasure nor mirth.

When Vanadis finished, Louhi said, "Beautiful words are rarely true, you were wise in having your brother speak first."

"You believe them, then?" asked Salli with baited breath.

Louhi regarded the siblings. Gamli stood bravely awaiting her judgement. Vanadis tried to follow but her gaze drifted apprehensively to behind the throne, where the dead, unseen by others, were still boiling.

Finally, the Queen answered, "I do." She waved and the horde of ghosts fell and dissipated like a fog. "Gamli and Vanadis, I remember your mother fondly and your father was a great hero of this hall.

It is because of this I grant you sanctuary."

"And the men outside?" asked Gamli.

"They may winter here but they will be closely watched."

"Thank you my Queen." Vanadis said with a bow.

Louhi turned to her brown haired daughter "Vilma, take Gamli and his men to the hall of your husband. Show them the best courtesy."

"Yes mother." Vilma answered.

"Salli, ferry Vanadis to my sanctum in the Sariola."

"What?" rumbled Gamli.

"Do not try me," Louhi warned, "I found your bluntness refreshing, but now it wears on me."

Flustered Gamli asked, "Why... My Queen, why can't she stay with us?"

"Better," judged Louhi with a fierce grin, to Vanadis she said, "it's for our protection. Your curse wiped out Kelifar, I have measures in Sariola that will prevent it from harming Pohjola."

"Then I'll gladly accept such lodging." Vanadis answered, doing her best to banish images of dismal, rocky dungeons.

"Don't worry," Louhi said to Gamli, "you'll see your sister again, but only after I have taught her to master her power."

Gamli looked to Vanadis, she touched his arm and said, "This is what we've been looking for. I'll be fine."

He hugged her, "Fine, but be careful."

CHAPTER 16

Memories are ice. / Over time they melt and change.
You can refreeze them but their patterns and cracks will be different.
You can let it melt but it'll won't vanish. / I'll be pool by which your image is reflected.
Bury it, boil it all away, it'll still be there, for you to breathe, for you to walk on.

Vilma descended from her mother's dais and said to Gamli, "This way, I shall lead you to your lodgings." Her manner was cool, as expected from her station.

Salli followed and to Vanadis said, "Come along, we have much to talk about." To Gamli she added, "Fear not for your sister, the chambers of Sariola are most pleasant."

"Take care, brother." Vanadis said as she was pulled off by an excited Salli.

"This way." said a bored Vilma.

"Good luck." called Gamli, and then quickly followed in Vilma's step.

Meanwhile, the hall had risen, many of the warriors greeted Gamli with cheers and smiles. Not understanding Soumi the best he could do was nod and cheer in return. When they reached the entrance of the hall they found a man waiting for them. He was tall, well dressed, and thin but his arms held a wiry strength. His brown locks and beard were banded in leather. A sharp copper axe rested on his belt and his manner was kind.

"This is my husband, Niklas." Vilma introduced, "He's Pohjola's greatest hunter."

"It's a pleasure to meet you." he said, his accent thick. He grasped Gamli's arm in friendship, "Your father was a great man. Many were the riches he brought to us from Alands."

"And your mother was kind enough to save my sister from the river of Tuonela." Vilma added.

"I wish I had a chance to know them." Gamli said. "I thank you for offering to keep us."

"We are glad to have you." said Niklas, opening the door for Gamli. He smiled at the waiting Vinglunr and his men, "Hello, you must be Gamli's friends. I am Niklas, come we have benches for you." He walked off swiftly, gesturing for Gamli to walk beside him.

Vinglunr eyed Gamli with concern. Before he could be swept away by Niklas' talk and walk Gamli answered, "Vanadis goes to the Sariola. The Queen says it'll help with her curse."

Vinglunr nodded and signaled for his men to follow.

***

They made swift progress down the hill, Niklas talking swiftly and pointing out the other halls along the way. Soon they reached his home, he called out and the doors were opened wide. His hall was long and spacious. On the walls hung many fine pelts. In the rafters were displayed skulls of his finest prey; elk, reindeer, bear, even a troll. At the far end hung a golden shield, behind it a shining golden bow.

After Lohi's hall, Gamli didn't bat an eye at the golden artifact. Vinglunr and his men however, paused and stared in disbelief.

Niklas noticed, smiled and guided them, so they could admire it further. "A gift from my Queen, in honor of the prizes I've brought back from the realm of Tapio."

"Tapio?" asked Vinglunr, his voice finally coming back.

"Yes, one of our gods, all forests are his domain."

"He's rewarded you richly." Gamli said, admiring the skulls.

Niklas grinned, "Yes."

"Louhi must have immeasurable wealth." gauged Vinglunr.

"It is the Sampo." Niklas said, "Every day it grinds flour, gold, and salt for us all." Clapping Gamli on the shoulder he added, "Before that we were very poor and relied on the likes of Gamli's father to take the wealth we needed." He laughed, "Admittedly some of it was from Alands."

"Yes," Vinglunr said dryly, "thankfully Gamli's father also set up trade."

"Yes, that was much better." Niklas agreed.

Meanwhile Vilma shook her head sourly as her husband shared Pohjola's secrets. She turned her attention to the slaves in her hall and instructed them to prepare a place on the benches for their guests.

Gamli stood and brooded on what little he knew of Kvistr Dusk Torch. The Kelifar tales he grew up with were not kind. Kvistr was a bestial conqueror, powerful but stupid and slow. Mjoll's rendition was more measured, she had told Gamli simply that his father was a warrior, quick to anger but he loved him and Vanadis very much. Then here, it was strange to hear Kvistr Dusk Torch praised. Gamli felt a hole inside him, one that gnawed with questions. "Niklas, tell me about my father."

"Gladly my friend." Niklas answered, he gestured to a bench. He, Vinglunr, and Gamli sat. The rest dispersed to speak with the house hold and sample the offered food and beer.

From Niklas Gamli learned that his father started off as a blacksmith, though he grew tired of his lot and chose to forgo forging swords to wielding them. With his Pohjalander brothers he raided both the Baltic tribes and the Alands, often coming back with great treasures. He was known for being world wise, even picking up strange customs. When Kvistr won Kelifar and chose to live there it had caused some anger with the Queen. Pohjalanders stick together, they do not forge separate kingdoms. In fact raids were set against Kelifar and Kvistr was forced to slay his own kin. That was until his beautiful wife, Hanne the Clever, snuck into Pohjola, the hounds were not as alert back then, and delivered a cure for Louhi's daughter Vargeisa. From then on Kelifar was a sister city to Pohjola and both prospered from brisk trade.

"That is until Steinarr killed your father. Please believe me Gamli when I say that some of us dearly wished to retaliate, but our struggles with the Lemminkäinen left us in no position for further war." Niklas finished, is demeanor both apologetic and fiery.

Gamli downed his beer, the last of a dozen. On his lap was the crumbs and scraps of a dinner of mutton and cheese. He clapped Niklas on the shoulder, teetered a little and said, "I understand, it matters not, we are now brothers."

The rest of the hall was similarly fortified. A Vinglunr's men mingled with the Pohjalanders some amorously so. Even the servants were in on the celebration. Niklas'son Kaapro sat on his lap. Vilma sat beside him, ever proper and watchful. Vinglunr swayed beside Gamli, his wakefulness succumbing to a full belly and the warmth of the fire.

Something sparked in Gamli's mind, "Niklas, Niklas." he said, nearly falling of his bench.

Niklas chuckled, "I'm here brother. What do you need? Quickly now before you drift off."

"Do you know Ransu the Fisherman? The Fire Wolf said he was friends with my father."

"Yes, I know him. He's also known as the Spider because he's so good with a net. He was a good friend of your father's, though a little strange. You may get into trouble if you visit him."

"I'll visit him anyway!" Gamli said with a victorious stand. Immediately he fell to drunken unconsciousness.

The next morning was hideous. Gamli sat at his bench, a bowl of cold water in his hands, from which he took little sips. He felt as if there were two invisible dwarves hammering his head. Most of Niklas' hall were in the same state. Vinglunr refused to wake, and instead kept his face to the wall and body as still as possible.

The only two who were active were Niklas and Vilma. Vilma had handed Gamli fresh clothes and his wonderful bowl of cold water, a task for which Gamli thanked her from the bottom of his heart. Niklas had already rushed out, had a winter's swim and returned.

As he dried his hair he said to Gamli, "Quick get dressed."

Gamli turned his head slowly and looked up at his host questioningly.

"We must depart soon or we'll miss Ransu."

Gamli grunted once and then focused all his will to move his limbs, to get dressed, and make ready for their journey.

When they left Niklas' hall it was still dark but the brightening east hinted the sun would be up very soon. Niklas was twelve steps ahead of Gamli, urging him onward. The brisk winter air was Gamli's salvation though the crunching though the snow was not. Soon enough they exited the northern gate to find many other halls stringed along the stony beach. Unlike the people behind the walls these folk were already up and about. Fishermen and their wives sat outside, watching the sunrise behind the Sariola while preparing their nets and boats.

Niklas suddenly seized Gamli's arm and pointed up. "There! Look, look!"

Gamli glanced up and staggered at what he saw. A black eagle, the size of a longship, drifted to the Sariola in a stately glide.

"It is Louhi." Niklas whispered. "She returns to her mystic chambers, there to teach you sister the ways of sorcery."

"Teach, not eat, correct?" Gamli whispered back apprehensively.

Niklas laughed, "I think you sister amuses the Queen too much to become breakfast." He slapped him on the arm. "Come, we must catch Ransu."

Niklas rushed down the beach and Gamli chased after him. Spying a boat already far down river

Niklas hollered "Ransu! Wait, I have someone who wishes to meet you."

"Tell Taika that she can keep her daughters." The distant voice sounded old and weathered.

"No!" Niklas pointed at Gamli, "Tika's daughters aren't this large. This is Gamli, Kvistr's son!"

"I am no woman." Gamli bellowed.

"Kvistr's son is dead." called the voice.

"No at all, I'm very much alive." Gamli winced again, yelling hurt.

"That rat Steinarr kept them as slaves! They've recently freed themselves and have come to Pohjola. Louhi flies now to teach his sister witchcraft."

"Stay right there!" replied the voice with urgency. With swift strokes of the oars the boat turned and sped back to shore.

"I think he believes us." said Niklas smiling.

Gamli nodded, kept silent and watched the boat approach. The boat looked old and dry. The oars were the same. So was Ransu. His body was corded, his skin as rough as twisted hide. Tattoos of harpoons ran down both forearms. His hair was long and black, streaked with grey. When boat ran a ground he turned, his eyes were a faded blue. He had but a stubble, no beard but his thick moustache, strong jaw and heavy eyebrows would prevent anyone from calling him boy. He stared at Gamli in shock. He stepped off the boat and walked forward in long strides. Without a word he seized Gamli's face, feeling his cheekbones with his rough thumbs. Tears beaded at the corners of his eyes "By Ukko, it is true."

"He has quite the resemblance yes?" commented Niklas.

Gamli seized the man's hands and removed them from his face. "You can tell me of my father, yes?" He said with strident purpose.

Ransu pulled out of Gamli's grip, "You didn't know him?" his mind raced, he pointed at Niklas "He said you were brought up a slave, is this true?"

Gamli nodded, "Steinarr's dead, my sister and I have been free ever since."

"If I had known..." whispered Ransu, fury suddenly lighting in his eyes, he clenched his fists. "If I had known I swear I would have sailed to Kelifar, slain every wretched Nibelung, and taken the two of you back home.

"What's done is done." answered Gamli.

"Please," said Ransu gesturing to his boat, "row with me and I shall tell you much about your father."

"I would like that." answered Gamli.

"I shall inform Vinglunr that you are in good hands." said Niklas, "Return at sundown and you'll have a toothsome dinner."

"My thanks." Gamli said with a nod.

Then Gamli and Ransu stepped into the boat and shoved off. With both he and Ransu at the oars, rowing north, Pohjola soon receded in the distance.

"I'm not much for words I'm afraid. If you would, tell me about yourself and your sister. If it weren't for Steinarr I would have been like an uncle to you."

The freshly brought up grief and regret in Ransu's tone moved Gamli's hart. "Very well," he said and he told Ransu about their life in Kelifar. How his earliest memories was being looked after by the other slaves and his sister. How he impressed the blacksmith Asvard who taught him how to work the forge, even though it was above his station. Gamli paused at that, he supposed it wasn't above him after all. He told Ransu about how he Vanadis and Flosi were inseparable, until recently. He talked about hard work and fear of the blot. He talked about how Vanadis had the worse of it until Dorte offered her favour. He suddenly realized how much this hurt, much more so than his previous hangover. "I-I can't go on." he rumbled.

"Then don't," Ransu answered with the ease of a trusted confidant. ", talk instead about how you got here."

Gamli did, he talked about that fateful night in Kelifar. Their meeting of Mjoll. The clash with Vargeisa and then the adventure in Myrkvid. Finally he spoke of the welcome the received here.

"I'm angry Ransu. At Steinarr, at Vargeisa... maybe a little at Vanadis." He felt sick admitting it. Both he and Ransu paused in their rowing.

"I would be very worried if you didn't hate your sister, at least a little." Ransu counselled. "Brothers who like their sisters too much..." he shivered, "you're Volsungs but you need not be like Sigurd and Signy."

"Uncle," the word sounded right, "how did you know we're Volsungs?"

"Hane was clever but not clever enough to keep it from Kvisitr, he and I shared everything." He paused in thought, "Shared everything except Hanne. A proper woman your mother, she wouldn't have had that." Ransu said with a fond smile.

Gamli chuckled, then added "I don't hate her, Vanadis I mean. I'm angry that I can do so little."

"That you're swept up in her story, yes?" prodded Ransu.

Gamli nodded. "Perhaps."

"I have the cure." The fisherman dropped anchor and pointed on the eastern shore. Before them was a rocky cliff, at the top of which was a stone platform. On top of the platform was a soapstone furnace and a steel anvil. No snow gathered on this platform. Waves of heat rippled from the furnace, though no smoke rose from it.

Gamli stared at it questioningly and then glanced around, regarding well both sides of the river. Cliffs rose on the other side, on top of them were snow-lined trees. The wind blew through them rustling their bare branches. No buildings were in sight, nor smoke from any cooking fires, no sign of people what so ever.

"Ilmarinen's Forge." Ransu explained, taking a leisurely seat in the bow of his boat. "To know your father you must stare into it."

"How so?" asked Gamli.

"Many years ago tensions were not so high between Pohjola and Kalevala. Louhi had a daughter who was so beautiful she was called the Rainbow Maiden and Väinämöinen's brother, the wondersmith Ilmarinen, wished for her hand in marriage. Louhi agreed to this as long as Ilmarinen could forge the Sampo, you've heard of it yes?"

"Gold from it lines Lohi's walls." Gamli answered.

"Ilmarinen tried many times to forge the Sampo but found the task beyond him. So he chose to reforge himself. He secured an ember from the blood of a foreign god and built the forge you see before you. You see, not only can it be used to produce wonders but it can bring about a wonderful change in a smith. Ilmarinen stared into its fire and was changed, the Sampo was no longer beyond him and so he was able to forge it and win the Rainbow Maid."

"That makes no sense. Everyone knows Kalevala and Pohjola are foes

Ransu chuckled, "There was peace for a few blessed years, but the Rainbow Wife, Louhi's eldest, was murdered in Kalevala. Our Queen blames Ilmarinen and Väinämöinen for failing to protect her, hence, our many troubles."

"What has this to do with my father?"

"Many of my countrymen have stared into the forge in hopes of becoming as skilled as Ilmarinen." Ransu shook his head, "Most see the image of the foreign god and go mad, those that can withstand the sight are cursed with visions, truths they are not ready for. These usually end their own lives, those that don't waste away as men with broken spirit." Ransu leveled an even stare at Gamli. "Once, in drunken idiocy, dared your father to stare into the forge. He accepted, he endured the foreign god and the visions. When he stepped down from that place he was no longer a smith but he was a far greater man. A fire had been lit within him, his new drive helped him to win Kelifar and marry a woman such as Hanne. If you want to know your father Gamli, stare into the forge."

Without hesitation Gamli dove into the water and latched onto the eastern rock face. He seized the rock in his powerful grip and began to climb.

Behind him he heard Ransu laugh. "What? Not even a thought for your own sanity? You are your father's son."

Gamli gritted his teeth and continued to climb, a hunger to find his own destiny driving him upwards. Finally he reached the top to find it as hot as a broiling summer's day. He pulled off his cloak, heavy woolen shirt and even his linen undershirt, dropping them in a pile at his feet. He climbed up the stairs of the dais, on the top step he paused. He felt a heavy presence watching him. He turned slowly around, his eyes sweeping the tops of the snowy trees but saw no one.

"Not so easy is it?" cried Ransu. "I once stood there myself and felt as you do. I backed away. Will you do the same?"

Gamli could feel his own heart beating, his instincts didn't tell him to step away; they told him to run, to flee. He closed his eyes and steeled himself. He reached out and the tips of his fingers sizzled on the furnace's surface. He hissed in pain, faced deliberately that way and opened his eyes.

He stood on a mountain ledge. A scorching wind whipped past him. Beneath him was a field of shining, dark stone, orange light reflecting off it. A river of molten metal ran through it. The river itself rolled down from the top of a great mountain of black, jagged rock. The sky was a fiery red. Standing before the mountain was a figure. His long hair was bright red, rolling flame. His cloak was a crimson wolf's hide. His skin was pale. His build mighty. At his hip was a sword with a golden hilt, shethed in obsidian. Gamli froze; his mind reeling for the warrior was the size of the mountain. He turned his head and glanced at Gamli. His burning eye seemed like a sun whose pupil was a dark moon. In its sight everything Gamli had known turned small, insignificant, and worthless...He felt a bitter, terrified laugh well up within him.

No, he clenched his fists and glared back at the eye. After everything he'd been through, all the pain, fear and grief, he would not fall to this. "Greetings," he forced himself to say, "I am Gamli Kvistrson."

A rumbling laugh, which was not unlike the boom of thunder, echoed across the field. The dark circle before Gamli grew to cover land and sky and then all was dark.

Gamli opened his eyes to find himself back in Kelifar. He stood behind the Great Hall in the bright midday sun. A roaring bonfire was before him.

"Kvistr, this is madness!" The voice came from the back door through which stepped Ransu. He was younger but no less weather worn. He looked exasperated.

Standing before the bonfire was a tall, broad man. His red hair and beard was exceptionally bright. He was dressed like a jarl. He wore iron gloves in which he carried a baby. The babe shared this man's blue eyes, and looked curiously at the fire. "Madness to you," rumbled the red haired lord, "but sacred duty to me."

"Kvistr, don't do this." Ransu begged. "Your wife, if her eyes don't kill you she'll poison your wine."

"This fire is fueled by ash wood. I have made the proper sacrifices. My dreams have blessed this day." said Kvistr, then, without hesitation he thrust his gauntleted hands, and the child, into the fire.

Ransu winced and turned away. So did Gamli. A roll of triumphant laughter drew their attention back. Kvisitr held the child fully in the fire, the flame licked his flesh but it did not burn. The child giggled and Kvistr held him up proudly. "Surt!" he called, "My master! Great Jotun of fire! I thank you for blessing my son. I swear he will live to do you honor!"

"By Ukko." swore Ransu.

His friend turned from the bonfire and held his son before him proudly. "Ukko has nothing to do with this. You witness an ancient rite perfected in the primordial realms, before your god even took to the sky."

"He would not ask us to thrust our children into flame." Ransu answered, with a wary look at his friend. "What if you had been wrong or your faith lacking?"

"Fear not," answered Kvistr, holding the child close, "I do not take Surt's gifts lightly. I only need one son blessed by the sacred flame and even then I would never be cruel or foolish enough to thrust him into a normal fire."

Gamli stood, in plain view, stunned. Ransu continued to berate the proud Kvistr and neither acknowledged his presence. Surt, he knew the name. The priests and skalds told of him with dread and fear. Surt, the king of the Fire Jotun, enemy of Frey, destined to burn the world. Gamli looked over himself with apprehension. Was this truth? Had he been blessed by the destroyer? The warrior by the mountain, it must have been him.

A shadow fell across Gamli, no, not a shadow, he was suddenly standing in the old smithy. He smiled with fond memory, seeing a younger Asvard before him. Before Asvard stood an awkward, sweaty boy whose long red hair had been tied back so as not to endanger him in the forge. He dipped the glowing hot chisel into the water, and after it cooled, he held it up expectedly at his master. Asvard seized it with his tongs and eyed it critically. This memory was bitter sweet for Gamli, he had enjoyed crafting the chisel very much but...

"It's serviceable but far beneath my works." The blacksmith judged. Both adult and child Gamli lowered their heads in disappointment. Asvard patted the child on the shoulder. "I'm sorry but keep at it. I'm sure you'll surpass me one day. Till then, I hope you find working in my service rewarding."

Younger Gamli nodded.

The world shifted and Gamli had to catch and hold a support beam to keep his balance. He was now inside the Great Hall, in Steinarr's very room. It was modest for the lord of Kelifar, furnished with only a small bed, table and dresser. However, these three were well crafted and sported etchings of the hunt and war. Steinarr and Asvard stood by an open door, examining something in the afternoon sun. Gamli stepped forward and peered over the Rogue's shoulder, they were regarding his chisel.

Steinarr flexed it his in hands, the chisel did not bend. He swung it lightly against the door and it sunk into the wood. "Kvistr's son did this?"

Asvard grinned and crossed his arms. "Aye, I must admit, I'm a little jealous."

"Can he teach you?" Steinarr asked.

Asvard laughed and shook his head "No, I've been teaching him. What we've got here is a wondersmith true, perhaps even another Wayland."

Steinarr frowned, "Like Wayland he's in bondage, should he ever wish to take revenge..." The jarl frowned darkly, "We all know what happened to Wayland's jailors."

"Ah," Asvard said with a primed, ready, answer, "where Wayland was a full grown free man our Gamli is my devoted thrall."

Steinarr didn't look convinced.

"While he's good with his hands, he's still a fool. Can't see the glory of his own work." sdded Asvard.

"What if he wisens?" asked Steinarr.

Asvard shrugged, "Then, I will free him and he marries my daughter, we both know his blood is worthy and I'll be proud if my grandsons share in his talent. In the meantime," he clapped Steinarr on the shoulder, "we can become very rich."

Steinarr snorted and smirked, "I find your argument convincing. We'll send his works to sell out West, that way he'll not hear of their quality. If the Norns be on our side this will make up for our loss of trade with Pohjola"

"You are clever as always, my lord." Asvard said with a bow.

The world was bright and Gamli stood back at Ilmarinen's Forge. His mind reeled, far more than it did at witnessing Surt. He felt adrift, alone, bereft of trust and familial love. All the pleasant memories of his smiling master were replaced by the greedy grinning man.

Gamli held his head and whispered "No." Yet every work he made at Asvard's forge returned to his mind. Every curve, line and grade. He recalled Asvard's tools and weapons and now, clearly recalled them as dust and grime in comparison his work. The realization of his own stupidity hit him with a force more painful than any claw or axe.

"Gamli," called Ransu, his tone concerned, "are you still with us?"

Gamli looked up to the heavens and screamed with unbridled hate. He then glared his hands flexing, needing to do something with them. At his feet rested tools, hammers, tongs, and crates of ore, the leavings of previous Pohjalanders who had hoped to become the next Ilmarinen. Gamli seized the gritty ore and shoved it into the forge with his bare hand. Then everything lit up in burning radiance and he was lost in its madness.

***

He came to on a rocky shelf at the bottom of the cliff. His legs and feet dipped into the river. The winter cut into his bare chest and face. In his lap lay a sword. The shining metal was tinted a slight green. The cross-guard was long and curved towards the grip, etched on it was the likeness of a biting serpent. The grip was a simple leather wrap. The blade was longer than most swords he'd seen, etched very faintly on it were runes. Gamli couldn't read them, yet while the script was elegant Gamli felt they inflected..."Scorn." He whispered.

"You've come back."

Gamli glanced up to find Ransu sitting in his boat staring at him in awe.

"I was gone?" Wondered Gamli. He searched his mind and ran into the vision, he frowned, and suddenly his blade's name seemed fitting.

"Quickly," said Ransu reaching out, "hand me the sword and climb up to dry off."

Gamli glanced at him suspiciously.

"Go!" Ransu urged pointing back to the forge. "If you tarry the cold will kill you."

Gamli shivered, despite his initial hesitation he handed Ransu the sword and quickly scaled the cliff. He found the forge wondrously warm and his dropped clothes nice and dry. Then it struck him, the silver stars and crescent moon were framed by the black sky, "By Frey..." Gamli gasped.

"Hurry!" called Ransu, "I would like to return to a warm hall."

Moments later, Gamli had dressed, climbed down, and boarded Ransu's boat.

The old man handed him the sword. "Here, I'll gladly row to keep warm, you watch for ice."

"Y-yes," said Gamli, he turned to keep his eyes on the water but also kept one hand on the hilt of his new blade. After a moment he asked "Ransu, what happened?"

Uncle laughed, "I thought you'd tell me."

Gamli gathered his thoughts, once they were ordered he said "The 'foreign god' is Surt, a Jotun King who wishes to burn the world."

"No wonder most lost their minds at the sight of him. What of your vision?"

"Betrayal," Gamli spat out the word, "and my own stupidity."

"Future betrayal?"

Gamli shook his head, "No, the past."

"Your sister?"

Gamli snorted, "Hardly. I was betrayed by a man I once respected. I do so no longer. After the vision," he frowned, "I suppose I did go mad."

"You were in a fury of the likes I'd never seen. You worked the forge like a god. Flame shot around you but it did you not burn. You bent and shaped the molten metal with our own hands. You hammered with such force the sky was lit by your sparks. The only reason no one came to investigate must have been they assumed you were Ukko angrily waving his fire sword. From the look in your eyes, I don't think they'd be far off. I'm sorry my friend but I nearly fled."

"Thank you for staying." answered Gamli gently. He held up the sword and looked back, "I forged this?"

Ransu glanced over his shoulder and nodded, "Aye, weeks of work and it only took hours."

Gamli held up the sword feeling its comforting weight. He ran his thumb lightly along its blade and winced as it cut him. He placed the blade gently on his lap and held his thumb until the bleeding stopped. He pondered, what did this mean? Was it the blessing of Surt or the workings of the forge?

"Ransu?" he asked.

"Aye."

"If I forged you a new harpoon, would you find me a forge and materials?"

"Why not go back to Ilmarinen's Forge tomorrow?"

Gamli shook his head, "The place is sacred, I wouldn't feel comfortable returning."

Ransu chuckled, "Very well, I know a smith, and for enough skatt he'll let you use his shop. Just try not to burn it to the ground."

Gamli considered his large hands with a new respect. "I'll do what I can."

CHAPTER 17

Midgard is ill-forged. | The dead suffer between its cracks
Seithkona give the dead a place within their own souls.
There the dead can rest | There the dead can act.
A seithkona's power is not her own, she conducts something far greater

The previous night Salli rowed Vanadis across the river, as they neared the eastern shore Mount Sariola loomed larger before them.

"Please," requested Salli, "tell me everything that happened between you and my sister."

"I just told the story to your mother, you were there." Vanadis answered, not getting what she was aiming at.

"I do not wish for a performance, I wish news. Please, it's been years since we've talked." Salli pressed.

"I'll do my best, though," Vanadis glanced at the dark Sariola that was pot marked with wounds of light, "I may be distracted."

Salli leaned closer and smiled, "Do your best and I swear you'll get the finest room."

"Very well." Vanadis replied. As Salli rowed she began to tell her everything again, starting at the battle of Traitor Bay. This time she chose a casual manner, and did not skip the details. She had wrapped up that part of the story by the time they got to the beach.

As they walked towards the entrance, Salli said, in grim contemplation, "I'm sorry about your Ansy Ironhair. I'm curious, if the fight had turned out differently, if you won outright, would you have killed Vargeisa?"

'I was out, the choice was not mine.' Seeing Salli's critical look though Vanadis chose other words, "No. I'd want to ask her why we were attacked, as such I would have requested Vinglunr to spare her." Vanadis surprised herself at the truth of these words.

Salli smiled, "Good, it seems you're destined to be her friend. This way."

Friends don't try to kill each other. Yet, again, Vanadis held her tongue.

***

When she stepped inside one of the bright doorways, all other sharp words were lost. She had expected a dank, rough tunnel, what she got was a hall made of smooth stone. On brackets, evenly spaced out, were flickering lanterns.

"Go on."sSaid Salli with a giggle, her voice echoing throughout the hall.

"Very well," As they walked Vanadis re-told her adventure in Myrkvid. Salli lead her through twists and turns, and up and down short flights of stairs. After the seventh twist Vanadis paused her tale and asked, "Are you trying to confuse me?"

"Sadly, yes." replied Salli, "It's a defensive measure, the Sampo lies deep within after all, it wouldn't do to have it stolen."

"I thought you trusted me."

"You admitted to being a liar."

"Then why do you want to hear more of my 'lies' about your sister?" Vanadis responded tersely.

"My apologises, I meant liar in jest." Salli answered, "As for these tunnels, they force me to take a twisting way. Mother trusts very few with the Sampo, it is why all paths in the Sariola are a maze."

Vanadis sighed and then added, in a friendlier tone, "This room best be worth it."

Salli giggled, "Oh it is."

She led on and Vanadis finished her tale along the way, just as they did so they came to a solid, wooden door.

"Your room." Salli took a key form her belt, unlocked the door and pushed it open. Vanadis staggered at seeing what was inside. It was a wide stone chamber with a large bed, wardrobe, desk, and balcony. The furniture was all dark pine. 9 tapestries hung on the walls. 7 of them were Lohi's daughters. Vargeisa recognized Vilma, Vargeisa and, of course, Salli among them. Each wore fine dresses and jewels befitting royalty. The last two hangings hung on either side of the bed. One was, a younger Louhi, a tall stately red haired princess. Beside her stood a proud looking blonde haired king who leaned on a longsword.

"I trust the accommodations are suitable?" Sallie said with the hint of a laugh.

"Your mother will kill me if I sleep here."

"Nonsense, she no longer visits here." Sallie walked into the chamber and touched the tapestry of the most beautiful of Lohi's daughters; she had great golden locks, a round majestic face and wore a shimmering dress that bespoke of summer and gold. "This was Marika, the Rainbow Maiden, she was married to Ilmarinen of Kalevala; she was murdered there." She walked to the opposite side of the chamber and touched the tapestry of another daughter, she had long brown hair, deep innocent brown eyes and wore a dress of midnight blue. "This was Esteri, my youngest sister. After Marika died Ilmarinen lost his mind and kidnapped her, we haven't heard word from her since." She pointed to where Vargeisa's tapestry hung, it was strange to see her outside of her armor, in a silken dress. She was less pretty than the others but far more striking, even in cloth her green eyes twinkled with mischief. "Vargeisa and mother had a falling out, she can never return to Pohjola nor can she ever stand to before the Queen again, to do so would end her life."

"I am curious about that."

Sallie shook her head, "I wish I could tell you but mother has forbidden us from speaking about it."

"Louhi's not here." Vanadis hinted.

Sallie turned fearful, "N-no, I cannot. Mother's power is very great, I won't push it."

"She would harm her own?" said Vanadis, looking displeased.

"N-no," Sallie paused in painful remembrance, "never intentionally." She glanced back up at Vargeisa's likeness, "However, my sister has a talent for invoking mother's ire."

Seeing the bittersweet expression on Sallie's face, Vanadis decided to drop it. "Very well. I understand, your sister does the same to me."

Salli smiled in thanks and touched the tapestry of the king. "My father Aleksanteri, Lemminkäinen slew him. He fled and hid while mother wrought terrible vengeance upon his people. All that did was bring more misery." She spun, with her arms spread, "So, no matter how beautiful this chamber is mother will never return here. It reminds her that we've lost nearly half our family."

Vanadis stood a moment in silence.

Salli laughed, "What, you do not ask why the great Louhi doesn't summon their spirits?"

'You ask me this, after hearing my story?' Vanadis' looks said as much but she added, "The dead are not the living. I was told my mother was loving and kind, her spirit is the opposite."

Salli looked ashamed for her question, "I see. My apologies." She drew a finger on the ornate but dusty quilt on the bed. "I'll shall summon dinner and a slave to clean this room. We shall eat, you shall have a bath in one of Sariola's beautiful hot springs and then a good rest. Mother will attend your training in the morning.

"I accept." Vanadis said with a smile.

Salli left Vanadis to instruct the servants. The young woman waited on the balcony. The view, the lit Pohjola underneath her, the river Tornio streaming out to the frozen bay, the surrounding mountains and forests, it was stunning. In the distance she heard a long lonely wolf howl but beyond that all was still.

Salli returned with two very healthy, well - dressed thralls, a man and a woman. They dusted and set the desk as a table. They put on it a bowl of savory stew, a pitcher of cold beer and two plates of dried fruit. Then, as the two ladies ate, they turned their attention to the room. Salli expressed delight at the stew, the fish and game cooked inside were fresh and tasty. Vanadis began to eat but her eyes drifted to the servants. The woman swept the floor while the man pulled the bedding off and left to gather fresh linen. Vanadis suddenly felt self-conscious.

"Is something wrong?" Asked Salli.

Vanadis opened her mouth but held back her honest words. Dressed as a ferry woman or no Salli held herself as a lady of high breeding. 'You wouldn't understand.' So, Vanadis put on a fake smile and said it was nothing. She asked Salli what it was like guarding the river. Salli grinned and shared stories of the colourful people she'd allowed in and turned away. She even told Vanadis about a border battle where Salli had shot a man with her bow. There was a honest hardiness to that which Vanadis liked.

After dinner, Salli stood and said with a bow, "Now, I leave you for the night. Reeta will attend your bath. Expect me late tomorrow, I wish to hear all about your first day of witchcraft training."

"I'll share everything your mother allows me to share." said Vanadis warmly.

Salli waved and stepped out of the room, saying as she left, "Turn someone into a rabbit for me." Then, she poked her head through the doorway and added, "Not me."

When she had gone, Reeta gestured for the door and said, "This way, mistress."

Vanadis flinched at the word. It didn't feel right.

"Are you well? Have I somehow offended you?" Reeta asked with sudden concern.

The young Volsung took her hand and said "Don't call me mistress; Vanadis will do."

"V-very well." Reeta answered uncomfortably, "This way, Vanadis."

Reeta lead her down another, but shorter, twisting way. They entered a steamy room. The walls here were damp and natural rock. Before them was a small natural spring, that bubbled and churned.

"You mean to cook me." Vanadis said dryly.

Reeta giggled. "Not at all." She slipped off her sandals and stepped in, completely unharmed. "See? This is a thing of great pleasure, not pain."

Vanadis looked dubious but none the less stripped. She stepped into the pool and hissed, it was hot. Retta took her hands and gently pulled her in. Ah, it was wonderful. Vanadis stepped in till she was up to her neck in water.

"Now, to wash you."

"I can wash myself."

"I insist." Reeta began to work. She did so with a professional casualness. It felt good to have the travel grime scrubbed off so Vanadis relented.

"Reeta, can you tell me of your work here?"

"I don't know where the Sampo is, if that's your aim." she said gruffly.

Vanadis raised an eyebrow at that. 'I would have never been so blunt to a guest.' "It is not." She said dryly, "I'm just curious."

"Very well..."

They conversed, it seemed Reeta did all the tasks that Vanadis did when she served Dortre.

"Don't pity my lot. This is a reward for those who prove themselves to the Queen. When I'm finished my tasks I have baths like this, sup on good food, and have a bed of my own. Think on that, a bed, for a slave. I wouldn't trade this for a royal marriage in a lesser country." She gasped, catching herself. "Of course, I mean no offence. I'm sure your country is just as glorious as Pohjola."

Wait...she speaks more than just Soumi. Vanadis suddenly felt incredibly outclassed. "None taken. In my country I slept on the floor."

Reeta paused, "Truly, a woman such as yourself?"

Vanadis smirked, "Back home they didn't know how to treat me."

"We'll soon rectify that." Reeta continued her scrubbing. "You'll find our hospitality the best in the East."

"Would such include lessons in Soumi?" Vanadis asked.

"It would be a pleasure to teach you."

After the bath Reeta guided Vanadis back to her chamber. Once there she lit the fireplace on the far wall and asked "Will you need anything else mistress?"

Vanadis winced again at the word but a little less. "N-no Reeta, I'm going to turn in."

The servant walked up to the dresser and tapped it, "You'll find fresh clothes, worthy of your standing, here. I'll check in regularly after sunup, if you need assistance dressing wait for me."

"No, that will be fine thank you."

"You can do your business down the hall to the right. Beyond that Salli requests that you do not wander Sariola. The Queen will visit early in the morning, I'll get you breakfast before she arrives."

"Thank you Reeta, goodnight."

"Goodnight mistress." She said with a bow, and then she made her leave.

Vanadis slipped into the bed uneasily. She found the mattress soft and the blankets warm. She also found herself wide awake. This felt wrong, in the back recesses of her mind she feared that, Dorte, not the monster in the woods, the living Dorte, would walk into the room and demand to know what she was doing in her bed. Furthermore, Vanadis knew she was not alone.
In the glow of the firelight she saw shadows walk both down the hall outside of the room and in the room itself. Dark presences that wandered with alert eyes and unshaking purpose. Spirit sentinels, part of what would keep her curse in check. 'Mother, we cannot afford you acting up.'

'I know dear.' Came the words right beside her ear. 'Get some sleep, we'll see what Louhi has in store for us tomorrow.'

Vanadis closed her eyes and opened her eyes to find the sun falling through the balcony's archway. She turned and nearly jumped out of her skin.

Looming above her, wrapped in a black cloak, long white hair falling down her shoulders, holding a cane with a carved eagle's head, a brooding expression on her long face, was Louhi.

"M-my Queen," Vanadis stammered crawling back in the bed, "I-I was given this room I'm sorry if..."

Louhi held her hand for silence. The old witch looked slowly around the room, "I shall discuss this with Salli."

The Volsung sighed with relief.

Louhi regarded her for a moment and said, "Your training begins immediately. I will wait by the door, get dressed and be quick about it."

As soon as the Queen stepped out of the room Vanadis leapt up and raced to the dresser. She threw on a red linen shift and belted it with a fine leather cord. She then quickly slipped on some sandals and was out the door.

Louhi eyed her and said, "You're a little too eager. Throw on a cloak, the Sariola's getting cold."

"Yes, Mistress." Vanadis answered.

Louhi seized her arm in a boney grip. "No." she said harshly "First lesson, never call anyone mistress. Spirits will not take orders from a slave."

"Y-yes, my Queen."

Louhi's smiled, "Better, now hurry."

Moments later, Vanadis returned, wrapped in a thick black, woolen cloak. The Queen marched off, her cane clacking on the smooth wooden floor, Vanadis followed close at her side.

"I thought long and hard on how to teach you, it kept me up." Louhi eyed her casually and added, "It seems you've little sleep as well."

"I am unused to sleeping with so many ghosts about."

"My silent, unseen watchmen. It took me years to gather and bind them." Louhi shot a sideways glance at Vanadis. "You however, have a similar troop following."

Vanadis glanced over her shoulder uneasily, expecting to see a spectral horde following her.

"Good." huffed Louhi, "You understand the seriousness of your predicament. Most young women with our curse need only worry about one or two persistent hauntings. You're the only one I've seen who, at such a young age, has an entire army hounding her. Mjoll was right to send you to me."

"They do not act like a horde my Queen. My mother rules and speaks for them."

Louhi turned thoughtful, "When I met your mother she did strike me as willful. She's our main problem then."

A question struck Vanadis 'Could you bind her?' but in in the back of her mind Hanne whispered 'Don't even think about it.'

"W-what will we do about her?" Vanadis asked instead.

"Through normal means it would take years, decades to sort out the mess you're in." Explained the witch, with a laugh she added, "I don't have time for such and I doubt you wish to be cooped up here for so long."

Vanadis seemed to consider it. 'It's a nice prison.'

'You promised a Legacy.' Her mother hissed.

Vanadis flinched, "Right." to Louhi she said "The sooner I can sort things out the better."

Louhi patted her on the back, "Good girl."
They came to a solid looking wooden door at the end of the hallway, Louhi grasped the handle and pulled it open. Torches flared to life inside, and Vanadis found it to be everything she expected form a witch's workshop. It was a vast circular chamber with a large fire pit in the center. Along the walls rested tables, on which lay scrolls, jars, candles, and skulls. Most of the skulls were animals, though a few were human. Along the walls, etched in gold, were the strange symbols Louhi had worn on her robes the night before. Louhi pushed Vanadis inside and gestured to a small, uncomfortable looking chair by the fire pit. Vanadis sat there and Louhi, after baring the door behind them, walked around to sit on the throne of bone across from her.
The Queen leaned forward and said "The intensity of your curse is unique but you are not alone. This world is ill-forged; many who die in it do not find eternal rest in the river of Tuonela. Your own people follow gods who deny rest all together, they either gather up souls for their fatal war or banish them to dismal Niflheim."

'Better active in another world than inert like some over bloated water log.' Vanadis mused, though she did not dare interrupt Louhi.

"Those dead who escape Tuonela and your vicious deities are trapped in a world ill-suited for them. They wander without skin, invisible and unheard by those they loved. Only we, 'lucky' few can converse with them and, as you know full well, they are demanding. However, fear not, for those who can control the curse can do wonderful and terrifying things with it."

Louhi straightened her back and closed her eyes. She then shuddered and moaned with three voices. She reached over her head and gestured to the dark recesses. Rolling out from it came a cloud of spectral bodies. At their head was the golden haired Rainbow Maiden, scarred with fresh fang and claw marks. Behind and beneath her drifted the golden haired king, his locks soaked in crimson blood. Clustered around them were ten other spirits, men and women of various ages. They undulated around Louhi and Vanadis like a flying river. Their mouths opened and they uttered a beautiful and terrifying choir in Soumi, the tune bespoke of loneliness and mystery. Louhi pointed at Vanadis and suddenly everything became larger. Her chair became mountainous and Louhi a titan. The river of souls coiled around the witch like a loving snake, then they and Louhi stared down at the tiny young woman. In the choir of voices she said "Behold the power of seith. It can be yours if you're willing to risk your life." She jabbed her finger at Vanadis, an intense pain twisted in her chest, she shrieked and everything went black.

***

Vanadis was awaked by a swift kick to the stomach. She rolled to her side and groaned. Suddenly a firm hand grasped her by the hair and yanked her up off the floor. Her eyes went wide and her heart pounded. She was back in the mill.

Stone walls surrounded her, before her was the hateful grindstone, with the turning leavers she knew too well. Sunlight streamed through the cracks in the roof. A large woman in a merchant's blue held Vanadis. In her other meaty hand was a sack of flour. "I return from Gotland and what do I find?

This?" she shook it in Vanadis' face, the sack was not as full as it should be.

"I'm sorry Mistress." Vanadis pleaded, "Marit sprained her ankle so we had less help with the grinding."

"You're clever, you should have found a way." With a flick of her wrist she sent Vanadis tumbling backwards. "Unfir, Lyting, get to work on her." The Mistress' two brawny sons stepped beside her.

"N-no!" Vanadis pleaded. "Without me, there'll be even less flour."

Miller stroked her chin, "Aye...You two." She indicated her sons, "Hurt her, but, don't break her. No funny business either, I'll be watching."

Her sons grinned and advanced on Vanadis.

***

Moments after the slave girl crawled out of the mill and curled up against the wall in the shade. Behind her the miller called "Think on that!"

Vanadis pulled her knees up under her chin and stared off at nothing in abject misery. The back of her dress was undone and several bloody, raw switch marks marred her skin. The nattering of voices did not shake her out of her brooding. As they got louder Vanadis was only half aware of what they said,

"Dote, don't go near her. She's dirty."

"She's liable to bite." giggled another.

"If I fear a slave, then I am not a worthy daughter. You there."

Vanadis recognized the tone of command and glanced up. Standing before her were Elina, Gerd and Dorte. Kelifar's most highborn daughters. Elina and Ingeborg regarded Vanadis as if she were a rat that just crawled out of the river. Dorte held an imperious curiosity about her. Much to Vanadis surprise she crouched down before her. "You, tell me what happened this instant."

The pain on Vanadis' back flared up as she considered how much harder she'd have if she put in a bad word about the miller. Avoiding Dorte's eyes she said, "I was lazy and given my rightful punishment." She bit back her anger at the lie. For the past few days she had worked harder than ever before but, without Marit, it hadn't been enough.

"There have been times," Dorte mused, "where I disappointed my father or mother and I too was punished justly, but never like this. Gerd, is it normal to treat thralls like this?"

"They can be treated however their owners want." She said with a shrug. "If they work hard their masters might free them."

Dorte looked over Vanadis with distaste. "I think it's monstrous. When I'm lady of Kelifar such things will not happen."

If word got back that Vanadis had put such an idea in the jarl's daughter's head..."My Lady," Vanadis said swiftly, "it's the way Heimdall as Rigg set up the world. Jarls rule free men, both own thralls. It seems harsh, personally I hate it, but we mustn't question the gods."

Dote frowned, Vanadis winced expecting a hit. No such blow came.

Vanadis felt a light touch on her shoulder, she opened her eyes to see Dorte regarding her with a smug, cunning expression. "Tell me, what's your name?"

"Vanadis."

"Vanadis, as filthy as you are, you speak well. If you were to be cleaned up I suspect you'd be quite striking. Sisters, do you not agree?"

Elina wrinkled her nose. "She would need much cleaning."

Gerd judged her but her expression was less harsh. "She knows her place, that's valuable in a slave."

"Vanadis," Dorte addressed magnanimously, "will you swear yourself to me? Promise to be eternally loyal and do everything I say? If you do I will buy you. Serve me faithfully and you'll never have to push the millstone again, and, if anyone so much lays a hand on you, they'll face my wrath."

Sudden hope flared within her. "Y-yes. Of course. I swear myself to you my lady."

Dorte paused, lowered her head and chuckled bitterly. Suddenly Elina and Gerd vanished. The sky darkened and everything turned to black. Vanadis and Dorte floated in starless, moonless, night.

"How I pitied you." Dorte said without looking up. "I had you tended, washed and stood you at my side. As my thrall you had far more renown than any common free woman. I used to get compliments 'She's such a well-mannered girl.' 'Where can I get a slave like her?' I was always kind to you Vanadis. I cared for you. I loved you like my own." She lifted her head and Vanadis saw it was purple and bloated, her blue eyes bulging. She jerked up as if being hanged. "How could you? Tell me, how did I betray you?" Her dead eyes, her purple lips didn't move. Her voice echoed from somewhere in her cadaver.

Vanadis let out a cry and staggered back. Tears rolled down her cheeks, "Y-you don't understand. It was my mother's revenge, not mine. You never betrayed me. I'm sorry I didn't warn you. Had I known...oh Dorte had I known I would have done anything to spare your life."

White cloth snaked around Dotre binding her body a burial dress. A long, white, silken shroud covered her face, Vanadis could see only the rise of her nose and the shadows of her eyes behind it. Dorte's fingers grew long, her nails became like claws. Her skin was smooth, white and lifeless. "Do one last service for me my thrall." She howled, seizing Vanadis' arm in a death cold grip. "Allow me to devour you."

Fear proved stronger than guilt, Vanadis kicked out, her heel hit solid flesh but the specter moved not. Dorte slashed and cut Vanadis' face. Dorte reached back and... out of nowhere Bera slammed into her shield first. The three tumbled through the ether.

Vanadis heard Dorte scream with rage. She then felt a gauntleted grip on her wrist and heard Bera urge, "This way my lady." The sky suddenly lit up with stars. A clear moon shone down and Dorte's screams went suddenly silent.

"We're safe now." Bera hung her shield over her shoulder.

Vanadis, now loosed from Bera's grip, looked around. They were back in Kelifar standing once more before the Great Hall. Its doors were shut but light, voices and music eminated from inside.

Vanadis took a moment to collect herself. "How did we get here? Last I remember I was in a chamber in the Sariola. Louhi was scaring me nearly half...to...death?" Vanadis suddenly noticed the faint silver aura around her and that her feet floated a finger's length off the ground. "I-I'm dead? The witch killed me?" Her voice sounded hallow.

Bera looked away sorrowfully, "Aye, I'm afraid so." Then her tone rose with courage and she slapped her on the back "Fear not, it's not so bad."

"I can't be dead. My brother, Vinglunr, they fought so hard to get to Louhi. No, I won't believe it!"

Bera rested a gentle hand on her shoulder, "I felt the same when I died but no amount of urging returned me to life.

"I..." Vanadis' keen mind disassembled her arguments. She remembered clearly her last moments and could find no other explanation. "N-no." she sniffed. She shook and then wept tears of anguish and rage.

Bera stood with her offering silent comfort, when her mistress' tears were spent she said "Coming to grips, that's the worst part. Once you accept it, you'll find being a spirit is easy."

Vanadis regarded Bera with disbelief, "Why be so kind to me? I promised you a grand life. I failed, why did you save me from Dorte?"

Bera grinned "I died protecting you, no need to stop now."

The shieldmaiden's words and smile were like a kick in the gut to Vanadis. She bore it and turned back to the hall to avoid her gaze, "I see..." The departed Volsung regarded the lively Great Hall, grasping it as a new, less painful subject. "Strange, after what happened you'd think no one would move in so soon."

"This?" Bera nodded to the great double doors. "This isn't the Kelifar. This is Hanne's Hall in the spirit world, I brought us here because Dorte' won't follow. Hanne won't allow it."

"Mother's domain?" Vanadis said in surprise. Then she frowned, "Perhaps we should go somewhere else? Her chiding will be unbearable."

"There's nowhere else to go. Come on." Bera grabbed Vanadis' wrist, kicked open the door and took her through. The music that echoed inside was slow, beautiful and stately. The singer was a woman whose voice was haunting and majestic. The band played drums, and flutes and strings. The dwellers looked well-dressed and hardy. The tables were set with sumptuous meats and freshly cooked greens. There was no fire but the silver spectral radiance from the spirts inside kept the hall warm and bright. At the end of the head table sat Hanne the Clever.

She noticed Vanadis immediately raised a glass. "Ah daughter, welcome to journey's end."

As one the crowd cheered. Vanadis found it eerie that they all moved on accord.

"Come dear, take your place beside me." She gestured to her left hand chair.

Vanadis glanced around, searching for the lord of the house and then, asked, "Where's father?"

"Watching over your brother." Hanne sighed. "He can be stubborn when it comes to Gamli. He'll be back momentarily."

"My lady?" Bera asked urgently, looking hungrily at the sumptuous feast that lay on the tables before them, all sorts of delicacies from roasted pork to honey drenched berries.

Vanadis regarded her mother and the rest of the crowd. Her mother's smile was very much at ease, the one a cat would make at finding a mouse. The other grins were forced; she saw hints of fear in the revelers eyes. She reached out and blocked Bera from going further. "Perhaps we should join father and watch over him, too, you know, just in case."

Hanne chuckled, "Nonsense, you've done enough harm. When he discovers your passing he'll be grief stricken. He may even try to foolishly avenge your death, and then we'll all be here."

Vanadis flinched at that. "How was I to know that Louhi would murder me?"

"She's a witch, dear, they excel at bringing people to bad ends."

"It makes no sense." Vanadis mused, "Louhi could have executed me on the spot. Why do it in the Sariola?"

"To hide her crimes, of course." Hanne gestured, the hall spun and Vanadis suddenly found herself sitting by her mother's side. Hanne pressed a drinking horn into her hand. "Have some mead, fret no more on this."

Bera dug into mutton with gravy and found it most pleasant.

Vanadis instinctually brought the horn to her lips but paused before drinking as a thought struck her. "She's Queen, her word's law, killing me would have been no crime."

"The Sariola's a sacred place to her. Perhaps you were merely a sacrifice?" Hanne handed Vanadis a piece of bread dipped in melted butter.

Vanadis opened her mouth to eat but again paused, in spite of her huger. "Then why am I here? Shouldn't I be one of Louhi's sentinels or a slave to a foreign god?"

"My power brought you here, it is as simple as that." said her mother, her tone cracking with impatience.

'That is most certainly false.' Fresh memories of Dorte's attack flashed in her mind. Vanadis stood. "Bera, we're leaving."

"I'd rather stay." said the shieldmaiden, her voice a deadpan. Her plate of food suddenly untouched.

Vanadis glanced back to see the hall's double doors barred and shut. The other spirits stood and pressed in close around her.

Her mother's smile turned cruel. "No you're staying. I am the lady of this hall. You'll kneel before me as a dutiful little ghost."

Vanadis noticed that out of the back of each spirit, even Bera, were spider web strings, these all lead to her mother, who stood resplendent in the center of the web.

Vanadis, retreated a step. "No, I'd rather have my own will thank you very much."

Hanne advanced. "It's the way of the world daughter. The weak serve the strong, you are the weaker."

The young spirit took another step back, glancing around fearfully, searching for anyway out, any small crack in the hall. Then she noticed her chest was heaving. She touched her cheek, it felt as if someone painted on it. Dimly she Louhi's aged voice chanting in Soumi in the background. A smile of revalation lit her face. "Mother, I'm alive. I can feel it. I don't belong here."

"I beg to differ." Hanne huffed. "I've thought long and hard about our 'legacy'. As a seithkona you would take charge of my hall. I will not have that." Hanne flicked her wrist and Bera stood and drew her axe. The host around her shifted their stance and scowled, ready for an attack.

"You'd do this to your own child?" Vanadis asked in indignation.

"There is nothing more natural." replied Hanne. "All parents wish dominion over their children, and they in turn struggle for dominance over them. Do you think you're worthy of leading us? You who have sworn fealty to the whore daughter of the Rogue?" She fumed. "I've had enough Vanadis. Submit yourself at once and you'll find me generous. You'll have an honored place at my side. Hesitate, even a moment, and I'll tear you apart and feed you to this hall."

Hanne's words stung and Vanadis' grey eyes flashed with anger. She seized some of the strings running to her mother. "No, no you won't." With a pull she broke them and half a dozen denizens reeled as if coming out of a sleep.

"You dare? Seizer her!"

Vanadis raised her hands and let a clump of the crowd pile around her, as they did she tore their strings. Their grip weakened and they staggered. Vanadis pushed past them, finding herself suddenly, inordinately strong, knocking them flying.

"I'm done cowering mother." Vanadis seethed. Unthinkingly she raised both arms and slashed them down. Her will enacted what she desired, a wind swirled around the hall knocking food, drink, bowls and cups everywhere. All the strings snapped and Hanne staggered back with a sudden look of fear in her eyes.

Vanadis advanced upon her. "You dare insult me? You, who were brought up in furs. You who were nurtured by dainties. You wouldn't last a single morning at the mill. I was cowed by you at first, but now... I've stared down Valkyries mother, you are nothing in comparison."

Hanne stumbled over a chair and fell. "You have no right to talk to me like that. I birthed you, I saved your life by hiding you among the thralls."

Vanadis laughed scornfully, "You were known as Hanne the Clever, how could you have not seen through Steinarr's disguise? Your stupidity tossed me and Gamli into bondage."

"I-I..." Hanne's demeanor began to change. The cruelness drained out of her face and she hugged herself cowering. "N-no. You speak falsehood. I did everything I could for you and Gamli, for my babies."

Vanadis glared at her mother, finding it hard to calm down. A power ran through every fiber of her being. She lifted her hands and found the spider strings of the spirits attached to her, she was now the center of the web.

"No." Vanadis brushed her arms and the strings fell away to nothing. Soon she simply stood as a bright, shining, living spirit. The denizens murmured and slowly came back to themselves.

"You're not my puppets, nor my slaves." She glanced around the crowd evenly, "I won't keep slaves," she then regarded her cowering mother. "I'm not like her."

"Forgive her, she knows not what she dose." rumbled a voice behind her.

All eyes turned. The double doors had been opened and leaning inside it was a powerful man with red hair, mustache and beard that flickered like firelight. He stepped inside with an air of pride and purpose.
"This is a blessed day. First and foremost, I break your mother's hold. Then, I witness your brother at the forge of Ilmarinen, full of mighty Surt's blessing. Then I return to free my people, only to witness my daughter doing it for me." He put his sturdy hands on Vanadis' shoulders. "You must forgive her. Hanne was not always like this, death has changed her."

At first Vanadis was too stunned to move. Stunned at the sudden appearance of her father and stunned at his mention of Gamli and Surt. His words on Hanne brought her back, she turned her gaze away and said "No, she went too far."

Her father clutched her chin and nudged her gaze up to him. With both a warmth and a fierceness he said "I was the stag welcomed as a guest in Steinarr's hall. It was my anger that strangled Kelifar, and it was their transgression against the laws of hospitality that revoked Freya's protection and allowed me to do so. While your mother forced my hand I do not regret the part I played, for it freed you and Gamli. So, do not judge your mother too harshly."

Behind her Vanadis could hear Hanne sobbing. With a huff the young woman said "As you wish." Turning to her mother she nudged the spirit with her foot. "Swear to me you'll never bind them like puppets again, and that you'll never try to drag me, or Gamli, to the grave."

"But this is my hall." Hanne pleaded.

Vanadis shook her head, "No. It's mine and I will rule it justly."

Kvistr squeezed Vanadis' shoulder "I am for this, as long as you do us honor with your life and offer sacrifice of food and drink every month. Do this and we shall thrive." Said Kvistr.

"Mother? Will you bow to my rule?" asked Vanadis.

Her father stepped beside her. "Hanne, it's only right that we give way to the living. We must support our children, not rule over them." He held out his massive hand to her.

Hanne glanced up at them warily. Vanadis regarded her with guarded conviction. Kvistr waited with loving patience.

"Fine." She seized Kvistr's hand. He pulled her up and Hanne turned to her daughter, "I will not bind my people. I shall not tarry you here nor seek to entrap yourself or your brother in the realm of the dead."

"Excellent, we have a pact." Vanadis concluded with a victorious grin.

"We have indeed." rumbled Kvistr and embraced both his wife and daughter in one hug. When he released them he admired them both. "Your resemblance is uncanny."

Hanne snorted, "It is, though I'd prefer it if she dressed better."

"I'll dress as I please." Vanadis shot back. Suddenly she realized that Louhi's voice was growing fainter. Holding in an edge of fear she said "I need to go," glancing at Brea she asked, "can you take me back to Louhi?"

Bera nodded, "Aye, spread your arms."

Vanadis eyed her dubiously but spread her arms. Brea smirked and suddenly rushed her, when she collided she vanished and Vanadis jolted back. To her surprise, her arms had become luminescent wings, her silver aura brightened.

Kvistr laughed, "Come," he roared, "Let us all see our young Vanadis off." He fell upon her and suddenly her wings grew brighter still and she floated a foot off the ground.

"I suppose this will be..." Vanadis cut off her words with a yelp as the entire barrow cheered and rushed for her. As they swarmed they became pure radiance that was absorbed by her wings, which now glowed as brightly as the moon on a clear night.

Only Hanne was left standing on the floor. She turned bitterly away.

"Mother?" Vanadis asked dryly, "Are you comming?"

Hanne smirked. "Tis better than staying in an empty hall I suppose." Suddenly she jumped at Vanadis and in a flash merged with her form. Then Volsung shot up through the roof of the barrow, passing through it like a ghost. She found herself high in the clear night. She flapped her wings once and shot up, breaking through the sky. As swift as an arrow she flew through the void between dreams. She was as radiant as a star, several volva would wake remembering her passing. Queen Louhi's chanting grew louder and louder until it resounded around Vanadis. Suddenly the darkness solidified as a dark sea and she smashed directly through it.

***

Vanadis gasped a ragged breath and her eyes snapped open. Instantly she was painfully aware of the chill air. She lay naked on a stone table in Lohi's ritual chamber. Her skin, from her forehead to her feet, was marked with strange symbols in charcoal. Immediately a thick cloak was wrapped around her.

"Easy," said Louhi, "easy. It's over, you've returned." The old woman held her up and rubbed her back.

"What," her voice sounded weak but her glare at the witch was sharp, "did you do to me?"

Louhi's blue eyes twinkled and she snickered, "Yes, that is the will I hoped for, the resolve that will make you great."

"What, did you do?" Vanadis repeated.

"Why, I killed you." Louhi said in a matter-of-fact manner. "However, it seems you've paid me back." She glanced over her chamber. The tables, shelves had been toppled as if a hurricane it the room. Coals had been flung everywhere, a few scrolls even burned and Louhi's robe smoldered. With a flick of her wrist she extinguished the errant flames. "Impressive, the wake of your power even disrupted a few of my guardians."

Vanadis found herself relying on Louhi's grip to remain upright. An exhaustion equal to sickness weighed down her limbs. "Why?" she asked, doing her best to keep what little strength she had, "Why, did you kill me?"

"Remember, I do not have the time to train you through normal methods."

"This was training?"

"Yes, it would have taken years to acquaint you with the spirit world."

"So you sent me there?" Vanadis asked incredulously.

"Aye," answered Louhi, "I extinguished all but an ember of your life. I planned to slowly fan it back but something went wrong, a spirit inside was tearing you apart. I attempted to banish it but it intertwined with your soul, I'm sorry to say, I banished you as well. The symbols on your body were meant to coax you back, but it seems you've returned on your own."

"I had a discussion with my mother and broke her hold on the ghosts of Kelifar. They brought me back."

"I see," mused Louhi, she cracked a smile "so you've already brought your spirit entourage under your command. You've turned a chore into a joy." She chuckled "I actually look forward to teaching you."

"I'm honored but, my Queen, but if you wish to kill me again, I refuse." Vanadis said dryly.

Louhi cackled and patted her on the back "Very well, though do not think your training will be safe. Now, it's time to rest. You've lost much strength and will need to recover it to face what is to come."

CHAPTER 18

Some say loyalty is owed. | I say loyalty is earned.
The arrogance of the highborn are poor wages.
Save your love for those who reciprocate. | Save your loyalty for those who've served you.
Louhi, you who taught me the ways of the seithkona, I would die for you.

Vanadis watched the spring dawn light Pohjola underneath her. The leaves were in full blossom. Fishing boats had already launched on the Torino. Birds greeted the morning with their songs. Vanadis breathed in the crisp mountain air and calmed her mind. She could feel several unseen presences around her, the spirts of Kelifar sensed her rising tension like the coming of a storm. Soon she would need them, but not yet.

Something caught in the corner of the seithkona's eye. She turned to see an ash-brown martin standing on the mortared balcony wall. In his beak he held a strand of red hair. The bird stared up at her with a cold black eye. Vanadis found herself absorbed by it. In its reflection she saw an impossibly tall stone wall with guards marching across it. She peered over the wall to see a field of crosses. Suddenly, she was back in the waking world. With a flick of his beak, the martin flung the red strand into the air; it caught in a gust of wind and blew away. The martin spread his wings and flew off. Vanadis frowned and contemplated what that meant.

Spider light fingers touched her shoulder and she jumped with a scream. Louhi, dressed in black, carrying her eagle head cane, stood before her. She peered at Vanadis quizzically. "Nervous, are we? It is expected; today's test will be trying, after all."

"It's not the test, my Queen." Vanadis answered. She glanced where the martin had flown. "I was struck by an omen."

"An omen? Well, you say you're clever, tell me of it and what it means."

Vanadis shared the omen with her. Louhi's expression dropped, and she brooded over it.

"It displeases you teacher?" Vanadis asked with concern. Then its meaning caught in her mind and her grey eyes widened.

Before Vanadis could speak Louhi waved off her concern, "We both know this has no bearing on today's test. Come." She spun on her heel and walked for the far door.

"Yes, my Queen." answered Vanadis, she followed.

***

Moments later, Vanadis and Louhi stood on a high up ledge on the Sariola. It curved around the mountain and out of sight. The wind blew strongly against the mountain. The sky was clear and the rock dry.

"To pass this test you must make it to the door on the other side. You may not summon Bera. Deal with any opposition harshly." Louhi instructed, pointing the way.

"Yes, my Queen." Vanadis said. She was equipped and prepared. She wore a dress of brown overtop of which was a light tan apron stitched with feathers and runes. A white fox fur cloak was draped on her shoulders, a necessity this high up on the mountain. She carried a solid, ash staff.

Vanadis considered the path carefully. She then pointed her staff forward and exerted her will, calling her spirits to open a path to Yggdrasil. The stone before her cracked and a glowing green fire flickered before her. Without hesitation Vanadis stepped through it and vanished.

Louhi cackled, "Very wise. I might not have to scrape you off the foot of the mountain after all."

Vanadis smirked but kept herself focused on the task at hand. She walked forward invisibly and cautiously, the flame dying out behind her. Slowly she crept around the curve of the mountain. On the other side she saw a large, closed, wooden door. Before it sat a horror.

It was as tall as a man. It had the face of a cone, the body of a warrior, two powerful, long arms whose firsts rested on the ground and six human legs. When Vanadis stepped closer it frowned and sniffed the air. There was not enough room on the cliff to squeeze past and, even if she could, she'd fail open the door before the thing had her.

Immediately a curse sprang to mind. 'To me.' Vanadis called silently, she felt the rush of a presence flood inside her. On its own her body shifted subtly and she lowered her staff in a defensive posture. She combined hers' and the spirit's strength and threw the curse at the creature with but a thought.

Sickening snaps and pops filled the air, three of its legs and an arm twisted and snapped. The creature let out a deafening howl but managed to stay on upright thanks to its many limbs

While Vanadis prepped another hex the thing charged in her direction. Suddenly, her body charged to meet it and swung the staff.

'No, no, no!' the Volsung mentally screamed.

The creature swiped forward and seized Vanadis' arm. It then cackled and threw the Seithkona with bone jarring force against the wall. It then leapt at her, its broken limbs flailing behind it.
With a glare, Vanadis tossed another hex. A vortex of shadow erupted around the thing, it spun with the screams of a dozen souls. The thing screamed in turn. Then the dark wind flooded off it and into Vanadis easing all her hurt.

The creature, its strength spent, lay still.

Vanadis' body stepped forward and hammered the ash staff into the prone thing, each blow ending with a sickening thud.

'Enough.' With a push of will Vanadis banished the spirit from her body and lifted her bloody staff from the corpse. The thing then melted like snow and left nothing but blood in its place.

Vanadis leaned on her staff and centered herself. After she caught her breath she advanced on the door. She reach out to pull its handle and hesitated right before touching it. Smirking the Volsung shook her head. 'This time I take no chances.' She stepped back, pointed her staff and spat a hex. The door rippled as if was flesh, then a dozen fanged mouths grew within it. They began to eat, smashing and splintering the wood until it was a pile of rubble before her.

Louhi stood on the other side. She regarded the splintered remains wryly, as if that last spell was overkill.

Vanadis stepped through and banished her shroud, becoming visible, a victorious smile on her lips. "Do I pass?"

"Not even a scratch." Louhi said in mock disappointment. "Aye, you pass."

"Shall we get to the next lesson?"

"No," Louhi waved her off, "I have the preparations of a feast to oversee in my hall. It'll require my full attention."

"Feast?" Asked Vanadis perplexed, "Today's no holiday. What reason do we have to feast?"

Louhi smirked, "I'm letting a treasure loose from the Sariola."

For a moment Vanadis looked even more perplexed, then her jaw dropped and she glanced at the Queen hopefully.

Louhi laughed and rested an affectionate hand on her shoulder. "This day you've proven your dominion over your spirits. Now only havoc you'll reign down will be at your command. I trust you not to harm Pohjola."

Joy flooded through Vanadis. During the long winter she had seen Vinglunr and her brother only a handful of times. Her rocky domain had grown tiresome. Many were the days she watched, with envy the denizens of the city wander about. However, one sour note struck her. "I'm overjoyed, but does this mean our lessons are at an end?"

Louhi stroked her chin thoughtfully, "I'm afraid so. You've put your own twist on you magic. If I taught you more we'd only bicker. It's best you learn the rest on your own."

"I understand." Vanadis said with resignation. "Still, I'll treasure your tutelage, always."

Louhi snickered, pushed the young woman forward and walked with her. "You make it sound so final. Pohjola is your home now, you can even keep your room in the Sariola as long as you don't grow tiresome."

At the worry left Vanadis at once, "I think I will. I'd hate to give up the bed and the hot springs."

Louhi cackled at that.

***

That evening, Louhi's hall was lit by torches and a fire pit. Dark, sturdy tables, laden with food and drink, went from the back of the hall to the front. Pohjalander men, women and children stood at their places. Louhi stood at the head of her table, wrapped in a dress of midnight blue and lined with silver. Vanadis, stood to her right, in a crimson dress with long black sleeves, whose lining was gold. Her hair was bound a gold chain. Vilma stood across from her in similarly stunning garb. Salli stood beside her. Louhi's other two daughters took the next places. Gamli was next, dressed in fine brown tunic, wearing a cloak of black bear fur. Vinglunr stood across from him, decked in respondent green and wearing a grey cloak. The rest of the guests were in equal finery.

Louhi gestured and the crowd fell silent. "Magic is our life blood. The magic of the Sampo fills our coffers and bellies. My magic and our warriors protect our boarders. It is good that we guard its secrets jealously, we must share it only with the worthy." Gesturing to Vanadis she said "A worthy stands before you." The hall cheered. Louhi smiled, "My student comes from our own blood, as such, Pohjola is her home. I trust she will use her spells in our service."

Vanadis bowed before the queen, and turned to the crowd. For a moment she was overwhelmed. Those before her looked upon her with an honest warmth. 'I love this place.' Vanadis was surprised at the truth of her thoughts. She found herself drying her eyes. Then she said "Gamli and I came to this place as outlaws, vargs. We hoped for a short sanctuary, a brief respite from our enemies." Vanadis choked on her own happiness. "You've opened your homes. You treated us with kindness and respect. So, of course my spells are at your service. I hope you will always consider me one of your own."

The crowd's roar of approval was their answer.

"Let the feast begin!" cried Louhi and the hall came to life. The denizens left their spots and mingled, feasting and drinking as they saw fit. Vanadis was pressed by the prominent Pohjalanders. A farmer welcomed her warmly. A merchant said he would be at her service. A few of the warriors pledged themselves as protectors as long as she remained in Pohjola's walls. Salli managed to pull Vanadis out of it and they, with her sisters, supped in peace. They five chattered and gossiped for a while, then the hall erupted into dancing.

Vinglunr stood on a bench, strummed his lyre and sang in fluent Soumi. They were lively tunes, accompanied by Pohjalander flutes and drums. Vanadis caught a few words, they were songs of harvest, mystery and humor. She and Louhi's daughters were pulled off to dance. Vanadis paired off with several, handsome, wealthy partners. She kept a gracious smile on her face though found it odd to be the focus of such attentions. She noticed her brother was pulled forward by several prominent women, including Salli. He danced cautiously, smiled little but those grins were genuine.

Finally Vinglunr took a break and an equally talented Pohjalander skald took his place. Vinglunr weaved through the crowd and met Vanadis. He offered his hand, "One dance, then we can sit."

"Very well." Vanadis answered graciously. Vinglunr moved smoothly, he even guided Vanadis so she seemed graceful. They made small talk, and found themselves immensely comfortable in each other's company. They had grown close over those few times Vinglunr snuck into the Sariola.

After the dance, he pulled Vanadis to a bench where her brother sat.

Gamli's face was flush with liquor, his eyes gleamed, pleasantly drunk. "I'm proud of you. Proud you've become a seithkona. Proud that you're dancing with other men."

Vanadis eyed him dubiously, "You expect me to dance with beasts?"

Vinglunr chuckled, "Pay him no mind. Rumors have addled him."

"Rumors? What rumours?" Vanadis asked.

Gamli waved his hand and left to get another drink.

"I'm uncertain you wish to know." Vinglunr warned with a hint of mischief.

"Tell me." Vanadis insisted.

Vinglunr laughed, "Very well. You see, word from the south as reached us. Word of the dreaded vargs Gamli the Serpent and Vanadis the Cursed."

"Wonderful." The seithkona commented dryly.

"Oh it gets far more elaborate. You see," Vinglunr put his arm around her and held out is hand as if showing her a grand horizon, "these two villains were the beloved wards of Steinarr the Rogue, but they turned on him in betrayal most foul."

"Beloved wards? How dare... you don'tt send your 'beloved' to the gristmill!" Vanadis fumed.

"That is not the worst." Vinglunr laughed. "Are ceartian you're ready for it?"

"I've made it this far."

"Furthermore, it is said that Gamli is to Vanadis, as Sigurd was to his sister Signy." Vinglunr finished.

Vanadis stared forward absolutely mortified.

Gamli sat down beside her with two full bowls of beer. "I'd rather sleep with a skunk."

Vanadis struck him, "I'd rather sleep with one of Louhi's abominations."

Vinglunr laughed. Gamli handed her the second beer bowl. Vanadis drank in fuming silence.

Once she had finished Vinglunr pulled out something wrapped in red silk. "So, now you understand why I hand this to you instead of your brother."

Vanadis took the present, something hard and circular was inside.

"Forged it myself." Gamli said, then pointing to Vinglunr he added "He bought the gold."

Vanadis unwrapped it and her breath was stolen away with what she found. A shining and gold circlet. It was smooth, unadorned but perfect in its simplicity.

Vinglunr held out his hands, "May I?"

Vanadis nodded and placed the circlet in his palms. Vinglunr carefully set over her head and on her temple. He gently pulled some of her brown locks out and let them drift forward. Gently, he commented, "It looks most beautiful on you."

Vanadis' eyes went wide as she felt a sudden thrum of power. She ran her finger along the circlet and felt tiny runes. "This is enchanted." She gasped. "Gamli? How?"

Gamli smiled proudly, "I've found my talent, sister."

"Indeed he has." Said Vinglunr, "Gamli here is a true wondersmith. He can forge great works in mere hours. Many of his creations hold magic."

Vanadis regarded her brother with a new found respect. "You haven't been idle. You must tell me how you learned."

"Will you allow me to do the honors?" asked the skald.

Gamli gestured for him to go ahead.

Vinglunr told Gamli's tale in true skaldic fashion. He told of Ilmarinen's forge, of the Pohjalanders ruined buy it, of Gamli's glimpse of Surt, of the vision of Asvard's betrayal and of the forging of the sword Scorn. He did not tell of Surt's blessing for Gamli had kept that to himself.

Vanadis listened with interest. At Asvard's part this she frowned and looked suddenly furious. When Vinglunr had finished she regarded her brother. There was something different about him, a steel in his eyes and a strength born of pain. She bit back her words of consolation and touched his arm. They shared a knowing look and left it at that.

The feast went on well into the night. Gamli eventually fell asleep, a beautiful Pohjalander maiden snuggled under his arm. Vinglunr sung a few more songs but otherwise remained Vanadis' charming companion. At the end of the night he saw her and Salli to her ferry.

***

Salli rowed Vanadis back to the Sariola and bid her goodnight adding, with a hug, "I am pleased you're one of us."

Vanadis wandered the rocky halls of the Sariola, now very confident of her path. She paused, however, at an archway that lead to one of the ledges. Standing there, was Louhi. She was staring up at the velvet night and stars, a look of grief on her face, tear marks stained her wrinkled cheeks.

"Teacher?" Vanadis asked softly.

Louhi jumped and turned to her with a scowl. Wiping her eyes she said "I throw you a feast and you dare ambush me?"

Undaunted, Vanadis joined her on the ledge. "You're thinking of the omen. It's of Vargeisa, isn't it?"

Louhi turned away, "None are to speak of her."

"I will." Vanadis said evenly. "I will because you need to speak of her."

Louhi shot her a glare. "Impudent child."

Vanadis crossed her arms and did not budge. "You're the childish one. Your bullying won't work on me."

Louhi dropped her guard. "Very well. We shall speak of this, once, but never bring it up again."

Vanadis relaxed her posture but promised nothing.

Louhi stared off, beyond Pohjola, beyond the Torino and began her story. "As you know, long ago my family was much larger, and happier. Vargeisa is my sixth daughter, she was so mischievous that I nearly foreswore further children. You already know of your mother's part in saving her life. Some would say Hanne's cure worked too well for, Vargeisa had boundless energy for boundless trouble. She would play tricks on her sisters. Pester the town and even found her way into forbidden parts of the Sariola. Some adored her for it, others despised her.

One day, she was working mischief with the fishing boats and one of the men pushed her boat, without oars, deep into the river and she was swept out to sea. I flayed the culprit alive. Then I took my eagle wings and searched for my darling girl. I soared for days above the wide ocean. I took the form of beautiful maidens and asked the southerners for rumor and help. I even spoke with your mother but all was for nought, my Vargeisa was lost.

Three years later, she returned. It seems one of your gods fostered her. She returned far more polite, far more controlled, and far more dangerous." Louhi grinned with fierce pride. "She was as beautiful as flickering flame but, cunning as the wolf. Those were joyous days."

Louhi' expression grew dark "Then one calamity struck after another. My eldest murdered in Kalevala. My husband killed by the vile Lemminkäinen. My youngest kidnapped, never to be seen again. On top of all this Vargeisa's foster god vanished."

"How can a god vanish?" Vanadis asked skeptically.

Louhi smirked ruefully, "When his brethren seize him and bind him in a dark place with the guts of his own son."

Vanadis was taken aback "Loki Laufeyson? Vargeisa was fostered by the trickster?"

Louhi nodded. "Aye, and Vargeisa was none too pleased about his binding. A determination burned within her to free Loki and she asked me to aid her." Louhi hugged herself as if beset by a sudden chill. "Of course I refused. Väinämöinen and his Kalevalen brood are foes enough, I do not need to endanger Pohjola further by incurring the wrath of the Aesir. Vargeisa was livid and we traded many harsh words. Finally she decided to strike out on her own."

Louhi gave her student a long, sorrowful look. "I tried to dissuade her on the docks. I said 'Vargeisa, if you leave now you shall never return. If you leave and I so much as catch a look at you, it'll be your end.'" Louhi closed her eyes and fought against churning regret. "Vanadis, you must always be cautious with your power, or you might do as I did and curse someone you love. This is why it pains me speak of Vargeisa. It reminds me of my own loss and foolishness."

The Queen went silent and Vanadis considered the story. She then looked to her teacher, Louhi had resumed her watch across the sea, seeming less the Sorceress Queen of Pohjola and more the grieving old woman.

"You should send a messenger. Tell her you love her and apologize. It'll do you good." Vanadis suggested gently.

Louhi snorted, "You think I haven't. She won't talk to a messenger of mine."

"She'll speak to me, I'll go." The words came before Vanadis could consider them.

Louhi turned to her surprised. "Truly?"

Vanadis paused before answering, she searched her soul and finally said. "Yes, of course I will. Two people in my life have given me respect, your daughter and yourself. That means more to me than you can ever know. Give me your message and I'll send it."

"You speak insanity. You know not where to look."

Vanadis' keen mind rushed back across the omen. "I think I do," she said thoughtfully, "the red hair the Martin held was in reference to Vargeisa. He landed on the wall of the balcony and then I saw a large wall and a field of crosses. Danevirke has a great wall and I've heard they battle Christians. She must be there and if not I'm sure I could pick up her trail. " Her conclusion sounded unlikely but it felt right.

Louhi considered this, "Yes...you're reasoning is sound." Then she shook her head, "It's no good, you're a varg in the south. They'll kill you."

Vanadis straitened her back imperiously, "I am the favoured apprentice of Louhi, Witch Queen of Pohjola; they won't succeed." She touched Louhi's arm and said, with urgency. "The thrush threw the red hair to the wind. Vargeisa may need help."

Louhi seemed torn.

"I will return." pressed Vanadis, then she added, with a smirk, "Though I will winter somewhere warmer."

Louhi regarded her student with pride and affection. "As you wish then, in the morning I shall fashion you with my message, a fast ship, and supplies. Strike out when you wish and Ukko be with you."

***

A day passed and the next humid morning found Vanadis walking towards on the docks of Torino with Salli, the spring wind whipped about their cloaks. Waiting for them on the busy dock was a ship. It was a brown karve, shorter and broader than a longship and much smaller and sleeker than a knarr. Its figure head was a reindeer. The crew, the seven men who had journeyed to Pohjola with them, were already packing her with sea chests and supplies. Among them was Gamli, Ransu and Vinglunr.

Vanadis nodded towards her brother, "He can take my sea chest the rest of the way." The porter walked up to Gamli and handed him the chest. Gamli eyed Vanadis and swung it a few times as if he were going to throw it into the sea.

"Don't you dare!" Vanadis warned.

Salli giggled.

"There's no reason for you to come." The Volsung maid hooked her arm around the skald's waist as he passed. "Because I have Vinglunr to protect me."

"I'm only catching a ship home," he laughed. Then considering Vanadis he added "Though I'll gladly be your champion along the way."

"I'm going," Gamli retorted, "and not just to keep an eye on him." He half glared at Vinglunr. "I'll search for new ores, and perhaps trade."

"Trading with those who'd trade with vargs is risky business." commented Ransu who took the chest from Gamli and placed it near the mast. "Yet it can also be a profitable." To Vanadis he said, "I'm Ransu the Spider, I was a close friend of your father's, it is a pleasure to finally meet you."

"Likewise, my brother's told me much about you." Vanadis said with a bow.

Ransu grinned "You're far more pleasant than your mother." To the three and the Vinglunr's 7 warriors, he said "Everyone on board. We set sail while the wind favours us."

Salli hugged Gamli and then Vanadis. "Be sure to keep my letter with you."

Vanadis tapped the scroll case at her belt. "I'll keep it and your mother's close," she displayed the bone ring on her finger, "until I deliver them to your sister."

"Please return safely, both of you, OK?"

"We shall." said Vanadis.

Gamli nodded.

As they stepped on board Vanadis asked her brother "What of Vilma and Niklas?"

"I've already bid farewell." Gamli gestured to a box secured to the stern of the deck. "He gave us lots of dried meat. We'll eat well."

"Excellent." said Vanadis and they both stepped on board.

***

Ransu cast off, the sail was unfurled and their ship made a swift exit from Torino. Vanadis sat beside Ransu at the rudder and regarded the crew. Vinglunr chatted with his men, who all seemed excited to be returning to the south. Gamli sat at his chest smoothing out a staff from a thin ash log. Beside Vanadis old Ransu relaxed guiding the ship with an expert hand. Vargeisa's purpose, the freeing of Loki, weighed on Vanadis' heart. Would Vinglunr and Gamli be so willing for this journey of they knew? Vanadis banished such thoughts from her mind. They weren't helping the Fire Wolf with her unholy task, just delivering messages. Vinglunr and her brother were better off not knowing.

A blue-grey goshawk took wing and followed their ship south for quite a distance. She then peeled off and flew south east. Her wings took her through the morning and she even glided through the night. On the following morn her course took her to the beautiful and sprawling Kalevala. She dove for the blue slatted roof of Väinämöinen's hall. She landed, knocked five times with her beak, and waited.

An hour later, after a light rain began to fall, a slow, rhythmic humming reached the bird. She took flight a short distance and landed in a window near the back of the hall. There stately Väinämöinen offered his hand. She hopped on it and he brought her inside.

"What news do you bring my fine friend?" he asked his tone full of welcome.

***

By midday, the rain poured down in a fury. Hardegon trudged down the muddy trail, the hood of his cloak pulled deep. Beside him walked a man shorter then him but nearly three times as broad. He had a wide face, a short but bushy light brown beard and a mane of unruly brown hair. He wore well used chain mail. An old but serviceable sword hung at his back. On his shoulders, he carried the corpse of a red wolf twice his size. The creature had many slash wounds.

"This weather mocks us." The large man huffed.

"Aye but soon we'll be warm and dry." replied Hardegon, pointing to the rich fields and outlying halls of Kalevala. The jarl's son squinted as he spied a hooded rider galloping from the city towards them.

The huge man spied him as well. "Hah! The addled fool rides towards sogginess and misery."

Hardegon signalled for them to stop "There must be a reason he does so. Perhaps it's ill news?"

"How I hope it is." roared the warrior. "A little sword play would warm my blood."

Soon enough the rider came upon them. Under his hood was the trim black beard and keen eyes of Starkad. "Hail brother, hail Lemminkäinen." He said with merriment.

"Ah the sorcerer!" replied the Kalevalen. "Excellent, perhaps you can banish the rain?"

"What brings you here brother? You sound as if you have news."

"Aye, old and trusty Väinämöinen has prepared Lemminkäinen's ship. Gamli the Serpent has made sail from Pohjola, if we sail north we can intercept him in a matter of a days."

A fire lit within Hardegon. "It appears our quarry is no coward. I shall reward his daring with my blade."

CHAPTER 10

To be invulnerable. / You must simply avoid danger.
Though such is the way of a coward.
To avoid cowardice . . . / You must shun safety.
Only cunning can bridge these contradictions.

They sailed south for several days. The weather was fair and windy so they made good progress. They visited no town or hall but Ransu's skill at finding the best camp grounds and catching fish and game ensured their nights were safe, warm and pleasant. Gamli finished whittling his staff and had his sister hold and wield it like a spear. When she inquired, he simply said he wanted her to be armed with something more substantial than her witch's stick. Vinglunr kept their spirits up with songs and stories. At night, Vanadis would share her watch with him and they talked of music, magic and philosophy.

One bright morning, Vinglunr had the rudder, Gamli and the sailors managed the sail and Ransu and Vanadis sat in the bow. The old man had been telling her stories about her mother while alive; Vanadis returned the favour by sharing some stories of her in death.

"So, Hanne's now what we feared she'd become." Ransu laughed.

"At least her shade is. I suspect her better half sleeps with her bones. I wish I had known her in life." answered Vanadis wistfully.

"You don't have to look far," he tapped her on the forehead, "You're Hanne with spells." The fisherman pondered her for a moment and added "However, there is one thing you lack."

"Oh?"

"Ambition, Hanne's drove her to become the Lady of Kelifar. If she lived she'd have maneuvered Kvistr into kingship and herself to queen. Don't get me wrong, I'm fond of Louhi, but, you could do much better than errand girl."

Vanadis frowned, somewhere in the corner of her mind, she could hear Hanne laughing. She was about to answer when Ransu suddenly stood.

He peered southwards, Vanadis followed his gaze and spied a boat. It was hard to make out at this distance. However, Ransu recognized it and did not seem pleased. He turned to the crew, panic in his eyes.

Gamli noticed and looked to him with concern.

Vinglunr noticed as well, "Ransu? What troubles you?"

The old man glanced from port to starboard, his faded blue eyes searching, they locked onto a river leading inland between a high set of crags. Pointing at them he said "Turn quick. If we dock far inland maybe he'll pass us by."

"Who'll will pass us by?" Asked Gamli.

"Lemminkäinen." Answered Ransu, as if it was obvious. "The ship," he pointed at the southward vessel, "It is the color of a cherry. The figurehead is a dragon with green eyes. We can't let him catch us on the open sea."

Vinglunr took the argument as sound and turned the ship.

"Men, ready the oars. If the wind fails us we must not lose speed!"

Fortunately the wind was kind and they sailed swiftly up the river. The red ship altered course and followed, it gained and grew slightly larger in the distance. Once the karve made it to the crags Lemminkänen's vessel vanished behind them.

"Keep sailing, the deeper we're in the better." ordered Ransu.

***

They sailed for an a few hours, in the meantime the sun rose high in the sky.

A pebbled beach appeared up a branching river to the northwest. "There, land us there." ordered Ransu. Within moments they docked. The old fisherman leapt out onto the shore and said "Grab only the essentials, leave everything else behind. I'll check to see if we've been followed." With that he dashed up the cliff.

Vanadis eyed Gamli and Vinglunr. Gamli shrugged and opened his sea chest. From it he pulled a rucksack, after donning it he strapped on his shield, it was painted as if it had green scales, the lower part of it was rimmed with iron spikes. Vinglunr did the same, prepping his sword and pack. The rest of the crew followed suit. Vanadis seized her pack, a large pouch of coins and double checked she had both Louhi's ring and Salli's scroll case.

Ransu skidded down and dropped himself off the rest of the way, he landed gracefully before them. "They follow, leave the ship, we'll hide among the crags."

"Why not ambush them?" asked Vinglunr, he gestured to the two paths that lead up the cliff face "You couldn't ask for a more perfect spot."

Gamli nodded, "Lemminkäinen's caused your people trouble, I'd love to stop him from causing more."

The memory of Louhi's lament on Sariola sparked an ember of anger within Vanadis "I've seen the grief he's caused the Queen. I want nothing more than send his soul howling to Niflheim."

The crew in turn bashed their shields in concord.

Ransu ran his fingers though his long black and grey hair in dismay. "We cannot win against Lemminkäinen. I witnessed his battle against our King, he was cut down like a child. We rushed him with twenty men and he threshed them like wheat. He only retreated when Louhi brought the army to bare. I know you southerners seek honorable death but facing him, with our numbers, is suicide. If we die like this your Odin will curse us for fools!"

The crew looked to Vinglunr who, in turn, considered Ransu's words carefully.

"Ransu's wisdom is sound." offered Gamli.

Vanadis glanced back to the ship. "We'll lose our vessel."

"Then we'll steal another and live up to our reputation as vargs." said Ransu, with waning patience.

"Ransu, how many men are with Lemminkäinen?" asked Vinglunr.

"Plenty." the fisherman answered.

"They outnumber us?"

"Yes." Ransu replied, again as if the answer was obvious.

"Then we flee." Vinglunr decreed.

Ransu turned his gaze to the sky, "Thank Ukko." He then gestured up the way he came, "Come, this way offers two paths."

The warriors settled their packs. Gamli joined Ransu and they clambered up the cliff. Vanadis shouldered her rucksack but hesitated.

Vinglunr touched her arm "Come, we must hurry."

"I don't like this, it delays our mission." she answered.

"Then we'll strive to make the delay as small as possible." Vinglunr said with confidence. He offered her his hand.

She took it and smirked, "I suppose I'm the fool this time around."

"I would have had the same sentiment if we were delivering a message for Mjoll." he answered pleasantly, then, the two fled up the rocky path.

Ransu lead them up the cliff and which reached a wide, rocky shelf. Beneath it was a carpet of evergreen forest. Before and above them rose pointed mountains layered with green brush. To their right the cliff dropped into the river. In the bright clear noon light they saw a great red longboat sailing it. The dragon head figurehead was ridiculously large. In the center of the boat sat a massive warrior whose girth dwarfed all others. He wore a tiny horned helmet.

"What a ridiculous helm," whispered Vinglunr, "is he the warrior of cattle?"

"Ridiculous or no he is fearsome, come, we must hurry." stressed Ransu.

Vanadis peered closer. Seeing the Jotunesque Lemminkäinen and the scores of men on his ship, made her suddenly thankful they had decided to flee. At the bow of the vessel she saw a noble, blonde haired figure. He had neatly trimmed and very short hair and beard. The way he stood reminded her of someone.

Gamli touched her on the shoulder, "Sister, let's go."

"Of, course." Vanadis followed.

They ascended the eastern mountain, staying on the landward side, and made good progress thanks to their swift pace and its gentile rise. In the distance they could hear the murmur of their pursuers and a booming laugh. The warriors glanced at each other with concern.

"They're swift." said Vanadis, swallowing her sudden fear.

Ransu paused and regarded the downward slope that lead to the forest. He then glanced upwards at a large cave. He wrinkled his nose and looked thoughtful.

"What's on your mind?" asked Gamli.

The fisherman nodded to towards cave. "Trolls, they'll be in deep slumber. If we're careful we could hide there."

Vanadis shared a sly look with him, "Daring, they won't think to look there, I like it."

"There's a difference between daring and foolish." said one of Vinglunr's men, an old veteran.

"I share your caution, Stefnir." said Vinglunr as he considered both options, "but I prefer Ransu's plan. If our pursuers follow us they'll have to contend with the trolls as well. Still, it if any of you wish to take to the forest instead, then, do so with my blessing. If we split our tracks, they may decide to split their forces."

The crew glanced at each other with uncertainty.

"Whatever decision you reach, do so soon." hissed Ransu.

"I'll take the forest." declared Stefnir. "If I am to be killed I'd rather it be at the hands of men." The rest of Vinglunr's men muttered in agreement.

A twitch of regret crossed the skald's face but he banished it with a grin. "Then farewell, I pray your flight is victorious." He clasped Stefnir's arm.

"I pray your strategy leads you to safety." answered the veteran. "If we both live let us share a drink in Mjoll's hall."

"If we both die let us share it in Valhalla." replied Vinglunr.

They said quick farewells. Gamli braced arms with each in turn and wished them well.

Vanadis said "My Freya guide you." with a formal bow. The two groups split, the 7 warriors heading for the forest, Vanadis, Gamli, Vinglunr and Ransu heading up for the cave.

***

Ransu lead them up with caution. In the distance, echoing in the mountain behind them, they could hear the troop getting closer.

"I thought we needed to hurry?" whispered Vinglunr, with a wary eye on their rear.

"Trolls don't leave sentries during the day, it is impossible, sunlight turns them to stone. They make do with traps." He pointed to a cluster of brush, Vinglunr peered closer to find it cleverly disguising a deep pit.

"Swiftly forward but cautiously then." the skald agreed. The four continued their accent, this time all eyes peeled for traps. Finally they reached the mouth of the cave. The daylight lit only a short distance, the rest was darkness. A musty scent wafted from inside. A dozen, polished human skulls were scattered on the floor before them.

"These are certainly not Valkyries." Vanadis whispered dryly.

"Uncle, what's your advice for not getting eaten?" asked Gamli.

"Light a lantern but keep it dim. Stick together and stay close to the wall. Don't touch anything. If the trolls awaken they'll smell us and we'll be doomed."

"Very well, we follow your words as if it were Odin's." answered Vinglunr.

Gamli lit a lantern, slid its cover mostly closed, and the four made a careful way along the wall. It was slow going. At one point they found a small string stretched at ankle level across the cavern, they stepped over that. At another point Gamli nearly trod on a long, black, serpent, they crept around it without issue. Then their way was suddenly blocked by a chasm. Ransu and Vinglunr seized Gamli just before he stepped over the edge.

Ransu nudged Gamli to follow along the ledge. They did so and soon came to a wide bridge of stone. There was no sign of brick, support or mortar in it, however, it was also too even and smooth to be natural.

"Troll magic." whispered Ransu.

Beyond the bridge rose and fell a choir or rumbling, wheezing voices. The musty smell was so overpowering that the four were forced to tie scarves around their noses.

"I take it we stop here?" asked Vinglunr.

Ransu shook his head, "It would be safer on the other side."

"Safer?"

"If Lemminkäinen ventures into these caverns the trolls will rush to meet him. They will not expect us to be hidden in the heart of their layer."

"I wish dearly to be away from this stench. Still, Ransu's plan has merit." Vanadis added.

"Wonderful, we'll be become the only fit companions for one and other, I fear this vile musk will never wash off." Vinglunr laughed. He and Gamli then lead the way across the bridge. It was wide enough that they had no fear of falling.

Once at the other side, Ransu nodded back towards the right. The four followed Gamli's light along the edge until they returned to the wall. They then continued their silent, careful, journey forward. The troll snoring echoed about the walls, from their deep breaths, and thunderous snorts it was easy to guess they were very large.

The four soon came across an opening on the right wall. Glancing in they saw it was dimly lit with flickering, embers. Gamli crept forward and the others followed. They found the embers were in a large stove built into the rocky wall. Hanging on hooks attached to the ceiling were pots and pans. Large wooden plates and bowls were staked in one corner of the room. In the other corner was a large pile of mixed animal and human bones. Lying beside the stove was a red dragon the size of a dog. It wore an iron collar with the spikes turned in, where they pressed through the chinks in his scales. He opened his green eyes huffed a small gout of flame.

The four froze, Ransu gesturing for it to shhh. It let out a pitiful whine and laid its head down on the floor. The small band let out a sigh as one.

"This is as good a place as any to wait." whispered Ransu.

"You mean the troll's kitchen?" asked Vinglunr.

"The smell of human is a common thing here." Vanadis mused.

Vinglunr considered this, "You make strong argument."

"Stay here." commanded Ransu. "I'll scout the mouth of the cave, see if our pursuers follow."

***

A half an hour earlier horn helmeted Lemminkäinen arrived on the branching path leading to the pine forest or the upper mountain and its ominous cave. He crouched low and studied the tracks carefully. Following behind were Hardegon and Starkad. Hardegon wore leather armor etched with an eagle on the breastplate, his trusty sword at his side. Starkad was fashioned in purple quilted armor, a sturdy axe was belted to his hip and he carried a shield. Behind them followed a group of Kalevalen warriors, tall and handsome.

"The tracks split. Seven warriors head into the woods, four enter the cave." Lemminkäinen surmised pointing out the direction each group took.

Hardegon considered the cave, "They must assume we'll follow the foresters and flee when we pass."

Starkad glanced at his gauntlet as if the ᛗ rune etched on it advised him, "I would not enter brother. Only death awaits us there."

Lemminkäinen glanced questioningly at Starkad, the then glanced at the cave and sniffed. He then snickered and laughed "Fools have stumbled into a trolls' den."

Hardegon frowned, "Then, our quarry has ended his life?"

Starkad stroked his beard thoughtfully, "Someone as cunning as Gamli the Serpent?" He shook his head, "I think not. If I were him, the only reason I'd enter that den would be to ward off pursuit."

Hardegon smiled in grim admiration. "A bold plan. One we must thwart." He turned to the warriors gathered before him. "Tarmo," he pointed to a sturdy man in studded black armor, "take 13 men and pursue those who fled into the forest. If Gamli is amongst them bring him back alive, slay the rest." The warrior bowed. "Juhani take 11 men, split into groups of four, spread out and scout the mountain. If you find an exit watch it. If you spot Gamli, follow his party and report back, do not engage. If you find nothing return before dark." Juhani bowed. To the rest Hardegon said, "We shall make camp here. When the trolls awaken we'll barter for our prey."

Lemminkäinen snorted, "I am not fond of waiting and barter. I thought your foe would give me better fare than this, my sword craves battle."

"Easy my friend," said Starkad, "if we win an early victory then we will be early to the victory feast. You'll be called as Lemminkäinen the Wise, who waited out his foe rather than rush foolishly into a troll cave."

The large Kalevalen chuckled at that. "It would be nice to be called wise for once. Very well, we wait."

With that, those who had been given missions rushed off while the rest made camp and watched the cave.

***

Later, in the trolls' kitchen, Vinglunr, Vanadis and Gamli waited. They sat, brooding in silence. Vinglunr sat with his arm around Vanadis, they both watched Gamli with shared misgiving. Gamli sat beside the dragon. He had pulled some dried meat from his back and offered it to the beast. The creature had eaten it and laid his head in Gamli's lap. The wondersmith stoked his back gently, as if he were a loyal hound.

"Your brother has a way with dragons." whispered Vinglunr.

"I'd scold him but I'd rather not anger his pet." commented Vanadis.

Ransu crept back into the kitchen and did a double take when he saw Gamli.

"My brother's found a friend." Vanadis whispered.

"I can see that..." said the astonished Ransu.

"What news from the entrance?"

Ransu crouched beside them, frowning. "Lemminkäinen has made camp outside. We must search for another exit before dark."

Vanadis suddenly turned thoughtful, "What if we sent the trolls after them?"

"You mean barter with them? Unlikely, they'll have us for breakfast." answered Ransu.

"No," said Vanadis with careful deliberation, "we won't barter. We stir them into a frenzy and direct them outside."

"I am not fond of stirring trolls into frenzies." commented Ransu.

"Hear me out, I summon a spirit to attack the trolls and then, have her flee towards Lemminkäinen's camp." From a dark corner of the room the seithkona saw Bera's disembodied face wearing a wicked grin. The little dragon let out a worried chuff. Vanadis smirked "Trust me, she's very eager to help."

"I like it." said Vinglunr. "At best, we finish Lemminkäinen, at worse we're torn apart, which, at least, would be a quick death."

Ransu considered this and cracked a smile, "It's better than anything I've got. We'll need to wait for sundown," he regarded how close Vanadis and Vinglunr sat, "though I suppose you won't mind."

Vanadis blushed. Vinglunr stood, "Actually Ransu, you sit. I'll watch for sundown." With that he stepped out of the kitchen and snuck down the hall.

The hours passed with steady tension. Once or twice they could hear a few trolls talking in their earthy language. One even trod their way, fortunately he was called back right before he entered the kitchen.

Finally Vinglunr returned, he seemed shaken "It is dark. They're discussing how best to summon the trolls in order to barter for us. We best act now."

Vanadis nodded and stood facing the pile of bones. "I'll send Bera, she assures me she can outrun them."

"Bera?" said Vinglunr with a start.

Gamli glanced up from his dragon. "Sister..."

Vanadis kept her focus on the gristly corner of bones and said, "I told you she was with me, didn't I? I'm summoning her but she won't be the Bera you know. Are you prepared?"

"Aye." said Ransu.

"Thank you Bera." whispered Vinglunr.

Gamli gently set the dragon's head off his lap and stood. He drew his green steel sword; it glinted in the ember light.

Vanadis closed her eyes and reached out towards the pile of bones. She breathed in deep; as she did she felt the spirit of Bera waft around her like a scorching wind. The force of her presence rippled Vanadis' dress and hair. The seithkona opened her eyes and they shone with an eerie bone white light. She uttered words with no meaning her voice interlaced with Bera's.

The bone pile rattled and out of it crawled a skeleton whose bones were a char black. She wore a dress and ritual apron that was similar to Vanadis', she carried a copy of her ash staff. Her braided golden hair fell over her shoulders.

The dragon skittered away from her.

Gamli stepped back, the point of his sword between her and him.

"By Freya." whispered Vinglunr.

Even Ransu looked shaken.

"Gentlemen," Bera's voice resounded as if she were in a faraway carven, yet her jaws and teeth did not move, "I am here to save you. Wish me well Gamli?"

Gamli lowered his sword "Aye... does it hurt? Are you in pain?"

"How sweet. No, I'm very well, happy to be of service." She chuckled and then, like a black wind, she rushed out of the kitchen. Moments later a cacophony of howls of rage rose within the depths of the den. Over top of that was Bera's cackle of malevolent joy.

Five huge green forms rushed past the kitchen. As soon as they were gone Ransu said "Now! On their heels! Run!"

Ransu, Vanadis and Vinglunr fled.

Before joining them Gamli said to the drake. "We both go." With but a single swing of Scorn, he broke the dragon's chain.

***

A few moments earlier, Hardegon, Starkad, and Lemminkäinen sat around a small fire. Gathered around them were their full complements of warriors. Juhani had returned with the scouts, they had found no exits from the mountain. Tarmo had also returned. At his feet was Stefnir's head.

"We are agree, then," said Hardegon, "we wait for the trolls to come to us, then, we talk."

"It is the wisest course." counselled Starkad.

"I wouldn't be able to stand the stench in there." grumbled Lemminkäinen "However, I pray we need not wait long."

A trembling chorus or roars from the carven answered Lemminkäinen's fears. The three leapt to their feet as one, their weapons drawn. Their men staggered back.

"You have your wish." Hardegon said with a glare.

Starkad reached out and drew in the air, in blue frost, the ◊ rune, it vanished and a wavering field of shimmering blue suddenly erupted and shimmered before them. A moment later an avalanche of black and green rushed out of the cavern mouth.

"Charge, send them to Hel!" shrieked a fearsome voice. Bera burst through the blue field, her bones covered with ice, her movement slowed. Even so, the leering skull smile framed in golden locks caused everyone to stagger back. Everyone except Lemminkäinen, who swung his great sword which shattered Bera into hundreds of pieces. Even so, her voice cackled with victory as trolls burst through Starkad's strange barrier.

They were five of them, each as large as a black bear. Their skin was green and warty. They had sunken eyes that gleamed red in the night. Each carried a huge weapon; a cub fashioned from a thick trunk of oak, a bolder headed hammer, twin obsidian knives as long as a man's arm, a rusted axe whose haft was the bar from a great gate and a Jotun sized bronze sword.

The troll with the sword rumbled something dark and earthy and swung his massive blade at Lemminkäinen. The bull headed warrior managed to block the blow and return one of his own.

Starkad drew N in the air, it shimmered, vanished, and a hurricane blast of wind sent the troll with the bolder maul flying.

Hardegon ducked the axe troll's attack but it mangled the Kalevalen warriors behind him. He darted forward and sliced up expertly with his sword, troll blood spraying over him. The blow did not fell his foe, who snarled and kicked at the swordsman. Hardegon leapt back, the troll's talon feet nearly disembowelling him.

"Hold fast!" Hardegon cried, "Make them pay for their aggression!"

Seconds flashed by and Hardegon fought with instinct. Each attack he stepped aside or ducked, returning his own viscous blows. Lemminkäinen was struck once with Jotun sword and returned a blow of his own. His foe fell only to be replaced by the tree wielder. The Kalevalen warriors fought valiantly, getting their own strikes in, but Two Knives was lightning quick and his blades were soon stained with Kalevalen blood.

Then, for a brief moment, time froze, Hardegon glanced between the clashing foes to see a small band running from the cave entrance. His eyes locked with someone he recognized. The thrall girl, she wore the dress and carried the staff of the skeleton that had assailed them. Hardegon's look turned form surprise to fury. Her look turned to sheer panic and she drove her troop to flee faster.

"No!" roared Hardegon. "They escape! Stop them!" He saw the long red hair of Gamli the Serpent as he fled down the path; he carried something red and scaly on his shoulder.

Before Hardegon could pursue the axe wielder nearly crushed him with the haft of his weapon. Hardegon drew back; his blade slicing his foe's arm, but the troll was hardy and still stood. With a cry of fury the swordsman pressed his attack, losing himself to battle. He and the Troll traded thrust and swing. Several deadly blows nearly landed on the jarl's son, each time the Troll was rewarded with another cut. Blood gushed from the giant axe man and he slowed. Hardegon landed a strike to the arm that nearly severed it and then a jab to the calf that dropped the creature to one knee. Hardegon then seized the Troll's collar, pulled himself up, and his sword poised to drive in deep to the foe's heart.

The Troll locked eyes with Hardegon and uttered something harsh and profane. The words washed over swordsman like a hot wind. Hardegon shook it off and drove his sword, and hilt deep, into the creature.

Then, the jarl's son came to himself, standing beside the corpse of his mighty foe. Hardegon glanced around to see gore soaked, grinning Lemminkäinen beside his two dead Trolls. He also saw his brother catching his breath, leaning against the corpse of the maul wielder. He also saw Tarmo leaning on his axe which rested in the back of Knives. The final Troll lay face down, five Kalevalen warriors standing around him. Beyond this, everyone lay slain on the blood soaked rocks.

"We must head to the ships." said Hardegon.

"Worry not." Laughed Lemminkäinen, "They have a good guard, four cannot face 10."

***

Moments later, the four reached the edge of the beachside cliff to find ten armed guards waiting for them.

Without missing a beat, Vinglunr screamed, "To battle!" and dropped down the short cliff. He raised his voice in a rumbling song whose tune spoke of evil and spite. The guards charged but as soon as they got within a few feet they cried in sudden agony.

Ransu tossed his spear and pinned two men through their torsos to the ground. Vanadis hunched over and raised her hands, from them shot beams of black and white that struck one of two warriors dead.

Gamli, gently put the weakened drake down and leapt off the cliff, he landed on one man and drove Scorn through another.

Within moments, the four had made quick work of their foes.

***

Minutes later Hardegon reached the same cliff. He saw the bloody remains his guards. He saw Lemminkäinen's ship broken and sinking. He saw the karve, in full sail, swiftly moving down the river.

"Gamli!" he cried, his voice reaching a higher pitch in his rage. "If you are a man, come back and face me. My uncle's blood cries for vengeance!"

After a pause, Gamli called out over the waters. "No."

"Your ancestor Sigurd would be ashamed!"

"We are of wiser a Volsung stock than Sigurd." called Vanadis, a hint of triumphant laughter in her voice. "Far wiser than your Hogni and Gunnar. We know well enough not walk into the arms of our enemies."

Ransu's laugher echoed across the crags.

Hardegon let out an inarticulate scream of fury. Which was soon followed by Lemminkäinen's when he saw that his ship had been chewed to pieces.

CHAPTER 20

It's easy to think ill. | To see flaws and silently chuckle.
I've done so often, and have usually been right.
Yet harsh judgement can be folly. | It blinds you to truth.
Be too cynical and you'll only realize true strength and beauty after it's gone.

Once they reached the open sea, they continued sailing, despite the darkness. Vinglunr, Vanadis, and Gamli attended the sail while Ransu's steady hand was on the rudder. The shining moon and stars in the clear night gave them enough light to go by. For an hour, they sailed on in silence, their joy at having escaped to thoughtfulness.

When the wind calmed and they had a moment to rest, Gamli pulled out his tools and worked the collar off the drake. It shrieked when he removed it, a gout of flame licking the wet wood of the boat.

"Easy," cried Ransu, "that beast will turn our ship to ash."

"He won't." insisted Gamli, tossing the spiked collar into the sea. "He's a gentile sort." He petted the drake and it stretched out in enjoyment. Gamli fed him some dried fish.

Vinglunr watched Vanadis, an uneasy question forming in his mind.

Vanadis sat on the port side and stared off into the waters, too tired for thought.

Then followed an awkward silence. Ransu regarded the brother and sister for a moment and asked "That was your first real battle yes?"

Gamli picked up Scorn and eyed the blood on the blade. "The first time I've killed. I didn't expect it to be so easy. I hate it."

"My magic...I felt his life snuffed out...it strengthened me." Vanadis said in disgust.

"I'm glad you feel regret, it's right to do so." he smirked at Vinglunr, "Though the Southerner may disagree."

"Make no mistake, Pohjalander, we value life as much as you do." the skald retorted. "After I made my first kill, I thought of the Curonian's child and wept." he said with humble remorse.

Ransu chuckled, "Good, good." Then after another moment of silence he addressed the siblings, "Worry not, dealing with killing gets easier. Though, I do recommend avoiding violence when you can."

Vanadis was eager to change the subject; looking up to Vinglunr she asked, "You seem to have something on your mind. Tell me, what is it?"

Vinglunr rolled his thoughts in his head and replied, "Bera..." the image of her skeletal form stole the rest of his words. Gamli looked up from tending the drake and listened carefully.

Vanadis took a moment to find the right words, to Vinglunr she said "She's been with us this whole time. You know her; do you think her spirit would have been happy to have merely watched?"

The skald grinned at old memories and answered, "Nay."

Vanadis shrugged, "I simply provided her the means to help."

"Sister, she was without flesh." rumbled Gamli.

Vanadis let out a short and bitter laugh, "Brother, if I could restore her fully don't you think I would have done so? I'm as happy with her condition as you are. What would you have me do? Refuse her aid? Let her seethe on the other side while we risk life and limb?"

"If you did, I fain she would haunt us." Vinglunr answered, his humor returning.

"Precisely."

"Thank her for us." added Gamli.

Vanadis considered the two of them and added, in a kinder tone, "I don't have to. She already knows and she'll return whenever I call."

"That's good to hear." said Vinglunr, "However, I have one request."

"Yes?"

"If I die and become one of your spirts, please never summon me like that." He sounded like he was only half joking.

"I'll only summon you in my dreams." retorted Vanadis.

Gamli glared at them both. "Easy now."

Ransu shook his head and chuckled.

The sailed long into the night and only docked when the sun began to rise. So exhausted were the four that they slept in their beached karve.

***

The next morning, late morning, Ransu and Vinglunr walked to a nearby town while Gamli and Vanadis hid. They sold their karve for a much smaller, more manageable skute, and had plenty of skatt left over. Ransu also wished to also sell Stepnir's and the men's belongings Vinglunr absolutely forbid it. Such would be saved for their return or placed in the barrow on Mjoll's island so their friends would not wander the afterlife as paupers.

Before they left Ransu eyed Gamli and his drake. "I suppose I can't talk some sense into you?"

"He's no mere creature." Vanadis said, stitching his neck. The drake stretched and let out a musical trill of pleasure.

"His name is Ormir." concluded Gamli.

"Wonderful." Said Ransu with a sigh.

With that they embarked on their journey south. A few more days passed with poor sailing. At first there was little wind. All four hit the oars and each day ended in ache. Ransu suggested summoning Bera to row, the others wouldn't hear of it. In the next few days the wind was fine but spring rains forced them to bail and then dock when the rain got too heavy. The sole blessing was this leading to a hefty fog, with which they used to sail past Kalevala unnoticed. Finally, their skute entered familiar waters and on the horizon they spied Mjoll's island. On this day, the blue sky was dotted with white clouds but otherwise clear, the wind filled their sails. As they got closer a feeling of relief and welcome washed over them. They all agreed to spend the night enjoying Mjoll's hospitality.

***

When they sailed past the barrow grove and saw the charred remains of the hall, however, all joy and anticipation fled. Gamli, Vinglunr and Vanadis stared, their heartache etched on their faces.

In a gentle tone, Ransu said, "I'm sorry."

"Take us to the docks, now." ordered Vinglunr, his voice hardening.

Moments later, all four had climbed the dock stairs to get a closer look at the ruined hall. A few, blackened, jagged beams jutted out of the ashes. No man, woman, child, or beast was there to greet them. However, around the ruined hall, Vanadis saw clearly the ghosts of Kelifar. Her father stood with his arms crossed, regarding them grimly. Her mother stood beside him and had an expression that seemed to say 'now, now, dear.' The rest of the ghosts gathered behind them. In addition Vanadis could see Ragnhildr. Mjoll, her warriors, her shieldmaidens and the rest of her servants were missing.

"How could you?" Vanadis asked, her voice trembling, "How could you know about this and not tell me?"

Ransu looked confused.

Vinglunr signaled him to wait.

Gamli watched his sister and listened, Ormir hiding behind him.

Vanadis stormed forward towards the spirits only she could see. "Well? What's your answer?"

"We don't really care about Mjoll, dear." said Hanne with a small shrug.

Bera charged towards her but Kvistr held her back with a fierce glance. He gestured to Ragnhildr who stepped forward.

"You were busy fending for your lives. Those of us who cared for Mjoll," she said with a glare towards Hanne, "felt that she would not wish you to worry."

"Where is she?"

The spirits looked at each other helplessly. "We were all burned together," answered Ragnhildr, "but her soul is not here."

"Then tell me how she died, this instant." The seithkona's grey eyes flashed with anger.

At that those words Vinglunr stiffened and said "Then share their story with us."

Gamli crossed his arms, a steady rage building in him.

"As you wish, dear." Answered Ragnhildr. With that she told her everything the spirits had seen. Everything from Mjoll's confrontation with Hardegon, to her sacrificing herself in her hall, to the people of Alands gathering the dead and paying proper respects, even to their foes, as was only right.

The story hit Vanadis hard, by its end, she had no words but "Thank you." She turned from the ghosts only to find Vinglunr and Gamli regarding her with grim expectancy. "Mjoll's gone," Vanadis' voice cracked but she held it under control. She then related the spirits' tale. Telling it was worse than hearing it. It brought pain to Vinglunr and Gamli, it brought crushing regret to her. By the end of her telling she had broken down in tears. Vinglunr embraced her, and joined her in sobbing.

Gamli had no tears; he simply stared at the remains of the hall. Ormir nuzzled his hand and he petted the drake absently.

Ransu stepped beside him. "What's on your mind?"

"Hardegon." Gamli rumbled with hate. "If I had known he started this, I would have accepted his challenge and he would have tasted Scorn." He patted the pommel of his sword.

Ransu clapped him on the shoulder, "Fleeing was the right decision. You'll have your chance to cross swords with him again, only next time you'll have the advantage. You can only savour revenge if you live."

Vinglunr held Vanadis who rested her head on his chest. "I'm sorry." she said, swallowing her sorrow.

Vinglunr grunted, "Why? You didn't cause this." he answered despondently.

She glanced up at him, "I misjudged her. I thought she was foolish, weak. What she did for us..."

Vinglunr forced a smile and rubbed the tears off her cheeks. "Well you now know what I've always known. Your Aunt was the strongest woman in Alands."

"Aye," she said staring at the remains of the Hall. "She's not with them, the lost spirts I mean. She's no longer in this world."

Vinglunr held Vanadis at arms, length so he could get a good look at her. In a deadly serious tone he asked, "Where do you think Mjoll is? Fólkvangr or Niflhiem? Please don't spare my feelings. I need to know what you know as a seithkona."

Vanadis looked over her shoulder at the gathered spirits. Bera grinned fiercely and pointed up. Hanne grinned malevolently and pointed down. Kvistr shrugged.

Turning back to Vinglunr Vanadis answered "I don't know," his expression fell, "but I can tell you one thing. If Siff hasn't welcomed Mjoll to Asgard, then she is no longer worthy of worship."

Vinglunr smirked, "Perhaps you're right. I know Sif, I know Mjoll; I choose to believe they are together." He said it with an infections conviction. Vanadis and Gamli smiled.

"Let us pay our respects." said Vinglunr, "

Together the four walked to the threshold of the blackened ruins. Piles of ash and soot lay everywhere but they had been swept into piles. Not a trace of bone or flesh could be found, the people of Neshraun had done a thorough job in tending the dead.

"So many people have visited her. Even jarl Truvor." moaned Hanne. "Everyone cried over her, even some from Neshraun, it makes me sick."

Vanadis shushed the spirit.

Vinglunr cleared his throat, looked over the ruins and said, "Mjoll, everything I have I owe to you. I will keep you close to my heart and after I finally enter Odin's Hall I will visit you in Siff's hall of Bliskinir and tell you the story of our lives."

"Aunt," rumbled Gamli, "Thank you for aiding us. I'll always remember you. When I meet Hardegon, I'll make him understand his crime."

Vanadis glanced at her brother, surprised at his sudden vitriol. He merely stepped back and motioned her forward. Vanadis did so and said "Aunt, I...I misjudged you. We owe you our lives and we'll make the most of them. I'll find strength in your courage, always."

With that, the four stepped away from the ruins. Then, they took Stephnir and the others' belongings and placed them by the barrow. Before leaving Vinglunr lifted his lyre, strummed a solemn tune and sang, his clear, powerful voice echoing across the island and the waters. He sang praises to Lady Siff and her husband Thor. He also sang of Mjoll the Gentle, who was a mother and healer to all of Alands.

CHAPTER 21

As children, we loved heroes and monsters. | Flosi once slew the Jotun Gamli and I laughed.
My brother's large, strong, uncomplicated, it was easy to put him in such a role.
I'll hex anyone who calls him a monster. | At darkest hour, he is always gentle.
His goodness then, may have been what drove him to the side of the Jotun.

They struck off, sails full of wind. It was late afternoon and none of them had the heart to stay on the island, their promise of home and welcome now ash and sorrow. Vinglunr, Gamli and Vanadis each sat silent, wrapped in their own thoughts. Ransu regarded them with concern.

"Skald," asked the fisherman, "do your people still host a thing in Gotland?"

Vinglunr looked up from his brooding. "Aye, Jarl Truvor will not break the tradition of his grandfather Jarl Rognvald."

Ransu smiled at fond memories. To Vanadis and Gamli he said "Your father and I attended every year we could. The music, the food," smirking at Gamli, "the women." Then, a little fearfully he said to Vanadis, "Only I partook in the women. Kvistr remained true, make sure Hanne knows that."

Vanadis snorted and smiled in spite of her grief. "She says she doesn't care. She says she'd only care if he sired a bastard, then she would have to kill it."

The fisherman swallowed nervously, "Thankfully, no such thing happened." Then, mastering himself he continued, "It is a time for the Harl to pass down judgement, but it is a greater time for celebration. We should attend."

All three looked at him as if he were crazy. Even Ormir grumbled musically at him.

"Ransu, the Jarl would pass judgment on us. Given the rumours we'd be lucky to receive a quick death." Vanadis said.

"Aye," said Gamli eyeing the staff he whittled, "I'm not ready to die yet. Too much to do."

"We're not going there to have judgment passed upon us." Ransu said as if they were fools. "We'll go there to have fun, something you lot desperately need."

Vinglunr shook his head, "It won't work Ransu. Me, Vanadis, or Gamli; one of us will be recognized. Surrounded by the whole Nibelung host, we'll wish we were back in the tender mercies of Hardegon."

"Then, we'll go in disguise. Surely, a man of your talent can hide our presence?"

Vinglunr chuckled, "Sadly, no, as the proud ward of Mjoll I've never needed to hide."

"I might have something." said Vanadis, looking thoughtful.

All eyes turned to her.

"I could craft us new faces with magic."

"We've spent nights in the cold for months and you tell us this now?" Gamli asked incredulously.

Vanadis shot him, the look. "My power comes from the dead brother. I won't call upon them in vain." After taking a breath, she continued, "Also, casting the spell has yet to be tested. There are... how can I say it? Certain risks."

"Go on." said Ransu.

"I'd bind a spirit to myself and each of you. They'd manifest over us and I'd mold their appearance. If it works the disguise would be perfect." she reached out and stroked the drake's nose, he hummed pleasantly, "Though I suppose Ormir would still recognize you Gamli."

"I won't need my appearance changed." Ransu said uneasily, to Vinglunr and Gamli he asked "How about you two? Are you two willing to wear ghosts for a night of celebration?"

"The risk," Vanadis cut in, "is that the spirit you wear may possess you. Also, if I summon my ghosts to power my spells the illusions will fade."

"Not the safest of options." mused Vinglunr.

"Nor pleasant." added Gamli looking ill at ease.

"As most hated vargs are you ever safe? As far as unpleasantness, what's more so, submitting yourself witchcraft or spending the rest of our days alone, in the wilderness?" asked Ransu.

Vanadis and Vinglunr looked dubious. Gamli scratched Ormir as if he had already decided no.

Ransu sighed, "Very well, pay this old man no mind. I'm all well and good living in the wilds. I'm simply afraid you'll lose your spirits."

"Have you ever been to the Thing Vanadis?" Vinglunr asked.

"A few times while attending Dorte." she answered, fond recollection in her eyes.

Gamli stroked his beard, "I've never been." he glowered. "Asvard went while I worked like a dog."

"I used to chide you for nearly killing yourself with exhaustion." In a gentler tone Vanadis added, "That must be why you're so skilled now."

Gamli and Ransu shared a look.

Gamli answered, "You have no idea sister." Then, in a determined tone he added, "I'm going. I'll buy supplies then I, not Asvard, will be the one to become rich."

Vanadis considered this and was moved. "If you go, I go as well."

"Then I go as well." said Vinglunr warmly.

"It's settled then." said Ransu with a grin.

***

The next few days of sailing dragged on with anticipation. The first night, Vanadis experimented with her spell by casting it on herself, Vinglunr and Gamli. She shaped their guises as the human approximations of the gods and goddess; Bragi, Frey and Freya. When Frey, who was Kvistr, possessed Gamli and reminisced old, leud tales with Ransu, Vanadis cancelled the spell

The next night Vanadis tried the spell again, giving each of a common, forgettable appearance. That night they approached and were welcomed into a farmer's hall. They supped on a hot meal and were served ale. They traded rumors. Vanadis told them of Louhi's new apprentice, some mysterious and beautiful woman. In return the farmers told of the strained relations between Truvor and his sons. They were certain that Gamli the Serpent and his harlot sister, were responsible for the wedge between them. Vanadis, Gamli and Vinglunr spent the night with their illusions on them. In the morning they found the skald had walked off. They soon found him, his spirit having made him climb a tree.

The next two days passed uneventfully. Each day Vanadis cast the spell again and found she had perfected it. The three could sleep without fear of wandering. She dared not throw a guise on Ormir.

***

The morning of the third day, they reached Gotland. It was a huge island of fields, forests, and short cliffs.

"It would take us the entire day to sail past her." commented Ransu.

Thankfully, the Thing was held on the northeast of the island and within a mere few hours, the four had arrived just off shore.

Beyond beach lay a city of brightly colored pavilions and tents, in the center of which was a large, thatched roofed hall. People from many towns rambled through the Thing, nobles, freemen, and slaves. The air was filled with songs and the cries of merchants. The scent of the sea mingled with roasting meat and even a hint of incense. Despite the cloudy sky, the atmosphere was one of relaxation and fun.

"Now," said Vanadis, "before we're spotted, let's put on our guises." She whispered soft enticements to the spirits and reached out towards Gamli. For a brief moment the shade of Bera embraced him, then his visage melted and reformed anew. His hair was shorter and black. His beard was trim. His eyes, still blue but he looked slightly older.

Vanadis whispered again and gestured to Vinglunr. Kvistr was about to embrace him but Vanadis shooed him away with a gesture.

"Something wrong?" he asked.

Vanadis cheeks turned red, "Nothing, I'd like to wander the Thing with you. Not my father."

Vinglunr chuckled and Vanadis whispered and gestured again. Samr, he had been a large man with a friendly face, embraced the skald. His visage changed. His hair was longer, blonde and tied back. His beard was braided. She kept Vinglunr's green eyes though.

"Sorli, really?" Gamli said in disbelief.

Vanadis glared at him. "Not Sorli, exactly, just his distant cousin. They share a resemblance."

"Whose Sorli?" laughed Vinglunr.

"A noble the girls of Kelifar fawned over." said the smith.

"Did you fawn over him?" asked Vinglunr.

"Perhaps a little." Vanadis admitted. "I work with what I know."

Vanadis gestured and Lene, one of mother's handmaidens, embraced her. Her visage morphed thus hiding her blush. When the disguise was complete Vanadis' hair was black and in braids. Her skin was paler, features kinder.

"You're all in fine form, proper enough to meet the Jarl." said Ransu, then, after a thought he added, "Don't meet the jarl, he's far too clever for us."

With that they sailed into Gotland, the pebble beach held a fleet of ships but thankfully there was more than enough room for their skute to slide in.

Ransu glanced up at the grey clouds rolling in the sky. "Lay down the sail, we can take shelter in the hall or one of the tents tonight." They did so, lowering the sail and stretching it taught over the hull.

"We'll meet here in the morn and continue to Danevirke, agreed?" confirmed the fisherman.

"Aye." said Vanadis. She took Vinglunr's arm and the two walked off to join the festivities.

Gamli watched them, pensive.

"You don't approve?" asked Ransu with a chuckle.

After a thought Gamli answered, "Actually, suppose I do. Vinglunr's like a brother, it's just," he shuddered, "I do not wish to think of what they'll do."

"There's but one cure for that." Ransu said clasping Gamli's arm, his eyes lighting up. "Find a women."

Gamli tossed his coin pouch into the air and caught it. "I'm after supplies, then mead. After that, if any woman wishes to keep me company, I won't turn her away."

"More for me. Good day to you, sir." answered Ransu. With that, they parted ways.

Gamli wandered into the Thing, Ormir following at his heels. Thanks to the drake he got a lot of stares, though no one approached. He wove through the crowd. His stomach rumbled so he bought a lamb haunch, he ate half and tossed the rest to the drake who devoured it in moments. After the lamb he was thirsty and so helped himself to mead from the many open barrels. At one point, he paused to watch a skald sing a lovely tune in honor of Freya. His partner dancer was a beautiful woman with golden tresses, she pantomimed the skald's story with perfection and grace. Gamli dropped a heathy amount of skatt onto the skald's mat.

Finally, he arrived at the merchant tents. Here men and women, seemingly from all over Midgard, sold everything from toys, to weapons, to furniture, to clothes. A few offered to purchase Ormir, Gamli politely declined. There was a lot of dazzling jewelry for sale but the smith found very little ore, and no tools that were superior to his own. He was about to give up when he stumbled across a red tent with a foreign feel. A husband and wife walked out, the husband holding a fine silver serpent arm ring. Intrigued Gamli walked inside.

The tent was spacious and lamps, on silver stands, kept it well lit. The tables were lined with both cut and raw jewels. In a box, near the front table, Gamli noticed interesting looking ore samples.

Sitting beside the table, in a chair draped in a wolf's hide, was a large man dressed in chain mail. He had a longsword and dagger sheathed at his hip. He was broad-shouldered and older than Gamli, his brown hair and beard greying.

The man behind the table caused Gamli to double take. He was the darkest person Gamli had ever seen; he had sharp features and even sharper beard and mustache. He dressed in green silk finery befitting a foreign king.

"Ah, welcome," said the man in green. His smile dropped to a gape of astonishment when he noticed Ormir. The lord in chainmail, for no mere guard could afford such armor, looked equally stunned. Ormir glanced up at them, titled his head, and let out a harp like trill in greeting.

The foreigner lifted a cloth divider behind him and issued commands in a strange, soft language. Two very large servants, dressed in a less ostentatious but similar style to their master, bowed and stepped outside the tent, closing its flap.

Gamli frowned, his hand drifted to the pommel of his sword.

An ambush. Hissed Bera in his mind. 'Kill the foreigner first, we can take the lord hostage.'

The armored man stood, held out his open palms and said "At ease, we wish to talk."

"Yes, your coming has been expected." said the man in green, in a nervous tone.

Gamli, his hand on the hit of Scorn, considered each of them. He felt Ormir nudge his leg, he glanced down at him. The drake, sat hound like and seemed perfectly at ease. Gamli, with some effort, 'Bera, let go.' released the hilt of his sword.

Both the foreigner and the chainmail lord relaxed.

"Excellent." said the main in green. He gestured to a third servant, a man with no moustache or beard but dressed in a similar style, and issued more commands in his strange tongue. The servant bowed, fetched a stool and brought it over to Gamli.

"Thank you." said the smith, and he sat. To his hosts he asked, "What's this about?"

"My friend," said the foreigner, "I am Zaidaan and this is my partner Krumr Vingfusson of Gotaland." The man in chainmail nodded. "We do no not know your name but your coming has been foretold."

"I'm Gamli." greeted the smith.

'Idiot.' sighed Bera in his head.

"You share the name of the Serpent?" questioned Krumr.

"Y-yes. It's like a curse." lied Gamli, badly.

His visage flickered. 'I'm leaving.'

Gamli pictured grabbing Bera's hand, 'Please don't.'

Bera sighed again and Gamli's guise remained intact.

Meanwhile the two hosts had stared in wonder and a little fear.

An idea struck and Zaidaan suddenly looked more at ease, "Ah, of course. This only proves further that he's our man. Djinn excel at misdirection."

"Surt is no Djinn." glowered Krumr. "Never mention him as such again."

Zaidaan chuckled and said something in his strange tongue, in soothing tones.

Krumr responded in the same language, his tone firm, with no room for argument.

Gamli cleared his throat.

"Ah, my apologies, you are not here to listen to us bicker." said Zaidaan.

"That you are the Serpent is of no concern to us." added Krumr.

"What's this about, Surt?" asked Gamli.

The partners glanced at each other, Zaidaan gestured to Krumr as if to say, you explain.

The warrior in chainmail turned to Gamli motioned for him to come closer. Gamli picked up his stool and obliged, Ormir curled up behind him.

"Long has my family paid homage to the Fire Jotun King. I paid little attention to their faith, and littler attention of the Aesir. I had no concern for the afterlife, my only desire was riches. So I traversed the Volga trade route, on it I allied with Zaidaan and together our trade has made us wealthy."

By this point Zaidaan's servant had poured both Gamli and Krumr goblets of heady wine. Krumr took a deep pull and so did Gamli.

"Wealth is the child of greed and envy is his wife. In the great trading port of Skiringsaal I learned this fully. Late one night our rivals barred the doors of our hall and set it aflame. That night, Zaidaan and I were to have died."

"Great walls of flame surrounded us." cut in Zaidaan, "Our friends, slaves and belongings were consumed by it. Krumr and I stood in the center, back to back, the heat already causing our skin to blister. Neither of us were religious men but even so, we both prayed." With a smile he added, "Your gods looked kindly on Krumr."

"The hall vanished and Muspelheim was arrayed before us.", continued Krumr.

"I thought it was my Hell. How I wailed." Zaidaan chuckled.

Krumr glared at him and he was silent. Then, Krumr continued. "The mountains shook and Surt loomed before us." He noted the sudden widening of Gamli's eyes and asked, "You've been there? You've seen him?"

"Aye." Gamli said, feeling the rippling heat about him, remembering the titanic warrior who stood equal to his mountain.

Krumr smiled "Of course you have. He wouldn't send someone who hadn't. Out of the sky flew a winged steed and on it was a most beautiful woman, a Valkyrie."

Gamli shirked back, "A maid of Odin, in Muspelheim?"

Krumr chuckled, "You have much to learn. Most Valkyries serve Odin but they are not his property. If Odin were master of death then he would not have lost Balder. This Valkyrie gathers warriors for the Jotun to fight in the final days."

Gamli frowned thoughtfully, remembering Vanadis' tale of Myrkvid. "I have heard some Valkyrie can be rebellious."

Krumr continued, "The Valkyrie informed us that Surt would spare my life from this fire in honor of the faith and service my family rendered him. Zaidaan was not part of this pact, however. . ." he gestured to his partner.

Zaidaan leaned forward and said, in a conspiratorial tone, "The Valkyrie informed me that my life would be spared also, if I swore to give up one of my treasures to a man I would meet. One who walked with a dragon."
With that, he pulled a small chest from under his table. He handed it to Krumr who held it while Zaidaan pulled a silver key from his belt and unlocked it. From inside he lifted a large smooth cube of bronze. Etched evenly on its surface were tiny runes, of the like Gamli had never seen. Each rune was eight lines, some whole, some broken. Zaidaan handed the cube to Gamli. It had a good weight. Gamli ran his thumbs across the runes. As simple as the cube was, it had an alien air. It felt, precious and holy.

Krumr placed the chest at Gamli's feet.

Zaidaan finished, "As you can guess, I accepted the deal. We were returned to the land of men and stood on the ashes of our hall, unharmed. My treasure, which is now yours, was also untouched."

"I saw the error of my ways," added Krumr, "Zaidaan and I recovered our wealth but ever since I've dedicated my life in devotion to Surt."

"Then you would know what I should with this?" asked Gamli, holding out the cube.

Krumr shook his head, "If you do not know already, you will in time. Keep it close until then."

To Zaidaan he asked, "What is this?

"A rare treasure from the far East, fashioned long ago in an Empire greater than Otto's. My mother purchased it and it was handed to me. I know nothing of its runes but I believe you hold the complete set. If you could translate them you would discover great secrets."

Gamli considered the cube, the bronze was of the highest quality; good ore backed it. His instinct was to melt it down, make something... he just didn't know what. He placed the cube in the chest and closed it. "Do you have other such things to sell?" he asked.

"Of course." Zaidaan laughed. "I'll even give you a discount."

Gamli looked over Zaidaan's wares. The materials in the box were tiny samples. Depending on how much Gamli bought he would send his servants with boxes of the ores to his ship. Like the bronze they were of the like he'd never seen.

"These were secured from mystic gates in your own land. Each is from a different world." He pointed each one out and described their properties. Ormir's neck snaked up the table and he sniffed a particular sample that was kept in an iron tray, it glowed fiery hot. Gamli hefted his coin purse and ran calculations in his mind. He bargained, but he could not afford usable samples of each. In the end he was able to get secure a small helping of red gold, which Zaidaan insisted was from Asgard, a small helping of mead iron, Zaidaan insisted it was the metal the dwarves use, and finally a little molten core, the same ore that Ormir was excited at, Gamli was unsurprised when Krumr insisted it was from Muspelheim.

"You're fortunate, the small supply of what you purchase is all I have. They are incredibly rare." Said Zaidaan.

Once the deal had been set, Gamli paid the merchant and gave him directions to the ship. Zaidaan then slipped out the back to gather the materials and instruct his servants.

Gamli turned to Krumr who had helped himself to more wine, while his partner and Gamli bartered. "Before I leave, I have a question."

"Aye?"

"You follow Surt because he saved your life, I get that. But won't he kill you during Ragnarok?"

The warrior snorted, and asked "Do you know how Midgard was made??"

"Aye, Odin and his brothers killed. Ymir. From his blood they made oceans. From his bones, the hills. From his hair, the trees. From his brain, the clouds and from his skull, the sky."

"Midgard then," said Krumr, "is a corpse lying in the branches of Yggdrasil. When we leave it three things could happen to us; become a refugee in Niflheim, slay each other for Odin's purpose and pleasure, or wander the world an unhappy ghost. I follow Surt because the way things are is pure madness. True my fiery lord will purge all nine worlds but from out of their ashes will rise better ones."

He clasped Gamli's arm and stared at him intently. "When the end times come decide for yourself, will you be on the side of tyranny or the side of rebirth?"

"I never thought of it that way." Gamli said with a frown.

"Most people do not. They swallow the Aesir's lies simply because it's what their parents told them." Krumr sighed. "Go with Surt's blessing and know you have an ally in me."

With that, Gamli left the tent. He found two hardy servants carrying chests with his purchases. He took the heaviest one, in the iron box, for himself and nodded towards the beach, "This way." Once they made it to the ship, Gamli sent the servants back to their master. He then stood and stared out at the sea thoughtfully. "What do you think Bera?" he asked.

He felt her stir in the back of his mind, 'I don't care.'

Gamli raised an eyebrow, "You're not horrified, I've been chosen by Surt?"

'I died in an act of loyalty to your sister, I serve her first. If she takes me to Folkvangar so be it. Though if we go to Muspelheim I would very much enjoy battling Ansy Ironhair at the end of days.'

"There are other things to consider." said Gamli, his thoughts going back to Niklas and Vilma and their children. His heart ached at the thought of any of them in mourning.

Orimir pawed Gamli's leg and let out a flute like wine. He nose-nudged the iron box in Gamli's hand.

The smith glanced down at him curiously. "You want what's in here?" He chuckled and opened the lid. He seized one of the molten cores. While it glowed red, it was not scorching to the touch, merely pleasantly warm. He tossed it down to Ormir. The drake caught it in his teeth, crunched, and swallowed. Then he flared like a campfire.

Gamli staggered back, nearly dropping the chest.

Ormir stepped away a few feet circled like a cat and lay down, looking contented. The flare of his fire leveled off and waves of heat emanated from him.

Gamli approached his pet cautiously. "Ormir?"

His drake's breath heaved inward and out like he was sleeping. The flames seem to pick on invisible harp strings, their mysterious tune swam in Gamli's head. Suddenly everything was consumed by a white hot glow.

Gamli soared over Muspelheim. From his vantage in the sky he saw shining cities of emerald, obsidian and ruby. He saw great forests of glass, from which ran deer of crimson flame. He saw a vast lake of fire resting at the foot of a volcano so vast that you could throw all of Kelifar into it.

He landed on a strange marble plateau. It was of the purest white and had gently sloping hills ridged by shallow trenches. Five pillars, towered around him. They curved inwards… Gamli's stomach dropped when he realized he was in a Giant's palm.

The sky boomed with voice ,"Son of Volsung, Son of Wayland, your blood is the alchemy that will break all bonds."

Gamli snapped back to the living world to find himself waste deep in the sea, his upper half drenched with sweat. He held a spear in his hand. The shaft was delicate, the one he'd been whittling and smoothing on his trip. The shaft was laced with red gold; the tip was made of the same.

"Burning Mind." Gamli whispered the weapon's name and held it up so that he could see better n the setting sunlight.

Behind him, he heard a crowd roar with approval. He spun to see that a large contingent of the Thing had gathered. They stood around the ever burning Ormir, lords, free men, and thralls. Men, women, and children. All cheered in excitement and exaltation, as if he had just performed a miracle.

Gamli stroked his beard and thought, 'I suppose I have.'

Then, he paused with sudden horror. His beard was red, Bera had fled.

CHAPTER 22

Loyalty is earned. | Duty is inflicted.
Often fate chooses our masters.
Service is not necciarily weakness | Freedom is bordered by the powers that be.
No matter who stands over you, hold close your pride.

Hours earlier, Vanadis and Vinglunr walked into the Thing arm – in - arm and mingled with the festive throng. Together, they sampled freshly picked berries. Shared a plate of honeyed ham. Sat and listened to the skalds sing of Hogni and Gunarr, their heroes of old.

"Of course you realize," Vinglunr whispered with humor, "my talents far exceed theirs."

Vanadis considered the songs. The strum of the lyre, the cry of the fiddles, the rich tenor and baritones, they were most pleasant to listen too. She smiled at the skald teasingly. "I'm not convinced."

Vinglunr gently put placed his hand on the small of her back, pressed her close and they kissed.

When they pulled away Vinglunr asked, "And now?"

She giggled, "I like your songs more."

The skald put his arm around Vanadis and she leaned in close. As a serving maid walked past he held out his hand and was rewarded with a mug of mead. He took a deep pull, offered Vanadis a drink and she did likewise.

Vanadis sighed contentedly, for once her expression unguarded. Sitting on this log under the open sky, her lover close and surrounded by her people in celebration. Vanadis recognized many of them; Hallvard the trader, he often visited Steinarr's hall. Old Marte, a kindly priestess of Freya who advised Kelifar. Saehilder, the finest weaver in Alands, her brightly colored dress showed as such. Within Vanadis stirred joy mixed with melancholy. "We should tell Gamli."

"Why the sudden change of heart?" asked Vinglunr.

Vanadis squeezed his hand and looked up at him, "We've gone too far to hide it any longer."

"Tis true." He said warmly and they kissed again.

Soon after the skalds finished their music, their head man, an aged fellow named Rannveig, announced to the crowd, "We end our playing for now to attend Jarl Truvor's council. However, expect more music and merriment during tonight's feast."

The crowd, including the lovers, cheered.

As the throng dispersed both Vanadis and Vinglunr turned thoughtful.

"Shall we attend the council?" Asked Vinglunr.

"Let's."

They stood and walked towards the hall hand in hand.

***

The hall was crowded. Those who secured benches stood on them. Vanadis and Vinglunr found a nice spot in the crowd, not far enough behind that their view was blocked, but also not at the very front under the gaze of Truvor's guards.

They did not have to wait too long. Truvor was announced and he climbed up on a wooden dais on which sat three thrones. He was dressed in red and purple finery. As grey as his beard was and as wrinkled as his visage was; he walked well and stood strong. Beside him was a tall woman, so tall that Vanadis nearly mistook her for a Valkyrie. Her red locks were bound in four of braids. She wore a green dress lined with gold. Vanadis knew of her, Thora, wife of Hardegon and defender of Truvor's hall. She surveyed the crowd with a look of authority. The hall cheered and the two sat, Truvor in the central throne, Thora to his right.

Truvor raised his hands for silence and the hall quieted. "Welcome to this council. In these troubling times it is good to see that our family and kingdom is strong. I call upon all to air their grievances, know that my judgment will be a just."

Then one by one crimes and conflicts were brought before the Jarl. A murder was accused, Truvor listened to the evidence and rendered banishment. Then a killing, the result of a duel, was brought before him, Truvor negotiated a blood price to everyone's satisfaction. There was also dispute on fishing waters which the Jarl settled soundly.

Then Asta was brought before him. She stood in a dress of blue, her auburn hair bound in bands of silver. Beside her stood a broad man with deep, unruly brown hair and beard. He was dressed in fine garb of green and brown, he wore a gold arm band.

"Asta Mistress of Neshraun, and Ogmund Bodvarson, grandson of Visin, master of Kelifar before Steinarr and before Kvistr." called the speaker. Asta and Ogmund bowed.

"Ogmund, I hear you have a grievance?" the Jarl asked.

"Yes, my lord." answered Bodvarson. "Last fall, due to an unfortunate circumstance, my deepest condolences, my lord, Kelifar's master and people fell to a man and the island has sat vacant. Vacant that is until this harlot," he jabbed his finger at Asta, "sent her folk to settle my land."

"Land which was rightfully given to me by your son, my lord." Asta cut in.

"Rightfully?" Ogmund fumed, "Hardegon had no claim on Kelifar. This trollkin is too powerful already. Why should she have both Neshraun's iron and Kelifar's trade?"

"Surely my lord, you will not listen to a man whose arguments include baseless insults and lies?"

Vanadis caught Thora giving Asta a look. The mistress of Neshraun sighed and calmed herself.

"I remember the days of Visin." mused Truvor. "He was an idiot."

The hall laughed, Ogmund turned red.

When the laughter died down Truvor continued, "Visin lost Kelifar through right of combat."

"It was taken by foreign hands my lord." pressed Ogumund.

The Jarl shot him a glare and Ogumund turned silent. "Foreign hands that increased our trade three-fold, that is until my foolish brother ended it. I have hosted Asta in my Hall in Öland and determined that she's capable of running both islands."

"It is unjust my lord." shrieked Ogmund.

Truvor looked upon the crowd "Tell me, which one of these is more worthy? Ogmund for his many," Truvor snickered "accomplishments? Or Asta who risked Hel's curse to get to the bottom of what happened to my brother and his people?"

"Asta." the crowd roared.

Truvor chuckled, "It must be near the end times for, again, my son and I are in agreement. Asta, you will retain control of Kelifar."

The crowd cheered, Asta bowed, Ogmund stormed off.

"Kelifar should be yours and your brother's." whispered Vinglunr.

Vanadis considered this and found, to her surprise, she was not moved. "I prefer Pohjola, even though I'm not the one to rule it."

Then a few other minor matters were brought before Truvor, afterwards this the hall quieted as the jarl prepared to announce the summer raids.

"I have deemed," he said augustly, "that we shall once again ally with Bjorn Eriksson to fight off Harlad Fair Hair's aggression. He may rule the west but he hall not rule us."

At this there was some cheering though quite a number of warriors scowled.

"My lord?" said a large man in simple garb but a pure silver arm ring. A scar ripped down his cheek, he wore only a goatee so a beard would not hide it.

"Yes Dunfall Rodrekrson?" addressed the Jarl.

"What of Gamli the Serpent? I hear he's holed up in Pohjola, we could ally with Kalevala and secure both riches and justice."

Vanadis' heart raced in anxiety upon hearing this.

"Yes, my son already thought of that." said Truvor dryly.

Asta, who stood in the front of the crowd, dared not meet his gaze.

"Then we should aid him." stressed Dunfall, many warriors grumbled in approval.

"I understand your sentiment Dunfall, you loved your sister and I loved my niece, both of which were claimed by the Serpent's poison."

Vanadis lowered her head and hid her shame behind her hand, the grief in the Jarl's tone cut deep.

Vinglunr rubbed the small of her back.

"However," added the Jarl, "we have much to lose by attacking Pohjola. Crafty Väinämöinen would use our heroes like a shields. While we bled he might conquer. If Louhi proves stronger our raiding parties would be lost and our great Nibelung clan weakened. We'd have nothing to offer King Bjorn and he'd leave us at the mercy of our foes in the Baltic Tribes."

"My lord, the death of Steinarr must be addressed." fumed Dunfall.

The hall watched with baited breath, hanging on each word uttered by the Jarl and the warrior.

"It has," stated Truvor, "the Serpent, his sister, and Mjoll's remaining warriors and servants have been declared vargs. Those that still live are trapped in dismal Pohjola, if they leave then any man may enact justice upon them."

"Not just any man should. Your son knows this." pressed Dunfall.

The crowd murmured in agreement. Truvor received a few glares, daring him to answer this.

Truvor considered Dunfall for a moment and then, he asked, "You doubt Hardegon's capabilities, then?"

The warrior staggered as if struck, "N-no, of course not."

"Still, you would have me throw an army behind Hardegon to kill a mere two thralls?" He shook his head, and chuckled, "You're either a fool or think Hardegon weak."

The hall considered this, there were a few laughs, and even more thoughtful expressions.

"If my son returns from his quest and is not cursed by our feud with the Volsung, then I will welcome him back. If the Serpent rears his wicked head in Alands, I will cut if off. We must not act rashly. King Bjorn is expecting our full support and he will have it. We cannot grant it if we divert ships on a vendetta against the unworthy."

The hall considered and then rumbled with agreement. Even the warriors who scowled looked convinced. Dunfall's comrades escorted him out to get smashed.

'Thrall? Unworthy?' Vanadis kept her gaze lowered so as not to glare at the Jarl. Vinglunr put his arm around her and they exited while the Truvor enacted further ceremony.

Once they had returned to the Thing grounds, Vinglunr lead the way to a pavilion where they served mead and pork. The lovers sat down at a table away from the rest and the skald whispered "We've made quite a name for ourselves."

Vanadis flashed him a determined look, "If they're not careful I'll show them how 'worthy' a danger we are. I'm the apprentice of the Witch Queen Louhi, I will not be looked down upon." She whispered.

"You'd rather they send a raiding party to Pohjola?"

This question snapped Vanadis out of her brooding. "N-no. Of course not, you're right." She sighed, "The Jarl's low estimation is a blessing."

"Best our home is safe." Vinglunr added.

"Our home?" asked Vanadis, "You'd live in a foreign land?"

Vinglunr hugged her close, resting his forehead on hers. "I'll dwell where ever you are safe. There's nothing left for me in Alands."

Vanadis kissed him and smiled at him lovingly.

"How about a meal and mead?" asked Vinglunr, "We can assuage one hunger," he then leaned close and whispered, "and then fill another."

Vanadis giggled, "Sounds wonderful."

Vinglunr stood "I shall return momentarily." He then walked towards the grill where a cook was roasting something that smelled savory and delightful.

Vanadis sighed with a grin, her spirit at ease with a feeling that all was right with the world.

Suddenly she noticed a figure on the roof of the pavilion. It was draped in a brown cloak with a blood red fringe. It was standing upside down, the cloak, strangely, falling upwards. The smoke from the grill wafted through it. Before the seithkona could react the thing leapt down upon her, she fell and everything was enveloped in darkness.

***

Vanadis was standing in a field and sky of black. Before her, illuminated by a silver aura, the same that surrounded Vanadis, stood the figure. She pulled off her hood. She had green skin that was stretched too tight against her face, and pointed ears. Her eyes were wide and red. She wore a sneer, all her teeth were jagged.

Vanadis breathed in deep, drawing on her will. She reached out one hand and prepared to drive the spirit from her.

The troll woman motioned for her to stop and grinned cunningly. "Ah, ah, ah. I'm the only thing keeping your spirit mask bound to your body. Banish me and you'll be revealed. Draw on your magic and your brother and sweet Vinglunr will also be unmasked. You'll all be in plain sight of your other foes."

Vanadis glowered dangerously at the invading spirit. "What do you want? Name your purpose. Be quick or I'll bind you to a shoe and you'll spend eternity sucking foot sweat."

"Just the sort of threat I would expect from a remorseless killer." sneered her visitor.

Vanadis laughed, "You're trying to shame me for Kelifar? I've moved well beyond that."

"Kelifar?" the Troll laughed back, "I speak not of Kelifar; I speak of Hofsfell."

This caused Vanadis to pause, "Pardon?"

The Troll shook her head in mocking disbelief, "Of course you never thought of it as a town. What would your kind call it? A cave, a liar? Its people, what would you consider them? Monsters? Beasts?"

Vanadis' haughty expression dropped.

The Troll's grin widened, "Yes, now you understand. You escaped Hardegon using the lives of my kin. While they fought and died you fled like cowards. You are as vile as they say, but not for the reasons they think." The corners of the spirits eyes beaded with tears, her anger was laced with a tone of shock at atrocity.

Vanadis saw the spirit for a second time, beyond her strange appearance, her grief and rage were very familiar. Guilt washed over the seithkona and she found it difficult to bolster her will. "I-I...I didn't consider."

"You Humans never consider!" the Troll answered clenched fists and a stomp of her foot. "My grandchild has fallen to Lemminkäinen's blade. From the grave I watched him grow strong only to meet this brutal end."

Vanadis' will faltered further, "I didn't mean hostility. I have no quarrel with your people."

"You imagine that makes it better? No, it makes it is far worse. If we were foes at least there would have been a reason behind the bloodshed."

"I was protecting my own. Wouldn't you have done the same if your brother's life was on the line?" Vanadis' tone was now pleading, her silver aura dimmed.

"I cannot answer that, I only know my own pain."

"You're here for vengeance then." stated Vanadis, grimly.

"Oh how I wished for vengeance. I prayed to Laufey of the Black Flame, I prayed that she would curse you. Would you know her answer?"

The name was familiar, Vanadis remembered Old Marte once uttered it as a curse, "Laufey take you." Swallowing her fear she asked hesitantly, "Yes, I would know if it."

"She requested you to pledge yourself to her." The grandmother laughed bitterly, "She was impressed with how you escaped Valkyries."

Vanadis stared at her blankly.

"If you accept I am to call off my vendetta against you. There is no justice." the Troll fumed.

"And if I refuse?" Vanadis asked cautiously.

The grandmother sighed, "Then there will be justice. I will reveal you, your brother and sweet Vinglunr to the Thing and you can witness the depths of your people's cruelty. I do hope they perform the rite of the blood eagle."

"There may be a third option.", mused the Seithkona. "I pay you a blood price."

The grandmother snorted, "I will not barter with the likes of you."

"Then why even tell me of your Mistress' offer?"

"After we've completed our business, because I have heeded her command, my grandson and I will be given a home in Muspelheim. Laufey is fair to those who are likewise to her."

"So my choices are slavery or 'justice'." said Vanadis with loathing.

With swiftness the Troll woman slapped Vanadis across the cheek. The seithkona recovered and glared at her, her aura once more shining bright.

The grandmother's was equally bright and her expression no less fierce. "Slavery?" she fumed. "Do jarls who pledge themselves to a king think of themselves as slaves? Laufey is a Queen among Fire Jotun. She commands legions of the living and the dead. Seithkona across Midgard bow to her in reverence and terror." She laughed bitterly, "She offers you a place in her service and you sneer? You're a fool!"

"I-I have not rejected her offer." Vanadis cut in, "I was taught by the Great Louhi; her river of Tuonela is distant from our heavens."

The Troll woman still regarded Vanadis as an idiot. "I have neither the time nor the inclination to teach you proper cosmology. I simply need to know, will you accept Laufey's mercy or shall we duel?"

Vanadis considered, her thoughts drifting to Mjoll and Vinglunr. What would they say? Vanadis huffed, she knew the answer. Her thoughts drifted to Pohjola, "I cannot betray my teacher."

"Why would the Mistress of the Black Flame care about a Pohjalander crone?" asked the Troll incredulously. "A better question, why do I care? Simply answer, yes or no. I'll hear nothing else."

Vanadis was twisted and torn. To duel would mean their deaths. To accept... 'Kings and jarls...' Vanadis mused. 'If I die...' She knew well death was not the end, yet fear still gripped her at the thought of it. What would happen to the others if her mask fell came to mind; 'What right do I have to decide Vinglunr and Gamli's fate?' She turned her gaze downward, clenching her fists. 'How I hate this'. To the Troll she replied, "I see no other choice. I pledge my service to your dark mistress."

The Troll grandmother's eyes widened in sudden fury. This actually made Vanadis feel a little better, had the Troll had gloated the she would have been truly doomed.

"Then I have no choice." seethed the Troll. "Welcome, to our sisterhood." She flashed forward and bit Vanadis on the shoulder.

***

Meanwhile, in the waking world, Vinglunr had laid Vanadis' comatose form on a table. The women in the pavilion and fetched a fox fur blanket and wrapped her in it.

The concerned cook frowned, "You're certain she doesn't need a healer?"

Vinglunr took the old woman's hands and squeezed them gently, "I am," he hoped his lie masked his fear, "she's had these fits all her life. She'll come back in an hour or so, she always does."

The cook regarded Vanadis, "Poor dear." Turning to Vinglunr she added, "You're good man to take such care of her."

"How could I not?" He answered.

The old woman patted him on the arm and returned to her duties. Vinglunr sat down beside his love and his mask of confidence cracked. He held her hand, "I know not what spirit holds you. Just know I will be here when you return."

Unseen by him, the Troll woman drifted up from Vanadis' body, looking ill-pleased. Meanwhile seithkona's hand grew unnaturally warm.

CHAPTER 23

'Our choices build who we are.' | I laugh at such 'wisdom.'
The Norns plant us in good or bad soil, this plots everything we become.
Those in an open field grow to their joys content. | The rest of us must twist around brambles.
Those truly cursed are forced to death or despicable crime.

Hours earlier, someone observed the Thing from a rocky hill. The afternoon sun shone through him, to the point that only the keenest eye could see his translucent body. The wight stood tall and proud, like a king. His image was drenched with signs of death. Skin hung from his face like a forked veil, his skeletal jaw naked between it. His stringy black hair was caked with dirt, as if fresh from the grave. His form, under his tattered, rusted armor, was gaunt. His red cloak was torn and muddy. He wore a crown of twisted iron and bone. His eyes were perfect and fierce, they observed the Thing with penetrating attentiveness.

He took it all in, the people bustling about; buying, selling, reveling. A few he played special attention to. The large brash man who inevitabley crashed through something. The skald and his sister, in their holy tribute to Frey and Freya. A young woman, as a little girl she had stumbled onto his tomb and he scared her away. Even now she fearfully glanced towards his hills. He let out a wheezing laugh, 'So amusing!'

The music reached his ears, the strum of the lyre, the beat of the drum the sound of horns and cheers. The songs were similar to what he knew when alive, but not quite. These little changes over time fascinated him.

Vaguely he wondered what the smells and tastes were like. He only had a shadow remembrance of such pleasures.

Suddenly someone wandering on the outskirts grabbed his attention. She was a creature like him. Her skin was paper white. She wore a fine dress silk and a shroud covered her face. He frowned and peered closer, something was wrong...Siggeir would smile in discovery if he could. Of course, she had no head, she was using the veil to replace it.

He gestured to her, curling his skeletal fingers up. "Come." he said, his voice, deep, resonant and powerful.

***

They both vanished and a moment later he and the interloper were on his ship. Its hull and mast were made of grey stone. Its sail was of pale, unblemished, human skin. The lines were twisted, hardened and dried innards. Sailing her were an undead crew, more skeletal than their master. The ship sailed through a sea and sky of earth and stone. The packed grave dirt was still, yet the ship seemed to sail and sway none-the-less. At the stern, there was a throne of twisted spirits, their ghostly bodies were bounded tight together. They screamed in silence, their eyes wide with pain and fear. Siggeir sat on them with an ease that bespoke familiarity.

His guest stood before him. She glanced, 'How quaint.' around the ship in confusion. Her 'face' turned and regarded the King. She took a fearful step back.

The wight leaned forward and addressed her, "At ease child. I have called you here as a guest. As long has you cause no offence you are as safe here as you were in your father's hall. I am Siggeir, rightful king of Gotland. Tell me, who are you, what is your station and what brings you here?"

The shade before him shifted her stance to a slight crouch, her hands raised as if on guard.

"Dorte Steinarrdottir?" he mused stroking his bony chin.

Dorte titled her head in confusion.

The King let out a rumbling laugh, "Oh I understand the silent tongue well. So please, tell me your story."

Dorte stood more at ease, her hand on her hip.

"I'm not merely interested in you." Siggeir said pleasantly. With a sweeping motion he indicated his crew, who had not paused in their arduous work. "I've heard all their stories."

The dead woman lowered her head and crossed her arms, pondering something.

"That's right." Siggeir answered. "Here your endless rage sleeps. Your story would be worthless if you could only scream. Now, please, tell me about yourself."

Dorte looked up at Siggeir and he listened to her tale. When she spoke of her death the wight sovereign nodded in sympathy. When she described her chase and clashes with Vanadis he straightened up in his throne, thoughts churned in his mind.

"A Nibelung lady slain by treacherous Volsung, how history repeats itself. We share much Dorte, it's almost as if you were my child."

Dorte touched the shadow of her chin and titled her head.

The king stood and drifted past her, "I know because I can see the woman at the other end of your string." He lifted his finger and draped on it was a golden strand that went from the small of Dorte's back and into the darkness.

"Your Vanadis looks very much like my Signy." He chuckled, and pointed to the sail, "As she was, not as she is."

Dorte regarded Signy's remains and retreated a few steps.

"Do not fear me, child. Yes, I can be cruel but only to my enemies. Signy betrayed me, her lawfully wedded husband. It was with her blessing that her brother Sigmund and their incestuous son Sinfjolti, slaughtered me in my hall. If it weren't for my preparations," he motioned to the ship they sailed on, "I would have descended to Niflheim."

Dorte stared at him for a long moment.

"The word for what you are is Haugbui. Though you're of a kind I've never seen. Haugbui are bound locations either their barrow or simply the place they died. You, however, are bound to a living soul. It's very fascinating."

Dorte clenched her fists.

"You make demands of a King?" Siggeir asked entertained.

She turned her head away, her bodily expression less fierce.

"Apology accepted." the wight sovereign laughed. "To answer your question, yes I could end your curse. However, there is a far more enjoyable way to go about it."

Dorte turned back to Siggeir and listened.

"Power," said Siggeir, regarding his open palm, "begs for use." He clenched his fist and then folded his hands behind his back. "I have plenty and have longed for the day I could test its limits. However, if I did, I fear Odin would hurl his spear Gungnir and vanquish me. Either that or Hel would find me and she would not be pleased." He regarded Dorte with a pleasantness, "If you, however, wreaked your own vengeance, the powers above and below wouldn't bat an eye."

Dorte shook her head evenly.

"True she is guarded by her ghostly kin but," he stepped beside her and, with one arm embraced her like a father. He swept his other hand as if showing her a grand vista, "this island is my army. Furthermore I will lend you a fraction of my strength. With this you can break through the Volsung's defences and, once you've devoured her spirit you'll be free. Is this acceptable?"

Dorte nodded slowly and turned to Siggeir, her veil marking a shadow of smile.

"Excellent," Siggeir said appreciatively, "I only ask that your draw out your hunt. The centuries have dragged on and I am in desperate need of spectacle."

***

Hours later Gamli stood waist deep in the sea holding his newest creation, the spear Burning Mind, its gold spiral inlay and pointed tip gleamed as the sun set behind the hills in the west. On the pebbly shore he could see a crowd of admirers, they stood in a semi-circle around the still sleeping, burning Ormir.

They had cheered for Gamli and now several in the crowd called him, "Sir, I would speak to you."

"It's Wayland, he's come to forge for us miracles."

Gamli didn't move, he saw clearly that his beard was red and his body to its normal girth and power. Thanks to the twilight shadows he couldn't make out anyone, so it was impossible to tell if there was anyone he knew in the crowd. He did note several men peering at him closely, Gamli griped the spear tight at the thought of any one recognizing him.

"Bera?" he whispered. He was met with silence, the spirt was gone from his mind.

"Easy, easy." cut in a familiar voice. "That's no Wayland, just son Edvin. He had the courage to look in Ilmarinen's forge and ever since he's had fits of madness where he creates wonders."

Gamli sighed, it was Ransu, the smith saw the fisherman's shadow step into the waters to stand between him and the crowd.

"Bring him over, I would have him forge me a sword."

"No, I have need of a bracelet of finest beauty, fit for a queen."

"Wayland can forge wings, can your Edvin? I'd like wings."

Ransu fished a heavy cloak from their boat. "Calm my friends, we mustn't aggravate him. We don't know if his madness has left. If not he could strike at any moment!"

Gamli flinched at that and glared at his friend.

"See, even now the rage grows, I shall try to calm him." With that the fisherman waded up to the smith, while the crowd watched.

Once he reached Gamli he hissed, "Am I correct, are you insane? What happened to your guise?"

Gamli rubbed the back of his neck sheepishly, "I... I witnessed Surt again, he must have scared away Bera. He has a purpose for me."

Ransu draped the cloak around Gamli's shoulders and pulled the hood low, saying loudly, for the crowd, "Calm, calm my son. Everything will be well, let's get you back to your forge beast."

In a whisper he added, "We'll discuss your holy quest later. For now, let's hope I can send your admirers away."

They walked closer to Ormir, the hood of the cloak so low that Gamli relied on Ransu to guide him. The fisherman gestured for the crowd to disperse, "Away with you, let my son collect himself. Once he is rested we'll take your orders."

A large man with the build of a warrior and the blisters of an iron worker eyed the two critically. "Stranger, has your son ever been to Kelifar?" His tone was suspicious.

Ransu laughed, "No, not at all. We're Pohjalanders through and through. This is our first time south."

"What's your game Ransu?" asked shrewd looking woman who pushed to the front of the crowd. An older woman who walked with her added,"You and Kvistr always used to come to the Thing, is that his son? Are you so daft as to bring him here?"

"The Serpent?"

"No, he wouldn't dare."

"Show yourself rogue!"

"N-now, now, no need to..." eased Ransu.

Gamli tore off his hood and lowered the spear at the throng. "I tire of this." H]he growled.

Sensing his master's displeasure Ormir awoke and hissed at those closest to him, the crowd backed away.

Ransu shook his head, and pulled his javelins and a spear from the ship. "By Hiisi, why did come to this?"

"You're no good at lies." grumbled Gamli.

"Says the one who banished his disguise."

Three of the men stepped forward. The young scholar who drew a long dagger. The blistered one, who wielded a hammer, and a one who had finished a duel before and as such was garbed in hide armor and wielded a still bloody axe.

The blistered man, Gamli recognized him as Osfrid, a contemporary of Asvard, said, "You dare come to these shores? You flee bitten thrall! You worthless dog! Asvard considered you a son." Fury lit behind his sneer.

Gamli's blue eyes reflected equal hate, "Never mention him again. I'm no slave. Know what you face, the blood of Kvistr, Signy, and Wayland flows within me. Know I've come out of the fires of the destroyer. Know the death of my aunt has enraged me. I mean no harm, but if you throw yourselves at me I will gladly send you to Hel."

Ormir stood beside his master and shrieked. The entire crowd, even the three brave ones, retreated another step. The word Volsung whispered among the throng.

"We mustn't flee," warned the young scholar, "we must take him alive, for only then can we force out of him how he poisoned us."

"He's right."

"This is Volsung revenge."

"What happened to Kelifar will happen here."

More men and women from the crowd stepped forward, they had no weapons but looked equally determined. They reached down to the beach and scooped up rocks. The rest, however, glanced at each in fear.

"Are you ready for this?" asked Ransu.

Gamli lowered his gaze at the crowd, "I am." he rumbled.

Before either side could strike a loud, eerie wail echoed from the west. Following it came screams of terror, then the sound of battle.

This chaos staggered the combatants on the beach. Osfrid glared at the Serpent, "This your doing? Have you allied with Harald or the Curonians?"

Gamli shook his head, staring beyond them with a look of concern.

"Vanadis?" Ransu asked.

"I'm not sure." answered the smith.

"Your sister? What does she have to..."

"Osfrid, look!" interrupted the scholar. All eyes turned to the Thing.

Revelers fled. Their foes were men of living wood. They were short and clustered with branches and leaves, as if they had just leapt out of trees. They were quick, swarming after the crowd like numerous wolf packs. They were fierce, they swarmed any they caught, slashing them to bloody ribbons with knife like fingers. As they ran they hummed a piercing, eerie tune that almost drowned out the screaming. Most of the revelers ran for the ships. Others fled through the tents, searching for kin or weapons.

Those on the beach watched in stunned terror. Gamli acted first, he slung Burning Mind on his back, scoped up Scorn form the ground and seized his spiked shield from the ship. With determined purpose he marched through the crowd.

"Hold." said the Osfrid, raising his hammer.

Gamli continued to stride, "My sister's in there; you won't prevent me from saving her."

The axe-man regarded the smith and a flash of respect crossed his face. "Very well Serpent, whatever our feud, it can wait until the monsters are slain." He turned towards the Thing and raised his axe, "To battle!" With that he charged.

Osfrid kept his anger on Gamli for a moment longer, then, with a snarl he wheeled, yelled "Odin!", and joined his brother.

The rest of the crowd dispersed, some racing for the ships, others racing towards the Thing, calling out names of loved ones.

"You'll be the end of me." sighed Ransu dropping his spear and taking up axe and net. Then he and Gamli ran towards the battle, axe aloft and sword drawn.

***

Vinglunr kept his vigil over Vanadis. Her expression was wracked with sorrow. She muttered sobs of anguish, eyes shut tight, trapped in nightmare sleep. She squirmed in her blanket wrap. Vinglunr rested his hand on her shoulder to ensure she didn't roll off the table. The skald watched her with deep concern, torn between waiting for her to surface or running for a healer. Thankfully their guises held.

The unnatural wail startled him out of his anxious stupor. He, and the rest of the pavilion, stared fearfully to the west, where it had come from.

"What in Freya's name?" swore the cook, looking beyond the tents and towards the setting sun.

Vinglunr stood, one hand on his love, the other drifting to his sword.

"Over there!" one of the cook's thralls pointed. Rushing towards them were a hoard of little wooden men, their claws bared, humming a maddening tune. They rushed into a group of revelers who'd been drinking in a pavilion beyond. With hissing shrieks they cut man, woman and child down, turning their celebration into a lake of screams and gore.

In one smooth motion the skald scooped up his love, her fur wrapped body burned against him as if she had a fever. "Find weapons! Group on me!" He called and then fled out of the pavilion. As he weaved around the tents he repeated his cry, "Find weapons! To me! To me!"

He turned a corner to find four warriors and a shieldmaiden had answered his call. He skidded to a halt amongst them and gently placed Vanadis down. He then sung out his Jotun magic, with a rumble and crack a semi-circular wall of ice arose before them.

"Those who can fight with me, those who can't stay behind us." he commanded.

The cook and her servants rushed passed him and his warriors stepped forward to stand shoulder to shoulder. Vinglunr's glacier was their fortress and the skald and his defenders the gate.

"I have your love dear." said the cook, who picked up Vanadis and held her as if she were her own daughter.

"I thank you." said Vinglunr.

Meanwhile the invaders swarmed forward. On closer look their faces were carved into skulls. Somehow their pointed teeth gnashed as they hummed their ghastly song.

"Stand firm!" shouted Vinglunr. "Stand your ground. For Odin! For Thor! For Frey!" He then called out a song, the language was breathy and loud like the wind through a dark wood. The tune was ominous. The creatures that raced towards suddenly reeled and shrieked at Vinglunr's words, holding their hands to their eyes. The others that leapt over them were similarly blinded but continued their rush, none-the-less.

Once one was in sword reach the skald struck with force. The wood cut and bleed like flesh. The creature screamed in pain and rolled furiously on the ground. Three more trampled over it to take its place. Meanwhile his four other defenders fought their own battles, similarly outnumbered by blinded foes.

***

In the Great Hall, Truvor's guards had a struggle of their own. Their situation was entirely less dire. The warriors' shields smashed against the wood effigies, their axes cut them in twain. Thora stood in the front lines, her dress stained in blood, fighting more fiercely than the guards. Truvor was beside her, his strikes slower but none the less steady. Behind them, backs to the wall, were the old, the ladies and the children of the court. Asta stood at the forefront, her daughter hiding behind her. Asta had one firm hand on a blonde haired child. He was Helgi Hardegonson, he watched the battle with wide eyed fascination. The air was full of cries, the clack of wood against shield and, muted beyond the walls, Vinglunr's song.

Then Dorte glided through the door like a plague wind. She pointed at a guard and he screamed as barbs of white bone burst from his flesh. He gurgled and fell to a bloody heap. The wood warriors closed ranks, hacking and biting with the ferocity of starving rodents.

"Stand firm!" called Thora. "We will prevail!" yelled Truvor. They pushed forward together and drove the ghastly warriors back.

Dorte drew a line with her finger. The air split open like a tapestry to reveal cold winter night, shrieks of torment echoed through. The rift only lasted a moment but it was long enough, four Nibelung warriors dropped dead, their faces masks of terror.

Thora broke through the effigies and charged Dorte. The Haugbui lifted her head let out a scream of anguish that halted shieldmaiden in her tracks. She dropped her to her knees. It was as if a despair, heavy enough to anchor a ship, held her down.

Truvor sliced the head off a foe, knocked it aside and rushed to her aid. "I know not where you come from fiend but you will not take my daughter in law."

The Haugbui looked down upon him and suddenly the Jarl went pale. "D-dorte?" he asked, he lowered his sword, "What happened to you child?"

The wooden effigies halted their attack and even Truvor's guards paused.

The Haugbui remained still and the jarl listened, Dorte's silent words heard by him alone.

He frowned, with a tone of wisdom and sorrow he said, "No child. Your curse is bigger than Vanadis. This is the power of our ancient feud with the Volsung. Relinquish your vengeance and find peace my dear girl. It has caused enough harm."

***
Deep in his tomb, on his ship of stone, on his throne of anguished souls sat King Siggeir. He held out his hand, tied to his fingers were five strings composed of tiny golden runes that lead off into the darkness. His mystic sight followed his strings where they rested, unseen, on Dorte's back. Siggeir watched all from just over her shoulder.

Dorte's bittersweet joy at reaching her uncle wafted over him. Her disgust and rage flared as she regaled him the reason for her predicament. Then confusion at the Jarl's answer. Then...then Siggeir felt the Jarl's words slowly take hold of young Dorte, swaying her dispare to hope.

"I think not." he chuckled. Then he flicked his index finger to release the Haugbui's unbridled rage.
"

***

Back in the hall, the jarl's niece stiffened and clenched her fists.

"Dorte be at ease." commanded Truvor with a fatherly tone of command. "You must rest, staying like this will only cause further pain."

Suddenly the Haugbui's long fingered hand the Jarl's forehead. Then Truvor screamed as his body twisted and snapped like dry branch and rivers of his blood soaked the floor.

Thora had recovered, she raced for her son. "We must flee!" she yelled. "Run!"

***

Vanadis floated in nothingness. It was unlike the void from before. It was a place where even color did not exist, not even black. She had no spirit or body. She was simply raw emotion, a strange, sharp, sadness. The sharpness was the jagged edges left behind from something torn from her. She saw freckles and clever green eyes, these brought first a remembrance of love and then a far worse bitterness. The weight of a child rested on her hip, the laughter of the young, the padded footfalls of grandchildren chasing each other; with these followed the realization they were no more, all stolen from her. Duty bound her in chains of frustration, she longed to find her children, set them free. Surt would not allow it, her place was in Muspelheim. So she fenced in her wretchedness and hid it behind aloofness and beauty. Still, it festered hate. For the Aesir, for the forces that hid her loved ones and even for her own kind; those traitors who'd had forgotten her children.

Dimly she heard Bera's excited words. "Mistress, come back. There is war."

Still lost in her mourning Vanadis didn't answer.

She felt Bera seize her arms and squeeze. Her voice grew louder, "Mistress, awake, you're in danger."

The sharp pain of her iron grip brought focus. "Gamli, why aren't you with him?"

"He drove me out mistress. Creatures of wood and blood run through the fair ground. Oh there is such a fight. We must hurry or we'll miss it!"

Vinglunr's voice reached Vanadis. He was singing but the words were strange and the tune dark. The kind of song he would only call only in a time of danger. Suddenly his singing chocked to a stop.

***

A few moments earlier, in the waking world, the creatures pressed their relentless assault in spite of their blindness and the small mountain of wooden corpses they had to climb to reach the skald. Vinglunr took solace in his brave allies, his ice wall.

Five more warriors had joined his line and all ten held firm. The blinded creatures could not break their guard, which was good for those who stood behind them.

The rest of the Thing was not so fortunate. Tents, pavilions and hall were set aflame. Many lay dead. The fairgrounds were a blood swamp.

Vinglunr spotted a weaselly looking effigy who climbed to the top of a collapsed pavilion. In his hands was a crossbow. He laughed, he leveled his weapon and fired. For a second the bolt seemed to hang in the air and the skald suddenly regretted not carrying a shield. It struck true and pierced Vinglunr's throat, he shuddered and fell, his song coming to an abrupt end.

Several things happened at once. Vinglunr's spirit guise left him him and his true guise was revealed. The wooden terrors slashing at them had their sight returned. The ice wall vanished. The horde of murderous effigies charged in. Those who relied on the wall, young maids, children, the old, were slashed, bit and torn asunder. The nine defenders were overwhelmed

It was at that moment Vanadis' eyes flashed open and her guise left her. The cook cared not for her throat was being torn out and her innards pulled into the open air. The warrior beside her screamed in agony, covered by a dozen wooden terrors biting into his flesh. Behind her a group of vile things bashed a little boy's head on the rocks.

When confronted with such horror a single spell surged to the Volsung's mind. In a panic she released it. Vanadis screamed and fire burst around her to become a sudden inferno. The flame was dark as char but it burned fiercely. Those being slaughtered and the creatures who killed them alike where consumed in a cacophony of anguish.

A second later, Vanadis realized what she'd done. Her grey eyes bore witness to the horrors and innocents being burning alive. She only witnessed it for a moment, for the fire was so hot, all, aside from her, were quickly turned to ash. Then, her flames flickered and died, leaving her standing in shock, in the smoldering remains.

Vinglunr stood before her. He looked at her aghast. Around him was a silver nimbus, the kind reserved for spirits.

Vanadis peered down and saw his sword sticking out of the charred remains. "No." she gasped, "No, no, no, no, no." she stared back up at him her face a mask of fear, regret and sorrow.

Vinglunr regarded Vanadis with a look of resignation and determination. "What are you doing? Go! Stop this madness." He then sank into his ashes. Vanadis' will shoot through and she screamed cried with rage.

***

Moments before, on the other side of the hall, a swarm of effigies guarded the rear exit; that is until Thora rushed through. She jabbed her spear through several of the creatures. Her shield crashed into several others, sending them flying. The two royal guards followed right on her heels, the rest clashed with the Haugbui. Thora and the guards engaged the horde while Asta, the maidens and children rushed past.

They did not make it far. Another, larger, pack of effigies rushed over the fallen tents and corpses to intercept.

Young Helgi grabbed an axe from a corpse and stood to face them.

"No!" commanded Thora in terror, "Helgi! Run!"

Helgi did not obey her command. He stood ready, hefting a weapon he could barely lift. Asta rushed in front of him, "My bord flee." But between the terrors Thora and the guard still faced and these fresh terrors, there was nowhere to go.

The swarm charred, chittering in anticipation for the slaughter. Asta closed her eyes. Helgi prepared to fight.

Suddenly Gamli, followed by Ransu, Krumr, and Zaidaan, crashed into the swarm. Gamli swung his shield down crushing several of the creatures and followed through with a lethal swipe from Scorn. Ransu tossed his net, entangling several of the effigies and then yanked them forward. Then the fisherman hacked them his axe. Krumr waded fearlessly into the hoard, his mail warding off their attacks, while he hacked with his sword. Zaidaan shouted a foreign battle cry and threshed through the creatures with a curved sword.

Without turning Gamli nodded to the north. "Go, the Nibelung rally."

In the distance, just north of the Thing, the smith, the scholar and the dullest waited, hurt but victorious.

"This way." The duellist waved. "We'll escort you."

Asta nodded, "Everyone follow me!" She fled, pulling Helgi with one hand and her youngest daughter with the other. The rest followed her flight.

Thora, who had dropped her spear and drew an axe, called back at Gamli, "You have my thanks."

"Then remember who aids you." Gamli huffed as he blocked a swarm of claws with his shield.

Thora smashed a creature who leapt at her, pulping it into a bloodly smear. "Who should I remember then?"

"Gamli the Serpent." The smith hacked down with Scorn, ending a cluster of the terrors.

Thora flinched at that but it was not enough to lower her guard. She swiped again, her blow sending an effigy flying. "These are not yours?"

Gamli blocked the creature's thrust with his shield, he answered with a sweep form Scorn that cut the thing in half. The smith shook his head grimly. "Evil follows my sister, but it's not her fault."

Suddenly he air shimmered and Dorte stepped out of nothing to appear between them.

Thora spun in an attempt to bury her axe into the Haugbui but Drote's curse was quicker. Thora screamed as her shoulder wrenched form its socket of its own accord.

Gamli turned, relying on Krumr, Zaidaan and Ransu to guard his back, and chopped Scorn at her; it cut a bloody line through her dress and across her alabaster flesh. Dorte raised her left hand and ʃ blazed, Gamli recoiled in pain.

"Enough." Called Vanadis in a choir of voices. She stormed around the hall, a nimbus of flickering ash flaming around her. She gestured and the reaming terrors were torn asunder by an invisible force.

The Haugbui turned to her and screamed with exultant rage. She pointed a long finger at Vanadis who responded by sweeping her arm in the air. The Haugbui's hex rippled of Vanadis' dusky dome of force; she winced as a small bone barb pierced the back of her palm. The seithkona responded by twisting her hand, a howling black vortex whipped around Dorte for a moment, ripping her dress and flesh, then, it flew back to Vanadis, who absorbed the black wind into herself and stood stronger.

Gamli and Thora rose. They struck at Dorte, Thora's axe thunking into her flesh and Scorn cutting another red line through her. Ransu tossed his axe and it buried itself in the Haugbui's shoulder. Krumr and Zaidaan swept around to get a better vantage.

Dorte shrieked with fury and made numerous slashing motions with her talon fingers. Several gashes ripped through the Vanadis but she still stood. She raised her hands and yelled, "Away with you." A beam of black and white flashed form her palms and struck the Haugbui, Dorte shuddered, rolled in the air and then vanished with a thunderclap.

Then, there was stillness. The wooden effigies returned to their nature, becoming stiff and lifeless, yet their blood remained. So to did the devastation. The Great Hall still burned, black smoke still rose into the sky. The mutilated bodies of revelers still littered the field.

"Where's Vinglunr?" asked Gamli, after he caught his breath.

Vanadis' grief stricken expression was all the answer he needed.

"No." he whispered, turning pale.

"We have all lost someone this day." said Thora with sympathy, regarding her two fallen guards and the massacre inside the hall.

Krumr clapped Gamli on the shoulder, "You should go. The survivors will blame you for this."

Thora considered and then nodded to the northwest, "Walk util you find a tree with five branches. Descend the sea side cliff nearby and you'll find a hidden grotto. Inside is a skute Truvor prepared should we ever need to escape, use that. It won't be safe for you to return to the beach."

Gamli shook his head, struggling to distage his thoughts form his mourning. "No, I cannot leave the ship. There is cargo I must..."

"I think I have it," said Ransu, he carried in one hand the chest that held the strange bronze cube. "Ormir dragged this all the way from the beach."

The drake followed at his heels and regarded his master with a sound that resembled a joyous horn.

Gamli took the chest patted Ormir's head affectionately, drawing strength from him. "Thank you."

"Vinglunr," Vanadis pressed, "we need to retrieve his lyre. It's not right that he doesn't have it." She spotted the skald's spirit waiting by the hall. He regarded her with a look that bridged anger and sorrow.

"At ease," said Thora kindly, "we are not monsters. If your friend fought with us he will be given full funerary rights. I swear a suitable lyre will be burned in his honor."

"I will supply it myself." said Zaidaan with a bow.

"If we are not to join Vinglunr should hurry." urged Ransu.

"Aye." said Gamli

Vanadis heard not. She had walked a few steps to confront her love.

"If there is to be a funeral I must remain here." said Vinglunr. "I must see if I am worthy of Valhalla. I will tell Mjoll of our deeds." his tone was curt.

"You could come with me." Vanadis pleaded, reaching out her hand.

"For the love of Ukko..." cursed Ransu, who only witnessed one half of the conversation. Gamli touched his shoulder and shook his head.

The skald took a step back, "Don't tempt me Vanadis. I know the sign of the black flame, you serve Laufey, mother of Loki. You have chosen a path I cannot follow."

"It was forced upon me." Vanadis cried. "If I refused we would have all died."

Vinglunr turned his back. "How I wish I could believe you, but I know well your skill at lying."

This jabbed into Vanadis' heart like a barb. "No Vinglunr, I'm not lying. Please, I didn't mean to cast that spell. I was frightened. Don't go."

As the skald walked away he said, "Know the love I held for you was the truth." He then vanished.

Vanadis pulled her hair and screamed in anguished frustration.

Gamli seized her arm, "Come on. We need to go."

She spun and glared at him but Gamli's will did not waver.

"V-very well." she said doing her best to hold back her tears and to her will.

To Thora, Krumr and Zaidaan Gamli said "It was an honor to fight beside you."

"I will remember you've done Gamli the Serpent." said Thora.

"Surt be with you." said Krumr.

"Farewell, I hope we meet again in a happer time." said Ziaadan.

"Thank Ukko." said Ransu.

With that the three left and their drake followed, fleeing to the hidden grotto.

***

Up upon his hill, his form slightly luminescent now that the sun had set, stood Siggeir. He watched the Volsungs flee.

At his feet lay Dorte, her hand twitched and clenched signalling that some unholy life was left in her. The King of Gotland regarded her kindly. "Be at ease child. You've entertained me greatly, in payment I will see you repaired and ready to enact your vengeance another time."

"My lord." called a soft voice behind him.

He spun and saw a spirit with sharp, regal features bow before him. She looked very much like that Vanadis, and also... "Signy?" he asked with a hint of fear. Siggeir's mind flew back to his stone ship, and he relaxed a titch; yes the sail was intact.

"No." replied Hanne. She stood closer and placed her delicate hand on his chest. She stood up on her tiptoes pressing herself closer to him. With a seductive grin she said, "Unlike Signy, I am Volsung willing to betray her own kin."

CHAPTER 24

When it comes to family, / take nothing for granted.
There is no bond that cannot be broken by suffering and woe.
Familial love is the bedrock of your soul? / Hah! It will turn to sand and you'll perish in the sea.
Still, better to live in a hall a short time, than to wander all your life naked under wind and rain.

Hours later, their skute sailed swiftly west across the Baltic, to the Gotaland mainland. The ship was small, swift and painted blue-grey. It had a stag figurehead. It was packed with supplies and a small fortune in skatt. Ransu had gleefully remarked that Thora, by directing them to this sweet little cache, had paid well for the saving of her son.

Then, the sky had opened up and rain poured down. Lightning flashed across the dark sky and thunder boomed. A mild storm, but a storm nonetheless.

While Ransu manned the rudder and Gamli tended the sails, Vanadis bailed. She summoned Bera to help. The black Skeleton moved swiftly and tirelessly. The seithkona did likewise, her grief numbing her exhaustion.

The storm seemed to last for an eternity. The downpour and drive for survival kept the three well enough awake. The storm abided when the sun rose behind them. At that point Gamli locked the sails and helped with bailing. When enough water had been tossed out the siblings collapsed on either side of the boat. With a flick of her wrist, Vanadis sent Bera back to the spirit world.

"I know some hidden bays in Gotaland." said Ransu. "We'll make for one of those. Then, we rest."

Gamli regarded Vanadis, who looked wet and truly miserable. "Sister?"

"It may not be the time Gamli." Ransu cut in.

"No, you a have a right. You both do." Vanadis swallowed her grief, and told truthfully her part of the tale. Both Ransu and Gamli listened with anxious attention.

Vanadis finished with, "When I awoke I was surrounded those things. They were killing us. We were all doomed. I-I was terrified, more so than I've ever been. I called on a spell, it burnt everyone around me, friend, foe all ash." Her expression cracked with guilt and grief, "It caught women, children, a-and Vinglunr, who'd worked so hard to protect us all." Finally she could stand no more and broke down into tears.

Gamli and Ransu looked to each other, then back to Vanadis.

"You did what you needed. It would have broken this old man's heart to lose both of you." said Ransu gently.

Gamli bowed his head in thought, his expression dark. Ormir hummed with concern and put his head in the smith's lap. Gamli snorted and stroked the back of his neck. "Truly, there was there no other way?"

"You think better I, than him?" Vanadis asked wretchedly. In truth she didn't know that answer.

"Not what I asked." said Gamli sternly. "If you hadn't cast it, are you sure you would have died?"

"I'm a liar," Vanadis spat out, "why would you believe anything I say?"

"Gamli..." Ransu cautioned.

The smith held up a warding hand and glared at his sister. "Well?"

Vanadis' mind went back to that terrible moment. The press of the wooden terrors was thick, the side of her face was covered with a poor woman's blood. "When I woke up the line had fallen. If hadn't been unleashed my spell, I would have died as well."

Her brother considered her for a long moment, he then turned and focused on the horizon, where they could see the thin line of the Gotaland shore. Then with a snarl he spun and punched the mast with enough force the wood cracked.

Both Vanadis and Ransu flinched.

The rest of the journey across the Baltic was taken in silence. Vanadis turned from her brother, pulled her cloak around her and sat in misery. Eventually exhaustion overcame her.

***

In her dream, Vanadis sat at her balcony at the edge of Mount Sariola. The sky was clear and beautiful, arrayed the full majesty of the silver moon and stars. Before her was a hnefatafl table, which was made of smooth obsidian. The king's piece was a brilliant red ruby, his guards were gold, and the raiders silver.

Vanadis slid a gold piece down and rested it beside silver. The silver was surrounded so she took it.

"With such a keen mind it's surprising you are mastered by foolish sentiment."

Vanadis glanced up to see Flosi. He wore a charming goatee. His black locks were tied back in the manner of a nobleman. His black garb was lined with silver. His eyes were a fiery red and luminescent.

A deep suspicion sunk into the Volsung. "Who are you?"

'Flosi' smiled and slid one of his silver pieces. "When the troll bit she ignited a spark, I am that spark." He snatched her king. "You lose."

Vanadis considered this and asked, "A spark of Laufey? Why do you look like Flosi?"

"I have no shape of my own so I chose one you find familiar." He stroked his beard and considered her with some amusement, "If you would prefer I could look like Vinglunr."

Vanadis' grey eyes flashed with anger, "Don't you dare. Get straight to your business then leave, I'm in no mood for games."

"You've become a sad sack of sorrow, completely useless to yourself and our mistress."

Vanadis balked at that, then came back with even more fury, "What do you expect?" she laughed bitterly, "I reduced my true love to ash."

"True love?" Flosi asked in mocking disbelief, "Are you a child? You knew the man a mere three seasons."

"I know my heart." screamed the seithkona knocking the hnefatafl pieces flying. Then, in a more subdued tone she added, "It's not merely that. Gotland was Kelifar all over again. I've tried so hard to control my curse, only for more people to die."

Laufey's spark considered her for a moment and said, "The magic you summoned was strange."

Vanadis glared at him, then her mind wound back and a realization hit her. "Those creatures, I've never seen their like."

"In all of Louhi's teachings did she ever show you magic like that?" prompted Flosi.

Vanadis thought, "No. Possession requires flesh. At best I can destroy wood and stone, I can't move it. "

"What does this tell you?" asked Flosi, waiting patiently for her conclusion.

"This was not seith. They were not summoned with my power." Vanadis answered with a faint hint of hope.

"Your are certain?"

Vanadis laughed, "Y-yes, yes I am." She smiled, "How was I so foolish? My curse couldn't have created the wooden beasts. That Dorte appeared...she simply took advantage of the chaos to get to me. "

Flosi responded with polite applause.

Vanadis suddenly locked eyes with the spark, her expression turning suspicious.

"You think our mistress sent them?" laughed Flosi.

The seithkona considered this and her suspicion faded. "No, you had me before they came. I see no reason why your mistress would attack. Unless the Thing offended her somehow."

"If it did Laufey would have wreaked havoc with the Nibelung long ago. Human politics concerns her not."

"Then who?"

Flosi reflected on this and answered, "The power that summoned the effigies was localized. Dorte will follow you beyond Gotland, but the curse of Gotland will not"

Vanadis thought on this and nodded, "Yes, I believe you. T-thank you. I couldn't bear the weight of another Kelifar."

Flosi regarded her smugly, "You're a little more useful to our mistress now, and I have advice that will make more so, if you would hear it."

"Your council has been sage so far." admitted the Volsung.

Flosi leaned forward and caught her grey eyes in his stare. "This next revelation will be unpleasant. There is something you could have done to save your skald."

A stone of guilt dropped to the pit of her stomach. "You cheer me one moment and now say this?"

"I do so your own good. Do you wish to know what you could have done?"

Vanadis tore her gaze away and said, "Alright, out with it."

"Listen carefully, for I know you better than you know yourself. When Louhi taught you your sole goal was to control your power. Oh you enjoyed spell casting but have always been hesitant in its use, a little less zealous in learning than you should have been."

"This curse isn't a game. If anything I should have been more cautious, then Vinglunr wouldn't have died." retorted the seithkona.

Flosi let out a mocking laugh, "Oh dear my Vanadis, ignorance is not control. Ignorance is how you lose it. If you had studied more you would have learned a spell that would have pulled you out of the knife fingers of your foes, without causing harm to others."

Vanadis exhaled and clenched her fists. Her thoughts racing to find some fault in Flosi's logic, she could find none. "Then I did kill him." she said in a dead pan.

"Yes, but you can learn from your mistakes. Embrace your gift, I can teach you our mistress' ways."

Vanadis regarded him warily, "You do this through the kindness of your heart?"

Flosi shook his head, "Oh no, I do this to show you my lady's benevolence. You remember what she shared with you, yes? It was a sign of favor and trust. Will you not return it in kind at all?"

Vanadis brooded on this and answered, "Vinglunr had a reason to distrust."

"Because he was blinded by Aesir's lies. You're cleverer than he, all I ask is that you keep your vow of fealty. In return, through me, our Mistress will help you rip the veil off the world and see things for how they are. With this you'll become wise and powerful."

"I won't betray Louhi, nor will I betray my brother." Vanadis warned.

"Your Queen has never offended the Jotun and her daughter strives to free Lauefy's son, what reason would Laufey possibly have to turn you against her? As for your brother," Flosi grinned, "you may find he's more sympathetic to our cause than you know."

Vanadis again considered, the ache of Vinglunr's loss was still fresh in her heart. If I apply myself, maybe I can lose this pain? "Very well, teach me what you will."

"Excellent," said Flosi with a bow, "in return our Mistress requests you allow me to examine your connection to Dorte." He held a golden thread whose one end went into darkness and the other went into Vanadis' back. "In all her long years she has never seen a Haugbui bound to a person."

"Will you share your findings?" questioned Vanadis.

"I see no reason not to."

The seithkona smiled, "Then we have a deal."

Flosi examined Vanadis' thread. On closer inspection they found it was composed of tiny golden runes that flowed back and forth from Vanadis like the tide. Flosi jotted down notes on a scroll. While doing so he asked many questions of Vanadis' past with Dorte.

"I thought you know me better than I know myself?" mused Vanadis.

Flosi sighed, "There are some things that must be expressed with words. Now, if you please, answer my questions."

The conversation and examination was lengthy. Flosi's voice was smooth and his manner polite and witty. Furthermore, the seithkona felt no exhaustion, hunger or thirst. The time flew, the sun rose and soon was setting again.

A question struck Vanadis and she asked, "How long have I been asleep? I'll need to eat sometime."

Flosi waved his hand dismissively, "Time here is different. I swear I'll awaken you long before you starve. Besides," he rolled up his scroll and, with a snap of his fingers, lit it. "I've complied my findings." The note burned to ash on the hnefatafl table and then blew away in the wind.

"So you've sent them to Laufey," Vanadis concluded, "what did you find?"

"It would appear you've cursed yourself."

"How so?" the seithkona asked incredulously.

"Think back to when Dorte died, you wished dearly that it was not so, yes?"

Vanadis thought on that, she remembered clearly Dorte's death rattle as she lay in her arms and the look of hurt and fear on breath starved face. "Y-yes, I suppose I did."

"That was your first spell. Your grief and will germinated the seed for Dorte's rebirth. When she awoke her last desire took hold, a desire for vengeance, on the one who had killed her."

"Is there a way to end the spell?" asked Vanadis

"Yes, Dorte's utter destruction or the death of she who slew her."

"Can't we simply cut the thread?"

"Very difficult but possible," mused Flosi, "however, you'd both die."

"Then maybe you could teach me a spell I could use to fight her?"

Flosi deliberated this, then, with a nod, he said "Our Mistress is pleased with what we've discovered. I shall share some of her wisdom, now, pay attention..."

Flosi began to instruct Vanadis. He waved his hand and spectral lines formed a map of the nine worlds on the game table. For the next five dream nights he taught her the nature of souls and of Yggdrasil. Again Vanadis was drawn in by Flosi's voice and words, which held significance and meaning. She learned much.

As dawn was ending on the fifth night Flosi sat back and closed his eyes as if exhausted. "I've finished. Do something more for our mistress and I shall teach you again."

Vanadis shook her head, and cleared her thoughts, "You taught me lovely theory but no spells." she said dryly.

Flosi smirked, "Think on what I've taught you."

The seithkona did. Flosi's lore mixed with the incantations, meditations and dark knowledge that Louhi imparted. Vanadis saw clearly how they intersected and then her grey eyes widened in discovery. "Yes...of course... The flow of souls," she reached out and whispered an arcane word that expressed night and transition, the Ruby king, who sat at Flosi's feet, and the silver raider at hers, they shimmered and switched places.

"It won't guarantee your victory against the Haugbui but, should you ever find yourself surrounded, such a spell will be invaluable."

"Yes, I agree. Thank you very much." mused Vanadis.

"Now off you go." Flosi waved his hand.

***

Vanadis awoke lying on a bench. Sunlight streamed through the cracks in the log wall, flashing in her eyes, intensifying her headache. She groaned weakly and rolled over.

She felt a hot huffing breath on her check and then he neck. She opened one eye and saw Ormir regarding her with his usual reptilian inscrutableness. She reached out and scritched his neck and the drake hissed and leaned closer.

"Vanadis?" Ransu was suddenly standing over her. "Thank Ukko you're awake. I thought we'd lost you." His eyes seemed strained but he smiled with relief. "Up you go." He gently helped her to a seated position. "Drink this." He pressed a wineskin to her lips, she drank, the cool water easing her parched throat. "Ah, ah, aaah, not too much." He pulled it away.

"Thank you." said the Volsung.

She glanced around. They were in a small hunter's cabin. Skulls of stags, a bear and fish hung on the wall, as well as tattered fishing nets. "Where are we?"

"A hidden place." answered, Ransu, "We've been here for three days. If you didn't wake up today I'd have had that idiot brother of yours carry you to a healer."

"Three days?" Vanadis regarded Ransu closely. His air was one of a father caring for his daughter, she hugged him. "Well I'm up now."

He patted and then rubbed her back. He sniffed, "Aye. You've returned to us, that's all that matters."

When she had recovered, she sat back down and asked, "Where's my brother?"

"Outside fishing." Ransu answered. Then, as Vanadis rose he clapped his hands on her shoulders and pushed her down, "No, you sit. I'll get him."

"Thank you." Vanadis answered, she gripped the bench so her dizziness would not overcome her.

Before he left, the fisherman paused at the door. "What happened in Gotland, it still bothers him. He may say things...I'm sure he won't mean them."

Vanadis snorted, "Trust me, he can't put me through greater torment than what I've already suffered."

"Aye, I suppose that's true." Ransu gave her an earnest look, "Just know, no matter what happens between the two of you, your Uncle Ransu will be here as long as you need him."

Vanadis smiled in full honesty, "Good, I think I will."

Ransu stepped out the door. After a moment Vanadis could heard him shout, "Gamli, get in there, your sister's up." Then, "How in Ukko's name have you caught nothing?"

A moment later Gamli stepped inside but paused to shake his head at Ransu. He then took a seat and snapped his fingers. Ormir snaked away from Vanadis side to lay down at Gamli's feet. The smith stared down at her, his expression guarded. "Sister, I'm glad you're awake." His tone was overly cordial.

Vanadis' words hung on the back of her tongue. She considered Gamli's coolness towards her. It's not good to be awake. She contemplated. She forced herself to match his gaze and found anger simmering behind those blue eyes. Her grey eyes narrowed, No, I won't run form this. "There is something you should know." she said matter-of-factually. "Do you want to here it?"

Gamli nodded.

"What happened at Gotland is not the same as what happened at Kelifar..." she repeated her deductions from the dream. How the wooden terrors were strange, not something conjured with seith. How they had no connection to her or him. She ended with, "I don't know who was behind the attack, but they weren't summoned on my account."

Gamli turned from her, his thoughts silent behind his brooding. Ormir huffed and stretched his long neck up and put his head in Gamli's lap.

"As for what happened to Vinglunr. I couldn't hear his voice when I cast my fire shroud. I...would say he died before the black flame but," she shook her head, "I'm afraid I'd be lying to myself. I'll never forgive myself for what happened. I don't expect you to either." She wiped tears from the corners of her eyes and forced herself continue, "Gamli, I need to know, do you hate me? If you do..."

He suddenly lunged and embraced her in a hug, she could feel his body shake as he wept openly. "It's enough." He said, "That you didn't cause this, it's enough. Just, by Surt, swear to be more careful with your spells."

"I swear." Said Vanadis readily enough.

The Volsungs cried in each other's arms, venting their grief, and once their tears were spent, they were stronger for it.

CHAPTER 25

To win at hnefatafl, / you must see the future.
Play move by move and you'll suffer swift defeat.
Your king will die. / Your raid will fail.
The same goes with life, whoever said 'live for the moment' is a fool.

They stayed one more night. Ransu cooked a fish stew mixed with dried vegetables from the supplies and a few things he found in the bush. He insisted Vanadis eat slowly but take extra helpings. She, thanks to her hunger, found the meal absolutely delectable. Gamli brought in fresh firewood and they sat that night around the fire pit. Their talk focused on Pohjola and colorful characters such as Niklas and Vilma. They avoided all mention of Gotland and Vinglunr. Early the next morning, just as the sun was rising, Vanadis found her strength had returned. While Ransu and Gamli slept she stepped out into the fragrant spring air. Their small cabin was deep in a copes of trees, no path lead to it. Vanadis saw a wide river beyond and she pushed herself carefully through the prickly pine branches to get there, along the way she found the skute, which had been overturned and covered in brush. Finally she reached the river's edge. See saw no sign of man, only cheerful bird song and buzzing insects greeted her. She took this opportunity to wash and refresh herself.

After her wash was finished, she checked the supplies under the skute. Finding them plentiful she took a breakfast's worth of dried meat and berries. She made her way back to the cabin and stoked the fire pit. As Gamli and Ransu awoke she sprinkled her breakfast with ash, said a prayer to her father, mother, their entourage, Bera and Vinglunr, and tossed her breakfast into the flames. The fire flashed and for a moment Vanadis saw her people feasting. Her father and Bera feasted in good health. Her mother was missing, in truth, she did not care. A warm feeling of gratitude washed over her from her spirit entourage. She felt nothing from her former love.
She stared up and whispered, "I pray you made it to Valhalla."

"I hear Asgardians are not freeloaders." commented Ransu, glaring at the remains of the offering.

Vanadis shot him a glare, placed her fingers on her lips and shhhed. "They'll hear you. I need their strength to power my spells and remember,Bera helped bale."

"Fine, I apologize." Ransu said staring around for ghosts. "Now, excuse me, I must catch breakfast for the living."

As he left Gamli sat beside his sister holding a spear, one that had a spiraling red gold inlay along the shaft and whose spearhead was the same. He offered it to her. "This is Burning Mind, it's yours."

Vanadis took it and regarded it with wonder. Despite its solid oak construction it felt mysteriously light in her hand. A thrum of power ran through it, the seithkona instantly recognized as a potent tool for spell casting.

"This is what you were working on when we left Torino."

Gamli nodded, "You need a better weapon than a staff. I finished it in Gotland when a madness came over me."

"A madness?" questioned his sister.

"The same I fell under when I forged Scorn." He answered, hefting the pommel of his sword.

"That's what Bera meant when she said you drove her out." admiring the spear further she added, "It is a rather useful madness."

"I comes for a dire source..." he frowned and suddenly looked guilty, "In light of it, I was wrong to be angry with you."

Vanadis touched his arm, "I was furious at myself. Vinglunr..." a pained expression crossed her face.

"What's done is done. We move on." her brother said firmly.

"Alright but can you tell me of your 'mysterious source'?"

Gamli looked even more uncomfortable, "N-no. I have to come to grips with it first."

'I heard you swear to Surt earlier.' Vanadis mused. Given her connection to Laufey, this didn't concern her. "Then I won't not press. When you're ready I will be here to listen."

"Thank you." said the smith. "I also have these." He reached into a pouch on his belt and brought out an axe, shield and wolf hide armor, they were tiny enough to be doll toys.

"I doubt they'll fit." observed Vanadis dryly.

"Take them." her brother grumbled.

"But I have no doll..." the words died on Vanadis lips as soon as her brother laid the miniatures in her hands, she felt a slight tremble of force from them.

"They're for Bera." Gamli muttered. "When you summoned her I noticed she wears the twin of your cloths and weapons. I'm proud of Burning Mind but I think Bera would prefer axe and shield."

Vanadis closed her hands around the miniatures, closed her eyes and felt out their power. She brought to mind the summoned Bera and saw her well equipped with hide armor, the shield and the axe. In the back of the Seithkona's soul Bera giggled with glee. Vanadis grinned at her brother, "She's very happy with them." She tucked the miniatures away into one of her own pouches."

Ransu returned with a large fish. "This," he shook it, "is for us. Don't give it to the dead."

Vanadis laughed, "Fine, let's eat."

Ransu cooked the fish to perfection, they ate and washed it down with a little wine. When their meal was finished the fisherman addressed the siblings. "We can't hide in this cabin forever. We need to go, the question is where? Should we can continue to Danevirke, or has this quest become too costly? South is fraught with danger." warned Ransu. "Öland lies very near. We can avoid it by sailing east and then south, but then we'll be betwixt that cursed Gotland and the Curonians."

Gamli looked to his sister.

Vanadis looked to Ransu, "You want to sail back for Pohjola?"

"It'd be the wisest course." the fisherman admitted.

Vanadis thought on this. She rubbed the bone ring Louhi had given her

"You were out quite a while. The Fire Wolf may might no longer be in Danevirke." added Ransu.

Vanadis tapped Salli's scroll case and ponded. Finally the she regarded both the fisherman and her brother, "I have to find her, for Louhi's sake. However, I won't hold either of you to this, if you wish to sail back home so be it, I'll find my own way."

Gamli snorted and Ormir huffed, "You won't be rid of me that easily. Whatever comes, we'll face it together." He shared a smile with her.

"This is Hiisi's road." Ransu cursed, but then, with reluctance, he added, "However, in honor of your father and mother, I'll stay with you, come what may."

"Thank you both." said Vanadis warmly. Then, leaning closer to Ransu she asked "Our choices are Öland or the pirates? I'd rather risk pirates. What do you say?"

Ransu stroked his bristled chin thoughtfully. "Neither will do." he said with distaste. "I suppose..." he seized the fire stick and drew a semi-circle on the dirt floor. Beside it he drew a small oblong and a larger one. Tapping the smaller, "Here's Öland," tapping the larger, "here's Gotland. We're here." He tapped the edge of the semi-circle slightly up of 'Öland.' "For now we can't sail, there's no way to avoid this." He drew several circles around the two islands. "We can ride." he drew a lined diagonally through the semi-circle "Here," he tapped the lower end of the semi-circle, "we can secure a boat and sail for Danevirke."

"We have no horses." commented Gamli.

"Between the jarl's skatt and our skute we have more than enough to buy them." proposed Ransu. "Then, when we find a southern town, we can sell the horses for a ship or passage."

Vanadis measured carefully Ransu's plan against the other options. "I like it, we ride."

***

With that, the three gathered their things and all the supplies they could carry. They then struck east on foot. They journey through the forest was hard going until Ransu found a path. They followed it and came to a prosperous farming town at dusk. Before they entered Vanadis conjured new guises. When they approached the great hall they were regarded with suspicion for word of the dread outlaw Gamli the Serpent had proceeded them.
    However, when Vanadis spun them a tale of how they were bounty hunters on the vargs' trail,

they were welcomed with open arms. It helped that Vanadis had perfected her disguise spell and she safely layered a spirit over Ormir. He was disguised as a huge dog, a sennenhund to be precise. They spent an evening in the hall where they were treated to a fine supper. In the morning they were given a hearty breakfast and fresh milk. Together Ransu and Vanadis secured two sturdy horses and a wagon for an excellent price with trade in of the skute.

The ride took many days. They kept to roads far inland. They stayed in a few other halls, each time in different guises. Along the way they were told all about the horrifying revenge of the Volsungs. How the witch Vanadis cursed the Gotland Thing. How Gamli the Serpent breathed life into the trees and sent them to attack his ancient foe. How the two made love on top of a pile of corpses; both siblings nearly lost their manner and meal after hearing that. Ransu thanked Ukko there were no such rumors about him. Finally the three reached a large port town. There they sold the horses and cart. With this money they bought a damaged knarr which Gamli swiftly repaired.

They set sail southeast, leaving Gotaland behind them.

One afternoon they sailed along the shore of Skane. Vanadis remembered well the Valkyrie Fastny's words "What I do know is that the Barrow Bowl can only be used in Skane. If one such as yourself were to search there, I'm certain you'd find it." The shore was wreathed in fog, beyond lay lonely shadows of stony hills. The air was still, aside from the occasional far too human bird cry. Figures fished on the shore, but when the fog thinned they vanished. In the back of her mind Vanadis could hear the whispered murmur of a thousand souls.

It took no small amount of courage for her to say, "I recall that Vargeisa has an interest in Skane. Perhaps we should dock here?"

"No." Said Ransu resolutely. "By Ahto, by Illmatar, and by Ukko we are not entering that land. If we do I am certain that Hiisi will stab out our eyes and we'll drown in the River of Tuonela. You have no choice, I am keeping course for Danevirke."

Vanadis glanced at her brother for support.

"I agree with Ransu." He rumbled.

So, they continued on.

They sailed along the coast of Zealand and found the towns friendly. The stories of Gotland reached here but they were told more with an air of wonder than one of terror. The weather became less rain soaked and sunnier. The three bought lighter garb and stowed away their winter clothes.

They left Zealand behind and found Jutland laying on the horizon. As they sailed closer the sun sank in the west. In the crimson sunset they beheld Danevirke. Before them was the eastern edge of a prodigious wall so tall that it dwarfed the port city of Hedeby on its northern side. On the southern end lay an expansive field that was littered with broken siege engines.

The siblings were gobsmacked.

Ransu chuckled, "Impressive, isn't it? Your father and I were also speechless when we first laid eyes on the Danevirke. We wondered if such a wall was necessary." He gestured to the broken tools of war, "As you can see they are. The White God won't not stand any other deities, so he sends his warriors to crush the strong and turn the weak."

"Can they not simply ride around?" asked Vanadis.

Ransu laughed, "Not at all, the Danevirke stretches across the peninsula. If the White God wants Jutland his followers must sail around and face a fleet on either end." He shook his head disdainfully, "Christians may wear the symbol of the fish but they're not sea folk like us; their ships are slow and useless."

Vanadis threw guises upon them again and they made camp on one of the northern islands. There they found a hall full of watchers and were questioned thoroughly. Vanadis' lie of wishing to see the home of their lost father, who fell on the wall, nearly failed. When the official hinted for a bribe, Vanadis acted aloof and insulted. The bribe was a ruse, having passed the test the three were given hospitality for the night and a promise of safe passage on the morn.

The next morn they sailed into the eastern port of Danevirke, the great city of Hedeby. Amongst the fishermen they found a few longboats making maneuvers. The watch hall provided a warrior to vouch for them, with her help, they avoided suspicion and docked in the busy harbor. The murmur of the crowd mixed with the cries of military drills.

Their guide handed the three leather cords on which hung an iron symbol of Thor's hammer. "Wear these always and all will know you are no Christian spy."

Vanadis examined the trinket closely, she felt no spirits course through it. She glanced at her brother who held it up and peered at it closely.

"This has no magic." he said, "What prevents them from wearing it?"

The guardswoman smirked knowingly, "The White god is a jealous one, should one of his own wear another's symbol, even in jest, even in ruse, he'll be tossed into Muspeiheim to burn forever."

The three flinched at that.

"Well? You're no Christians, yes?" asked the guard.

The three donned the symbol.

'This won't anger Laufey, will it?' Vanadis thought to her spark.

'Don't be foolish. You may wear whatever trinkets you like, as long as you do not mock our Mistress.' answered Flosi.

The guard smiled at them, "Good to see you're right minded. I pray you find the solace you seek and perhaps," she said eyeing Gamli, "a new purpose? We welcome all brave men who come to defend the North."

"I'll consider it, thank you." said the smith.

The guard smiled, bowed, and made her leave.

When she had gone Gamli held the amulet out, looking ill at ease.

Vanadis nudged him and whispered, "Pretend it's not there."

"That'll be hard when Thor smites me for being blessed by Surt." he whispered back.

"Thor's got better things to do than to pay us heed." hissed Vanadis.

"Children," cut in Ransu, "let's focus on our quest. The sooner it's done the sooner we return home." He turned his attention to the wall and the siblings did likewise. Up close it was awe inspiring. It was as wide as a hall and as tall as four. It was constructed out of huge blocks of mortared stone. Towers ran up it at regular intervals. Guard houses leaned against it. It stretched along the southern end of the port town and presumably well beyond.

"You're omen, did it show you where in Danevirke we might find Vargeisa?" asked Ransu.

"Sadly no." Vanadis answered with concern.

"We'll have trouble finding her then. The Danevirke stretches west all the way to the Orse Sea. The Fire Wolf could be in anywhere in between, even inside the wall."

"Inside the Wall?" questioned Gamli.

"Aye, it holds many chambers and corridors. That way warriors may assemble on the ramparts, or sneak out to lay waste Christendom."

"How do you know this?" asked Vanadis.

Ransu smirked, "I told you that your father and I visited Danevirke, yes? We fought many Christians for skatt. Back then we lived by our might, wits, and the providence of our gods, they were good times." He chuckled, "Your lie could have easily been truth."

"If Kvistr died on the wall, we would have never been born." Vanadis answered dryly.

"I'm glad he survived." added Gamli.

Ransu laughed, "So am I. Now, what's your plan?"

Vanadis paused, her thoughts churning. Finally she said, "We'll travel west and ask for Vargeisa in every hall. We'll claim our party and hers found the lost treasures of Wayland Smith in Myrkvid. We feel Vargeisa won too large a share and now we want to renegotiate. This way we'll catch word of her and she'll catch word of us. We'll seek each other out and, when we meet, we complete our mission."

"A sound plan." mused Ransu.

"We'll start our search here."

With that, the three split up and explored Hedeby. Ransu walked amongst old haunts, visited some old loves, and asked of the Fire Wolf. He was welcomed warmly but found no information. Gamli toured the merchant stalls looking for specialized ore. He found nothing that compared with Zaidaan's wears. He asked about Vargeisa and also found nothing. Vanadis weaved her way through the clustered houses and massive crowds to visit affluent halls. Her guise, manner, and dress with the silken sleeves, fit in nicely. She inquired on Vargeisa but found no information. However, she was invited, with her companions, to spend a night in a jarl's hall. She and her brother accepted the invitation. Ransu spent the night with an old friend. A pleasant evening passed. In the morning Vanadis and Gamli's host bought their knarr for a generous sum and sold them horses at a discount. With that the three rode off along the wall, Ormir rushing beside them, once again, in the guise of a hound.

As the sun set, they came across a well-armed, outpost. They were questioned, Vanadis answered with her story of chasing Vargeisa. The guardians were less than impressed, until Ransu offered a donation for the wall, then the three were welcomed in heartily. They spent the night. Vanadis inquired once more about the Fire Wolf, offering another donation as she did so.

An old guardsman, Gusir, stroked his beard and answered, "I recall her. Fair and tall she is. Her companions are a scraggly burglar and a mysterious seithkona."

Ransu and Gamli looked up from their meal and heeded his words.

"Yes, that's them." Vanadis answered, leaning closer to the old man. "Though be cautious of her and her companions, they're much stronger than they look."

The veteran chuckled, "Aye, this I already know. This past winter my patrol ran into Vargeisa and her strange war band on the south side of the wall. The Fire Wolf carried Leofing's head."

"Leofing?" asked the hidden Volsung.

"A warrior in service to the hand of the White God, Emperor Otto. Leofing gave us much trouble, he sent many of my brothers to Valhalla. It was good to see him dead." the vet chuckled.

"Vargeisa slew him then?"

Gursir nodded.

"Where is she now?"

"She offered fealty to King Gorm, and, given her deed, he accepted. As far as I understand she's stationed at the castle."

"Castle?" Vanadis enquired.

"A stone fortress, its make and build stolen from the Christians. It's as tall as Danevirke and as vast as an entire village. Like a Jotun's home." The vet's tone grew reverent when he mentioned it.

"How?" cut in Gamli, looking flabbergasted. "The wall, this castle, how was it all built?"

The old vet stroked his beard, "Before Gorm the Danevirke was no wall, merely a line of fortifications. When Gorm took the throne he demanded resources and men from King Harald Fair Hair in the north. Already embroiled in conflict with Bjorn Eriksson and not wishing to face a Christian onslaught, he acquiesced. Men, supplies and stone were brought down and the wall was built. Free men designed her and many thralls gave their lives craft the Danevirke."

"I find it strange this could be built in a lifetime." Gamli muttered.

"Yet there it is, we lie in its very shadow," challenged Gursir.

Vanadis cut in before her brother could respond, "It is the wonder of Midgard. Thor must have blessed its construction."

The old veteran considered this and nodded. "Of course he did." To Gamli he added, "Now, you have your answer."

Gamli glared at his sister but asked no further questions.

The night passed. In the morning, they were treated to a flavorless but filling breakfast. When it came time for them to leave, their host instructed, "Follow the Danevirke west for one more day. At evening you'll reach the castle, if your Vargeisa isn't there someone inside may know her whereabouts. Need I warn you about starting trouble?"

"You do not." said Vanadis politely. "We'll keep our negotiations civil."

"Good to hear." said the vet with a smile, "Now off with you."

With that they struck off.

Danevirke Castle came steadily into view. They first saw its tower which rose three times as high as the wall itself. It brought to mind the lonely high seat of Odin, Hliðskjálf, from which he watched the Nine Worlds. "Gorm thinks highly of himself." chuckled Vanadis. Then the fortress came into view and Gusir's words proved true. It was as tall as the Danevirke and as big as a village. It was incomplete. Large holes were open in some of the upper walls, and, in many places, wooden scaffolding hung naked. At its feet lay a guard city. There were numerous halls, outside of which warriors sparred and practiced. There were farmer fields which lay dark, seeded and ready for growth. In the center was a maze of market stalls, much noise and chatter arose from them as the workers on the castle arrived to spend skatt for good food and drink.

Vanadis rubbed her eyes in disbelief at the sight.

Ransu observed it with a quiet admiration.

Gamli glared at it and then at his sister. "You must believe Thor constructed this himself." He fumed.

Vanadis sighed, "You were annoying Gusir. Yes, he seemed civil, but he'd just as soon murder us if we proved too much of a bother."

"It's true." added Ransu with a yawn. "I slept with one eye open all night." Then a thought struck him and he asked the smith, "Why so doubtful? You yourself forged a sword in a mere hours, is it so hard to imagine an army could build this wall and fortress in a few years?"

Gamli snarled and shook his head, "An army of Waylands and Ilmarinens perhaps. If King Gorm had access to such he would have wiped out the Christians and had no need for his wall."

"Then perhaps it was the hand of a god?" Vanadis suggested.

Gamli frowned and peered at the Danevirke distrustfully, "This is of neither god nor Jotun. There's something wrong about it, it should not be."

"Should not be?" his sister laughed. "It's sitting right before us. I trust you have a better argument?"

Gamli scowled, "It's not something I know, it's something I feel."

Vanadis was about to retort when Ransu singled them both to hush. He nodded down the road.

Riding up it were a troop of a dozen warriors, fully armed.

"Let's make way." Vanadis suggested. The three and Ormir stepped off the path to let the soldiers by.

As the troop drew close the man at their head, one who wore chain mail and carried a sword on his hip, raised is hand and the warriors halted. "You there, strangers, what brings you to Danevirke Castle?"

"A business partner awaits. We hope to speak to her." answered Vanadis.

"Who is this partner?" the commander demanded.

"Vargeisa the Fire Wolf." statedd Vanadis. "She has something of ours, we wish to peacefully negotiate its return."

The headman looked stunned, but only for a second. "Arrest them."

The warriors leapt off their horses and drew their weapons. Scorn flew out of Gamli's sheath and he hefted his shield. Ransu had his crossbow out, somehow already strung and ready.

"Hold!" cried Vanadis, stepping between the two groups. She glanced at the commander and said, "Let me guess, she's caused trouble?"

"You could say that." he answered guardedly.

"How typical." Vanadis scoffed. "Vargeisa brings chaos wherever she goes. If you're after her you'll need us."

The commander regarded her dubiously.

"Must we fight?" asked Ransu, his aim leveled at the nearest foe. "If we do you'll kill us but I guarantee we'll drop half of you in Tuonela."

Gamli yelled and hammered his shield, causing the warriors to jump back.

Ormir lifted his head and let out a choir like roar, most strange for a hound.

"Vargeisa is very good at making potent enemies." Vanadis said, her voice echoing with grim confidence. "Why kill each other? We should work together."

The commander pondered this and then sheathed his sword. "Ketill, Raudr, Thorgir, escort them to the Castle. I trust the King would like a word."

"Most wise." answered the Seithkona.

The commander grunted, then yelled "Onward!" and galloped off. The rest, aside from Ketill, Raudr and Thorgir rode off after him.

"Right then," said Thorgir, a large man with a scarred face, "off to the castle."

Ransu tucked away his crossbow, Gamli sheathed Scorn. Vanadis giggled, "You heard him. Let's meet the King."

The three guards rode slightly ahead and deigned not to talk to their guests.

Ransu nudged his horse closer to Vanadis and whispered, "Are you daft?"

Gamli closed in on the other side and added, "We are Vargeisa's allies...aren't we?"

"We are." whispered Vanadis determinedly. "This way we can keep an eye on her foes."

"I'm ill at ease with this plan." rumbled Gamli.

"Be cautious," advised Ransu, "Gorm's no fool, he won't be easily deceived."

***

Soon enough they were in the shadow of the fortress and the yawning cyclopean gates lay before them. Their escort rode in casually. The three, however, could not help but gawk as they followed.

"This is one place I've never been." said Ransu. Then, in a quitter voice he added, "I pray I'll be able to leave."

"Not right." muttered Gamli.

Vanadis was about to tell the two of them to cease being children when suddenly she was knocked off her horse. The mare reared above her, her hooves came down, just missing Vanadis' head. The horse kicked back and then ran, miraculously not trampling the seithkona. Vanadis had no time to rejoice, her body thrashed out of her control. A howl of fear issued from her lips in a voice not her own. She caught a glimpse of both Gamli and Ormir in their natural appearances, their masking spirits having fled.

***

Suddenly, her spirit and senses sunk into the floor and all went dark. She felt cold, hard hands seize her arms and legs. Her heart racing she cried in fear and tried to wrench out of their grip. She was unsuccessful and the hands pulled her further downward. Terror rose within her...

'Fear will be your end. You must move past it or die.' Lohi's words. In the early months of Vanadis' training she had been plagued by night terrors, they weakened her defenses and spirits ran her through the Sariola. One in particular, a nasty haunt, one who had starved in Sariola's maze, nearly tossed her off the balcony. Louhi had pulled her from the brink.

The memory gave Vanadis strength and she banished her terror. The seithkona breathed and ran a Pohjalander's child's song through her mind. The spell complete the she shank to the size of a doll and slipped the grasping hands. Vanadis then clapped her palms and willed the black flame; it flared around her releasing a cacophony of screams from her tormentors. She silently commanded the fire to turn white and it radiated out a bright luminescence. What she saw boggled the mind.

The grey stone around her flexed and relaxed as if it breathed. A groaning echoed about her, not unlike wood twisting and stretching, but also not unlike souls in agony. Before her the stone was blackened, out of it hung twisted, charred hands. Beneath her the stone sunk like a long, deep throat, which no doubt led to something more ominous in the gut.

'This is insane! Stone doesn't breathe, doesn't burn.' As she thought this the rock melted away and she witnessed. . . It was beyond description, she struggled to understand, the Volsung's mind and perceptions were stretched to the tearing point.

'I must return.' Vanadis urged herself awake. The force of her will shot her soul upwards at incredible speed. She struck the waking world with the force of one hitting the sea form a long dive. She gasped awake and, for a moment, was addled.

***

"Welcome back." The voice was unfamiliar. It sounded rough and confident.

Sight came back to Vanadis and she saw a stone ceiling a short distance above her. She laid on her back on a hard bench. She touched her temple and to her chagrin found her circlet missing. Otherwise her clothes were intact. The air was cold and stale. Light from flickering torches illuminated the wall beside her.

She turned to find a middle aged man standing before her. He was tall and lanky. His clothes were of noble cut and of crimson and black. The crest of a red eye was stitched on his breast. His nose was long. His black mustache was thicker than his short beard. His head was smooth and bald. He regarded her pleasantly. "Impressive, seithkona who succumb to the Wall hardly ever return."

Vanadis glanced around and confirmed that they indeed shared a small cell.

She slowly pushed herself up. "Who are you? Where's my friend and my brother?"

"Drafli the Eye, godi of Heimdall and sorcerer of King Gorm of Jutland." He gestured behind him.

Standing beyond the bars was a commanding man with long grey hair and beard. He had severe features and a severe expression. His eyes were keen and intense. He wore a steel crown adorned with three rubies. Flanking him were six guards in leather armor, carrying swords.

"Sire." Vanadis with a bow.

"You who know Vargeisa. Who are you?" Gorm's tone bespoke of power and an intolerance for delay.

""Vanadis the Cursed." the seithkona answered honestly.

"'The Cursed'?" asked Gorm. "You make light of your situation?"

"My lord?" asked a guard at his side.

"Yes, Forni?" responded the King with slight annoyance.

"I've heard of her. She's an Alands' varg."

"An outlaw?" the King chuckled, "I suppose then the name fits."

Vanadis bit her tongue so as not to add you have no idea.

The King turned back to her, "So varg, how do you know the Fire Wolf?"

Start with the truth, spin falsehood out of it, plotted Vanadis. "We had a joint venture in Myrkvid."

"Go on." urged the King.

Vanadis told her tale from the encounter in traitor bay. Gorm urged her to be brief. Vanadis responded with only the barest facts. Her desire for sanctuary in Pohjola. Vargeisa's quest for knowledge. Their encounter with the Valkyries.

"Valkyries?" Drafli commented in disbelief. "You seem hardly worthy."

Vanadis reigned in her glare. She paused in thought.

"If this is a waste of time your punishment will be severe." warned the King.

"I spoke to Alruna, Wayland's lost love." she said, watching close the King's reaction.

He frowned in thought and looked to Drafli. The godi gestured for her to continue.

"They hide in Myrkvid because they've fled Odin's service. To move out from the fog they need to wear human skin."

The guards regarded Vanadis with sudden disgust, she had hurt their piety. Gorm and Drafli however, shared a knowing glance.

To his guards, the King ordered, "None of this leaves these walls."

"Yes, sire." they said as one.

He turned back to the seithkona, "Continue."

Vanadis told of how her lies saved her and the confrontation with Vargeisa. She told of Vargeisa's binding of her and Fastny. She lied in saying Vargeisa asked how to revive her lost sister, the Rainbow Maiden. She told the truth of Fastny's words on the Barrow Bowl. She lied by claiming Vargeisa left Vanadis to rot.

"I see, so that's how the Fire Wolf discovered it..." mused Drafli.

Gorm nodded. He then asked the seithkona, "How did you survive and what brings you here?"

"My brother and Ransu found me and cut me loose. We escaped Myrkvid and survived a hard winter. In the spring we found ourselves with no sanctuary and no prospects. Vengeance is all we have left. So we've tracked the Fire Wolf through rumor and vision here to your steps." Vanadis drew on her still grieving heart to season her words with bitterness.

"Quite a tale." commented Drafli.

Gorm stroked his long beard and pondered. None dared interrupt his thoughts and an ominous silence hung.
Finally, the King regarded the Volsung and said, "It was through no small effort that Drafli found the Barrow Bowl. We used it to gather the Nameless Volva's wisdom with which we built the Danevirke. The Bowl is priceless, if you aid Drafli in retrieving it, and if he succeeds in returning it, you will find sanctuary here."

"Can we trust one such as this?" The sorcerer asked.

"I deign we can trust her more than your Alands apprentice." Gorm shot back.

Drafli flinched.

Gorm gestured to Vanadis and said, "This varg and her companions have nowhere to go. They cannot cause any more damage than Starkad, and even if they spill our secrets none would listen to them. Loyalty to us means vengeance and life for them."

"I cannot find fault in your wisdom, my lord." answered the sorcerer with humility.

Gorm locked gazes with Vanadis and said, "I will free you, your brother, your friend, and yes, even, your beast. I will return to you your treasures and arms. However, understand that this man," Gorm pointed to Drafli, "holds your fate in his hands. You wish to find favor with me, find favor with him. Fail this and I shall bury you in the Wall myself."

"I understand perfectly, my lord." Vanadis said with a deep bow, a slight tinge of fear in her voice. To Drafli, she added, "I am at your command."

The sorcerer regarded her for a moment and said "Very well, come with me."

CHAPTER 26

Glory and duty, | they are not the same.
Those who say otherwise merely wish to use you for their own ends.
The good are not glorious. | It takes evil to shed blood for the sake of fame.
Heed well my blasphemy, use it to tell false friend from true.

Many nights earlier, Lemminkäinen stood on the pebbled beach glaring at the remains of his ship, an aura of rage about him. Pieces of the red hull, seemingly chewed apart by human teeth, floated in the moonlit bay. The figurehead, a ridiculously large red dragon maw, lay on its side in the shallow water, one green eye staring balefully at its master. Beside him lay one of the Kalevalen warriors, his head had been crushed. Above the corpse was Lemminkäinen's right hand, soaked in blood and specked with bits of brain.

Hardegon sat on the short cliff behind him. In lantern light he examined his drawn blade, the stain of Troll blood still on it.

Starkad leaned on the rocky wall nearby. "We should leave." he hissed, "I myself have delved into the depths of madness and understand well enough to know that he," he nodded towards Lemminkäinen, "is not sane."

Hardegon frowned at his sword. Placing the Lantern down he once again ran his cloth, a scrap taken from one of the troll shirts, along his blade. The stain was not touched, it was as if the metal had always been crimson.

"Hardegon!" Starkad urged. "Do you not heed me?"

'I prefer the shine of steel. Still the mark of a troll death is a mark of glory.' He sheathed is weapon.

"Everyone else has left. If you do not answer, I will go as well."

"Lemminkäinen," called Hardegon, "Starkad and I are leaving this Troll's nest. Will you join us?"

The huge warrior grunted and moved not.

"You will pay Vertti's family well, yes?" asked the swordsman. "He was simply trying to talk sense to you."

Lemminkäinen let out a heavy sigh but did nothing else.

Hardegon stood, "Let's go brother, mayhap we can find a town and a new ship?"

"Finally, you show wisdom."

***

With that, the two struck off. They went the wooded way and traveled east until they reached the shore. They then followed it south all night and for the entire following morn, out of wood and around crag. In the afternoon they stumbled upon a port town. When they reached the master's hall they were welcomed in, given a bench and both fell into a deep slumber.

They were awoken that evening for supper. It was a modest but hearty meal. Hardegon told the master of the town about his quest to slay Gamli the Serpent. He also showed the mark of troll's blood on his blade.

"Such a wonder." Master Berg commented as he ran a wetted cloth along the sword blade. Its perfect deep crimson was unmarred. It smelt slightly of corrupted metal, blood. He handed the sword back to the jarl's son. "A poisoner and a Troll wife, I pray that you continue to peruse such villains, Midgard would be better without them."

"Even if they were to run into Jormungand's maw, I would follow." said Hardegon with a fierce grin.

"I would not." added Starkad. "Because, Jormungand's fangs and poison would be sufficient to see justice served."

The hall laughed.

"You know where they head next?" asked Master Berg.

The swordsman shook his head, "We only know what Väinämöinen's told us. They have left

Pohjola to work more evil."

"The old wizard has done so much and we have repaid him only with the death of his countrymen. I'd be loath to ask him for more." added Starkad.

Hardegon nodded "Aye. This is business is between Nibelung and Volsung, Kalevala need no longer be involved."

"Just as in the old days." Berg said with admiration. A thought struck him, "I have council if you would hear it."

"Of course." answered the jarl's son magnanimously.

Berg leaned in close, as if sharing a prized secret. "If you heed my advice I shall supply you with a ship and crew. Find a Helsingland volva by the name of Ida Loftrdottir. Pay her well and she will ask the gods where you might find the Serpent."

At this Hardegon looked to his brother.

Starkad shrugged, "His words are sound. Of course, I will cast the runes as we journey but I doubt my skill will exceed a volva's."

Hardegon stood and clasped arms with Berg. "We shall heed you friend. Know that when skalds sing of my quest your kindness in it will not be forgotten."

***

The next morning Master Berg outfitted the brothers with a karve and 10 men to sail her. With a sturdy ship, abundant supplies and a hearty crew they struck off. The spring rains would have slowed them down but Starkad drew the N rune and held its power, filling their sails with wind and ensuring swift passage.

When they reached Kalevala, they found the sight of the beautiful city refreshing but it also brought the brothers regret and sorrow. To the crew's chagrin, they ordered the ship to pass her by.

Every few mornings, Starkad cast runes and each toss resulted with him brooding over the stones.

"Ill tidings, brother?" Hardegon asked.

"I'm uncertain." answered the sorcerer. "Ask our questions to the volva and her answer may reveal if my fears are proven or lifted."

Eventually, they turned west and sailed down a wide river into a thick forest. Soon after they came upon the logging town of Lofot which rested in a manmade clearing. When greeted Hardegon asked of Ida and was directed to a winding path into the woods.

While Berg's men took advantage of Lofot's hospitality Hardegon and Starkad followed the trail. They walked its meandering way through the afternoon and to the sunset. They had just considered setting camp when they stumbled upon a large hide tent at the top of a tall rocky hill. Sitting outside was an old woman whose dress and manner was rough and sturdy, as if she had lived out in this wilderness for years. Before her was a camp fire, hanging over it was a pot, from which she stirred a thick stew.

She glanced up at the brothers, "You're just in time for supper. Please sit." She gestured to two chairs that were set by the fire.

"You're Ida?" asked Hardegon.

"Aye." she said, "I already know what brings you here, meet my price and I'll aid you."

Hardegon grinned, "Then we are pleased to share a meal with you."

The brothers sat and Ida poured them stew. As they ate Ida asked them of news of the outside word. Hardegon told her of the Nibelung alliance with Bjorn Eriksson and their successful battles with Harald Fair Hair and their successful raids against the Baltic Tribes. He told her of the uneasy truce between Bjorn and Harald Fair Hair. Starkad shared tidings from Danevirke and Kalevala. How Danevirke secured funds and aid from Harald and how Kalevala was still locked in a deadly stalemate with Pohjola. Hardegon finished with the tale of his uncle's death and the details of his quest for justice on Gamli the Serpent.

Ida sopped her stew with black bread and devoured it. "I thank you for the tidings. I get few visitors and spend precious little time in Lofot."

"Why not simply live in the town?" asked Hardegon.

Ida laughed bitterly. "I always tell the truth, whether it be good or Ill. I predicted the misfortunes of Lofot's current master, he knows I am useful but cannot stand my presence. I also know he shall outlive me, so I live here." She gestured to her camp and the vast woodland expanse it overlooked. In a gentler tone she added, "Still, it's not so bad. Skadi has been kind to me, life here is exhilarating and true. Not like the soft lives of the loggers downhill."

Hardegon smiled, "The Goddess of the Hunt and Mountains, wife of Nord master of the sea. A fine patroness."

"Aye," Ida shot Hardegon a knowing look. "As a Jotun she is an outsider to the Aesir, such as I am an outsider in my home. Such connection is comfort." She then stood and lifted the flap of her tent, "Hardegon the Trusted, enter, pay my price and I shall tell you where you may find Gamli the Serpent."

Hardegon rose, to Starkad he said, "Wait here, when I return we shall know where our quarry lay."

***

Hardegon and Ida entered her tent. It was spacious and tidy. Hanging from the support pools were feathers and tiny squirrel and rooster skulls. In the very back was a small fire pit. The volva walked around this and sat at the far end. She gestured for the jarl's son to sit across from her.

"You are no simpering prince." She said amicably, "Therefore I charge you a mere 250 skatt, half my normal price."

Hardegon flinched at that. Still, he opened his pouch and pulled out a mixture of coins, gems and an emerald ring. "Will this suffice?" he asked holding them out to her.

Ida accepted the cache and examined it closely. With a smile she said, "Yes, indeed it will."

"I mean no offence, I'm merely curious, but why would one such as yourself need a princely sum?"

Ida considered him for a long moment and stated, "Your reputation precedes you, Hardegon. I know that at one time you were bribed a considerable amount to betray Bjorn Eriksson on behalf of Harald Fair Hair. I also know you delivered the bribe and the briber to the feet of King Bjorn himself. Now that I see your manner I believe such a tale, you can be trusted. Therefore, I feel comfortable telling you that this skatt is not for me."

"For your kin, then?"

Ida shook her head and said, "I collect it on behalf of Skadi. She has deemed that a destined warband will brave these woods when Ragnarok fills them with wolves. The destined shall stumble across my cache and gain fortune that will spring them to greater deeds in the end times."

Hardegon laughed approvingly. "I see, then, I am happy to have contributed to such a noble cause."

Ida used flint and tinder to light her fire. "Your generosity will be rewarded; I will direct you to the Serpent." She frowned and dropped bundles of herbs and flowers into the flame. "I warn you, I may see other things as well, terrifying portents, you will gain the knowledge you seek but may leave worse for it."

"Odin himself has blessed my quest, for his favor I will brave anything." Hardegon answered resolutely.

Ida raised an eyebrow but did not challenge his claim. She waved the rising smoke towards her and closed her eyes. "Then sit and listen Hardegon. I shall fall into the weave of fate and see where your thread leads."

Hardegon waited in silence as the volva sat and drew in the bitter fumes. After a few moments she began to mutter in a strange tongue. Her words sometimes soft as flowers, and sometimes harsh as bristles. She then began to sway from side to side, she let out a guttural groan. Finally her eyes flashed open, they were milk white. She opened her mouth and spoke as if far away. "Hardegon Truvorson of the blood of Gunnar and Helgi. You shall face your Volsung foe in the Mounds of Skane. If that be not sufficient throw all your will into the hunt and you will find him again. However, beware Truvorson, for whether or not you find Gamli your thread is short. Next year you will most certainly die be it by sword, spear or sickness. Your path to Valhalla will be determined by what you do in the few seasons you have left."

Her words washed over Hardegon with an undeniable certainty. He felt a shock of fear run through him. So soon? He thought. How can I build a legacy worthy of Valhalla in such a short time? The answer was obvious, he remembered Odin's raven tossing him the king piece, he recalled the Serpent running just out of his grasp.

He felt a light touch on his shoulder. He glanced up to see Ida, now returned from her trance, regarding him with sorrow. "I'm sorry," she said, "I choose not what see, I merely relate it."

"What did you see?" Hardegon asked, a tremor in his voice.

"I saw you clash with large man with red hair, wielding a green sword in the Mounds of Skane. I saw you clash with the same man on a mighty longship. I also saw you trembling and pale with sickness."

Hardegon swatted her hand away, "How can I fight and be ill?"

Ida drew herself up with hurt pride and answered, "It is the ultimatum of the gods. You must find a worthy death soon or be condemned to Niflheim."

These words rung true to Hardegon. "O-of course. It is the same with everyone. I simply have less time."

"Seek the Serpent." Ida urged. "Killing him will please Odin. Then seek to die in the same battle or the next. That is the surest way to Valhalla."

Hardegon nodded, "Yes, of course. You speak Frigg's council." He knelt before the volva and grasped her hand. "From the bottom of my heart I thank you. You have told me both what I wished and what I need. I shall prove no coward in the face of death. I will rush with gladness to the Serpent's slaughter and my own."

"You are a true Nibelung Hardegon. Know that tonight you are in no danger of Hel. Sleep out under the stars and strike off on the morrow with the gods' blessing." said the volva with full pride.

***

Hardegon left the tent to find Starkad staring at his cast rune stones in the firelight. When the swordsman's shadow fell over them he glanced up. "Well? What did Ida have to say?"

Hardegon considered his brother whose look held deep concern. 'If I tell him the full truth he will insist on a fruitless quest to save me.' "Tomorrow we strike off for the Skane mounds."

This elicited a sour look from his brother. "That is far too close to accursed Danevirke for my liking."

"It is the will of Odin, hold firm in devotion to him and you will not fall again into madness." urged Hardegon.

Starkad considered his runes again and said, "I wish to stop at the Gotland Thing along the way."

The swordsman sneered at that, "Why? So we can observe father cower in the face of our quest?"

Starkad shook his head, "No brother, it's the runes," He gestured to the stones before him, "every time I toss them they tell me there is trouble."

"He speaks true." said Ida, who had stepped out of her tent to stand beside Hardegon.

"How did you not see this?" asked the swordsman.

Ida shrugged, "I was focused on your fate, not your family's. I could ask the gods for further wisdom but it does little good to pester them."

The thought of Thora and little Helgi came to Hardegon's mind and his heart ached. He crossed his arms in resignation. 'I have some time.' "Very well, we'll stop at the Thing, though father might not let me off the boat."

Starkad gathered up his runes and chuckled, "How is it possible that father approves of me more than you? It must be a sign of Ragnarok."

Hardegon looked off over the cliff and onto the moon illuminated forest. "For some it is always the last of days."

***

They spent the night outside the Vovla's tent, under the stars. The fire kept them warm. The sky was cloudless. They awoke covered in morning dew. Ida cooked them a simple breakfast of oatmeal and berries. To drink the volva shared some red wine. Then, after saying their farewells, the brothers struck off down the path.

***

They returned to Lofot midday and found Berg's men waiting for them. They sat near their vessel playing dice, their manner surly. In the distance the chop of the loggers' axes could be heard. When the brothers approached the crew's headman, Thrain, greeted them.

"It is good to see both of you. We would return to Norrland but not without hearing of your quest, Master Berg would be most cross if we returned with no word on it."

Hardegon clapped him on the shoulder and said. "I shall fight the Serpent in the Mounds of Skane."

"Though, we must first away to Gotland, there is trouble for our Nibelung clan." added Starkad grimly.

"What sort of trouble?" asked Thrain.

The sorcerer shrugged. "I'm uncertain. The runes urge us south with all possible speed. I fear calamity."

Thrain stroked his brown, curly beard thoughtfully. "Sorcerer, with your wind spell we would make great time."

"We?" asked Hardegon.

"Aye," answered Thrain, "the master of Lofot is miserly and dour, I doubt he'll sell you a ship, let alone lend you men to sail her. Our Master Berg, on the other hand, would most likely wish us to aid you further, especially if his generosity is reciprocated."

Hardegon regarded the crew who looked to him with baited breath. He noted their shields and weapons stowed under the karve. "I would gladly put in a word with Bjorn Eriksson for any man who helped us reach Gotland. Who knows? He may request they join the summer raids?"

At that, the crew cheered. Thrain laughed and clasped arms with Hardegon. "A word is all we ask. The summer raids would enrich our hearth sgreatly."

With that settled, they flipped the karve back into the water and set sail. Starkad drew ᛀ in the air and its magic filled their sails with wind, ensuring a speedy voyage. They made great progress until Gotland appeared across the horizon, that night a storm hit and they were forced to take shelter.

***

Starkad stood outside of the tent, drenched in the rain staring balefully across the churning waters towards Gotland.

Hardegon walked out to stand beside him. "Brother? What ails you?"

"A sick feeling brother." Starkad answered, "Gotland has the same air as Danevirke; all it lacks is the accursed wall."

"Sickness?" Hardegon asked, a hint of fear in his voice. "You think our clan suffers plague?"

"Not our clan, the island. It suffers a spiritual malaise, one that stirs... things from rest. You remember when we sailed past Gotland last fall, yes? How I struggled to dive into the sea? In my madness I thought you were returning me to the accursed Danevirke. Now that my senses have returned I see clearly the root of my panic."

"The Gotland Thing, Thora and Helgi are there." Hardegon concluded in sudden panic, "We should stir the men, sail there in spite of the storm."

Starkad kept his eyes on the Gotland shore, "I'm afraid we are too late. I've tossed the stones, they speak of only sorrow. Whatever calamity has happened, it has passed. All we can do is witness the harm." He clapped his brother on the shoulder, "We should wait for the storm to end. As soon as it has we will sail for the Thing."

Hardegon took strength from his brother's resolve. "Very well, I will heed your wisdom."

***

With that they spent an anxious night waiting out the storm. It cleared just after sunrise. At the brotherss urging the karve was flipped back into the water, Starkad summoned the winds and they made all haste for the northeastern shore.

When they beached the karve, they saw before them the remains of the Thing. The many colored tents were torn and trampled into the mud. Bodies of warriors and traders, in addition to their children, lay scattered about. Groups of men and women, on the brink of grief and exhaustion, gathered the bodies. At their center was Eir, an old woman garbed in black, a priestess of Hel, also known as an angel of death. She directed the corpse gathering with a sacred, solemn air. Beyond them could be heard the many voices of others who searched for the dead. One rose to prominence.

"Search the southern hills but be back swiftly. Once everyone is accounted for we sail for Öland. Yes even the corpses, I won't hold a funeral here."

"Thora." Hardegon exclaimed.

"Go to her," Starkad urged. "I'll introduce Thrain and his men to Eir."

"We are at your service." Thrain said sombrely.

Hardegon nodded in thanks and ran towards Thora's voice. The corpse gathers paused and stared in surprise as they saw the jarl's son rush past.

"She's in the western field." Eir said.

The swordsman nodded in gratitude and wheeled west. He darted around a pile of fallen tents and halted when he saw Thora.

She was caked in mud, she aided in the corpse gathering herself. Around her stood a troop of Öland's finest, their expensive clothes also soiled in muck and mire. A few had bruises, cuts and bandaged wounds, as if they had just come from battle. One of them spotted the swordsman and signaled the others. They all turned to him.

"Hardegon." Thora cried in disbelief.

"Thora." the swordsman rushed to her. The karls and their men made way. The husband and wife embraced.

"What happened?" Hardegon asked. "Who did this? Where's Helgi?"

Thora rested her forehead against his and smiled with relief. "It'good to see you husband. Helgi's safe, he's in the hall."

"It was Gamli the Serpent." spat karl Hak. "He and his witch sister stirred the ghosts of Gotland. I saw them make love upon our dead!" he cried with rage.

These words slammed into the Nibelung hero like a hammer. He recalled how close he had been to catching them. 'If I had been quicker, cleverer...'

Karl Hjalti touched Thora's shoulder. "Go, show him the remains of Truvor. Tell him all that has transpired. We'll manage here."

"Remains of Truvor?" Hardegon asked, his heart sinking.

Thora grasped his hand and looked into his eyes. He saw the strain behind her mask of strength. "Y-yes. Your father was slain." She tugged him towards the north end of camp. "Come, I will take you to him."

"S-starkad." Hardegon stuttered. "I've brought him with me. He should know."

Thora glanced back at Hjalti.

"We'll have someone send for him. You need only give the tidings."

***

Moment's later Starkad sat in the muck, his back leaning against the Fortune Gale, his father's flagship. His cheeks were tear stained, his look shocked and haggard.

Hardegon sat on a rock on the beach, he stared off past the rolling waves of the Baltic, his mind s reeling from the sight of his father's twisted corpse and from Thora's words. "Starkad my brother," he pleaded, "you know of magic. What possible sense is there in this story?"

"This island's cursed, I'd wager it has been such for a long time." answered Starkad in an exhausted deadpan. "As malevolent as they are, the Fallen Volsungs could not have caused devastation on this scale."

"They had the 'malevolence' to save our son." stressed Thora. "If it weren't for their actions Dorte would have slain all of our children, our entire future gone."

"Nonsense!" Hardegon yelled. "Why would Dorte attack her kin? My cousin was full of life and love, she would never do such a thing. The witch must have forced her hand."

"Then why did the witch face her? Why did she use her spells drive Dorte away?" Thora shot back.

"Have you not heard? Our people cry for blood!" stressed Hardegon.

"Baseless fear drives them." Thora retorted. "I know the truth."

"Spirits are not the same as what they were in life. They act not with thought but on instinct and emotion." Starkad cut in. His tone held less vitriol than either of them but was still weighty enough to cut through the bickering. "Dorte had pleasant memories of the Gotland Thing, we all know this, we watched her grow up from a little girl to the fine woman she became.Her ghost must have been drawn here. Then the cursed magic of this place corrupted her. In her confusion she lashed out and the evil followed. She knew not what she did and father paid the price. That is the best I can piece together of these happenings."

"No, the Serpent's presence here could not have been coincidence. He set this up and saved our children so as to deceive us." Hardegon accused.

"There's a simpler, more truthful rationale." cut in Thora. "Gamli and Vanadis are not monsters, they're simply people. Anyone of us would jump to the aid of a child, even the children of our most dire enemies. Frigg's love drives us all, it's simply our nature."

Hardegon scowled and skipped a rock across the sea.

"The more pressing question, is what now?" queried Starkad.

"We took census after the attack. We found out that, of those who attended the Thing, half of us survived." Thora scowled. "Out of them, the smith Osfrid riled up five good men to hunt the Serpent. Of course," Thora chuckled ruefully, "they have no idea where he hides. Thankfully karl Freystien and Bosi could not attend, they are loyal and their holdings and their people intact. Still, King Bjorn expects a Nibelung contingent in his summer's battle with Fair Hair and we have few warriors to spare."

"A Norrland crew took us to these shores, ten men strong. They have expressed interest in Bjorn's raid, they are a worthy addition to our forces." said Hardegon.

"If they prove worthy we could marry them to our daughters and bolster our numbers." added Starkad.

"A wise suggestion." said Thora.

A thought suddenly struck Hardegon, "Thora, does Asta still live?"

"Aye, she and her daughter. She cares for them and our son in the Great Hall."

"Starkad, after you put father to rest, see her. She is wise and Mistress of both Neshraun and Kelifar."

"I? Don't you mean 'we,' brother?"

Thora regarded her husband incredulously, "Surely, you're not thinking of joining Osfrid, are you?"

"I am." answered Starkad sternly. "Steinarr must be avenged and our people will not rest until the fallen Volsung are put to justice."

"King Bjorn's expecting you." stated Thora in exasperation. "Pray tell what will he think when we present him half our promised warriors without you?"

Suddenly, an idea came to his mind. The summer battle, if he proved his mettle and died gloriously, King Bjorn would reward Öland richly. Thora and Helgi would be given wealth and renown, in this way Hardegon's death would lift the Nibelung clan back into prominence in Midgard. Then he recalled Odin's raven tossing him the king piece, felt its weight in his hands. He recalled Ida's words. Falling in the battle against Fair Hair would win fame and renown, but the path of the Serpent offered true immortality. I would be legend. He stood, "Starkad, you're Jarl of Alands."

"What?" gasped Thora.

"Brother, no. I'm not suited."

"I think you are." Hardegon insisted. "Strong, powerful, wise. You have discovered the strength of the runes. Our clan will prosper under you as jarl. They need you. I, I must go to face the Serpent, it is simply my fate."

"Are you mad?" asked Throa. "What of our son? You have given away his legacy."

"When word comes back of my slaying of the Serpent my renown will fall onto Helgi. He shall be a child of saga and glory."

Thora regarded him closely, "Do you not plan come back from this?"

Hardegon tried to calm the storm of passions within him. Thora's pained, betrayed expression was too much. "Farewell." He turned and stormed off.

"Hardegon! What of your son?"

"Brother, you must reconsider."

The swordsman ignored them and continued down the beach.

Thora was about to rush after him but Starkad grasped her shoulder and held her back. She shook him off.

"We both know him, once he's like this he cannot be swayed." said Starkad.

"Y-yes, but what shall we do?" asked Thora.

"Bjorn will not accept the aid of a sorcerer. You're the best choice to go to him. We'll gather what warriors we have, with the Norrland folk hopefully that will be enough. I, I will try to hold our clan together." suggested Starkad.

Thora brooded over this for a long moment and said, "Very well. Let us push my husband out of our hearts. A man who chooses vengeance over his own son is most unworthy." she seethed.

"The seat of jarl is yours if you wish." added Starkad. "You have more right to it than I."

Thora shook her head, "No, if not Hardegon, Truvor would have wished for you to take his place. Of that I am certain."

"You will always have an honored seat in Öland. I will treat Helgi as my own son." said Starkad warmly.

***

A few evenings later, Osfrid and his warband of five sat around a fire on the shore of Gotaland. They had searched forest, hill and hall but found no sign of their quarry. Pain, grief and rage fueled them, they were far from finished the hunt. They sat in silence, eating a meal of fish and rabbit.

Osfrid glanced up and saw a shadow stride towards them along the beach. "Brothers," he warned, nodding in the figure's direction, "someone approaches."

The warband rechecked their weapons were close at hand, then, all eyes turned towards the approaching figure. Soon enough, he stepped into the campfire light.

Osfrid stood. "Lord Hardegon."

The Nibelung hero greeted the warband with a fierce grin. "Friends, I've come to join you on your quest."

"Funny, it was your wife who hindered it. She forbid us from going." said Rodrekr, a cunning eyed warrior who sat across the fire.

Hardegon sat down beside him, "She was moved by womanly sentiment. I am not. Besides," he clapped Rodrekr on the back, "we are now on the path to glory. Bringing the Serpent to justice will please the Gods."

"Aye," Osfrid said with a laugh, "it is right you are with us Hardegon. Steinarr would want it this way."

The rest considered this and then cheered as one.

The swordsman regarded them all with pride. "Thank Odin that I find myself surrounded by true brothers in arms. In the morning we head for the Mounds of Skane. The gods have relieved to me that this is where the Serpent shall nest."

CHAPTER 27

Betrayal is a poisoned arrow. | That you notch and loose when the time is right.
The poison is the death of truth and honor, oh it is a powerful toxin.
Plant in your soul the seed of distrust. | Laugh at the fools who believe your words.
Yet, all the while cherish those who you care for; this is the unholy paradox.

"He sends you with vargs to recover what was stolen. Gorm must be mad." proclaimed Griss Draflison. His long nose and intense brown eyes were similar to his father's. Though his build was broader and his dark locks fuller. On the back of his hands he sported ᚺ and ᚦ respectively.

"We should be the ones to accompany you. Let the witch and her brother rot beneath the wall." added Griss' wife Ingvild Grave Shield. She was a severe looking young woman. Her long hair was snow white, her eyes an icy blue. She held the build and dress of a warrior.

Drafli pulled on his thick leather tunic and secured it. Stitched in the supple leather was a lining of runes. "It is the King's choice and, given Starkad's flight, and the theft of the Barrow Bowl, I'm in no position to argue."

They stood in an armory deep inside Castle Danevirke. Lining the walls were shields, weapons and tunics of thick fur and leather. It was illuminated by two tall lit braziers on the far wall.

"Starkad's weakness was not your own." offered Griss.

"As for Vargeisa," Ingvild struggled with her next words, with a shrug she said, "admittedly you were the fool. Blue eyes and red hair are no reason to trust."

"Aye." Sighed Drafli as he seized a mace whose head was inscribed with ᚻ, he hung it to his belt.

"Which is why I fail to understand why Gorm takes this risk with the vargs." Ingvild pressed, "He's devoted to Thyra, I'm surprised he falls for beauty and youth as easily as you."

Drafli strapped a leather gauntlet on his left hand, on it was inscribed ᛗ. "He is less the fool than I." He turned to his son and daughter-in-law. "The vargs have nowhere to go, by helping us they help themselves. If they perish we lose nothing. If they survive we win powerful allies. Either way we keep our two greatest treasures secure." he clapped both on the shoulder.

Griss shook his head. "Father, I'm no longer a boy who needs protection. My spells are as strong as yours."

"Then, this job's beneath you." said Drafli.

Ingvild crossed her arms and huffed, "Our King, always hiding his true strength."

Drafli chuckled, "Aye, if the Christians knew what they truly faced would they be so bold in their attacks?"

***

Meanwhile, Vanadis, Gamli, Ransu, and Ormir sat in a room in the upper chambers of the castle. The noon sun filtered through the arrow head shaped window. The room held a small bench with a chair sitting across from it. Vanadis and Gamli sat on the bench, Ormir lay at Gamli's feet, Ransu sat on the chair.

"We'll follow Drafli for now. When we find Vargeisa we turn on him." said the Volsung witch.

Gamli shook his head, "I don't like it."

"We have enemies enough already." added Ransu.

"Should we take Gorm up on his offer then? Turn on Vargeisa? Louhi will become our new foe. I won't have that." snapped Vanadis.

Ransu looked torn, "I don't want either as my enemy. Perhaps we can simply 'lose ourselves' in the mounds?"

Vanadis shook her head, "Then we'd lose Gorm's favour and allow Vargeisa to die. The worst of both worlds."

"There's nothing worse than a traitor." rumbled Gamli.

Vanadis sighed "Gamli, once Gorm has the Barrow Bowl, he'll tuck us away. Oh he'll allow us out to do his bidding, but as soon as we return we'll be locked away again. We'll no longer be free, merely part of his horde. If he can ever profit from turning us in, he will do so without hesitation. I've spoken to him, you haven't. I both admire and fear his cunning and conviction."

Gamli said nothing, he simply petted Ormir's head absently.

"You said yourself this Danevirke should not be." Vanadis pressed. "I agree, I've been in the wall and witnessed its horrors. Imagine what unspeakable acts King Gorm and Drafli committed to raise this monstrosity. All right minded folk should stand against him."

"Do what you wish sister. I won't kill a man in an underhanded manner."

Ransu shrugged, "I will. Being underhanded is how I reached this age. Still," he considered Vanadis closely, "what drives you to this Vanadis? Why risk so much for Vargeisa? Didn't she try to kill you?"

Vanadis paused and said haltingly, "You wouldn't understand."

"Vanadis, you owe us an explanation." pressed the fisherman.

Vanadis brooded over this a long moment. Gamli touched her shoulder and stared at her with gentleness but also determination.

"All my life," Vanadis started, "I've been looked down upon. In Kelifar the only people I respected were Dorte, Steinarr and Gerd."

"Not me or Flosi?" Gamli asked hurt.

Vanadis touched him his arm. "I loved and trusted you both. However, that's different from respect. Now though? You're no longer the little brother I watched out for, you're Gamli the Smith and I hold you in great esteem."

Gamli humphed. "By Surt, it is something to hear you say that."

Vanadis squeezed his hand and then, continued her speech, "Back in Kelifar none of the people I respected shared respect for me. That's until Louhi. She suffered none of my weakness. Over the winterI came to understand this wasn't because she was cruel, but because she expected much from me. Until I met her I was a cursed thrall, she made me into who I am now am. There is nothing I wouldn't do for her." Vanadis hugged herself and lowered her gaze. "I fully admit to you two..." Ormir let out an annoyed hum, Vanadis cracked a smile, "you three, that I have been stupid. I thought we could simply slip Nibelung and deliver the Queen's message. I didn't count on Hardegon. I didn't count on whatever attacked us in Gotland. However, this is something I must do. Again I say, if either of you wish to turn from this path I won't begrudge you."

Gamli shook his head, "I can't turn my back now. I won't backstab for you, but I will protect you."

Ransu chuckled, "I did say this was Hiisi's road did I? Now that I'm on it I see no easy way off. Perhaps, when we return to Pohjola, the Queen will shower me with riches?"

Vanadis laughed, "I'll ask her to conjure you a castle of gold."

Ransu leaned back casually, "A simple hall will do."

***

An hour later, the three stood at the massive gates of Castle Danevirke, with them were Drafli the Eye and 12 soldiers bedecked in heavy leather armor and carrying fine shields, axes and spears. Standing on a balcony above them was Gorm the Old. At his side was his beloved Thyra, an imposing woman who regarded the troop arrayed before her with a keen eye. Flanking them were Griss Draflison and Ingvild Grave Shield.

"I see before me a collection of honest men and rogues. This is good." the King chuckled. "Drafli uses these vargs to catch their fellows. Vargs, serve us well and you will be outlaws no longer. Go forth and return to us both our lost treasure and the head of the Fire Wolf. Let her be an example, all who steal from Danevirke will join the Christians who adorn our wall."

Drafli bowed, "We shall not fail you, my King and Queen."

The soldiers gathered at watch, who witnessed these proceedings cheered.

With that they struck off east at a maddening pace. They reached Hedeby by late evening. Drafli had them rest in the guard hall. The next morning, in a sequestered section of the hall, he ordered

Vanadis to share her story with the assembled warriors. Vanadis did, keeping to the same truths and lies she told Gorm. The men were shaken by the tale. One, who was a young man named Ulv Hungbogason, commented "Valkyries can rebel? These are ill tidings."

"There's more to this tale." said Drafli. "As many of you know the gods speak to Thyra, many years ago they warned her of a coming dark age where Jutland would stand alone against a sea of troubles, where the Danevirke would fall to Christendom if it lacked strength. Many northerners would laugh at such a claim but we know well Christian numbers and tenacity. Thyra and Gorm sought a way to protect Jutland against the coming troubles. They found me. I sought the artifact the seithkona mentioned; the King and Queen aided me in return for sharing the wisdom of the Nameless Volva. We succeeded on our quest, one night in the Skane Mounds Thrya and I used the Barrow Bowl to contact the Nameless One. In exchange for a blot in her honor she taught me the secrets of the runes and Thyra how to summon an ancient power that would aid the defence Jutland. The Danevirke we know, thrives on this power's blessing."

"What is the nature of this power?" asked Vanadis.

Drafli considered her question and answered, "The sorcerers mentioned in your tale. These sovereign lords have extended their magic beyond the grave and it has been of great use to us."

"This sounds profane." stated Vestienn Glamrson, a large warrior with a forked beard.

Drafli laughed, "You think so? Is it so different from the seithkona's magic?" he asked gesturing to Vanadis.

'Entirely different.' Mused Vanadis silently remembering the living nature of the wall. She winced in pain as her mind brushed against the memory of what lay beneath it.

"It's not like your magic?" asked Ulv, who had noticed Vanadis' expression.

She felt Drafli's gaze upon her "It's very much like seith." she lied. "The spirits possess stone as opposed to people. In the face of right minded folk, like you and me they sleep. In the face of Christians, they inflict a baleful curse. In truth I'm a little envious."

The warriors nodded, pretending to understand, and seemed a little more at ease.

"We have an advantage on the Fire Wolf." continued Drafli, "It took us days to find the exact location, in the Skane Mounds where the Nameless One can be summoned. It'll take the Fire Wolf no less time. If we hurry we'll catch her. Steel yourselves for a swift journey northeast."

"Aye." said Drafli's troop as one.

"Let us be off." answered the sorcerer. With that they stood and headed for the docs.

The three followed.

Ransu shook his head, "Landing in Skane after all." He glared at Vanadis, "How bitterly I'll laugh when we fall into the River of Tuonela."

"We would have had an easier time if we landed their earlier." retorted Vanadis.

Gamli and Ormir stepped between them, before Ransu could take a swipe at the seithkona.

***

The troop seized one of the King's longships, a fine, sleek vessel. They set sail and made excellent progress across the coast of Jutland and then along the coast of Zealand. Every night they stayed in a friendly hall. They kept their business secret. Despite their lack of guises none recognized the Fallen Volsungs, though their crimes were still on many tongues. In private the siblings insisted to the troop they were not lovers. Their visible disgust at such elicited both belief and laughter. The troop was curious about the real happenings. Vanadis filled them in: They were Steinarr's thralls, not wards. Gamli did not poison Kelifar; it fell to a curse that was brought upon by Steinarr's crimes. The siblings did not summon the creatures that attacked Gotland. She left out Dorte entirely. Drafli was polite and cordial throughout, though his eyes often drifted to the Volsung sister. However, he made an effort to avoid more than polite conversation.

'He was stung by Vargeisa.' Vanadis mused.

Ransu got along well with the crew, even teaching them a few tricks with the net and crossbow.

Gamli remained apart and often brooded alone, watching Ormir's flickering flame. Vanadis explained his surliness as piety. "He holds a deep connection with Sigurd. He's often lost in thoughts on our illustrious family."

When she confronted him on his behaviour Gamli merely said, "I won't pretend friendship with those we're going to kill." He said no more for the rest of the trip.

***

Eventually they approached Skane's shore. The fog had lifted leaving an innocuous sandy beach in its wake. On either side were tall, rocky cliffs. The path up from the beech lead into a thick forest.

Ransu rubbed his eyes and stared again. He whispered to Vanadis, "What we saw here before. Did our senses fool us, was it a dream?"

The seithkona peered beyond the woods, to the lonely rocky hills that rose above them. In the back of her mind she heard the murmur of many spirits. She felt their gaze from the mounds. "No," she whispered back, "the fog brought them and pulled them back. They're in the hills, waiting for us."

"Wonderful." groaned Ransu.

They beached their longship in the late afternoon. Once the ship was flipped and the warband ready Drafli addressed them. "Past these woods is a land close to Niflheim. If you would not bench Hel's Hall stay together. We shall reach the summoning nexus by nightfall. Vargeisa and her sister are powerful seithkonas. Their brother is an Ulfhednar, a man who can turn into a wolf. Fear not, for mine and Vanadis' magic will protect you, and we outnumber them five to one. If we are swift and silent Heimdall will bless our hunt, and Odin will grant us victory."

The crew cheered not, for fear of giving away their position; instead, they muttered in agreement and stood alert and prepared.

Vanadis approached Drafli. Her manner confident and ready. Wearing her gold circlet, carrying her spear of red metal. Wearing feathered earrings and a cloak of fox fur. Her grey eyes shone and her lips were curved into a smile. His eyes were upon her again, and she hoped his mind clouded. "I look forward to seeing Vargeisa again. I will sing her to sleep with curses."

"If all goes as planned our battle will be quick and simple. Still, I look forward to seeing your spells." Drafli replied.

Gamli turned away looking displeased.

Ransu chuckled quietly.

With that the warband headed into the woods

***

Moments later, Rodrekr rushed into camp. It was tucked into a tiny clearing well away from the beach, a thick ring of leafy elm hiding it from prying eyes. It held a few small tents with a small fire pit at its center. The pit was dug low, so as to hide any flame.

Hardegon sat on a stump beside the pit. He drank slowly from his water skin and pondered. For the past few nights he'd been plagued by dreams. In them he shivered and sweated. He wheezed and his throat was nearly closed. He couldn't lift his sword. He fell and the last thing he saw was the hem of a dress, half black, half white. In the waking world he sat and paid apt attention to his body. Yes, he had aches but they must have been from how he slept. The vovla said he might die of sickness, that was the fate that waited him if he did not die in battle. How soon would it claim him? How long did he have?
'Curse Ida's vagueness.'

"Sire." Rodrekr addressed.

Hardegon snapped out of his musing. "Yes?"

"The Serpent has landed in Skane." said the warrior.

Rodrekr's words arrested Nibelung hero's full attention. "Excellent, you are a fine hunter. Everyone gather, Rodrekr has news." he said in a joyous tone.

The seven gathered and Rodrekr informed them of all he had seen from the cliff.

Hardegon stroked his beard, "A well-armed warband from the west, sailing in an expensive longship."

"They sound too well equipped for bandits." mused Osfrid.

"I agree," said the swordsman, "they're forces of a King."

"They must have allied with Harald Fair Hair." said the young Orm excitedly.

"Nay," answered the Nibelung hero. "I have fought Fair Hair's forces with Bjorn Eriksson, they are honorable folk. No, these feel more like the machinations of Gorm the Old."

"Have you an inkling on their purpose?" asked Rodrekr.

The swordsman chuckled, "Only that they are driven by evil."

"Tell us your plan my lord." said Osfrid.

The nobleman looked to his troop who all regarded him with anxious readiness. For a fleeting moment he thought of their families and guilt soured his elation. He brushed the guilt aside. 'If we simply attack we would inflict grievous harm but lose. I would most certainly die in in such a combat...' he frowned, 'No, this would not attain Valhalla. Odin would see such a tactic as foolish and unworthy.' "As much as my sword thirsts for the Serpent's blood, we must hold our fury. We will follow them, watch them and, when an opportunity presents itself, we will strike."

***

An hour later, Drafli's troop found themselves deep within the Skane Mounds. The ground was dry and barren. The hills were tall, eerie and rocky. They sky was clear but the silver moon and starlight made the Mounds seem even more unearthly. The occasional shrill and sudden bird cry rose up from the hills.

Vanadis' grey eyes caught movement there. Flashes of silver light as spirits glanced up from behind the stones and dried out trees. Her ears heard them speak

"I'm lost help me."

"I can't go back, I will freeze."

"Mother?" A question was asked and then, there wasa shriek of terror.

The seithkona summoned her own spirits to stand watch; they posted an invisible guard around her. They comprised of Kvistr Dusk Torch, Bera, and four of his stout Kelifar warrriors.

'What? Mother's not here?' Vanadis thought dryly.

'I know not where you mother dwells.' answered Kvistr. 'She mopes, I suppose, she's never accepted your ascendancy.'

'Poor her.' Vanadis quipped with a smirk.

Drafli lead them around a tall pile of huge flat stones that stood like a marker for an unknown grave. Once the warband was around he gestured for a pause.

"Is something wrong?" Vanadis asked.

"This," he pointed to the ᛗ rune on his gauntlet, "warns me of danger, ambush and betrayal."

"Really, what fascinating magic." Vanadis commented, swallowing her sudden fear. Behind the troop, she could see Ransu step back a pace and raise his loaded crossbow.

Drafli regarded her with seriousness, "We're walking into a trap."

"We are?" Vanadis queried, mentally readying her deadliest spells.

"We are followed - by vagabonds hired by the Fire Wolf." answered Drafli.

"How close do you think they are?" Vanadis asked, ready to release her curse.

"Close, I've spotted them in the southern hills."

Vanadis inwardly sighed.

Ransu lowered his crossbow.

"At first I thought they were spirits but spirts do not try hide."

"They do not." Vanadis agreed.

Drafli considered his troop. "Ulv, Hevard, Hosvir, Klyppr, Havarr, Ransu; lead the bandits off a distance and then face them."

"Yes sire." answered Ulv, eager to prove himself.

"I'd rather not." challenged Ransu, "I have no desire to sup with your Hel."

Everyone turned to the Spider, the warriors with disgust, Vanadis with a glare.

"I'll go, I insist." said Gamli.

The troop and their master turned their attention to him.

"We don't know their numbers. If I go we have an extra man." He patted Ormir's head, the drake let out a shrill trill.

Drafli looked dubious.

"If startled Ormir will burst into flame. Good for drawing attention, not so good when sneaking up on the Fire Wolf."

"You speak wisdom." concluded Drafli. "Very well, those I mentioned and Gamli, draw and then face our trackers. The rest will head with me for the summoning nexus." He glanced at Ransu with disdain, "When we fight Vargeisa I expect you to comport yourself like a warrior."

"Aye," said Ransu brandishing his crossbow, "I'll have your back."

Vanadis approached her brother with obvious worry "You're better suited for this task, but still, be careful."

The smith hugged her and then held her at arm's length. "I'm Gamli the Serpent, my sword is Scorn, I have a dragon at my side. I won't be the one in trouble."

Vanadis grinned. "Very true. I'll see you when our tasks are done."

Gamli kissed her on the forehead and then turned. To his warband he said, "Come." The other five fell in line, the six strode off with Ormir following behind.

Drafli stepped close to Vanadis and said, "I thought little of your brother until now. He is remarkable. Nearly as much as his sister."

Vanadis smiled and leaned on him lightly, "Thank you. I promise, when you witness my magic you will not be disappointed."

The three warriors glared with disdain.

Ransu rolled his eyes.

Drafli remembered himself, took a step away from the Volsung sister and said, "Let us be off. We're very close now."

***

Rodrekr lay on the top of a hill many strides away. He kept his gaze focused on the rocky pillar where his quarry hid. From his vantage he could see every which way they could exit. After a moment he saw a group of six, plus the red drake, dart out from their cover and rush for a northwestern hill. He then spied the other six racing to the west; one of these wore a long dress. Rodrekr slid back and raced down to his waiting companions.

"Six men and the drake make for the northwest. Then, including the witch, make for the west."

"The one with the drake that must be the Serpent." concluded Osfrid.

"Aye," said Hardegon thoughtfully. "We must choose between him or Vanadis."

"We could split up and track both." suggested Rodrekr.

'The seithkona is no doubt up to villainy and using her brother for a distraction. If we don't stop her, no telling what evil she'll unleash.' mused the Nibelung hero. That thought satisfied his suspicions but his heart pulled him elsewhere. "No, we have a chance to kill one of them. Best take it, we pursue the Serpent."

"I was hoping you'd say that." said Osfrid, drawing his war hammer.

"There comes a time when a hunter must strike." said Rodrekr, he unshouldered his bow. "Now's as time as good as any".

"Then let us make haste, to the northwest." said the swordsman.

***

Hardegon's warband darted from their concealment and swiftly and silently raced for the northwestern hill. When they rounded the corner Rodrekr spied the drake's tale scoot around the corner of an escarpment of jagged rock. They chased that as well. When they reached this destination they spied someone peering out from behind a sickly tree, when spotted he let out a cry and ducked behind another hill.

Hardegon held out a hand to signal a halt. "Be cautious, this is most likely a trap."

Osfrid and four others readied their shields. Rodrekr notched an arrow. Hardegon drew his sword and dagger. Then the warband cautiously walked around the hill, alert and anxious for combat.

When they got to the other side they found the drake wreathed in a bonfire. Standing before it were six figures with their weapons drawn. The large one, the one who wielded a sword and shield, whose fur cloak flared out behind him asked in shock "Hardegon?"

"Gamli the Serpent." The swordsman greeted with perverse glee. He advanced, his six warriors at his heels. "I much prefer meeting you like this, as opposed to watching your fleeing backside."

"I was no coward when I saved your son." Gamli rumbled.

"All part of your plan I'm sure. You won't fool me Volsung swine."

"You call me swine? After what you drove Mjoll to? Under Steinarr I felt the lash of Nibelung 'mercy'. Under Asvard I was paid with Nibelung 'generosity', and you show me Nibelung 'gratitude'. I shall pay back what you're owed." Gamli's tone was dark, ferocious. Ormir let out a trumpeting roar.

***

Moments before, Drafli's warband hurried west. They crested not the hills but wove around them so as to remain unseen. In the distance Ormir's trumpeting bellow echoed across the mounds. Vanadis looked back worriedly.

Drafli cursed. "Quick, make all haste for the nexus!" he cried and drove his warriors to a sprint.

Within moments, they rounded a knoll to find a large, stony, and crescent drumlin. Inside this crescent was a thin pillar of fire that shot up as tall as the drumlin's highest point, it had been hidden by the mounds until now. A shadowy figure knelt before it, her head back, staring up at the sky.

"The Barrow Bowl!" Drafli exclaimed. "We've arrived just in time. Forward men, kill the Fire Wolf, and retrieve our treasure."

***

Back in the northwestern hills, the two warbands let out battle cries and charged.

Osfrid raced forward and pulled his massive hammer back. Gamli shunted, stabbed Scorn deep into him, and then booted him off his blade knocking the smith far backwards, a look of despair on his face, trailing a stream of blood. A second warrior swung his axe only for it to be blocked by the Serpent's shield. Gamli responded by slicing Scorn downward and cutting his opponent's shield in half. The warrior pulled his axe back but was too slow, before he could attempt another strike the smith loped off his head with his green blade. Ulv rushed towards Hardegon who swung an expert strike with his sword, knocking Ulv's mace out of his grip. He then sunk his dagger between the young man's ribs. Ulv gasped with sudden, deathly fear. The swordsman shouldered him into Havarr's spear thrust. Hardegon then drove forward and thrust the tip of his sword through the Danevirke soldier's breast.

Rodrekr loosed an arrow and it found a home deep in Hosvir's throat. As he fell Ormir rushed forward and flared brighter. He raced between two of Hardegon's men, his flame biting into them and spreading. They let out sheiks of terror and pain, the smell of their burning hair filled the air, and the doomed men fled fast from the fiery drake.

Hardegon pulled his sword out of Havar's standing corpse and sprinted towards Gamli. The smith raised his shield but the swordsman took a knee and sliced, cutting through the smith's thick fur to trail a line of blood. Gamli let out a grunt and swung Scorn down, Hardegon spun out of the way and his Troll blood blade swooshed for the Volsung's head. Gamli barely got his shield up in time.

Hardegon laughed, "Come now, Serpent. Surely, you can do better than this?"

Gamli snarled and swung again, Hardegon parried it and got a solid stab into Gamli's shield arm. The Smith cried in rage and cuffed the jarl's brother across the side of the face with his sword hand. Hardegon reeled and Gamli chuckled, the satisfaction of the blow enough to dull the pain of his wounds.

Hardegon wiped his bloody lip and grinned. "Yes, this is how it should be." He lowered his blade and shifted his stance to something more aggressive. "Come Volsung, we will have such a battle that the dead who haunt these hills will sing of it to the living."

"Aye." scowled Gamli. "I'll send you to Mjoll so you can explain yourself." With that he rushed forward.

***

Moments before, as the Danevirke warband charged, Vanadis shot Ransu a glance. She closed her eyes and focused her will. 'Come to me.' The spirits of Kelifar flooded into her, her body jerked and lurched, she rushed a few steps forward. Ransu took careful aim at the sorcerer.

The ᛗ burned hot in Drafli's gauntlet. He quickly drew ᛁ in the air, suddenly his skin turned blue and hard as ice. Ransu's bolt hammered the back of his head and bounced flying. He turned in surprise and glared at Ransu, the blue sheen on his skin falling back to normal flesh.

Vanadis twisted and stretched weirdly from spirits flowing within her. She raised the point of Burning Mind at Drafli and released their power through her weapon. The curse struck the sorcerer, a mouth opened up on his arm, on his leg and on his torso, they bit inward and he screamed in pain at the bloody tearing wounds. Then, his expression hardened and, with an act of will, he banished the hex, but his injuries still remained.

The sorcerer was about to order his men to wheel and attack when he heard a snarl behind him. He turned to the side and, with a quick glance, saw a red wolf the size of a horse bound past several of his men to lock his jaws around one of his veterans, the old warrior let out a scream of pain, the Wolf shook him, his neck snapped, and he screamed no more.

Katla stepped out of the shadow of the drumlin, her cat Moldan at her side, giving the charging soldiers a baleful glare. She raised her hand and a twisted mass of spirits rose from the ground in front of two warriors. It had two heads comprised of seven faces each, they both had gaping maws that snapped down and ripped two young warriors apart.

Drafli drew ᛉ, it flashed red and exploded in rock dust which he ran through, a he did his flesh became like living stone. He charged forward shouting. "Fools! You know not the enemy you face."

Vanadis' left hand twisted up and she clenched her fingers around a ghostly skull that suddenly appeared in her palm. She pointed Burning Mind again and tossed the spirit skull uttering a craven snarl. The grinning haut collided against Drafli exploding into a black vortex. Its wind cut through his rock skin, causing him to flinch in pain but he continued his charge.

Ransu drew two javelins and tossed both, one at a time. One speared through a warrior's head. The second sunk through another's leg. As he gripped the shaft and screamed Wolf bit his head off.

Katla's monstrosity vanished as swiftly as it came. Two soldiers shouted cries for glory and charged her. The seithkona raised her hands and swiftly chopped them down. One of her assailants was engulfed by a cloud of wispy grey smoke. He vanished and Katla emerged out of it with dagger in hand. His companion skidded to a halt and swung his axe, it thunked in her head. As she fell, she gave him a leering smile. When her body hit the ground the illusion vanished and the warrior saw only the corpse of he who had been swallowed by the smoke. He stood frozen in grief and horror.

The two remaining warriors drove their spears into Wolf who howled in agony.

Vanadis jabbed Burning Mind at the sorcerer, his staff grew a mouth and bit his hand. It crunched only rock. Drafli swung his mace, the ᚺ rune on it flared; he hit Vanadis with enough force to knock her flying. He raced forward and lifted his weapon high, glaring down at the seithkona. "Worthless varg my King offered you purpose and you spit in his face."

Vanadis grey eyes had turn blue. She leered up at the sorcerer and said, in a voice not her own,

"My lady chooses her own purpose, fool." With a cackle she added, "Why serve a King of Horrors when she has horrors of her own?"

Drafli was about to strike when the head of an axe crashed into his arm with enough force to shatter rock and bone, spilling a river of his blood from his now broken limb. A black, skeletal hand gripped his shoulder and threw him to the ground. Bera stood over him with her ever present skull grin. She wore hide armor and had a shield at her back. She admired her axe. "Your brother does good work." she sighed pleasantly.

Vanadis rose, her stance off as if multiple ribs were broken. She lowered the point of Burning Mind at Drafli. The hex hit him, his eyes went wide and, highlighted by his terrifying screams, his body and limbs twisted and warped his bones shattered inside him. Within a moment, he lay still, his stone magic spent, a disgusting lump of blood, flesh, and bone.

Meanwhile, Ransu put crossbow bolt into the back of one of the soldiers who fought Wolf. The Ulfhednar stood on top of his freshly slain foe, lapping up his blood and seeming to grow stronger for it.

'Now rest.' Vanadis commanded. She felt the spirits within her swirl and then slow.

"When you next battle, summon me earlier." Bera chided before her bones and equipment fell to the earth and dissipated as dust.

The seithkona blinked and her were eyes once more grey. Vanadis let out a hiss as the pain of her injuries slammed into her. She staggered, thrusting Burning Mind forward to save her from falling.

Ransu approached, "You must have used witchery to convince me to attack such a sizeable force."

"We won." Vanadis huffed. "Besides, I knew Vargeisa would be guarded." She gestured to Wolf, who had resumed his lanky human form, and Katla, who had reappeared behind the grieving brother to stab him multiple times in the back.

"Aye." admitted Ransu. He regarded the Seithkona with concern, "It seems I fared better than you."

Vanadis was about to respond when the puddle of blood and skin that was Drafli stirred. Despite her injuries she scooted back a step. The other eight corpses began to thrash and writhe. Their mouths locked open and they wailed as one.

"By Ukko." Ransu swore, growing pale.

Wolf jumped. Moldan arched his back and hissed. Katla became shocked and confused.

Spectral hands shot up from the earth, grabbed the corpses and pulled. They were torn asunder and their grizzly parts dragged under the solid ground as if it were mud. The wailing dimmed underground until all was silence. Only the whoosh and flicking of the Barrow Bowl's flame could be heard. The only sign that a battle ever took place were Vanadis and Wolf's injuries and a broken spear that had been left behind.

Suddenly, the flame in the Barrow Bowl winked out and Vargeisa fell off her knees and to the ground, she moved not.

***

Moments before, in the northwestern hills Rodrekr lay a burning corpse. Ormir lay beside him, breathing deep, with an arrow stuck into him. The rest of Hardegon's and Gamli's warbands were slain by axe, by spear or by fire.

The Nibelung and Volsung still fought. Hardegon's dagger lay nearby shattered. Gamli's shield arm hung useless. They circled each other, both breathing deep, both suffering from light but bloody wounds. Scorn and Hardegon's sword pointed at each other, while their masters sought some weakness in the other.

"I did not expect a thrall to put up such a fight." Hardegon admitted with a determined satisfaction.

Gamli grunted and took a swipe at his foe. Hardegon stepped out of the way and returned with a slash. Gamli ducked back, the tip of troll blooded weapon shaving off a tuft of his beard.

"That sword." he mused aloud. "There's something wrong with it."

"It's marked by Troll blood. I have you to thank for that honor." Hardegon returned through gritted teeth. He swung up and Gamli blocked with Scorn. The swordsman glanced up at his opponent in surprise, the blow should have sent the smith's blade flying, instead Gamli held Hardegon's two armed strike with his one.

"Troll's End, it's an evil thing." Gamli huffed, regarding the red stained blade.

"For you, perhaps." replied the swordsman, he stepped back and drew his blade free. Both opponents raised their weapons.

The sudden shuddering of corpses brought pause to their fight. As in the western drumlin the slain's jaws locked open, and they wailed. Ormir whimpered and skittered back from the burning Rodrekr as the ghostly hands claimed him and the rest.

"What is this? Your sister's vile magic?" cried Hardegon.

Gamli watched the dead get dragged into the earth and replied, "No. I have no idea what this is."

"It's as if Hel's laid claim to them." hissed the Nibelung hero.

"Hel or these hills." replied the smith glancing around warily.

The corpses vanished and silence reigned.

"Well," said Gamli raising Scorn, "want to see who's swallowed next?"

Hardegon glanced at Gamli as if he were mad. "Nay, this is no fit battlefield. We are here to prove our valor to Odin, not to have our souls dragged into the earth."

Gamli glanced where Ormir lay bleeding, his flame extinguished. He still breathed but it was obvious he would not for long. Gamli sheathed Scorn. "Then we par heret." He walked for his beast, right past Hardegon's naked blade.

The swordsman watched him with incredulity. For a moment he seemed torn, then he sheathed Troll's End. "Y-yes but I will find you again and we will finish this."

Gamli knelt and heaved Ormir onto his shoulder. "I'll pay for my crimes?"

"This is bigger than your crimes, bigger than both of us. We are Nibelung and Volsung, we are destined to fight." stressed the swordsman.

Gamli considered him for a moment, huffed, turned his back, and began his walk south. "You're free to follow but I warn you my companions hold no value in honor. Vanadis will curse you and Ransu will finish you off with a bolt."

Hardegon watched him go with an expression of ragged desperation. He then snarled, turned away, and marched off, anxious to get out of the wretched mounds.

CHAPTER 28

I am a master at a craft. | I excel at making foes.
In the sagas, you kill and it is right, but make no mistake, each death marks you.
That is why the first victory is the hardest.| The first splash of blood is shocking, not so much when
you're soaked in it.
For every victory you leave someone in grieving, and they'll rightly wish to make you pay.

Vargeisa came back slowly. Her will swam forward to the waking world through a sea of inky black. She was dimly aware of conversation, she recognized Vanadis' voice. The Fire Wolf chuckled remembering Katla's prediction 'The scourge of Gotland will aid us in the Mounds of Skane.' She opened her eyes to find herself lying in her tent. A flickering fire outside shone through the canvas. Without moving she rolled her eyes to the side. Beside her sat the shadows of Katla and Vanadis. The Fire Wolf squeezed Katla's hand to signal she was awake. After Katla squeezed back she suddenly rose. "Why good evening."

Vanadis shrieked.

Vargeisa giggled.

A shadow fell across the tent and Gamli asked "Are you alright?"

"Yes." Vanadis replied, catching her breath. "Though I'm considering murder."

Moments later, the three were gathered by the campfire. Gamli, Ransu and Wolf, sat on the other end. Nearby Moldan was curled up by the peacefully sleeping Ormir. They were camped on a cliff face that overlooked a river and waterfall. Fields of Northern Skane and Sothern Ranrike were arrayed before them. Clusters of lights signified where the towns lay.

"So we parted ways." finished Gamli.

"You were fortunate they sent a small party." mused Ransu.

"My thoughts as well." added Vanadis, "Perhaps, after Gotland, they have few warriors to spare?"

Vargeisa daintily sipped a bit of Ranu's delicious rabbit stew. Then she commented "Quite a journey." She regarded Vanadis kindly, "I'm truly sorry about Vinglunr, he was a good man."

"What's done is done." answered Vanadis, an edge of grief in her voice. "What's important is we're together and I can give you these." she removed Louhi's ring from her finger and presented Vargeisa with both it and Salli's scroll case.

The Fire Wolf regarded them with trepidation. "You realize the old witch most likely cursed the ring. She hates me."

Vanadis shook her head with a look of certainty. "I swear she hasn't. Your mother regrets her actions deeply."

"She's a cunning old crow." huffed the Fire Wolf.

Vanadis smirked, "But, she's no liar."

"Then, you could be lying." Vargeisa shot back.

Katla squeezed her arm and gave her a stern look. Vargeisa glanced at Wolf.

He shrugged, "If they wanted to kill you they could have done so already, when backed by Drafli and his men."

"Very well." Vargeisa seized both the bone ring and the scroll case. She held the ring above her finger and declared "If I am slain it is on all of your heads." She slid it on her finger and suddenly the camp and the world was lost.

Several memories flashed in her mind. She was nursing a babe with red hair, her loving husband at her side admiring one more beautiful daughter. She saw the child years later rushing through the hall giggling, a young Rainbow Maiden chased her, scolding her for stealing her comb. She was on wing sailing over the sea her heart aching for her missing child. She was joyous for her child had been returned, now a grown woman with eyes as cunning as a wolf and beauty like an open flame. She was on the docks of Torino, glaring at the same child who stood arrogant and defiant. She said 'Vargeisa, if you leave now you shall never return. If you leave and I so much as catch a look at you, it'll be your end.' Then, the child did just that. She turned her back, on her own mother, and stepped onto the Sapphire Haunt. Louhi spun on her heel and stormed off, she didn't get far for she felt the spirits inside her swirl and in a rush as they obeyed her command. She felt the invisible connection with her daughter twist and corrupt, she heard Vargeisa cry out in pain. Quickly, driven by fear, before she could look at her daughter she spread her wings and flew off to the Sariola. Then, many years later, she stood at a ledge of her mountain and stared up at the stars, fresh grief had been thrust upon her.

"Teacher?" Vanadis asked softly.

Louhi jumped and turned to her with a scowl. Wiping her eyes she said "I throw you a feast and you dare ambush me?"

Undaunted Vanadis joined her on the ledge. "You're thinking of the omen. It's of Vargeisa isn't it?"

Louhi turned away, "None are to speak of her."

"I will." Vanadis said evenly. "I will because you need to speak of her."

Louhi shot her a glare. "Impudent child."

Vanadis crossed her arms and did not budge. "You're the childish one. Your bullying won't work on me."

Louhi dropped her guard. "Very well. We shall speak of this, once, but never bring it up again."

Suddenly, the memories weakened and her own thoughts returned. In the back of her mind, she heard her mother say, "I was wrong, my dear one, dreadfully so. If I could lift my curse I would, even if it meant incurring the wrath of foreign gods. I pray to Ukko that you are safe and in good health. Free Laufeyson if you must but survive the ordeal. Survive and find joy. This is my wish for you. Please forgive your foolish mother."

The Fire Wolf blinked tears from her eyes. "I-I apologize, I must be alone." She said, her voice torn with sorrow. With that she stood and rushed away from camp holding in wretched sobs.

"Is it safe for her to be alone?" asked Gamli.

Wolf snorted, "I pity any soul luckless enough to cross her this night."

Katla watched where she ran with an expression of concern but also relief. She turned to Vanadis and offered her a small, thankful smile.

"I delivered this for my teacher. Though I have to admit, I admire Vargeisa. I hope the message brings her comfort." Vanadis replied.

***

The next afternoon greeted with a light summer rain. Most of the party gathered under the pavilion where they tossed dice. A significant pile of skatt lay before Ransu. Off to the side, tucked away from the rain, and weighted by sturdy rocks lay the contents of Salli's scroll, a wool embroidery of her and Vargeisa holding hands. Beside it sat the Barrow Bowl, a simple vessel made of reddish clay, tiny runes were etched along its rim.

Gamli held Wolf back, "I swear he's not cheating."

Ransu just smiled innocently and said nothing.

Katla covered her mouth to hold in laughter.

Vanadis and Vargeisa sat a distance away, under a maple tree which, for the most part, kept the misty rain at bay. They picked at their breakfast of cheese and berries. Vanadis had filled Vargeisa in on the state of Pohjola. She spoke if it with great pleasure and spared no details.

"You are most fond of my homeland." commented the Fire Wolf with a grin.

"I consider it my own." Replied the Volsung sister with unwavering certainty.

"Long ago, Väinämöinen washed ashore and was a guest at my mother's house. At the time he was most welcome and he could have stayed, but he considered it better to be in filth and rags than in luxury and silk in a foreign land." Vargeisa chided.

Vanadis snickered. "Väinämöinen has never been in filth and rags. I have, I would never go back." She munched a bit of cheese and consider this further, "Truly, I hold no love for Alands. My time there was a sea of misery. You mother welcomed me, taught me to be a free woman and a powerful seithkona. My home will always be Pohjola."

The Fire Wolf chuckled, examined a bright red berry before popping it in her mouth. "My mother's teachings never took root in me. Oh she tried but my will was too strong. My pledge of fealty is to Loki alone. His laughter, tricks and stewardship fashioned me into what you see before you. I treasure deeply the time I spent with him, even more so than Geirroth and Agnarr treasured their time with Odin and Frigg. " She arrested Vanadis with a hard look, "Which is why I must free him. So I must know, will you stand in my way?"

"Would you believe my answer?" Vanadis shot back dryly.

"Your lies will find no purchase with me, not in this matter." the Fire Wolf said with deadly seriousness.

Vanadis chuckled, "I serve Laufey, my brother is a chosen of Surt, I can't, in justice, fault your quest."

"Be not so naïve." the Fire Wolf hissed. "Loki has many enemies, even among the Jotun. I must do things to free him that they will not stand for."

"Such as end the world?" Vanadis queried.

"Of course not!" Shot back Vargeisa, "Who gave us the prophesy of Ragnarok? Odin! Since when has he proven himself trustworthy?"

"Sometimes even deceivers tell thre truth. The Nameless Vovla gave him the prophesy, didn't she? You spoke to her, did she verify Odin's claim?"

This halted the Fire Wolf's tirade, "I..."

Vanadis touched her arm gently. "I've told our tale of Myrkvid many times. When I have done so I've purposefully left out all mention of Hvergelmir. I haven't spoken of your true quest to anyone, not even my brother. It's none of my business. If you can swear to me that your quest will not harm us or Pohjola, even indirectly, then I won't stand in your way."

Vargeisa sighed, "Hvergelmir is deadly; in opening its seals I might release...things that will wreak calamity and woe. However, I do swear that I will strive to ensure these evils do not plague Pohjola."

Vanadis weighed these words carefully in her mind. She looked and reflected on the Fire Wolf who seemed anxious. "I'm no saviour." she started, placing each word with precision. "I'm only moved by the welfare of those I care about. I'll do anything for them, even set Midgard ablaze. In that regard I understand you Vargeisa Fire Wolf. All I ask is that you act with caution in freeing Loki. Do this, and we can be friends." She opened her arms to her.

"Friends." Answered Vargeisa much relived. Then, they embraced each other like sisters.

***

That night the rain let up but the sky remained cloudy. The party sat around the campfire once more, this time supping on fresh fish from Ransu's net.

"On the marrow, we must leave for Ranrike." announced Vargeisa. "We are to meet a secluded sect of Jotun worshipers, with luck they will aid me in enacting my great work."

"What work is this exactly?" asked Ransu.

"We have spoken of it." cut in Vanadis. "You wouldn'tt like it."

"But we are going with them, aren't we?" retorted the fisherman wryly.

"No," answered Vanadis with a quirky smile, "tomorrow we're heading north, back to Pohjola."

"Thank Ukko!" cried Ransu staring up at the sky. "You finally talk sense."

Vanadis shovelled in a bit of trout, savoured it and said "There's no reason for further danger." To Vargeisa she added, "If you have a message for your mother and sister give it to me and I'll make sure they receive it."

"The message is simple. Tell my mother I forgive her. Tell my sister that I am well and hold close to my heart my love for her." answered, the Fire Wolf. "However, I suggest that you listen to my council and wait to deliver."

"I promised Louhi we'd return. We can't go with you to Ranrike." Vanadis answered.

"Return to her you shall," said the Fire Wolf, "but only if you heed my words." She gestured to the Baltic and swept her hand northeast. "If you sail that way you must pass Öland, Gotland, and Kalevala. You will be most welcome, for they are eager for your deaths. They wish you to answer the killing of Steinarr, the Troll attack against the Kalevalans, and the travesty at Gotland."

"We have an understanding with Thora." said Gamli.

"Yet Hardegon perused you." answered the Fire Wolf.

"We've passed Kalevala before twice without incident." said Ransu.

"That was before their warriors failed to return to their grieving wives." Vargeisa pointed southwest. "Forget not that you have earned the ire of Gorm the Old. He will send a fresh party to the Mounds, Drafli's son will summon his father who will lay your crimes to bare."

"Crimes spent in saving your life." Vanadis snarled.

"I'm grateful. Which is why I advise you." said Vargeisa nonplused. "Given your reputation there is only one place for you." She pointed east. "You must stay a while with the Amber Tribes."

"Barbarians and pirates? You mean to kill us." stated Ransu.

Vargeisa giggled, "The swiftest way to Tuonela is to call a Curonian or Samogitian such. The east is vast my friends. Find a secluded grove, with Ransu here you'll live comfortably. If you manage to get on speaking terms with the tribes Gamli's wears would be in great demand. Play this right and you may return wealthy and to a homeland embroiled in other matters than your crimes."

"Perhaps we just need to sail against the eastern shore?" suggested Vanadis. "That way we'd avoid our enemies."

"Until they discovered you in Pohjola. Fresh in their grief three kingdoms, Jutland, Alands and Kalevala, would demand your heads. Mother would refuse and we would have war in the north." the Fire Wolf's tone held a harder edge.

"Then we'll head east." said Gamli. He turned to Ransu, "We'll need you though, otherwise we'll starve."

The fisherman frowned in thought. "I suppose Curonians and Samogitians are no less deadly than any of our other foes. I've always wanted to prospect for amber. Very well Fire Wolf you've convinced me."

"Vanadis?" asked Gamli.

"Do not let your mind be clouded by your heart." pressed Vargeisa. "Think of what's best for yourself and the ones you love."

The seithkona looked away, brooding. Her keen mind dissected Vargeisa's logic, looking for a flaw, scraping for a reason why they couldn't head straight back for Pohjola, for home. She found nothing. "Thor's balls." she cursed. Then, with a sigh, she added "East it is. We'll make our home in the wilderness. When the time's ripe we'll return to Pohjola."

Vanadis rubbed her back. To Wolf and Katla she asked "Shall we give them our knarr? We need it not for our journey to Ranrike."

Wolf and Katla glanced at each other.

"Aye," Wolf said, "they saved our lives which are worth more than any ship."

Katla nodded sagely.

***

The next morning the six gathered at a hidden Skane cove. The sky was grey and windy. The sea choppy.

"Should we keep camp?" asked Gamli.

Ransu studied the clouds, "Nay. Ukko's reigned them in up high. They won't give us trouble. The wind blows east, this is a good day to set off"

"As for us," said Vargeisa, now weighed down by her pack, tucked securely inside was the Barrow Bowl, "we must be off." She embraced Vanadis and then, she held her at arm's length. "May Laufey watch over you."

"She watches over all her investments." Vanadis said with a smirk. "Best of luck to you, as well. I hope find whomever you seek."

"Farewell." Said Gamli with a nod.

"It was a pleasure to meet your acquaintance Vargeisa. You are far less dour than your mother." Ransu said with a bow.

Wolf nodded in farewell.

Kalta waved.

With that the three boarded the knarr, Gamli unfurled their sail and they struck off across the Baltic.

Wolf watched them go, "They might have been useful. We could have pressed them to come with us."

Vargeisa giggled. "Oh they're useful enough. We'll whisper rumor and embellishment. Outrage at their villainy will mask our own crimes to come."

Katla glared at her.

Vargeisa laughed and then, she looked 'hurt,' "They'll be safe enough. No one will think to look amongst the Tribes. Next year, we'll warn them away. The following?" she shrugged, "I pray it'll be safe for them to return, but by that point it'll be out of our hands."

Wolf chuckled, "You are a cold woman."

"I simply know how to best to use both friend and foe." replied the Fire Wolf.

***

The three sailed south east, making excellent progress, and the western shore swiftly sank on the horizon.

Ormir let out a flute like whine. Gamli patted him reassuringly, "Aye, we're going straight across. Be good, we can't afford a fire this far out."

"If he sets us ablaze it'll be on your head." warned Ransu, who sat at the rudder.

"Have you ever made this trip before?" asked Vanadis uneasily.

"No." the fisherman answered abruptly.

"I see." Vanadis said, as she swallowed her fear.

Ransu considered her unease and Gamli's look of doubt. "Don't be concerned. I was born on a ship. I've sailed all my life. This route is new to me but I'll get you to the eastern shore safe and sound."

They sailed all day, when night fell there was no sign of land, just the rolling, dark Baltic.

"Shouldn't be there by now?" asked Gamli.

Ransu laughed, "Not at all. I've heard tell that such a journey could take days."

"We have enough water, right?" asked Vanadis who was about to take a swig.

"Aye." Answered Ransu. "I checked our stocks before we left. Though, it helps that the beast drinks not."

Ormir trumpeted in annoyance.

Vanadis took a deep pull from the water skin. "Oh he drinks, just not water." She knelt, summoned a weak spirit who lit a black flame in her palm. She offered her hand to the Drake, who licked the fire thirstily. The drake let out a pleasant hum and then nuzzled his head into Vanadis' hand.

Gamli sighed with relief. "I'm glad we all can eat."

They sailed on through the night, each taking a shift at the rudder. In the morning, Ransu cursed out Vanadis for steering too far north.

"That there?" He pointed to a small dot of land beyond the waves. "That would be Öland. We must go no further."

"The wind changed." said Vanadis. "I thought tacking north would be faster."

Ransu frowned, tested the wind, and grunted. "Very well, we'll head northeast. Just pray no one spot us from land."

They sailed for two more days. The third and fourth days of their journey had less wind and more heat. The three broiled in the summer sun. Ransu forced the siblings to wear light clothes and don sea water soaked hoods and hats.

"Out here, the sun will kill you. Drink sparingly."

While not on the rudder, Ransu fished. Each evening, he pulled a fine feast for them which they cooked on Vanadis' magic flame. The result was surprisingly pleasant, the taste seemed more lively, like it had a bite of its own, but too much would numb the lips and tongue.

Vanadis awoke Ransu early the next day. Before she could say a word he motioned her to hush. He stood up, his face dropping to sudden fear. The air was still. He looked to the west and saw a heavy, dark, anvil shaped cloud, at the head of several misty dark clouds. They were approaching fast.

"Ransu? Does that mean what I think it does?" ssked Vanadis with a tremor in her voice.

He glanced down at her "Yes, waking me now was most wise." He raced over and shook Gamli. "Wake up! Now!"

As Gamli rolled and staggered to consciousness. Ransu ordered "Vanadis, tether yourself and the beast to the ship. I'll secure myself and your brother."

Once the smith was awake and the crew secured Ransu then ordered "Take the sail down. Secure the beam. Drape it over the side and secure it like a tent. Blast! I wish we had another hand."

"We do." said the Volsung sister. She cried "Bera, you are needed."

A cloud of ash swirled up from the deck and out of it stepped the grinning, skeletal shieldmaiden.

"Ah hah!" Ransu laughed. "Never have I been so happy to see you."

"You old charmer." said Bera in an eerie voice.

"Now quick, help me secure the sail. Gamli turn our ship to the waves. Vanadis secure our oars." The fisherman had to yell this as the wind was picking up to a roar. In the distance the anvil cloud flashed bolts of lightning and thunder boomed across the waves.

"Thor is angry with us." said Gamli.

"Nay!" said Ransu, "It is Ukko, he warns us that we haven't much time."

In moments the sail was taught across the beam and secured port and starboard like a large tent.

"I'll hold the rudder." said Ransu. "Gamli, Bera to the oars but pull them only at my direction. Vanadis to the bow, keep your eyes peeled for land. If you see it warn me."

Soon after that was said, the storm hit. Rain lashed down on the karve and the waves rolled the boat swiftly up and down. Ransu held the rudder steady and yelled for Galmli or Bera to row, both used their utmost strength to help keep their ship upright. Vanadis, in the bow, gripped the gunwales tight.
In the face of the violent sea, in the fierce lighting, in the deafening thunder, she was terrified. More terrified than when her dead mother first visited her. More terrified than in the darkest of Louhi's lessons. More terrified than when she had been swallowed by the Danevirke. Yet, in spite of this, she held onto her wits and kept her eyes peeled.

They battled the storm for what seemed like hours, it did not abate. At times Ransu ordered Gamli and Bera to bail rather than attend the oars. Vanadis offered to help but Ransu insisted "Keep your eyes on the bow."

It was good she did, for suddenly, through the driving rain and the lurching waves, loomed a shoreline. "Ransu!" Vanadis screamed. "I see it."

"Gamli! Take the rudder!" Ransu switched with the smith and ran for the bow. He knelt beside Vanadis and peered hawkishly ahead. The hilly shore stretched in either direction as far as the eye could see. It was close, close enough to see a hut, whose fire flickered in the darkness, far inland. Lightning flashed but Ransu did not blink.

"I'm sorry." Vanadis cried. "I don't know how it could sneak up on me."

Ransu squeezed her shoulder firmly, looked her straight in the eye and said "To Hiisi with your apologises. I need you sharp. Can you stay sharp?"

Vanadis mastered herself. "I can."

Ransu slapped her on the back, "Good girl." He then pointed to the distant hut. "You see that?

"Yes."

"I'm beaching us just port of that." He pointed to a speck of land to the left. "Keep your eyes on that, guide me so I may guide the ship."

"Won't we crash into the rocks?"

"Not if your eyes are keen, my hand steady, and Ahti is kind."

He then raced for the rudder. "Get to your oar."

Gamli obeyed. Bera sat ready.

"Turn starboard!" shouted Vanadis.

Ransu heaved on the rudder, the ship lurched.

"We're not far enough!"

"Gamli row!"

"Too far! Too Far!"

"Gamli halt. Bera row!"

The ship lurched side to side. As Vanadis gave directions and Ransu guided the craft. Water flooded into the knarr. Twice the gunwales almost submerged.

Finally, Vanadis yelled, "We're striking land!" and she braced herself. The rest of the crew did likewise.

The knarr slid into the mud with such force that Bera shattered and the ship skidded overland with great speed. The three screamed. Ormir let out a trumpeting cry. Thankfully, its momentum soon ground to a halt, a mere few strides north of the house, which, upon closer inspection, turned out to be a great tent with a foundation of mud.

For a moment all was silent except the rain. Then lighting flashed and a boom of thunder rolled across the sky. Ransu let out a joyous cheer. Gamli and Vanadis followed suit. Their laughter was desperate and thankful. Ormir lay curled up in Gamli's lap, still frozen with fright.

Vanadis wiped her drenched locks out of her eyes and sighed. Suddenly she was assailed by strange words. She shirked port to find a young boy chattering at her in wide eyed excitement. Beside him was a bare - chested gangly man with dark wild hair and a beard braded with tiny bits of amber. He looked to the crew with concern and asked a question whose words Vanadis could not understand.

She looked to her companions. Gamli and Ransu shrugged.

The boy grabbed Vanadis' sleeve and pulled, pointing to the tent. His father likewise gestured for them to follow him inside.

Ransu stood. "I'm not one to refuse an invitation. Come let's get out of this rain."

Vanadis chuckled and followed suit, "Agreed." With that, she let the child guide her to shelter from the storm.

CHAPTER 20

In home, there is love and safety. | There is also no awe, no wonder.
One who always stays near hearth, even if he is wealthy, is really a pauper.
Midgard is our world. | Best go out and see it.
But be warned, travel too far abroad and you'll grow roots in a foreign land.

The three were lead into the tent to find it a humble, but clean and spacious affair. A fire pit lay in the center, on a tripod hung a pot from which boiled a soup. Reed mats and furs were rolled out for sitting and sleep.

To the left of the entrance, a weather beaten old man, wrapped a wool blanket was laying. His eyes were closed and he muttered incoherently.

Beside him, knelt a thin woman who cooled his forehead with a wet cloth. She wore common but well-kept clothes. She glanced up in shock at the strangers. Then she glared behind them at her husband and said something that sounded like a scolding.

When Gamli stepped inside, set down Ormir and the drake snaked for the fire the mother screamed.

The father staggered back.

The son laughed with amazement.

"It's alright." Gamli said, his hands spread out peacefully. "Ormir means no harm."

The drake curled around the fire and let out a pleasant whisper that sounded like pan pipes. Then the serpent breathed in and out in a relaxed manner, letting out light, soothing music. The family paused and regarded Ormir with wonder. Vanadis nudged the mother and gestured to the grandfather. His look of pain was gone and he slept peacefully. The Mother gasped with sudden joy. She squeezed Vanadis' arm and thanked her. She turned and patted the drake gently. Before the son could let out a tirade of amazement, she shushed him.

The father smiled at Gamli and gestured for him to sit. The smith did so gladly.

The storm soon raged its last, petering off into a misty rain and then stillness. Ransu took charge of the soup, and ladled it out in a manner that satisfied the mother. The two groups ate and spoke amongst themselves. They also communicated to each other in smiles, gestures and slowly repeated words. Through this the family learned the party's names. They in turn learned the family's. The father was Edgaras. The mother was Gryte. Their son was Juras and the grandfather was Merkelis. When they slept Vandis, Ransu and Gamli kept a watch but found, with this family, they had no need of it.

***

The next morning Ransu surprised them all with a large catch of fresh fish. After a hearty breakfast the party and Edgaras stepped outside to take stock of the damage to the knarr. The storm clouds had vanished. The sun coaxed fog from the muddy sand veiling the land in white.

The knarr's hull was missing more than a few planks. Gamli's oar, the rudder, and the keel had all snapped. The sea chests, and their contents, were fine. The sails and packs were soaked.

"She'll take care and time to dig out. Once we do we'll know if we have a ship or drift wood." said Ransu.

With that, the three pulled everything out of the knarr, Edgaras pitching in to help. Once the knarr's cargo was neatly stacked by the tent the three began to dig out their ship, Edgaras lending them shovels. They finished in the early afternoon, Ransu regarded the 'vessel' which was now ripped full of holes. "This is Hiisi's work." He looked to Gamli, "Any ideas?"

Gamli stroked his beard and looked over the craft closely. "I'm good at patching ships but that's a far cry from fixing this. I'm uncertain Surt's blessing applies to things of the sea. Maybe Wayland's blood will be enough? "

"Ransu, Gamli!" cried Vanadis. The fog had lifted and she had scaled a dune to get her bearings. "Come up here, take a look."

"We're busy." huffed Gamli.

"This will take only a minute." urged Vanadis.

"What do you think?" Ransu asked Edgaras. The amber adorned man glanced up and Vanadis and seemed to take cheer in her bewildered look. He glanced at his two guests and chuckled, then, he walked back inside the tent.

"I take it there is something to see." commented the fisherman who raced up the dune. Gamli sighed and followed. When they reached the top both of them fell into astonishment.

The fog had lifted and from their vantage the three saw they were not on an island, not on the mainland, but instead on a strip of sand and dunes that stretched north and south as far as they could see. To the west the blue Baltic rolled onto the horizon. To the east was another body of water whose length, north and south, continued beyond sight. When they squinted east they could see lush, green land on its far shore. The sand and sky was dotted with numerous sea birds whose cries filled the air.

"What is this?" exclaimed Gamli.

Ransu glanced in both directions and along the wasteland strip in disbelief. "In my long years I've been to many places and heard of many things. This? This is strange to me."

Vanadis considered the tent beneath them and their ruined knarr. "Strange as it is, we're stuck here. Ransu, could you aid our hosts while Gamli repairs our ship?"

"Aye, they've lent us a hand, I'd be happy to do the same. What will you do?"

Vanadis gestured and a shimmering field of green rippled before her. She stepped through it and vanished. Her voice came out of nothing "I'm going to wander about, see what this land has to offer."

"Be careful." warned Gamli.

Vanadis giggled, "Fear not, Bera's with me."

"Then, you are in good hands." surmised Ransu. With a bow, he added, "Bera, if you can hear me, thanks for your help in getting us onshore. We were all needed and without you we would have perished."

"She has heard you and asks, if you could portion out a meal for her." answered the ghostly seithkona.

"Of course," chuckled Ransu, "Making offerings to the restless dead is never a waste of time."

***

The day passed peacefully. Gamli worked on the ship with hammer, axe, board, and nail. When he needed to lift or turn the ship, he did so with Ormir's help, the drake acting like a wedge or pulling rope while Gamli heaved and pushed. By the evening he had patched the hull but would only consider his task complete after he tested its seaworthiness.

Ransu, Edgaras, and Juras struck out to the shore with shovels and sieves. They prospected for amber along the western beach, finding likely spots, digging up the sand, and sifting the amber out. Ransu's keen eye helped them find key deposits. When they returned at sunset their baskets held many precious, yellow gems. Ransu took half of his share for himself and gave the other to Edgaras, who accepted it graciously.

Vanadis struck off and walked north along the eastern shore unseen. Along her path, she spied other amber prospectors, some took their goods to small horse headed ships and rowed them across the lagoon. Other's rowed back, their vessels laden with supplies. She walked among them unseen, they seemed decent, hardworking folk but she could not understand a word they said. All the while the summer sun shone brightly and the sand dried. The seithkona thirsted and, seeing the natives drink from these eastern wasters, she did as well. She found it refreshing. Vanadis returned to their hosts at twilight.

Gryte tended Merkelis who came out of his stupor twice, long enough for her to feed him. He had regained some strength thanks to the peaceful night before, but was still unable to stand. He regarded the guests with a little fear at first, but calmed when Ormir hummed the song that had eased him the night before.

Ransu took over cooking. He presented a dish of roasted fish with vegetables and seaweed. They washed it down with beer. It was a solid, tasty meal.

That evening the three conversed together, slightly apart from the family.

Vanadis told Gamli and Ransu everything she had found and concluded with, "This place is nice but I'd feel safer on the other side of the lagoon. Sadly, I don't think we'd be welcome there."

Ransu considered their hosts; Edgaras had stepped out into the windy night. Gryte talked pensively with Merkelis. Young Juras sat by Ormir, feeding him burning sticks, as a way to deal with the obvious stress about them. "They might vouch for us but, right now, they seem to have other concerns." Then, after a thought, he added, "Could one of their ghosts translate?"

Vanadis shook her head, "The dead speak what they did in life. The ghosts here wouldn't understand not my commands let alone heed them." She chuckled bitterly, "If Vinglunr were here I'm certain..."

Her brother took her hand, "He's not, but you have us."

Vanadis sighed in appreciation. "For which I'm thankful. The question is..."

Suddenly, Edgaras burst into the tent, accompanying him was the distant roar of wind. He urgently spoke to his wife. Gryte replied by shaking her head and pleading with him. Old, sick Merkelis grasped her arm and entreated her, tears in his eyes. Juras ran to his grandfather and hugged him, weeping with fear.

"Must be something out there." said Ransu.

Gamli stood grasping the hilt of Scorn. "Best to go meet it." With that, he strode for the exit.

Vanadis followed and asked, "Brother, perhaps, we shouldn't get involved?"

"They sheltered us from the storm, we side with them." Gamli rumbled.

Edgaras made way for the smith but was too embroiled in the urgent discussion with his wife to pay much heed. Ormir snaked away from the fire and followed his master out. Vanadis was close behind and Ransu after her.

They found the beach empty. Even the southern wind touched them not thanks to the nearby dune.

"Strange." commented Ransu.

"Perhaps, a higher vantage?" Suggested Vanadis as she climbed the sandy mound. Gamli and Ransu followed. They peered south and their breath caught in their throats. A massive cloud of sand blotted out the landscape and even the stars. It rolled forward, howling like a great beast.

Vanadis regarded it and then, turned to the tent. "The storm will knock down this hill and bury them."

Ransu paused in thought and added, "The ship, we'll carry it out of this dune's shadow. Then we can hide behind it. We'll have to dig it out but it's better than being buried alive."

"Merkelis," The seithkona said, "if we move him out this weather will kill him." She frowned, "I have no spell that can move the tent."

Ransu considered "Perhaps if we put him under..."

"N-no." said Gamli, "I'll deal with this."

"Brother how?"

Ormir suddenly ignited with such brilliance that Vanadis and Ransu were startled and fell rolling down the dune.

"The madness." cried Gamli, "Keep our hosts in the tent. They won't need to move."

Vanadis spit sand out of her mouth and glared up at him. He was a shadow lit from behind by Ormir who had become a bonfire.

Ransu lifted her to her feet. "Best to let him be. I don't think we can stop him."

With that, the two rushed into the tent. Edgaras was imploring his wife, seeming ready to seize her and drag her out.

Vanadis glanced at Ransu with uncertainty.

Ransu merely urged, "Trust Gamli."

She sighed and lightly touched Edgaras' shoulder. He spun and glowered at her.

"Be at ease." Vanadis said in a confident tone. "My brother will save us."

The amber prospector did not look convinced.

Suddenly, Gryte shrieked. All turned in her direction and saw the wall of the tent lit buy a immense fire outside. She cried and shielded her father. Edgaras rushed forward and seized her.

The seithkona shuddered and sneered at him. "I told you, be at ease!" she snarled in a voice not her own.
The Volsung sister pointed at their host and he suddenly vanished, leaving his clothes behind, which dropped to the floor. The mother and son, still embracing their protesting grandfather, didn't notice. The air filled with the ominous, deafening moan of the wind, the lilting music of Ormir, which seemed to sing in defiance of it, and the whoosh of flame. This light and fury rose to a cacophony of pandemonium and then, as suddenly as it began, it faded. The burning light shank and died, the wind still blew but the tent was still. Gryte's cries and screams ceased. Merkelis said something in a questioning tone. Juras looked around in dismay for his father.

Ransu, who had covered his ears, closed his eyes and braced for the worst, slowly came out of his shell and looked around. "It's done. We best check on him."

"Aye."sSaid Vanadis, who was herself once more.

The two rushed out of the tent. Seeing them go, and after her father's blessing, Gryte and her child followed. They found Gamli lying outside the tent, he breathed heavily, catching his breath. Ormir lay curled up beside him. A wall of black volcanic glass, twice as tall as the tent, split the dune in two smaller parts. It was curved slightly outward, so as to direct the sand to either side, away from the dwelling.

Vanadis, Ransu, Gryte, and Juras stared up at it in awe. The seithkona, still staring at the wonder, knelt and dropped a small white mouse she'd been holding onto the stand. She stepped back and suddenly it vanished, in its place stood a naked Edgaras, who, in the face of Gamli's wall, found himself unable to notice his nakedness, nor even complain at his previous, sudden, transformation.

Ransu knelt beside the smith, laughed and clapped him on the shoulder. "By Ukko that is something."

Gryte dropped down beside him, tears in her eyes thanking Gamli profusely. Gamli pushed himself up and smiled at her, looking pleased to have helped. Juras rushed forward and hugged him, the smith patted him on the head. "My proudest creation." he said, gesturing to the wall.

Edgaras walked carefully up to it and held out his hand, nearly touching it, but not quite. Heat shimmered about him. He turned and asked a question in a tentative tone.

"I think he wants to know why we didn't burn." said Ransu.

Gamli petted Ormir. "He directed the heat away from the tent." Then, with a sudden frown, he asked, "Why is he naked?"

"I turned him into a mouse." answered Vanadis.

"You should have turned the old man into one instead, we could have sheltered him with two hands." suggested Ransu, making a cupping motion to demonstrate.

Vanadis shook her head, "The spell would have killed him. As for our host, I needed a way to disable him that didn't involve shattering a leg."

She knelt in the sand beside Ormir and regarded her brother with a profound respect, "Still, my mouse trick is nothing compared to that." She nodded at the wall. "I am at a loss for words Gamli. All I can say is, I'm proud of you."

"Ho." Gamli laughed. Glancing at Ransu he said, "Remember this, you're my only witness."

"I am proud to be of service." answered the fisherman with a laugh.

***

In the morning, after a quick breakfast, Gamli and Ransu stepped outside to once again to dig out the knarr. This time it was easier going, for they dealt with sand, not mud. Vanadis and Gryte followed to dig out the tent and knock sand from the roof. Edgaras and son left early with a full basket of amber, they bid good day and struck off east. Merkelis stayed in bed but was well enough to call out when he needed care.

After a morning of hard work and after a quick swim and wash in the sea, they returned to lie inside the dwelling. Gryte shared a snack of dried fruit and a generous helping of beer. Grandfather, no matter how much he begged, got only fruit and water

Suddenly Ransu sat up. He cocked an ear and motioned everyone to hush. "Footsteps, lots of them."

Gamli reached for his sword but Gryte held his arm and shook her head. She seemed calm and eager. She spoke to him in a soothing tone.

Gamli hesitated and glanced at Vanadis.

She stood, "Take it with you but let's hope you don't have to use it."

Gamli grunted and nodded. "Don't worry." He said to Gryte. " It's merely a precaution." He belted his weapon but held out his palms to show he did not mean violence. Gryte relented but looked pensive.

Vanadis considered Ransu, "Ransu, I stored your javelins in the knarr, rush out there and be ready. Don't throw them unless you have too."

"Aye," said the fisherman and he raced out.

The seithkona focused herself, reaching out with her will to her milling spirits. 'Still no mother?' 'No,' returned the voice of her father, 'but we stand ready and will heed your call.'

"Thank you." She said out-loud. She turned to her brother, "We'll see if they're peaceful, if not, we fight and then run."

Gamli glanced at Gryte worriedly, "We won't have to kill them, will we?"

The Volsung sister rolled her eyes and pulled her brother out the door, "I'm a pragmatist, not a monster."

Once outside they heard many voices approaching and the trudging of many feet in sand. Then, off to the left, near Gamli's wall walked Edgaras leading a troop of warriors. They wore heavy leather armor, carried shields and axes. At the center was a tall, stately woman with long black hair. Her bangs were held back by an amber band lined with gold. Around her neck was a gold collar adorned with amber horse heads. Under this was a cloak of red, which draped all the way down to her sandaled feet. Upon seeing the wall of volcanic glass, the troop paused in astonishment.
Edgaras chattered excitedly and gestured to it. The woman pushed her way through her guard and reached out a delicate hand, "By Neringa," she whispered in awe. She favored Edgaras with a smile, "You boasted naught. This is great magic."

"By Ukko." stammered Ransu, "She speaks Soumi."

"No," said Gamli, "She's speaking Orse, as I am now."

"Shht!" hissed Vanadis.

The troop turned their attention to them. They muttered to each other in their strange tongue, braced and ready for battle.

Gamli raised up his hands and took a step back. "We mean no harm."

Ransu ducked behind the knarr and, with his hands out of sight, seized a javelin.

Vanadis regarded the woman and bowed. "Hello, I see you admire my brother's wall."

Edgaras chattered to both groups nervously.

The woman gestured for calm and said to the prospector "Be at ease." Her blue eyes locked on Vanadis and she seemed to measure her worth. "I am Lonija, holy priestess and daughter of Malvis High Chieftain of Courland. Who are you and what brings you to the Couronian Spit?" Her voice was rich, cultured and confident.

Now that she had turned to face them Vanadis noticed the left side of Lonija's cloak hung a little too close to her body. 'She's missing an arm.' Whispered one of her spirits. Vanadis chose not to remark on it. As for the priestess' questions, a number of likely stories rose in her mind, Vanadis pushed these down though and decided to start with the truth, she would lie, as needed. "I'm Vanadis the Cursed. This is my brother Gamli the Serpent, and the man hiding behind the boat his Ransu the Spider. We were shipwrecked by the storm. Edgaras and his family graciously sheltered us while we repaired our vessel."

Gryte stepped outside and fell to her knees in the sand. She pleaded with Lonija and gestured to their guests.

The priestess smiled at her and answered, "At ease. I am here to talk, not fight." She looked at the group, "I trust you are the same?"

"Aye." said Ransu, stepping around the boat, leaving his javelin behind.

Gryte looked very much relieved. Juras raced out from behind the troop and prattled excitedly at his mother. She looked helplessly at Lonija.

"You are dismissed." She answered graciously. She turned to Edgaras, "You may stay while we barter or leave as you wish. You were wise to bring this to my attention."

Edgaras answered cordially and took a step back, watching the proceedings.

"How can you talk to all of us?" asked a confounded Gamli.

"Brother," Vanadis cut in, "we are on their land; we answer their questions, not the other way around."

She could feel her brother glaring at her behind her back. Some of the troop noticed and chuckled.

"Right, you are," said Lonija, well - pleased, "and I shall ask them. For instance, how are you cursed?"

Vanadis laughed, "I have many foes. My brother and I are Volsungs, our Nibelung enemies wish to kill us. They've been at our heels for the past year. We've just escaped them."

Lonija turned thoughtful at that, "Yes I've herd of Volsungs. Dragon slayers are they not?"

"Our great ancestor was Signy, aunt to Sigurd who slew the dragon Fanfir." answered Vanadis.

"I have also heard you are a line of sorcerers, is this true?"

Vanadis remembered well the songs Vinglunr shared with them on their journey, tales of their blood. "Yes, our ancient mother Signy was a powerful witch. Her brother, Sigmund, and his son. Sinfjötli. could turn into wolves. My brother crafted that wall," Vanadis nodded at the glass construct, "and I turned poor Edgaras into a mouse."

Lonija giggled at that, "As I have heard and now that I see the wall, I believe. Your foes, the Nibelung, will they follow you here?"

Vanadis smiled craftily and shook her head, "No, they wouldn't think to look east. They consider your kind blood thirsty barbarians. We, on the other hand, know you to be reasonable." At least Vanadis hoped that Lonija was reasonable, she'd soon find out.

"You seek sanctuary, on our lands?" she asked with sudden disbelief.

An idea struck the seithkona, a smile came upon her lips, the words just began to roll off her tongue, then she paused. She glanced back at her brother who watched the parlay with growing dissatisfaction. To Lonija she said "Not quite, we planned to hide in an uninhabited grove and wait a year before returning. We hoped to avoid your detection but the more I think on that, the worse the idea seems."

"I would say so, we would find and kill you." said Lonija tersely.

"I have a much better idea," offered Vanadis, ", but it will only work if my brother agrees."

"What?" said Gamli, sounding dubious.

"Brother," Vanadis said with the utmost care, "would you consider starting a business here?"

"You mean working for the right to live?" Gamli spat, "I had enough of that with Asvard."

"No," Vanadis shook her head, "I'd never ask that of you. I'd die before doing so. What I mean is for you to set up a business here so the Curonians can pay a fair price for your works."

Gamli flinched as the idea struck him. He regarded Lonija, "Your people would be willing to have me?"

Lonija snorted, "We have our own smiths."

Vanadis removed her golden circlet and offered it to the priestess. "Not like this, take a look."

One of her guards, a large man with a think brown beard and icy blue eyes, asked Lonija something while glowering at them.

The priestess considered both offers – from Vanadis and her bodyguard. There was a tense pause, Edgaras pleaded something but the huge man shouted him down. Finally, Lonija said, "No Izidorious, I would hear them further." She then gestured for Vanadis to hand her the circlet. The seithkona did so and the priestess weighed it, and tossed it spinning in the air, watching it as it glittered and she caught it again.

She looked impressed, "Perfectly smooth, no sign of mark or clasp. Simple but supremely beautiful. There is a magic to it too."

"Yes there is, it strengthens my spells. My brother crafted it for me as a symbol of freedom from Nibelung bondage. It's my greatest treasure aside from my brother and Ransu."

Lonija tossed the circlet back to Vanadis. "Show me more."

Vanadis looked aside to the fisherman. "Ransu, could you bring out my spear from the knarr? Move slowly and hand it to me haft first."

"Aye." Said Ransu and he slowly complied. Vanadis carefully took Burning Mind from him and presented it to Lonija.

Lonija lifted it in her one hand and rested its butt on the sand. She looked closely on its twisting gold inlaid surface and eyed the sharp spear point. "A fine weapon." she surmised. "It too holds power."

"It's a talisman through which I can channel seith." answered Vanadis.

The priestess handed Vanadis back her spear and then she regarded Gamli. "I am curious about your weapon, it holds an interesting hue. Would you allow Izidorious to examine it?"

The Couronian warrior looked intrigued at that.

Gamli and Ransu looked uncertain. Vanadis seemed calm but inside she panicked. She foresaw the Izidorious drawing her brother's sword only to stab him with it. Then then rest of the troop would attack.

"Well?" Lonija pressed, her deep brown eyes locked on Gamli with a hint of humor and judgement. "If we allow you on our lands it will take a significant amount of trust. Will you not show trust in kind?

Gamli's expression turned determined. "You're right."hHe rumbled. With that he unbelted his sword.

"Gamli are you sure about this?" asked Ransu.

"Brother, perhaps..." said Vanadis.

"Enough." hnterrupted the smith. "It's my decision, if it dooms us it'll be on my head." He held his sword out by its sheath and offered the hilt to Izidorious.

The Curonian stepped forward, grasped the hilt and drew the blade.

A hex was held in Vanadis' mind, she was about to release it when Gamli glared at her.

"No." he said. His intensity startled her. She dropped the spell.

"Well?" asked Lonija inquisitively to her guard "What do you think?"

The large man marveled at the sword's green sheen. He then frowned at it questioningly. He turned and swiped it in the air a few times and found its weight and speed to pass his judgement. Then he smiled wolfishly and asked Lonija a question. The rest of the warriors laughed. Edgaras protested.

"No, Izidorious. We have honor."

He snarled and retorted something dismissive.

"Because we are better than that. Honor is not easy but," she gestured at the weapon, "it can be rewarding."

The troop considered her words. Some muttered among themselves. Izidorious, reluctantly chastised, sheathed Scorn.

Vanadis, Ransu and Edgaras sighed with relief.

"Are my works to your satisfaction?" asked Gamli.

The priestess turned to him smartly and said, "They are indeed. You will be lent a scrap of land to hide in and given our business for as long as what you forge us is of equal quality to what you've shown me here."

"I can't promise they'll all be magic but I swear you won't find my merchandise lacking." said Gamli with a simple honesty.

Lonija considered this and answered, "Fair enough gather your things, we'll be moving inland."

Izidorious looked livid at that, Lonija touched his arm and guided him and the troop away, whispering in his ear as she did so. The brawny warrior snickered.

"We can still make for the sea." suggested Ransu.

Vanadis considered that but asked Gamli, "What do you think?"

The smith shrugged, "If she wished to betray us I'd lie bleeding on the sand."

"You still might" mused Vanadis, "but, I don't know of a better place to hide. We're in no less danger with them than we are out west."

"You make a good point." Ransu sighed.

***

With that, they gathered their belongings and stepped inside the dwelling to say farewell to their hosts. Edgaras presented Gamli with a chunk of amber the size of his fist. It was sleek and spotless, not a bug or a leaf inside. The smith tried to refuse but Edgaras wouldn't hear of it. Vanadis embraced Gryte who pressed a bundled pack of provisions in her hands. The seithkona then hugged Juras, who was in tears. She then kissed Merkelis on the cheek. The old man smiled, he was now strong enough to sit up on his own. Ransu also embraced Gryte and Juras.

Then the fisherman nudged Merkelis and said, "Don't worry, I'll watch over these young ones." Both old men chucked.

After giving Juras some time to say a sorrowful goodbye to Ormir and feed him another burning stick, the party left their hosts and struck out east.

They reached Lonija, her troop and her ship as the sun was setting. The ship was a dark, sturdy horse headed boat.

"Big enough to stow prisoners." whispered Ransu in Vanadis' ear.

"I know," she whispered back. Invisibly her spirit entourage stood at guard and traces of their power eked into the seithkona, occasionally lifting the hem of her cloak or a tuft of hair.

"You certainly took long enough." commented the priestess.

"Juras found it hard to part with Ormir." said Gamli, gesturing to the drake that stood by his feet.

Seeing that troop jumped back, hands on the hilts of their weapons.

"He's a pet." stressed Gamli. He knelt and rubbed the bottom of Ormir's snout and neck, "As good and loyal as any hound."

Ormir fluted pleasantly.

Lonija regarded the drake with fearless interest. "Fascinating." To her warriors she added, "Lower your guard. If they meant for the beast to attack it would have done so already."

Her guards, reluctantly, followed her command.

She nodded to the ship. "Come, let's paddle across the lagoon and I will bring you to your hideaway."

The party, Lonija and her guards boarded the boat. They pushed off with the oars and paddled across the still, dark water. The atmosphere was tense. The guards eyed the drake with caution while they paddled. Gamli and Izidorious watched each other like hawks.

Lonija yawned, as if such posturing bored her. To Vanadis and Ransu she said, "It is the time for your questions. What would you know?"

"First, how do you speak Orse, Soumi and Couronian all at the same time?" asked Ransu.

Lonija giggled, "Why that's simple, I am a priestess no? My god has blessed me so that I understand all that is spoken, and all who hear me understand my words."

"Our gods do no such things." commented Vanadis.

"That is because your gods dwell far away," Lonija pointed to the sky, "while ours dwell with us, close but unseen."

"Truly? Then tell us of them." Vanadis said diplomatically.

At that Lonija looked troubled. "Sadly, I cannot. Our sacred trust prevents me from telling you of them. However," she mused regarding the western beach that became more and more distant as they paddled on, "there is an exception. If you'd like I can tell of one goddess and how she created the spit. It is one of the few tales I am allowed to share."

"Please." said Vanadis with a polite grin.

"The spit is like nothing I've ever seen." Ransu admitted.

The honest admiration in fisherman's words caused the priestess to smile. She told the story. "Deep in this lagoon lives the Laume Neringa. She is more powerful than any warrior and more beautiful than the night sky. The dragon Naglis took a fancy to her and begged her hand in marriage, but Neringa loved him not and staunchly refused. This angered Naglis, and in his fury he destroyed many villages along the coast. Neringa tried to crush him, but he was always too fast, he could always retreat into deeper waters, into his domain where Neringa was not foolish enough to go. Then one day an idea struck her. Neringa gathered in her apron a desert's worth of sand and, before the next sunset, used it to wall off Courland bay. The next time Naglis swam to wreak vengeance, he found his way barred. The only entrance to the new lagoon was too narrow and he could not survive on dry land. So he swam away defeated. Yet still he pines for her, still he sends our Neringa yellow gems from the ocean floor, the amber you've seen our prospectors gather. However, Neringa will never fall for Naglis' charms for the blood of her people forever stains him." She gestured to the spit, "That, my friends, his how what you see before you was formed."

"She must be a Jotun." Ransu, surmised as he stared at the beach whose ends were beyond sight.

Gamli stroked his beard, "Ever since we were young we've been told Jotun only cause evil." With that he abandoned his watch on Izidorious and fell into brooding.

They paddled on, Lonija and Vanadis exchanging pleasant chit chat as they went.

***

Finally, after the stars were out and the crescent moon hung in the sky, their ship drifted to an abandoned dock. It belonged to the remains of a tiny village that lay at the edge of a twisted, dark, swamp. Most buildings had collapsed, aside from a stone hall which had a tiled roof that was riddled with holes. It looked wet and dismal.

"Your home." said Lonija with an amused grin.

"I knew there was a catch." cursed Ransu.

Vanadis peered closer and her witch's sight caught glimpses of silvery ghosts looking back at them. "It's haunted." she said dryly.

Gamli waited for the priestess to explain.

"This is Kintai. Those who lived here once rebelled against my great, great grandfather. He crushed them but their spirits refuse to rest. We've tried to reclaim it but our efforts proved for naught. We are no longer interested in Kintai, which is why I shall lend it to you." The priestess smiled at Gamli as if daring him to find fault with her gift. Her troop snickered and chuckled.

The smith turned to his sister and asked, "Can you do anything about this?"

Vanadis stared long at the village, its dead stared back at her. A few brandished weapons. Many screamed insults in Couronian. She glanced to her side, at her own shining host.

Her father smiled broadly and rested his hand on her shoulder. 'They are nothing to us.'

"It won't be pleasant, for them." the Volsung sister said with a chilling confidence. She turned to the priestess, "If you give us this place I will be forced drive them into the swamp."

The seithkona's intensity took Lonija off guard, "O-f course. Do what you must, they dared rebel against my family, and deserve far worse."

Gamli regarded Kintai with a discerning eye. He saw piled stone, he marked the rotted carcasses of boats, and he caught a glimpse of what might have been a smithy. "This will do." he said, stroking Ormir absently. "Set us on shore, come back in a week and I'll have something to sell."

The priestess regarded the three with disbelief, even Ransu now seemed eager to disembark. "Very well."sShe huffed. She turned to her troop, "Bring us on shore."

As they approached, Vanadis saw the ghosts rush forward to await them. They were a rag tag, desperate group. In hatred, they chanted as one, this rippled into the living world as a tangible aura of dread. The seithkona stood and thumped the butt of Burning Mind onto the hull of the boat. She then pointed its tip at them and her ghostly entourage formed up around her like giant wings across the waters.
"You wish to test me?" she called, not caring if they understood.
"Very well!" she swished her spear down and her ghostly warriors flew across the water and crashed into the native ghosts like a scythe through wheat. Those foes who were not torn apart fled deep into the swamp. Suddenly, the ruins lost their malevolence, they were merely empty and still.

The guards stared at the seithkona in fear and awe. They had not witnessed the assault but the water had rippled against the wind and the clash of steel and cries of the wounded had echoed across the shore.

"We're ready to disembark now." Vanadis said demurely.

They quickly docked and as soon as the three, and Ormir, had left the boat the warriors pushed off.

"I'll remember our deal." Gamli called to Lonija, "Return and I'll have wonders for you to buy."

The priestess kept an even gaze on him as she drifted away, "I will Gamli the Serpent. I expect great things."

Once the horse-headed vessel was out of earshot Ransu smirked and commented, "Looks like they misjudged us." He turned to the ruins, "I feared we'd be living in of tents and trees. This, this I can work with. Come you, two, we're making this ruin a home."

***

A week passed. Word of the visitors spread through the Courland halls like wildfire and many laughed at the trick their priestess had played on the foreigner sorcerers. Kintai town and swamp were cursed, none could survive it. Yet, this merriment soon turned to disquiet. Every day smoke rose from the ruins. At night, fires could be seen on shore and the swamp trees reverberated with eerie pipe music. So, Lonija returned to Kintai in a swift boat with just as many guards. This time they approached the ruins in the broad light of day.

From off the shore, they found that, while the grounds still looked overgrown, most of the debris had been cleared away. The rotted boats were gone leaving a clear space for their vessel to beach. The fisherman rose from the depths and waved, "Hail!" he called cheerfully, "I'll let Gamli know you're here." He walked up into the sand naked, seized his breeches and walked to the hall. "Gamli! Get your wares out, they're here."

"Hmph," Izidorious grumbled, "we should have known that filthy Alanders would thrive in a cursed place. What should we do, my lady?"

"We have nothing to fear, let's see what they have to offer." responded the priestess. Which was true, tucked in her belt was a wand from the sacred grove and she felt her goddess close by.

They landed and approached the remains of the hall, the troop closing ranks around Lonija. The crumbled doorway had been removed leaving a clear archway. They stepped through and found Vanadis there to greet them. For the briefest moment they saw a lily white little Courland girl holding the seithkona's hand. She glanced at them shyly and vanished, her giggle dancing along the walls. Everybody, including Lonija, froze.

Vanadis smiled cordially, "Greetings, I'm pleased to see you."

Lonija glanced around slowly, looking for other spirits that might be watching. She saw none, the open hall had an air of serenity about it. "You've given them peace.

"They wouldn't leave. Rather than waste my power fighting I offered a sacrifice of provisions instead. Now they're quite content with us living here." said the seithkona, her lip twisting into a smirk. A thought struck her and she added, "Though they were your enemies, yes? They're not suffering but, I assure you, they won't cause rouble either."

'Unless you command them to, witch.' Thought the priestess. Still, she had her wand and her Goddess was close, "See to it that they don't. We do not wish to spoil our barter."

"Of course," said the seithkona with a bow, "these are your lands, we shall respect your rule. Please," she gestured past a cloth divider, "this way. My brother's waiting for you."

They followed Vanadis beyond the divider, the western wall had been mostly removed, and sunlight streamed through several large holes in the roof. Under one patch that the roof covered sat a table, behind it stood the red haired smith. He was dressed in merchant finery, and wore a sliver arm ring on which was a stylized tree. "My lady," he said with a simple courtesy, "this is what I have for you."

She and her troop stepped forward to find a score of arrows arrayed on the table. The fletching and shafts were straight and true. The arrow heads were spectacular. They were bronze, iron and stone. Tiny, intricate etchings were arrayed on each, each one was a separate work of art.

Izidorious snorted, "They look pretty but will they strike true?"

Gamli glanced at her questioningly.

"Izidorious marvels at their beauty but wonders if that's all there is to them."

The smith chuckled. He swept the arrows up with one hand, pulled a stone headed one out of his fist, held it up as high as he could and dropped it. Thunk! It embedded in the table as if it had been fired. He repeated the motion, dropping each and every other arrow with the same result.

Izidorious turned to Bronislovas the Archer. "What say you?" he couldn't hide the awe in his tone.

Bronislovas stroked his long moustache and appraised the arrows, "With these I'd be match for Naglis himself."

Gamli noted their manner, smiled at Lonija and asked, "Now that you see that I'm true, what do you offer for these wonders?"

The priestess regarded the arrows thoughtfully. She glanced up at Gamli and his sister, they seemed comfortable and healthy; she had expected them to find them raving and starved. Back in her boat was a little vegetable, meat, fish bread and cheese.

"Don't mind me." Ransu suddenly walked past carrying three large silver salmon, he hung them on a rafter at the far end of the hall.

Lonija loosened a pouch from her belt and emptied it on the table. A few smooth amber stones landed there

Gamli eyed them and glanced at Ransu.

Ransu took a close look and said, "It's a fine offering but not for all of them."

The smith glared at Lonija.

"They're for the three iron ones." the priestess answered.

Ransu nodded, "That's fair."

"And the rest?" said Gamli, losing patience.

"We'll be come back next week well stocked with iron and bronze, enough materials for you to make tools, weapons and armor. I trust that will be more than sufficent for the rest?"

"Aye." said Gamli cautiously.

"Excellent." Lonija answered with a smile. "I expect future trade will be mutually beneficial for all of us."

With that Lonija and her troop took their arrows and made their leave. The three saw them to the dock.

Before disembarking she turned to her men and said, "Gentlemen, present them with their gifts."

"Gifts?" asked Izidorious.

Lonija nudged a basket of rations with her foot. She leaned closer and whispered, "We make a good impression on this foreigner, he makes further weapons for us, weapons we can use in driving other foreigners from Courland."

The guard chuckled and grinned. "You prove wise as ever, my lady." He said with a bow. He then seized two baskets and nodded to his men to take up the sacks of food. He stepped off the boat and made his offering to Vanadis who accepted it graciously. His men placed their cargo neatly before Gamli and Ransu.

"Your generosity abounds." said Vanadis with a bow.

"I look forward to seeing you next week." said Gamli in measured tones.

"As do I." answered Lonija. "Farewell for now."

***

Another week passed, albeit far more pleasantly thanks to the Courland rations. As promised Lonija returned and, true to her word, she brought iron and bronze ore. Gamli gladly exchanged his remaining arrows for this.

And thus, their year truly began.

***

During the hot summer, Ransu explored swamp, lagoon, plain and forest, always returning with fish, berries and meat. With Vanadis' help, he cleaned and preserved everything he found. His pelts were used for winter clothes or further trade with the Curonians.

During the fall, Ransu took stock of their supplies and found them ample thanks to trade and his own hunting. Given this, he told the siblings he was off to explore the Courland. Vanadis advised against it, Ransu did not heed her. Gamli wished him well. The fisherman traveled far and saw many things, while keeping out of the way of the natives. He witnessed a Courland funeral, where the deceased's belongings were scattered and the community raced on swift horses to see who was quick enough to claim them. He walked by sacred groves and found them beautiful, especially in the fall when the leaves were crimson and gold.

However, Ransu felt invisible eyes watching him so he did not enter. Ransu caught a glimpse of the Romuva Shrine, colorful, towering wooden poles rose up form it, each ending in the head of a god; the Horse God, the Bear God, the God of Man, and many others. These gods seemed to regard Ransu balefully, the fisherman dared not approach. On the northern border Ransu witnessed the Curonians battle the Samogitans, they charged each other on horses and the plains rumbled like thunder. They fought with staggering ferocity, many men died. From Ransu's prospective, the Curonians won, he noted well the gleam of a Gamli forged sword in the hand of their High Chieftan.

When the first snows fell, Ransu returned to Kintai. He made a game of it and snuck in just as the Hall was having supper. Lonija, her maids in waiting and her guards had joined Gamli and Vanadis for a feast. The fisherman startled the Volsung sister by suddenly sliding onto the bench beside her.

After the Hall chuckled, and the seithkona glared, Lonija addressed him "I hope your tour was memorable."

"Aye," said Ransu, shovelling honeyed pork and cheese onto his plate, "Courland is beautiful."

"I know." answered the priestess. "You're lucky we didn't catch you, because if we did, we would have killed you."

"I'm safe here though, yes?" Asked Ransu with concern.

"That remains to be seen." quipped Vanadis. The Hall laughed but Lonija did not answer Ransu's question.

***

The year was different for Vanadis. Soon after Lonija' first visit, she had a dream. On another starry night, she sat on her balcony in the Sariola. Sitting across the table from her was Gerd, the famed child of wisdom of Kelifar, the last time Vanadis saw her she was curled in a ball, cowering in fear, wheezing her last. This Gerd was different. She sat straighter, with grace and poise, her straight mousey hair had a sheen to it and she wore a red and gold dress that put all of Dorte's wardrobe to shame. Her eyes glowed a luminescent red.

"You're the spark aren't you?"

Gerd poured herself and Vanadis a goblets of red wine and answered, "I am."

Vanadis accepted the drink, sipped it, found it good, and asked "Why this form? Did you tire of Flosi?"

"Not at all. I chose Gerd because you respected her, a rival intellect, one from which you would take ready instruction."

"More lessons then?" Vanadis asked with a hint of pleasure. "What would you like in exchange?"

Gerd giggled, "You've already made the payment." She grinned wolfishly, "The death of Drafli. He was blessed by Heimdall; his demise furthers our mistresses' work."

A tiny sliver of guilt jabbed in the seithkona's stomach. "I didn't do it for Laufey. I only wished to save Vargeisa. If there had been another way..."

"Liar!" Gerd laughed, then, with a conspiratorial look she added, "You planned his murder as soon as you set out with him. When he failed to die easily you reveled in testing you magic against his. Your power was sufficient but you want more."

The seithkona looked troubled at that. She hated it but part of what Gerd said rung true.

"Be at ease. True, Drafli was a kind father but he also fed innocents to that abominable wall. If Midgard knew his true crimes you would be regarded as a hero. Unfortunately, men are fools and your reputation has become black as soot. So to balance things out let me teach you something useful." With that Gerd spilled the contents of a velvet pouch on the table. Small rune stones clattered on it.

Vanadis picked ᚱ and regarded it, her curiosity dulling her guilt. "You're teaching me Drafli's magic?"

"Would if I could." answered Gerd, "No, I'm simply teaching you how to read. Once you understand then we'll travel to a place where such knowledge will grant you great power."

A memory came to mind of Steinarr staring hard at a scroll, then chuckling as if it spoke to him. When no one was looking Vanadis managed peak, all she saw were incomprehensible runes. It infuriated her that she'd never understood them.

"That will be more than enough." Vanadis said with pleasure. She toasted Gerd and they began her lessons.

Learning the runes took far more effort than learning a spell. The first dream seemed to go on for eternity with Vanadis grasping their very barest meanings. When she awoke she found Gamli and Ransu staring down at her with concern.

"It's been three days." prodded Ransu.

"There will be more to come," Vanadis answered with a very dry throat, "but first could you bring me something to eat and drink?"

After her meal she explained her dream and drew out runes in the dirt to demonstrate her knowledge. Neither Gamli nor Ransu got any of it.

Still, the fisherman answered "Let me find some comfortable bedding. Just remember, your choir debt stacks while you're out."

"I don't like this." said Gamli. "What if you drift off and never come back?"

"I'll be cautious." Answered Vanadis warmly. "Trust that I will always return." Then, with a smirk, she added, "One way or another."

"Don't you dare haunt me." Gamli said with a nervous laugh.

Vanadis would fall asleep for days on end, returning to her Sariola to follow the instruction of Gerd. As the weeks passed the seithkona grew paler and thinner, yet, in spite of this, was always in good spirits. Whenever she awoke she'd eat and drink ravenously. At times, Gerd forced a break of a few days. During this time, Vanadis regained her strength, helped fix and maintain their home, offered feasts to her spirits and the Courland ghosts, and assured her brother that all was well. Then it was back into the dreaming school. By the beginning of winter and by the time Ransu returned from his autumn journey, Vanadis had become most fluent in reading and writing.

Then one early winter night, Vanadis dreamed to find herself not in the Sariola but in someplace dark. There was a biting chill in the air and a steady, windy moan, echoed throughout. The seithkona's silver aura lit a few feet ahead of her, she saw snow covered ground. She was wearing thick fur clothing, on her feet were strapped snowshoes. Suddenly, with a whoosh, a disembodied orange flame flickered before her.

The flame spoke, "Good, you've made it. You are now ready to put your reading to use." her voice was both powerful and seductive.

"You are?" asked Vanadis, she reached out to her spirits but they did not heed her.

"I'm your spark, I speak with the voice of the Mistress. We are in Niflheim."

"I am dead?"

"Are you truly that stupid?" retorted the flame dryly.

"It's an apt question." Vanadis shot back.

"No," the flame sighed, "we merely visit here. When you awaken you'll return to Midgard."

"I thought Hel never let souls return."

"We are in Niflheim, and while we shall approach Hel's hall we shall not enter it. Now follow." With that the flame, which was the size of a bright touch, moved forward.

The seithkona walked with it. She glanced around but could see nothing beyond the flame's light. Though the air was frigid a grey mist hung over the place. The only sound Vanadis heard was her breathing and the crunch of her snow shoes. The spark gave of some warmth and Vanadis was well bundled up, but still the cold got through. "So we are here," ventured Vanadis, "to read something in Hel?"

Vanadis' troch chuckled, "Of course, where better to learn seith than at the footsteps the true Mistress of the Dead? You're fortunate to be one of Laufey's adepts. We are only allowed to approach because Hel is her granddaughter."

Suddenly a grumble, like a falling mountain, echoed through the darkness.

"What was that?" Vanadis asked her heart racing.

"Hel's hound Garm, do not worry, we'll not approach him."

Moments later, a wall loomed, in the dim light and mist it was impossible to tell how tall or wide it was. When they came closer they found it comprised of boulders mortared by bone. Gleaming white skulls were fitted between the cracks.

"In the Heavens and the underworld, the spirits are fashioned into useful items. Only the worthy keep their will and forms. I like to imagine that Flosi was made into a cup, from which a cherry lipped Valkyrie drinks. I'm sure he would approve." laughed the spark.

"You're lying." said Vanadis, mortified, "This," she gestured to the wall, "is simply to scare invaders away."

"Perhaps I am. I do so soften what is about to come, behold." The spark floated up and revealed that one of the stones had writing on it, chiselled in with a fine hand.

"It's just words." scoffed Vanadis. She glanced up and read. These words were terrifying. The spoke of dark truths and while the seithkona understood what was said her mind reeled at its implications. They were things she could never speak of, concepts she could never quite grasp. The seithkona fell to her knees, tears freezing on her cheeks.

She awoke with a gasp. Gamli, who sat across from her, jumped in fright.

"Sister?" He asked.

Vanadis just stared ahead, the frightful philosophy churning in her mind.

"Please, drink." Her brother said, pushing a mug of water into her hands.

Her lips were dry, her throat parched, she took an even sip of the cold water and it rolling down her throat and into her being brought her back to life. She glanced up at her brother and said, "I've been to Niflheim Gamli. What's written on Hel's wall..." She closed her eyes and sobbed.

Gamli hugged her, "Five days...I'd nearly given up on you."

Vanadis hugged him back and then, she gently pushed him away. "I-I'm fine." she stammered. "I just need time to think."

"Of course," said Gamli. "Ransu is out hunting, he'll bring us a fresh catch and after a good meal, I'm sure you'll feel much better."

Ransu did come back, he held several rabbits. When he saw Vanadis awake, he smiled and said, "Thank Ukko, the two of us wouldn't have been able to finish all of this."

Vanadis found her brother's words to be true; the succulent rabbit mingled with mead warmed her body and soul. It cleared her mind and she pondered her journey.

Several days passed, when she slept she felt the flame waiting at the back of her mind, calling her to read Hel's wall again. While awake the fear she felt faded, she turned the dread writing in her thoughts and found she understood seith a little better.

Finally curiosity overcame terror and she told her brother and Ransu, "I'm going back into the trance."

"Sailing the river of Tuonela, it's not a good idea." cautioned Ransu.

"No." said Gamli, "You're staying here with us."

"I'll do what I want brother." answered the Seithkona, "You have your forging," she gestured to a rack the held a dozen finished bronze head axes, "I have my dreams. I'll come out stronger."

Ransu sighed and clapped Gamli on the shoulder. "When she gets like this you know there's nothing we can do to alter her course."

"All I ask is that you keep watch over me and, unless I begin to rot, don't stick me on a funeral pyre."

Gamli snarled, shook his head disdainfully and stormed out of the hall.

"I'll talk to him." Ransu said and shot off after the smith.

Vanadis lay down and closed her eyes. She soon found herself back on Niflheim's frozen plain.

Her spark was there to greet her. "Good, you've come. I hear most who see Hell's wall consign themselves to despair."

The seithkona trudge forward, "I'm not most. Let's see what else the wall has to say."

Her torch led her to the stone and writing. Vanadis continued reading from where she left off. This time she was cautious and read slowly. Further understanding dawned but with it her soul ached. When she couldn't stand it anymore, she said, "Enough!" and found herself back on her bench in the waking world.

Ransu was cooking fish, "Ah, back to three days this time. Much better." He served her a tasty meal.

Gamli shook his head and grumbled.

Vanadis shrugged.

He sat down beside her and huffed, "Your ways are strange."

Vanadis snickered and nudged him; he nudged back, nearly spilling her form her seat. They laughed and ate.

Vanadis returned to Hel's wall three more times that winter. Each reading got easier and brought more clarity. They were lies, meant to sink the reader into complete dread and hopelessness, if one could endure them and sort the falsehoods from truth they could gain a deeper understanding of seith. That is exactly what Vanadis did. This knowledge opened a whole slew of new spells for her. She could draw on anguish and despair of the spirits within her to turn her spit into acid. She could mold spirits with her hands and focus their rage into a weapon. She formed a connection with Svartalfheim to blind those who displeased her or shroud the land in darkness.

Then, one day, while the winter snows began to melt, she summoned her spark dream and found herself back on the Sariola balcony. Her spark once again sat across the table from her as Gerd.

"No journey to the wall this time?" Vanadis asked, a hint of disappointment in her voice.

"I'm afraid not, Hel granted us only a winter to study. If we were to return we'd have to face her guardians." Gerd shook her head evenly, "We do not want that."

"No." mused Vanadis. She poured herself and Gerd some mead, the spark took it gratefully.

After taking a sip Vanadis regarded her Gerd thoughtfully. "Something's been bothering me. Drafli's death, it was well worth the knowledge of how to read, but was it truly worth tutelage at Hell's wall? Was he hated that much?"

Gerd grinned and shook her head. "No, he was worth far less than Hel's wall."

Vanadis frowned, "What do I owe her?"

Gerd considered her words carefully before answering. "Power begs for use. Our mistress hopes you use your new spells in a worthy service, one she cannot speak of, but would please her non-the-less."

This brought to mind the emotions that washed over the seithkona when she first pledged herself to Laufey. The Jotun Queen's sorrow and pain at losing her child. The disgust at her peers for turning their backs on him. The pinch of her binding duty that prevented her from saving him. Vanadis emphasized but this also struck a chord of anger within her, "I see. You're forcing my hand."

"Of course not," Gerd scoffed, "our mistress merely sees what decision you will reach before you make it. Granted it's not guaranteed that you'll survive..."

"As soon as I'm able I plan to return to Pohjola and never leave." Vanadis cut in.

Gerd choked on her mead and barely avoided snorting it out. "Truly?" she laughed, "What do you plan to do there?"

"Live free, without fear." Vanadis stated dryly.

Gerd giggled, "Come now, do you even know that that means?"

Vanadis' defiance stalled at that question. "Well I..."

Gerd leaned closer, her brown eyes locking the seithkona in an appraising stare. "Will you take up knitting? Make a quilt, a tapestry perhaps?" Gerd snickered. "Will you marry a fool husband? Watch your children seize the glory you were too scared to take? Grow old and die to become a faded, useless spirit full of regret. Oh no," Gerd shook her head, "you couldn't do that. Ever since you were a child you've strived against your betters, survived with will and wits. Your greatest joy is in deceiving your foes or ripping them apart with your black spells. So, why not join forces with the worthy? Why not take your place in shaping, not just the future of Midgard, but of all the nine worlds?"

"Hah!" Vanadis scoffed, "I'm not so callous. What's the future in Vargeisa's quest? None! It'll usher in Ragnarok which will kill everyone I love."

"You're clinging to foolish sentiment and you know it." Gerd said slyly. "You think neutrality will protect the ones you love? Nay, you would merely consign yourself to helplessness. Far better to wield the sword than be its victim."

With that Vanadis was pushed to wakefulness. She screamed out in frustration.

"Sister?" asked Gamli.

"What ails you?" asked Ransu.

"Nothing." The Seithkona huffed.

Vanadis attempted to return her Sariola but found only peaceful dreams, highlighted by her spark's laughter. It stayed as such for the rest of the spring. Leaving Vanadis to brood over her future.

***

Three seasons earlier, after the trade of the arrows, Gamli set to work on the many fine materials that Lonija provided. Gamli found the roof of the old smithy sound so he cleaned it up for his workspace. Here he used Ormir's flame to forge new wares. He made the anvil ring and produced tools, weapons and shields, all of excellent quality. True to her word Lonija came back and bartered for them with amber, gold, silver and provisions. Ransu acted as Gamli's trade adviser making sure the final price was fair.

In the fall, Lonija came not only with wealth to barter but custom orders, as well. Gamli plied his skills to their fullest, even weaving enchantments into a few orders. The High Chieftain ordered armor and a sword. Gamli forged a matching set. Wind, a set of chain mail whose wearer could run as fast as a steed. Storm, a bronze sword as strong as steel and hit with the force of a Troll. They were beautiful creations, the shoulders of Wind had horse head ornamentation. The hilt of Storm was etched with swirling filigree.

When Lonija arrived to pick up the set Izidorious was most impressed. So much so that he lent Gamli his blade to touch up.

Lonija regarded Storm with a grave curiosity. With a serious demeanor she said "You realize my father will use this to kill your countrymen, and the armor will save him from reprisal. Why are you so ready to craft such for us?"

Gamli crossed his arms, "My 'countrymen' stole my first works from me. They profited and I remained a slave. They're unworthy of my works. Your tribe has paid fair price and I am no cheat."

Lonija regarded him with a sly interest, "I see. What of your return? Will you be forced to sell your wares to the unworthy?"

Gamli turned away shyly, "I..." he sighed, "The Pohjalanders were kind to my sister. I have no qualm working for them."

"You sound reluctant to do so." the priestess remarked.

Gamli considered his anvil and forge. He considered Ormir who slept peacefully by the fire. He glanced over Lonija's shoulder at the wrecked hall he called home. "We're strangers here." he said reluctantly. "Eventually we shoul leave."

The priestess glanced at Izidorious who watched them with very close attention. Reluctantly she took a step away from Gamli. "You will. However," she added with a note of hope, "these arms will please my father, I'm certain he will have much work for you."

Gamli regarded her kindly and said, "For that, I'm thankful."

Malvis did have much work for the smith. As the first snows fell Lonija arrived with several boats filled with ore. Malvis requested that Gamli forge him an entire armory for the next summer's raids. Gamli returned to Izidorious his improved sword, he was most pleased. Then, the smith set to work. For days, he spent long hours in his forge, crafting with impossible precision and speed, his hammer strikes accented by Ormir's piping song. Heat rippled from the forge, so much that neither snow nor ice could touch it. He paused only once, when his sister seemingly lay dead. When she revived but then insisted on continuing her folly, Gamli went back to his toil.

Spring returned, thawing the Curonain Lagoon and melting the snow. With it five ships sailed for Kintai. They were sleek, fine, horse-headed vessels. Their crew warriors whose shields were painted with bright heraldry and woman dressed in resplendent finery and children who chattered with excitement. Instead of a mast each ship sported a totem with a godhead. The Horse God, the Bear God, the Stag God, the Raven God and then, the God of Man.

Ransu spotted them first and altered the siblings.

"With that many men, they wouldn't need to purchase the armory, they could seize it and offer us as sacrifice." surmised the fisherman.

Gamli frowned at the procession, ill at ease.

Vanadis considered the ships for a good long moment and said, "I doubt it. If they wish to kill us they would come at night and not bring their families. They're either passing by or plan to celebrate their purchace."

Both the fisherman and smith glanced at her in shock.

"You? Assuming the best?" said Ransu staggered.

Gamli peered down at his sister. "Are you possessed?"

Vanadis glared at them both. "I'm possessed with a desire to hex you." she huffed. After they snickered she added, in a less angry tone, "I state what I see. Still, we should be cautious. Just in case, I'll rally the ghosts of Kintai, if Lonija betrays us I'll unleash their fury."

"Ah, that's the seithkona we know." Ransu laughed.

Gamli nodded, again staring at the procession. "Very well."

The docking of the tiny fleet was proceeded by the proud blast of horns, which drove Ormir into hiding. The first ship docked and out of it stepped Lonija, followed by Izidorious. The three waited for them, dressed in their finest. In the back of Vanadis' mind she held her spectral forces at ready.

"Greetings, smith." Lonija said with a polite bow. "My father and his chiefs are here to inspect the armoury. I trust this won't be a bother, will it?"

Gamli glanced over the other ships. They carried much cargo wrapped in sacks and locked in chests. "You bring more than the chiefs."

"My father has decided to hold a Thing in Kintai, to discuss the summer raids. It is his right, cursed or no this land is his."

Gamli regarded the priestess with great scrutiny. Her words were smooth but her expression was tense, as if pleading the Gamli to please play along.

"I don't need to welcome him to his own land." Gamli said. "Have him come to my warehouse, I'll show him my wares."

"Thank you." said Lonija with relief.

The ships docked and the Curonians disembarked, with an air of caution and curiosity. Ransu and Vanadis greeted those who spoke Orse and directed them to the best place to set their tents. Meanwhile, Lonija led a small group of dignitaries and their many guards, to the far hall where Gamli stored his weapons.

As soon as the priestess entered she announced "Malvis, High Chief of Courland." She gestured to a man who was taller and broader than even Gamli. He had log braided hair and a thick beard the color of night. He wore red and gold woollen finery, his cloak was embroiled with horses, it was of such quality that merely looking at them made the smith feel wind blowing across his face. He wore Gamli's gleaming chain mail and Storm was strapped to his back. He regarded Gamli with deep judgement.

Gamli stared back with pride but also respect. He gestured to the hall. Standing on the racks were a score of wicked bronze headed axes. On another were five gleaming swords. A score of sturdy round shields adorned the hall, each emblazoned with a Courland Crest. Three suits of chainmail lay on the table.

Secretly there was even more. Hidden in his hall was a suit of mail named Mountain, a shield named Just, and a sword named Fire Heart. These arms Gamli had crafted for himself.

Upon seeing the armoury, the chiefs and their guards murmured in wonder. Malvis snorted in surprise. He turned to Gamli and clapped him on the shoulder with such force the smith nearly toppled. The Courland High Chief gave him a brilliant grin and shouted a gruff order. Servants rushed through the dignataries and dropped three chests before Gamli, they opened them, inside gleamed amber and gold. Malvis turned to his daughter and said something in a grand fashion.

She smiled demurely, bowed and said to the Gamli, "My father is most pleased. You and your sister may dine with us tonight. Furthermore, you are welcome to stay in Kintai for another year, if you continue to forge such wonders for us."

At that Gamli grinned as wide as Malvis. He bowed deeply and said "Tell your father I'm thankful, and happy to continue my work for him."

***

The evening was spent in a grand pavilion whose walls were stitched with scenes of hunting and celebration. The chiefs, their wives, and children all gathered inside. Servants cooked a boar to perfection. Beer, mead and wine flowed freely. Lute, drum, pipe, and voice rose high in the tent, even Ormir joined in.

Gamli was seated near to the High Chief, beside Lonija. Vanadis was seated by Izidorious who flirted with words she did not understand. The seithkona, remained elegant and kept a polite distance between him and her. Izidorious was a little gruff for her tastes.

Though Ransu had not been invited, he wormed his way in none the less. Fortunately, no one seemed to mind.

At one point he had sat himself with Gamli and Lonija. A little drunk he asked, "A query my lady. Something I must know. Did you lose your arm through accident or were you always as such?"

Gamli, also a little drunk, glared at fisherman and balled a fist as if to strike. Lonija held him back with a touch. "It's alright," She stressed gently, "I'm surprised none of you asked earlier."

"It would have been impolite." Gamli fumed.

Lonija stared into his eyes and arrested his attention. "You're right, but now that it's been asked, I have no regret telling you. I came out of my mother's womb like this. Because of such, I was placed in a sacred grove for the gods to claim." She smiled kindly. "They did not take me away, instead the priests heard my cries as speech, knowing that I had been blessed I was welcomed back into the arms of my mother and father." She gestured to Malvis and his raven haired wife.

"They meant for you to die, because of this?" Gamil gestured to the part of her cloak that hung limp, where her left arm should be.

"I hear your people would have done the same." Lonija answered with firm patience.

Gamli closed his eyes and breathed in deep. Suddenly, he stood and stated, "Ormir, come!" and stormed out of the tent.

Malvis noticed and called after him with a hint of outrage.

"What does he think he's doing?" gasped Lonija.

"I've seen this before." said Ransu with sudden anticipation. "It's the madness, the same kind drove him to forge the wall on the spit." He stood and laughed. "Come, this is something you will won't want to miss."

Ormir's voice rose outside like the sound of godly horns and the tent was illuminated by the brilliance of a great fire. The crowd gasped and rushed out of the far side of the pavilion. Malvis, Lonija, Ransu and Vanadis raced forward towards the light. A pillar of fire rose in the open square of the town. In it they could see the shadow of Gamli hammering on Ormir who sat as still and sturdy as an anvil. Occasionally he'd gesture and gold, iron and amber would fly from his storehouse and into the flame.

Malvis held both his daughter and his wife close. Izidorious stood before them sword and shield ready. The rest of the chiefs and their folk gathered around, staring in wonder.

Vanadis gawked and yelled over the roaring of the flame, "I've never seen him like this."

Ransu bit into some roasted boar and grinned. "This is going to be great."

They watched Gamli's shadow forge dance and listened to the horns of Ormir for hours, completely entranced. Eventually the drake's song reached a tremendous crescendo and then died off. As it did the flame lowered, finally ending in a small campfire that Ormir slept in. Gamli, staggered forward, carrying his newest creation.

He fell on his knees before Lonija and held it up to her. "It's yours. For everything you've done for us." He said with the peak of exhaustion.

"Is this a jest?" Lonija asked incredulously.

Gamli held an arm forged out of iron which ended in a delicate hand whose knuckles were gold. It had the slimness of a shoulder length glove worn by a royal lady of taste. It was studded with bits of gleaming amber.

"No jest. Wear it, you'll see." he pressed it forward.

Malvis uttered a hate filled curse.

"N-no father." said Lonija. "He means no offence, let me try it on."

Carefully, with an expression of hope and awe, Lonija fitted the arm under her cloak. She suddenly uttered a sharp cry of pain.

Malvis and Izidorious drew their swords.

"No!" cried Lonija, holding up both hands, her living one and her iron one. "I am..." she stared them shocked. She opened and closed both perfect hands. She turned to her father and placed her new left palm on his arm. "How is this possible, I... feel?" She gasped, she felt his cloak with her new thumb and fore finger, "This arm...it's as if it were real. As if it were mine." She covered her mouth with both hands and cried for joy.

Lonija's mother embraced her, also filled with happiness.

Malvis glared down at Gamli. He dropped his sword and dragged the drained smith into a hug, tears in his eyes. He then held him out at arms, length and made a declaration.

The crowd roared with approval.

Ransu and Vanadis stood there stunned.

"W-what? What did he say?" asked the seithkona.

One of the old chiefs who stood nearby answered, "That your brother is now his son. You are now one of us." The old man said proudly.

"Wonderful." Vanadis answered, regarding Gamli's look of pure happiness. "We've lost him, Ransu."

The fisherman watched Gamli as Lonija embraced and kissed him, "Is that really such a bad thing?"

Vanadis had no answer for that.

***

Many months earlier, Hardegon rode along the leaf carpeted road towards Enga. He slouched in his saddle as if a heavy yoke burdened him. His brown hood was pulled deep, hiding his sallow visage. His breath was laboured. Despite his weakness, he still wore his armor and Troll's End hung on his side. His horse carried on, unencumbered by his rider's sickly weight.

An acrid smell curled into the swordsman's nostril and he let out a hacking cough. When he recovered he peered down the forest road. Before him were the remains of Enga. Her halls were charred and ashen. Her once ripe fields black charcoal. The ground was churned and disturbed. Yes, an army had been through here but only to gather corpses.

The Nibelung hero kicked his steed forward and trotted down the hill. Hardegon's sunken eyes swept desperately the remains of the town, seeking something, anything that would point his way to the Serpent.

They rested on a long bearded old man sitting in a ruined archway. He was dressed in battered grey, his wide brimmed, pointed hat hiding his eyes. A staff leaned beside him. In spite of the ruins he sat casually, smoking on a long stemmed pipe.

"Old man." called Hardegon. "Are you a survivor of Enga?"

The old one glanced up at him from under the rim of his hat. "Me? I'm simply sitting here to pass the time. The name's Gangari, sit a while and talk." He patted the step beside him.

Hardegon stared off across the town. "I have no time." he answered. "I must find Gamli the Serpent."

"Oh? He and his witch sister were here. They burned Egna to the ground, I saw them."

"Truly?" asked the swordsman with sudden, keen, interest. "Do you know where they fled?"

"Unfortunately no," said the vagabond, "though if you sit and share your wine with me I'll tell you everything I saw."

Hardgon considered him and then considered the wide ruin. He dismounted his horse and tied his reigns to a branch. He then sat beside the old one and handed his wineskin. "Drink as much as you desire, then tell me what you saw."

Gangari drained the wineskin in one pull. Then, after wiping his mouth, he told his tale, "I stumbled upon them three nights ago. Jarl Svadi held a great harvest feast in his hall, all were welcome. I, of course, took him up on his offer. He put forth a fine meal and mead flowed for all. Then, about midnight, a red haired beauty swept into the party. She held herself well, had the manner of a noblewoman. She sat with the Jarl and they made a game of guessing who she was. When all had failed she revealed herself as Vanadis the Cursed and broke the Jarl in half with a touch. Of course, his men at arms rushed to defend him but then Gamli the Serpent took his wolf form and rushed the hall. Following him was a twisted thing of spirit and horror. The Jarl and his men all fell. The women and children fled, Gamli nipping at their heels till the edge of the forest. Then the vargs burned the hall and the fields. That was a bleak night. If it weren't for Krumr of Gotaland's plentiful stores, many would starve this winter."

Hardegon listened but as Gangari's story progressed he looked more and more sour. Finally, he shook his head, sighed, and said, "All this way for naught. Vanadis the Cursed has hair as brown as a field mouse. Gamli the Serpent cannot take the shape of a wolf." He coughed hard and then, after steadying himself, added, "Still, I thank you for your tale Gangari. You've convinced me to search elsewhere."

The vagabond gripped Hardegon's arm and entreated. "I've told you a tale, now tell me yours. Tell me why you search for the Serpent."

"I have no time." said the Nibelung hero, though he found the old one's grip like iron and could not rise.

"You have time enough. Sit, give me your tale and I may give you council."

Hardegon eyed the old man and considered running him through. 'No.' he thought. 'Even desperate there are some lows that are beyond me.' "Very well..." with that he told his entire, sorry tale. Of the death of Steinarr, of Mjoll's trap, of the battle with the trolls, of Ida's prophesy, of his battle in the Skane mounds. He finished with "I searched for the Serpent in Danevirke but it turned out he betrayed Gorm. I offered my services in finding him but the King of Danevirke is finished with trusting foreigners. So I've searched on my own, following crime and rumor."

"It runs a toll on you friend." judged Gangari. "If you continue like this, whatever ails you will kill you."

Hardegon laughed, gods it hurt to laugh, and replied, "No amount of medicine or rest will save me. It is the fate Ida predicted, I must die of sword or sickness. I choose sword, but not before I finish my quest."

Gangari put a gentle hand on his shoulder and shook his head, "No, you should head home. You must have a wife, a son. Spend your final days with them in the comfort of your hall surrounded by your kin. There you can die in peace and dignity."

Gangari's soothing words planted a yearning in the swordsman. How he did wish to embrace Thora again. How he wished to see Helgi and impart on him what little wisdom he'd gained in his short life. To be in Öland with his people, with his brother, one last time...

Hardegon forced himself to stand. "Do not tempt me." he screamed. "I shall not go quietly, for that is the path to Hel. I shall see Thora again but it shall be in Asgard. Helgi shall learn not from me, but from my saga. My name in glory will serve my people far better than my life."

Suddenly Gangari was gone. In his place was a stately old man garbed in black. Two ravens landed on each shoulder and two wolves lay at his side. He glanced up and Hardegon saw one ice blue eye, and a dark, empty, socket where the right eye should be.

"Odin." the Nibelung hero gasped and fell to his knees.

The Aesir stood and towered over him like a black standing stone. An aged but sturdy hand landed on Hardegon's shoulder. In a kindly manner Odin said, "Return to Danevirke and seek Ingvild Grave Shield. She will grant you a place to winter. Withstand your curse until the summer. Then, if you can face Bjorn Eriksson, you'll be given one more chance at the Serpent."

His message relayed, the Aesir King vanished.

CHAPTER 30

The truth will always come out. | I laugh at such sentiment.
The crimes of the night are often buried.
They are not seeds that will grow righteous fruit. | They are corpses that rot to nothing.
Nay, only rage, lies, and greed turn the wheels of justice.

King Bjorn Eriksson sat on his Svealand throne. He was a solid, strong man whose long blond locks and short beard gave him a gruff look for a monarch. Though dressed simply he wore a gold arm ring, an iron crown and carried himself with a majestic fury, a fury which he focused on the cowering man before him.

"Skapti, you worm. You swore the fallen Volsung were in Grimsdalr, Rogvaldr here tore that town apart, one of my towns, and found nothing."

Skapti, a weasel of a man with thinning brown hair, shrugged helplessly. "I understand naught my lord. I made Thrasi scream truths until his soul and body were spent. The Serpent must have been there. Either Loki himself stole them away or," he jabbed an accusing finger at Bjorn's right hand "that man is incompetent!"

Skapti's accusation stopped Bjorn's anger in its tracks. He chuckled and glanced at his friend. "You hear this? Yonder rat questions your skill."

Rogvaldr's expression was hard to read behind his dark bushy eyebrows and thick beard. However, he made his displeasure clear by drawing his sword. "Permission to demonstrate, my lord."

Bjorn smiled pleasantly, "Granted, as long as not a drop of worm blood stains my pelts."

"N-no, my lord! I'll find new witnesses, I'll further my investigations, I'll wring...."

Rogvaldr descended the King's dais. Skapti attempted to flee but the watching crowd roared with disapproval and threw him back. The king's man then dispatched the coward with ease. Rogvaldr bowed and Bjorn laughed and applauded with his people.

After the commotion had died down, and Skapti's corpse was dragged away, and Rogvaldr returned to the king's side, a veteran warrior bedecked in finery approached the throne and said, "What then, my lord, are we to do about the fallen Volsung? Barekr's murder, the fire of Enga, the stealing away of Kott's daughter, not to mention the massacre of Gotland and Kelifar. I speak true my lord when I say many jarls cannot, in good conscious, accompany you in this summer's raids, when doing so would leave their homes unguarded against the likes of Gamli the Serpent."

Bjorn glowered at him but the old warrior held his ground. The assembled nobles and freemen watched with baited breath. Bjorn breathed in deep and exhaled, reigning in his rage, "Be assured that my dearest wish is to see their heads mounted at the entrance of this Great Hall. Therefore I triple their bounty, and call forth my best trackers to find them. I will not rest until their evil is no more."

The veteran nodded with satisfaction. "Thank you my lord."

"Now onto other business. Erlendr step forward, I have come to a decision on the jarl of Alands."

In a dark corner, her form a mere shadow within shadow, Hane the Clever watched with wide, excited grin.

"King Siggeir," She whispered, her words trailing into the spirit world, "awaken my love. The time for our great game is upon us."

***

Weeks later, King Bjorn trudged over a white, sandy dune. This sandy waste stretched an island's length to either side, both ending in endless sea. It stretched forward and back for eternity. The hot summer sun beat down upon him; his throat and tongue were deathly dry.

A woman's voice reached his ear, sweet and melodious; she sang a song of sorrow for the fate of Sigurd and Signy of old.

"Hah." Bjorn coughed, "Even now, Volsung plagues me." Still, he turned to the right and followed the lay.

The short walk took nearly all of his strength. His skin blistered and every breath was hot pain. However, Bjorn refused to admit defeat, he trudged on defiance smouldering in his blue eyes. He made his way around another dune and there he found his songstress. He halted and gaped.

She stood with royal grace and sharp royal features. Her light brown hair was arrayed in pearls and gold. Her full lips smiled with pleasure as she sang. Her gret eyes regarded him with merriment. However, her most beautiful feature, to Bjorn's heat addled mind, was the pitcher she carried.

He stormed forward and she relinquished the vessel into his trembling hands. He tipped it to his lips and cold, refreshing, water washed down his tongue and throat. The sensation brought a look of pure joy to Bjorn's face. He guzzled it until he was sated, when he turned the jug back he found it as full as ever.

The lady giggled and gestured for her pitcher back.

"Of course, thank you." Bjorn handed it to her.

The noblewoman smirked, stood on her toes and tipped the vessel over Bjorn's head. He huffed in as the cool water drove the wretched heat from him and healed his burnt skin. She then tilted the pitcher back and held it close once more.

Bjorn shook hair like a wet dog and laughed. His lady giggled, the water marred her not.

Bjorn took her full measure and said, "Greetings. I am King Bjorn Eriksson, Sovereign Lord of Svealand. Whom do I have the pleasure of seeing before me?"

"I am Signy sister wife of Sigurd." Hanne lied.

Bjorn's pleased expression dropped. "Of course you are. The gods have not cursed me enough. Are you also here to cause trouble for my kingdom?"

"You speak of my children?" Hanne asked with an enigmatic smirk.

"Who else would I speak of? Your serpent and witch have caused me nothing but trouble. Your quenching of my thirst will not prevent my swift and inevitable justice."

Hanne laughed with mirth.

"You mock me?" Bjorn growled.

"Nay," said Hanne good naturedly, "I'm merely amused that you assume to me to have maternal love."

Bjorn eyed her curiously.

Hanne put a delicate hand on his chest, leaned in close and said "Have you not heard the tales? I had my own sons killed when they proved too weak."

Bjorn, as big and strong as he was, staggered away from the witch. "Y-yes." He said, composing himself, "I had heard of that, though, till now, could not verify the truth of said tale."

"Then it should surprise you not that I hold no love for cowardly descendants. Gamli the Serpent and Vanadis the Cursed do nothing but blacken my family name. Which is why I shall tell you their whereabouts."

The King grinned at that. "Do share."

Hanne gestured across the nearby lagoon, "They are in Courland. Gamli lends his wicked strength, and Vanadis her vile magic, to the Couronian cause."

Bjorn looked unamused and doubtful. "Truly? From my perspective they lair close to Svealand, all the better to spite me."

"Yet, you cannot find them in Svealand." answered Hanne in a lilting tone.

The King still seemed suspicious.

Hanne stepped over to him, placed both hands on his bare chest and leaned in close. Looking up at him she smiled and said "Within three days you shall have three unexpected visitors to help you on your quest. They will be proof that my words are true." With that she stood on her tip toes and kissed his cheek.

Then Bjorn awoke with a start. He sat up and touched his cheek, where he could still feel Signy's kiss.

***

An hour later, Bjorn had donned his mail, sword, and shield. He, Rogvaldr, and 20 other men rode swiftly down the mountain road to Port Garor. There they saw three strange ships in harbor. Two were sturdy white longships with proud dragonheads. The third was red and dwarfed both of them; its dragonhead was so large that it sank her bow into the sand. The three crews, all together a small army, awaited them the town square. They were tall, handsome folk who sported fine shields and weapons, but these were not drawn at ready. At their center was a warrior so large he must have been troll blooded. He'd be completely terrifying it weren't for the tiny horned helm that rested on his crown. He stared up at Bjorn and roared something in Soumi.

Bjorn glanced at Rogvaldr who answered, "He sends greetings from Kalevala, my lord."

***

An hour later, the Kalevalens enjoyed a welcome feast at Bjorn's expense. In return they brought forth lyre, pipe and drum and performed lively, wondrous music. All of Garor attended to listen, cheer and clap along. The troll blooded one did not sing but he did feast. He had emptied several casks of mead by himself and devoured a whole roasted ox.

Bjorn sat back from the affair. He was more for raiding wealth then counting, still he well understood what harm this celebration would cause his treasury.

Rogvaldr joined him on his seat at the upper hall. Gesturing to the large man he said, "That is Lemminkäinen."

"I've heard of him." answered Bjorn, "Tales of his avarice have now been proven."

"He says," Rogvaldr struggled to make the next part, less ridiculous, "he's here for vengeance, for his boat."

"Oh?"

"Apparently Vanadis the Cursed hexed it and he was forced to build anew."

Bjorn gestured to the musicians, "They stand for this as well?"

Rogvaldr shook his head, "Nay, they are here to avenge their countryman. It would seem Vanadis not only sleeps with her brother but also with Trolls. They claim her Troll husbands slew their brothers."

Bjorn shook his head, "What madness drives one to such depravity?"

"I know not my lord, though I suggest the mercy of a swift death for such a troubled soul. Perhpas she'll find solace in Hel?"

A thought struck Bjorn, "Rogvaldr, do they know where the Volsungs hide?"

"Sadly no, my lord." answered his friend. "They were directed here by Väinämöinen, who advised they aid in our search"

"So this is that wizard's doing." Bjorn glowered, visions of Lemminkäinen feasting his way across Svealand haunting his mind.

"Perhaps we should tell them that we have it on good authority the Serpent hides Harald Fair Hair's court?"

"Hah!" Bjorn laughed slapping Rogvaldr on the back. "No, I have too much respect for old Fair Hair to set such a curse upon his lands." A thought suddenly struck the King and he added, in a more thoughtful tone, "Tell our Lemminkäinen that I'm waiting on word of the Fallen Volsungs. Ask him to tarry here for at most three days, by then I will know where to strike."

Rogvaldr regarded him with surprise. "Truly my lord?"

Bjorn shared with him an enigmatic smile, "I have spoken to a volva, if her prophesy proves true then we shall hunt vargs and raid at the same time."

***

A day later, while Bjorn sat on his bed breakfasting on brown bread, cheese and mead, his matronly wife stepped into their bedroom and announced "We have a visitor."

Noting her aloofness Bjorn snorted with laughter, "Who? The Signy from my dream?"

"Nay," answered Maeva the Wise, "it is Ingvild Grave Shield."

That threw Bjorn for a loop. "A dog of Gorm the Decrepit? Here?"

"Aye, sporting full arms and amour, as if she's about to go to war."

"With us?" laughed Bjorn in amused disbelief.

"30 of her men are docked in Lysa." answered Maeva in a deadpan.

Bjorn flinched at that. "Has the old fool lost his mind?" he roared.

Maeva smirked, "Ingvild claims she's here to talk, that we have a common purpose, the Fallen Volsungs."

At that Bjorn's temper cooled to interest. "Truly?"

"Your Signy did say we'd receive aid from unexpected sources."

"True enough, I will see her."

***

An hour later, Bjorn and Maeva sat on their thrones. Before them, under a substantial 'escort,' stood Ingvild Grave Shield. She was garbed in black mail. On her hip was a sword with a bone hilt. On her back was her famous shield inlaid with the crest of three red hawks. In her gauntleted hands she carried a small bronze box and finger bone wand. She stood tall, proud and fearless. Her complexion was young in spite of her stark white hair. She regarded the king with reserved respect.

"I am surprised," began Bjorn, "that Gorm did not send one of his sons to treat with me. Does he regard me so little? Where be Canute and Harald Bluetooth?"

"Canute lends his sword to King Sitric in Ath Cliath, Harald Bluetooth captains a patrol south of the wall. As for why I'm here, while Canute and Harald are worthy princes, I will be of more use to you as one who hunts monsters." answered Ingvild astutely.

Bjorn considered this and mused, "Yes, I've heard of you Grave Shield. Two years ago Gorm woke up something foul under Danevirke, they say you stood against a horror that turned your hair white and the hearts of your brethren to quivering puss. In truth, I am pleased to meet you. Especially since my Maeva tells me you come to help quash our Volsung plague."

"Indeed, your majesty. The Witch Vanadis killed my father-in-law. I am here to avenge him."

"Yet, his son is not?" commented Bjorn dryly.

At that Ingvild stiffened. "My King considers my husband too useful to spare on this mission. My Gris is duty bound, but do not think he does not chafe under such an order, as wise as it may be."

Bjorn guffawed and slapped his knee. "Leave it that old husk to dampen a tale of righteous vengeance." Turning to Maeve he added, "I like this one. What say you?"

"She has her charms." the Queen said, her imperious expression unreadable.

"Tell me," said Bjorn, turning his attention back to Ingvild, "what is this chest and wand you bring?"

"They are gifts from Queen Thyra." Ingvild answered, holding them up. "The chest holds a ravenous spirit to devour the witch and the wand is proof against her power. We shall find them useful when we confront her and the Serpent in Courland."

Bjorn flinched in surprise, Meava's lip twisted in an intrigued smirk, Ingvild's escorts huffed and laughed.

The King gestured for silence. Leaning forward and regarding Grave Shield intently he asked "What makes you think they're in Courland?"

"The night before I was sent here Queen Thyra had a dream. In it King Siggeir, the eternal Volsung foe, came to her on a ship of stone. He was incensed at the evil the Serpent and the Witch had wrought on Gotland. He begged my Queen to send a force to avenge him. Drafli the Eye, my father in law and the man whom Vanadis killed, was a dear friend of Danevirke so my Queen readily agreed.

King Siggeir presented these artifacts to her, when she awoke they followed her to the waking world." She held up the grim wand, "This holds the spirit of the Witch's mother, if one breaks it in Vanadis' presence, her magic will be for naught." She held forth the small chest, "This contains a wraith of Kelifar, not only will it devour the witch but it can also lead us directly to her."

"How so?" asked Bjorn with growing interest.

"A golden thread of fate links the wraith to the witch. Those, such as myself, can see it. Even now it trails across the sea towards Courland. If you doubt my words summon one of your volvas and she'll vouch for what I claim."

Bjorn glanced at Maeva. The queen peered closely at the chest and then nodded. "I see it. She tells truth."

"Keep the artifacts." answered Bjorn. "For I welcome you and your men on our Courland raid. Use these sorcerous gifts to dispatch the witch before she can curse us. As for the Serpent, leave him to me and Lemminkäinen. "

"Reckless Lemminkäinen, the bane of Pohjola?" asked Ingvild in surprise.

Bjorn grinned, "Aye, the same. He too seeks revenge against the Fallen Volsungs."

"For the troll incident? I thought that mere rumor."

"The only truth with those two is villainy." answered the King.

Ingvild pondered this, "Your majesty, if I may be so bold, there may be one more deserving of ending the Serpent's life than you or Lemminkäinen."

***

Moments later Bjorn strode out of town with Ingvild at his side. He had left with such haste that his crown still adorned his head. He ordered his men to stay behind for there was one he would confront alone.

They had walked a short distance from town when shieldmaiden paused and pointed. "He's there your majesty."

'He' was a vagabond wrapped in a brown cloak. The tip of a sheathed sword peeked underneath the hem of his cloak. He leaned on a thin elm, its thick leaves sheltering him from the summer drizzle.

Bjorn grunted and strode forward. Without turning he said to Grave Shield "Return to Lysa and await my command. We sail as soon as I can gather the jarls."

"Yes your majesty." Ingvild answered with a polite bow. Then she struck off ahead, giving both king and vagabond a wide birth.

Bjorn stormed up to the man. "Hardegon, you dare show up here after rejecting your place in last summer's battle?" he snarled.

Hardegon pulled off his hood. His skin was sallow, the hands that held his cloak were thin, his eyes sunken.

Bjorn halted. "By Thor, what's wrong with you?"

"Have no fear." Hardegon wheezed with a grin of greeting. "This is a curse, not a sickness. It is my burden to bear alone."

The king recovered himself and said, "Tell me, my 'trusted one', what do you know of last year's clash?"

Hardegon laughed wretchedly, "I know nothing of it. My search for the Serpent has been all"

"Nothing? You care not for your kin?"

"Oh, I care for them but I feared that, if I cared too deeply, I would be distracted from my mission. As much as it has pained me, I must admit that I've driven them from my mind."

Bjorn considered him closely, then, with an air of severity he said, "I will drive them back. Your Thora is dead."

Hardegon closed his eyes and grappled with the painful news.

"She attended the battle in your stead. My forces clashed with Prince Guttorm of Rainrike. Her Nibelung troop flanked them, but Fair Hair's forces proved stronger than either of us expected. Still, she and her small band's actions drove the enemy into disarray, though she was slain her spirit surely found Fólkvangar that night."

The swordsman smiled that. "You do me a kindness by telling me such."

"I speak simple truth." said Bjorn flatly. "I also speak truth when I say there is no more alliance between our people."

Hardegon staggered at that.

Brjon grinned fiercely, "Since Alands no longer has the strength to stand on her own she is mine."

"What of my brother?" the swordsman asked, steel in his tone.

Bjorn smiled at that, "I dislike sorcerers, however, in honor of Thora he is still jarl as long as young Hogni is well. When Starkad can no longer be jarl, Hogni will succeed him"

"Is Hogni is well?" asked Hardegon in a trembling voice.

"I am informed that Starkad considers him like his own. Hogni is growing strong and proud, though I hear he holds little love for you." answered the King.

The swordsman chuckled with pain. "As is just, I sacrificed his love after all. Do you know of a woman named Asta of Neshraun? She did me a service, do you know how she fares?"

"She is Starkad's wife, together they have a daughter." answered Bjorn.

The jarl's brother regarded Bjorn quizzically, "Why comfort me with such news? Did I not betray you?"

Bjorn's fierce expression fell to one of kindness. "Oh I was furious at first, but the more I thought on it the more I understood that; had it been my uncle and my people who suffered, I would have done the same in your place.

Hardegon, I took Alands as a matter of kingship, not as a matter of vengeance. Know it was a bloodless seizure and your Nibelung clan are among my proudest subjects."

A smile of relief and joy lit the dying man's face. "For that I am grateful. I know I have no right to ask, but I must. Allow me to sail with Grave Shield to Courland. I swear, if I am allowed to confront the Serpent I will regain my former strength and do my King proud."

Bjorn put his arm around his trusted friend and led him back towards town. "You shall not sail with Grave Shield, you shall sail with me, Hardegon. I shall grant you your chance at Valhalla on the Courland sands."

CHAPTER ƎI

Many have a child's view of the ancient tales. / They see them as tales of heroes and success.
This is because, as children, the truth was told with lies.
Be righteous and strong. / And your name will live on.
In truth all legends end with a corpse.

Fire surrounded Gamli, Ormir sung as he worked hammer and tongs. The glowing hot bronze danced on his anvil, each time he struck a strange rune vanished and a new one took its place. The smith's deep blue eyes watched it, he felt each vibration up the hammer and gauged how it rung on his tongs. Finally, it struck just the right way, it rang true. Far off distance a gong echoed across the sky. He lifted the hammered metal from the anvil, one rune shone clear: Q.

Many moments later, after he chiselled, tapped, ground, and sharpened, the fires died and his work was done. He sat outside his smithy in a circle of charred grass; before the madness struck, he had carted his tools out as to avoid the loss of his shop. Ormir curled up and lay sleeping behind him. Gamli held his newest work in his hand and frowned, as all his works, it seemed flawless, but, something was wrong. It seemed like the work was a little too complete.

"All that for a knife?" laughed a pleasant voice nearby.

Gamli turned and quickly gestured her not to approach. "Be careful, it's hot."

He walked over to Lonija, placed his creation down and opened his arms. They embraced.

"It's good to see you." Gamli said with truthful joy.

"And you as well husband." answered Lonija pleasantly.

"I am thankful your Goddess has spared you some time."

She squeezed Gamli's hand and stared up at him warmly. "I'm happy to have a husband who understands the duties I owe my people."

She ducked under his arm and considered the newly forged knife. Its handle was chiselled from Edgaras' unmarred amber. Embedded in it was an iron clasp that held a blade, doubled edged which tapered to a point, made of Zaidaan's bronze. The curious rune, Q, was clear and black on the blade as if painted in ink. "What a strange thing." she commented.

Gamli lifted the dagger to have a closer look at it. "It's called Dispersal, a deep foreign magic is within it. I fear that it'll bring trouble."

"Then why did you forge it?" Lonija asked shrewdly.

Gamli shrugged, "In my madness I craft whatever the Norns deem fit."

"Can you not get rid of it?" asked the Priestess.

Gamli chuckled, "No, as troublesome as she may be, I'll usher her towards her purpose. She's one of my children. However," He grinned at her and held her iron forged hand lovingly, "she's not my favorite."

Lonija admired her hand and said, "Such a useful, loyal daughter. One day we shall forge something together, shall will we not?"

Gamli grinned wide, "Of course, we can start now if you wish." With a smooth motion he swept her up and kissed her.

They lingered like his, simply enjoying each other, until Lonija finally pushed herself away. "Soon," she promised, "but first I must tell you that your sister and Ransu head for Klaipeda."

"Of course, my sister," sighed Gamli, reining in his passion, then, after a moment of thought, he asked, "Where is Klaipeda and will they get into trouble by going there?"

"Be at ease. Klaipeda is a fortress which lay where the lagoon meets the Baltic on the northern end of the spit. A certain Gotaland trader by the name of Rennir, one whom we have good dealings with, has arrived early and brought with him a guest, a certain Vargeisa the Fire Wolf. I traveled here mostly to see you, but also to tell you of such, however, you were in the madness. Vargeisa's presence moved your sister so I gave her and Ransu leave to see her, they ride with two of my men who will vouch for them."

Vargeisa's name brought a troubled look to the smith's face. He turned, "I should go."

Lonija touched him gently on the arm, "Or not." She said, with a gentle pleading.

Gamli regarded her quizzically.

Lonija steadied herself, as if preparing for something rehearsed, and said "I love your sister and I find Ransu...amusing. However, they do not belong here." She grasped his hand, "Not like you do. If Vargeisa is here to fetch them, perhaps it's wisest to let them go?"

Gamli was startled at that, "You would banish my sister to unfriendly lands?"

"No." Lonija urged, "Not at all, but I've seen the look she hides form you. She's not happy here. If this Vargeisa has a way for them to return safely, then I say let them do so, but please," she shook her head, "do not go with them."

Understanding dawned on the smith and it brought a tender look upon him. He reached down, lifted Lonija's chin and kissed her again. "For as long as you wish me here, I'll never leave."

She smiled sweetly. "Good."

Gamli then looked north, "As for Vanadis, you're wrong. All her life she's sought the best for us." Gamli laughed and gestured at their home, "Now, we have it. Wealth, freedom, and prestige. If I wished to leave, which shall never happen, she'd join you in convincing me to stay."

The priestess looked troubled and dubious but answered, "I will not stop her staying. As long as she never approaches our sacred groves. Your sister is kind, but her magic is evil."

"I'll warn her, she's wise enough to take heed." Gamli said with confidence. He then looked over his wife with a deep longing, "I wish we could leave them to their business."

"What about it concerns you?" asked Lonija.

"The Fire Wolf is..." Gamli searched for the right words, "dangerous. It's best we watch her."

Lonija regarded his seriousness and straightened her posture and her dress, "I see, I thank you for this council husband. We shall ride after them straight away."

***

Ransu, Vanadis, and Vargeisa sat by the wooden palisade wall of Klaipeda. A barrel acted as their table and they shared a jug of beer. Beyond them, near the main hall, black and silver haired Rennir bartered with a crowd of Curonians.

"The memory of your crimes still lies fresh on the minds of those in the west," announced Vargeisa. "They call you curse bringer, troll wife, hall burner, and banisher of maidens."

Vanadis looked shocked, insulted and downtrodden. She searched the Fire Wolf's eyes to see if this was in jest. Then Vanadis turned furious, "Hall burner?" she asked, "Banisher of maidens? Since when have we done such?"

Vargeisa broke into a grin, "Yet, you don't deny Troll wife?"

Vanadis stood and glared down at her, "You...you've been using our names to cover your own crimes, haven't you?"

"Why of course not," the Fire Wolf with feigned innocence "only a student of Loki could be so cruel."

"I will hex you." stammered Vanadis. "Rip out your soul and bind it to a boar's ass."

Vargeisa controlled her humor and held out a hand for peace. "At ease, I did not come all this way only to tease you. I bring good news, you can return to Pohjola this year, in fact we should do so as soon as possible."

"How can I, when you've stirred all of Midgard against me?" Vanadis hissed.

Vargeisa eyed the staring crowd and gestured for her to sit. "I will explain but this news is... sensitive."

Ransu stood and approached the bargaining table. In Couronian he said helplessly, "Women, close as sisters one moment, at each other's throats the next."

The crowd chuckled at that. Ransu walked over to trade, leaving Vargeisa and Vanadis to chat.

"Explain." Vanadis whispered.

Vargeisa, turning once again serious answered, "I admit guilt in blackening your reputation further, but understand that I had no wish to put you or your brother at risk. The Fallen Volsung name was simply cover for a year. I was confident your foes couldn't find you. In another year, the people's rage would swing back to an older foe; the Samogitians, perhaps, or maybe Harald Fair Hair? Once that happened trust that I would have signaled for your return." Suddenly, she smiled at Vanadis in admiration. "What I didn't expect was for you to become such close allies with Courland. You must tell me how you did it."

"It was my brother." Vanadis answered simply, "His honesty and forge magic charmed them." She snorted, "He even married the High Chieftain's daughter."

Vargeisa tilted her head curiously.

"Enough of that. How do we get home to Pohjola?"

"Ah!" said the Fire Wolf, then, leaning closer and lowering her voice she continued, "What I also didn't expect was for King Bjorn Eriksson to discover your hiding place."

"Why would Bjorn care about us?" asked Vanadis.

Vargeisa just gave her an apologetic look.

The seithkona's eyes flashed with anger but she held it in. "Go on."

"Bjorn plans to raid Courland. With him sail Kalevala and Danevirke. All of them are united by hunger for Courland amber and pledge their vengeance against the Fallen Volsung."

That struck Vanadis hard, for a moment she was stymied as she realized just how many, and how powerful her foes were.

Vargeisa squeezed her hand and smiled, "Fear not, for this is a blessing."

***

An hour later, Vargeisa, Vanadis, Gamli, and Ransu stood by the docks of Klaipeda. To the south, across a wide dark river, lay the sandy dunes of the Couronian spit. To the north, sat the wooden fortress of Klaipeda. To the west, the rolling Baltic. The river flowed southeast, splitting the mainland from the spit until it met the Couronian Lagoon. Horse-headed boats fished in both the Baltic and along the river. It was a bright, late afternoon. Further down the dock was moored a longship of western make. A few sailors idled by casually watching, but too far away to spy. Sea birds sailed the skies or hopped around, hunting for fish or a hand out.

Vanadis held Gamli's hands and looked up at him in joy. "It's all set out. We'll return with Vargeisa and Rennir to Gotaland. There we'll meet with up with Katla and Wolf and also a man you know, the merchant Krumr. We'll negotiate passage to Pohjola. Meanwhile, our foes will search for us here in vain."
Vargeisa stood with her arms crossed, looking self-satisfied at her own cunning. Ransu considered the plan and it seemed to him sound.

Gamli looked troubled and then determined. He pulled away from his sister. "No."

Vanadis staggered back. "No?"

"Are you daft?" Gamli asked. "We've everything we need here. We're respected, loved. We have a life."

"We also have one in Pohjola." Vanadis shot back. "There's no reason why you can't do there what you did here."

"It's true." added Ransu, "You'd be richer in Pohjola."

Gamli stood his ground and shook his head, "I would be worse; I'd be without Lonija."

"You've only known her a handful of months." Vanadis argued. "There will be others."

"You knew Vinglunr not much longer." the smith retorted.

Vanadis flinched as if struck

Seeing the pain across her face, Gamli sighed. He placed both hands on her shoulders, locked eyes with her and said, "I can't help how I feel. This is my home now."

"Remember, you were born in Kelifar, we both were."

"We were slaves." rumbled Gamli, "So, here I chose to stay."

"Not wise." stated Vargeisa. "Three kingdoms raid this land; take yourself and your Lonija out of it."

"I'll warn Malvis and we'll stand and fight." stated the smith. "Hearth, family, there's is no better reason to risk my life. I'd rather die than be without either."

"Gamli..." cried his sister.

The smith suddenly pulled her into a deep hug. "Now listen here. I want you to take that ship with Vargeisa and Ransu. Go back to Pohjola, your life is there. Just know, I'm always your brother, I'll always love you."

Vanadis pushed herself away and glared at him, tears in her eyes, "There's no convincing you is there?"

Gamli stood firm. "No."

Vanadis shook her head. "You're insane." Then, after steadying herself, she added. "I will leave you. I'll go back to Pohjola, make no mistake about that, but first... first I'll ensure you and your wretched Courland are safe."

Gamli blinked in surprise, then, he recovered himself and said, "I'd feel better if you left."

"That's your concern." Vanadis huffed. "Either leave with us now or we fight Svealand, Danevirke and Kalevala together."

Gamli looked to Ransu.

The fisherman shook his head and stood beside Vanadis. "I hear Tuonela nice this year." He muttered. Then, in a braver tone he stated "I go where she goes."

Gamli looked to Vargeisa.

The Fire Wolf raised her hands helplessly, "I merely bring news, and a ship with which to escape. You must choose, will you and your sister die here or shall we all go back to civilization together?"

Gamli lowered his head and brooded, "I will not leave."

"Fine." huffed the Fire Wolf. "Come Vanadis, we're going."

The seithkona stayed where she was.

Vargeisa glanced at her and urged, "Vanadis, I do not think he can be reasoned with, it is no longer time for bluffing."

Vanadis looked longingly at the ship but moved not. "I-I...can't. He's my brother." she explained.

"Regin had a brother, Fanfir, he turned into a dragon and drove him from home. Aganar had a brother, Geirroor, who stole his oars and pushed his boat out to sea. You have a brother whose foolish sentiment will get you killed. He himself wishes you to leave, so do so. Come with me." Vargeisa snapped.

The seithkona's expression hardened. "No, if you could have stood with your sister who was killed in Kalevala, would you have not? It's the same here, I must protect my family."

Gamli put his arm around Vanadis.

The Fire Wolf stood there and stared at them incredulously.

Gamli waked up to her and drew a bronze dagger form his belt, the one with Q on the blade. He pressed it, amber handle first, into her hands.

Vargeisa glanced down at it and up at him. "What's this?"

"Its name is Dispersal." answered the smith. "It's a tool of ill-omen."

"Is it cursed?" asked the Fire Wolf, with a suspicious sneer.

Gamli chuckled, "No. It's foreign magic, one that can open any lock and cut any bond. I suspect you'll use it for ill." He regarded her warmly. "You have it with my blessing. Consider it payment for the warning you've given us."

The Fire Wolf's sneer dropped and she considered the knife closely, weighed it in her hand, and a slight smile curved on her lips. "Why thank you, yes, this will come in most handy." She glanced up at the three.

Gamli walked back to his sister and put his arma round her shoulders and guided her towards the fortress, "Come, Lonija must know of this."

Ransu gave Vargeisa a curt wave and followed.

The Fire Wolf thumbed the handle of Dispersal. She lifted and looked at the bone ring that the Volsung sister delivered from her mother. She let out a sigh of frustration and rushed to catch up. "By the Norns your stupidity is catching."

"Glad to have you with us." Vanadis said with surprise. "Can you convince Rennir and his men to help?"

"Not a chance." Vargeisa laughed.

***

Many days later, framed in the setting sun, a fleet of seven longships glided towards the narrow gap between the spit and the mainland. They were at full sail and silent.

Torchlight flickered in the fortress of Klaipeda. Watchful men walked her ramparts but the orange brilliance of the sunset hid the ships until they were very close indeed. When they were spotted, a long, low blat from a horn sounded out, echoing across the lagoon.

At this, a cheer of fury arose from the invaders. Oars were set, sails were lower and the fleet raced across the waters with alarming speed. A score of Curonain warriors rode out of the fortress to meet them. The longships did not engage. They rowed past. In his fine ship of darkest green Bjorn Eriksson stood and laughed mockingly at the defenders. They were not here for them; they were here for riches and the vargs. The defenders rode after but were helpless to stop them.

Meanwhile, in a hidden bay nuzzled into the spit waited five horse-headed ships. They were smaller than the invader vessels but another five waited were hidden on the mainland. Malvis, Gamli and Izidorious watched from a dune. All three were dressed in chainmail, all three carried fine shields and swords, works of deadly art crafted by the Serpent. They heard well the Viking roar, and they saw well the fleet speeding past the fortress and striking for the wealthy villages of the Lagoon.

"We should attack." Gamli rumbled impatiently.

Izidorious pulled him back to the sand and motioned him to hush. Malvis watched the invaders with a look of expectant glee.

One ship, a ridiculous red vessel with a dragonhead far too large raced out ahead. At the rear sat a giant of a man, so large, in fact, that he rowed a set of port and starboard oars by himself. He laughed and sung out, somehow making lyrical Suomi sound hideous.

Gamli gripped the hilt of Fire Heart which rested on his hip, on his back was sheathed Scorn. "Lemminkäinen." He whispered with spite and awe.

Suddenly, the Reckless One's ship lurched to a stop as two enormous hands shot out from underneath the water and seized bow and stern. The ships behind them sank their oars deep and lurched causing the ships to crash together into a tangled mess.

"What?" Cried Lemminkäinen, his booming voice sounded louder than thunder.

Malvis chuckled and then, he bellowed out in laughter.

The three could feel Lemminkäinen's look of rage upon them. The Kalevalen warrior drew his enormous sword.

Suddenly, a loud crack snapped and those onboard Lemminkäinen's ship staggered.

"What?" cried the great warrior again.

Another crack as Neringa pressed her hands up and inward.

"No!" screamed Lemminkäinen. "Nooo!" He raised his sword to chop at one of the hands but too late. His ship snapped in two, sending her crew, including the Reckless One, toppling into the drink.

Izidorious slapped Gamli on the back and said something with rapturous glee. The smith understood a few words and understood that Naringa had taken her tribute.

Malvis lifted his horn to his lips and blew. The eastern shore answered. Then the three rushed onto their waiting boat and shot off.

***

Ten small Curonian ships rowed swiftly on either side of the disarrayed fleet. Within moments the two Curonian small fleets crushed the western alliance between them, and the pirates raced onboard the floating battle ground.

Malvis changed in the forefront, leading his men. He swung Storm and it crashed into his foes like thunder, sending them mangled, bloody and flying into the sea. Thanks to Wind Malvis moved swiftly and any blows that got through his guard were deflected by its steel.

Izidorious was close at his side; he smashed his shield into the face of an invader, breaking the young man's jaw. His horse hilted sword swung swiftly and lopped off the arm of another attacker. He strode fearlessly into the carnage.

Gamli followed his Fire Heart burned through the enemy's swords and shields. Three invaders attempted to pile onto the smith but he knocked them aside with a single blow. He followed close behind the High Chief, striking down all who would dare attack his father-in-law.

The Couronian pirates fought with swiftness and viciousness born of defending their home. The westerners barely had time to raise their shields before they were cut down. The Couronian chiefs and their guards, wielded Gamli's weapons, which proved far superior to the western steel.

Bjorn, like the rest, had been stunned by the lagoon Jotun's attack and also by the sudden Couronian raid. However, his battle hardened mind quickly recovered. "To arms!" he roared. "Fend the invaders off!" He hefted his shield and longsword and rushed across the boats to fight those on the western front. His fearless assault carried him straight into the enemy line. It drove those nearby to rally behind him.

Ingvild Grave Shield, reacted next. "Warriors of Danevirke rise!" She raised her shield and invoked its magic, the three red hawks etched on it flew off, coming to life as birds of steel. They swept into the Curonians, their very wings causing horrendous wounds. The Danevirke guard fought with precision and skill and hurt the Curonians sore.

The Kalevalans, who had flanked the fleet in their white longships, had taken the brunt of the pirate raid. Many lay dead, but those who survived lifted their voices as one. Their song was a fast, brave tune. It bolstered the westerners, driving them to speed and vitality. Allowing some to turn deadly Curonain strikes aside and live to mount a counterattack. After but the first cord the rest of the fleet joined in. As the Kalevalens sung, they also fought with amazing skill, delaying the pirate advance.

Though his body was a wreck of twisting pain Hardegon forced himself to follow his King, Troll's End in one hand, a short sword in his other. Though he moved like one of the dead his strikes were strong and determined. He fought like a madman, slaying many foe. "Serpent!" he cried, "I'm here for you! None save you can stop me."

In the first initial moments the Curonians assault slew many. However, now that the invaders had rallied, it was obvious that a Curonian victory would need to be hard fought.

***

Meanwhile Vanadis, Vargeisa and Ransu waited in a horse-headed ship on the eastern bay. They were flanked by Curonain warriors. Lonija waited on shore, Ormir, who had been ordered to protect her, at her side. Beside them was a second boat. As the sun dipped below the horizon they watched the chaos unfold and listened to the Kalevalen song highlighted by war cries and the clash of steel.

Vanadis glared at the battle, "It'd be useful if Neringa sunk the entire fleet."

"She has played her part and we are thankful, but, to be strong, we cannot have her fight our battles." answered Lonija sagely.

"Does that apply to us as well?" asked the Fire Wolf who sat aboard, cleaning her nails with Dispersal.

"Not at all," answered Lonija patiently, "as reserve you'll fight but you must wait till the right moment."

Vanadis shook her head in frustration. "Your father's a fool. I could have sunk three of their ships by now."

Lonija chuckled at that, "Perhaps, but we hope to seize their lives and their ships; a fair price for invading Courland."

"It's good we held back." said Ransu, his voice tinted with fear. "Behold."

The party turned and saw, crawling up on shore, the enormous form of Lemminkäinen. Once on land the Reckless One spun on his heel and faced the water, holding his shaking sword before him. Even in the dying light, they could see his wide eyes staring into the lagoon. He had lost his shield and stood as if injured.

"Looks like he escaped Neringa." chuckled Vargeisa.

The memory of Lemminkäinen cutting down Trolls surfaced to the seithkona's mind. To Lonija she urged, "We can't allow him to rejoin the battle or attack villages."

Vanadis' words shook the priestess out of her shocked state of disbelief. "I-indeed." To her men she ordered, "Attack the large one!"

The Curonain defenders leaped out of their ship and charged across the sands at Lemminkäinen.

"This will be fun." Vargeisa giggled and joined them.

"Bera!" Vanadis called, with a gesture the skeletal warrior rose out of the sand, axe and shield in hand, and, with a cry of vicious joy, she chased after the warriors.

Ransu stood where he was, leveled his crossbow and fired one of Gamli's bolts.

The warrior shouts drew the Reckless One's attention. He spied them, and behind them Ransu. The enormous warrior whipped his arm up to shield himself, Ransu's bolt shot through the mail and arm. "Ah!" Lemminkäinen laughed, "This is more like it!" With a wolfish grin he charged the defenders. When they met he swung his massive sword, it cut in a deadly arc splitting open three Curonians in a shower of blood. Bera leapt forward and chopped, several blows striking hard against Lemminkäinen's mail. Vargeisa slid behind him and jabbed her sword into his thigh. The surviving Curonians fell upon him as one.

The Reckless One roared and knocked several foes flying with a sweep of his hand. He chopped down with his sword and it split Bera's shield in two, crashing the skeleton to the ground.

"How are you still standing?" cried Vargeisa as she chopped at his calve. Her blade merely sunk into his thick boot.

Lemminkäinen guffawed, seized one of the standing guard and threw him down onto the Fire Wolf. As she lay stunned he raised his blade.

Ransu was still loading his crossbow.

Vanadis swayed as her spirit host possessed her. Through green eyes she saw the Reckless One about to strike, she reached out; suddenly the groaning warrior on top of the Fire Wolf vanished, Vanadis stood in his place. Before Lemminkäinen could strike, she snarled and jabbed Burning Mind into the ground causing a sudden flash of darkness.
The Reckless One reeled back from it, covering his eyes. "What's this? I can't see! You stole my ship and now, you steal my sight? Die!" He chopped his sword down but it was a little too far to the left, it sunk merely into sand.

The Volsung sister vanished. Vargeisa rolled out of the way and ran.

"Now!" shouted Bera, "Kill him now!" The black skeleton charged and sunk her axe deep into Lemminkäinen's side. The few Curonians that stood followed suit, they raced forward and struck at the troll blooded man, their weapons hitting soundly causing bruises and spilling blood.

"Enough!" snarled Lemminkäinen. He swung wildly with his blade; it clipped a defender, slicing him in two. He swept his foot and smashed Bera to pieces. He shook his head and cleared his eyes only to see Ransu staring down at him across the tip of his bolt.

"To Tuonela you go." the fisherman huffed and let fly.

The bolt thunked into the Reckless One's forehead, directly above his left eye. Lemminkäinen gawked. Everyone paused, even Vanadis, who had returned to her place beside Ransu. and returned the Warrior on his place in the sand.

Lemminkäinen plucked the bolt's shaft form his forehead, the point still embedded into his skull. He then screamed with rage.

Ransu looked up to the sky and said, "Ukko, surely, this is unfair."

Vanadis released a curse, the black vortex ripped into the Reckless One's flesh but he did not take heed. The Curonian defenders charged but Lemminkäinen cut them asunder. Vargeisa stood a ways away, completely and absolutely flabbergasted. The Reckless One seized one of the defender's axes and hurled it with inhuman force.

It struck Ransu full in the chest, the tip of the edge sticking out of his back. The fisherman coughed blood and fell to his knees, his face locked in an expression of surprise.

"Ransu!" screamed Vanadis, she knelt to his side.

Lemminkäinen, who had finished with the last of the guards glowered at the shore side ship and the witch. He bent his head and torso and was about to charge when the Fire Wolf leapt on his back and jabbed her sword deep into his shoulder. The Reckless One bellowed like a dragon and attempted to shake her off.

Meanwhile, Vanadis stared at her old friend in horror. He lay in the bottom of the boat, his blood soaking her dress. He breathed not, he saw not, the seithkona felt his spirit stir loosen inside his body. She turned her gaze to Lemminkäinen, who had thrown Vargeisa off and now slashed viciously at her, the Fire Wolf barely dancing out of the way. The seithkona's expression turned to pure rage.

'Come.' She reached out her will and the ghosts of Kelifar flooded her being. She floated an inch off the boat, her back arched, a moan of a dozen voices echoed from her lips. She then dropped and stooped, glaring behind her hair. She raced across the sands and let out choir of shrieks. Hearing this Lemminkäinen turned to see the seithkona thrust forward Burning Mind, a hoard of howling, ghostly skulls blasted from it and struck him full on. The warrior screamed, thrashed and then fell. Laying still

Close by, only a small distance off shore, floated the black Danevirke longship. Only five of Ingvild's warriors, and one shieldmaiden, remained. Grave Sheild assessed the battle with Lemminkäinen, wraith chest and bone wand in hand. She considered the seithkona with a look of respect and caution.

"You all stay here." She raised her shield; her red hawks flew to it and, with several clanks, returned to being mere embellishments. "I shall face the witch and the Fire Wolf alone."

***

Meanwhile warriors continued to kill each other on the island of boats. Several Curonain ships and three of the longships had broken off, their crews mere corpses. A handful of Kalevalens remained and Bjorn's forces had been cut in half. The defenders fared little better; they still outnumbered the invaders but, not by much.

The battle was fiercest on Bjorn's flagship. Izidorious had fallen, Bjorn had knocked him overboard and his heavy armor and weapons dragged him to Neringa's domain. Malvis roared and clashed with the king himself, while Gamli fought Rogvaldr. All around them pirate and Viking fought a bloody clash to the death.

Rogvaldr's axe clipped Gamli's sword arm but the smith's mail deflected the blow. Gamli swung Fire Heart and it singed deep into the veteran's shield.

"You fight well, traitor," grumbled Rogvaldr. He twisted his shield to the side, pulling burning mind from Gamli's hand. He then swiped at the smith's head, Gamli ducked back, the edge of the veteran's axe shaving some red whiskers.

The smith grunted and drew Scorn from his back, he stepped forward and jabbed its point into Rogvaldr shoulder. "You know nothing." he rumbled and then sliced up nearly severing the Svelander's arm. He crashed his shield against Rogvaldr's driving him back. "Courland's shown me greater honor than Alands, Danevrike or Sveland ever has."

The veteran sneered back, "That I die fighting your evil is the greatest honor."

Gamli obliged by shoving Scorn through Rogvaldr's torso and then yanking it out, letting the harry warrior fall in a fountain of blood.

Bjorn and Malvis shared vicious grins

"How long has it been?" yelled Bjorn as he hacked down at Malvis shield? "Three years? It's good to fight you again."

Malvis replied with something that sounded like respect, shunted in closer and nearly stabbed the Sveland King's face.

Bjorn knocked the blade aside and returned a thrust; it drove Malvis back but pierced not Wind. "That's some armor." he remarked.

Malvis nodded towards Gamli and swung a mighty slash with Storm, Bjorn blocked it with his iron shield, and stood firm. "The Serpent crafted it?" He laughed, "Lucky for me, 'old friend', I have a master smiths as well." He sliced up under the Couronian chief's guard and cut into his beard and chin.

Malvis shook it off, his face a bloody mess. In spite of this his eyes gleamed and he flashed a wolfish grin.

Bjorn pulled his sword back for a strike and chuckled. "You've cost me dear but this fight is worth it."

Suddenly the din of battle was cut by Hardegon's cry, "Serpent! I have come."

Bjorn raised a hand and nodded to the swordsman, "Hold on, I want to see this."

Malvis kept his guard up but eyed the swordsman.

Hardegon stood drenched in blood, his short sword just as crimson as Troll's End. He breathed heaving breaths. His expression was one of bearing great pain.

Gamli turned and eyed him, "Hardegon? You look unwell."

"I'm well enough to slay you." The swordsman hissed.

"Hold on!" called Bjorn. His men paused.

Malvis issued a similar command and the pirates broke off.

Both the Chieftain and King watched the two with keen interest.

Gamli nodded in thanks to Malvis and strode towards Hardegon, a discerning eye on Troll's End. "Ready to answer for Mjoll? You'll do so quickly with that blade."

"You fear this?" Hardegon laughed, hoisting his sword and sliding into a fighting stance.

"No." rumbled Gamli, he then shunted forward, smashing Hardegon with his shield and knocking Troll's End flying. The swordsman crashed to the deck and found himself without the strength to stand.

***

Meanwhile, Ingvild strode fearlessly out of the lagoon and towards the waiting Vanadis and Vargeisa.

"Grave Shield." the Fire Wolf greeted pleasantly with a small wave.

"Harlot." Ingvild greeted back, then, with a look of respect to the seithkona she added "Vanadis the Cursed, I'm here to end your life, in response of your murder of my father-in-law."

Vanadis floated an inch off the ground, the ghosts of Kelifar still swirling within her, her head was bowed, her lips moving in some sort of muttered, repeated curse. Vanadis' voice came somewhere within her body. "You'll lose. You can't face us both and I am in no mood for mercy." Suddenly, the stars and moon seemed to darken and the beach was covered in ominous shadow.

Ingvild gave her a thin-lipped smile. "Be not so sure, have I come prepared." With that, she dropped the chest and snapped the bone wand. Appearing before her floated the spirit of Hane the Clever.

Vargeisa flinched in surprise.

"Mother?" asked Vanadis.

Hanne smoothed her dress and floated towards her. "Daughter." She greeted. Then, turning to Grave Shield, she said, "Thank you for returning me home. I'm so sorry for what we're about to do to you."

"What?" stammered Ingvild, "Thora was told you'd...."

Hanne cackled, "All a lie. I simply needed to be free of a certain captor." She floated into Vanadis' form and merged with the spirit gestalt. "I am, of course, only loyal to my family."

"Perhaps you should run?" suggested the Fire Wolf sweetly.

***

Meanwhile, Gamli sheathed Scorn and lifted Troll's End off the deck, holding it with pure distaste.

Malvis laughed. Bjorn shook his head in disappointment.

Hardegon lay on deck, with only the strength to breathe. He stared up at the sky, a look of horror on his face. "I'm consigned to Hel." he bewailed.

Gamli scooped Fire Heart from the deck, then threw Troll's End high into the hair. He pulled his sword back and struck the blood blade. It was a perfect strike and Troll's End shattered, leaving only the hilt.

Suddenly Hardegon shot up. He was gaunt no longer, his skin was sallow no longer, he lifted his arms and stared at his hands, now once again steady. He leapt to his feet in, his old limberness returned. "How?"

"Your sword was cursed." Gamli answered. "I've lifted it." He pulled Scorn from his back and tossed it to Hardegon.

The swordsman caught it and stared at the smith incredulously. "Why? Do you not wish to avenge your aunt?"

Gamli shifted his stance to something aggressive and glared at him fiercely. "Make no mistake, you're not leaving this ship alive. Your uncle used a cursed sword to kill my father, thanks to that I was thrown into thralldom. You'll have to answer for that and the death of Mjoll, but I won't slay you using cheap tricks."

Hardegon laughed with joy. "You see Bjorn? Before us stands a true Volsung." To Gamli he added, "You are no poisoner. I would take back your name if I could."

"All I request," rumbled Gamli, "is once this is done, no matter what the result, this feud is over. I will have no other Nibelung hounding myself or my family. Agreed?"
"Aye." Said Hardegon eagerly, "Once one of us falls the feud is satisfied. Bjorn, you are my witness."

"Aye," said the King with an expectant grin, "these Volsung will find no trouble from me, as long as they stay away from Svealand."

"Good." Huffed Gamli. With that, he charged at the swordsman.

***

Meanwhile, Ingvild thrust her shield forward and her three hawks flew from their perch, streaking towards the seithkona.

Vanadis reached out and made a crunching motion with her hand. The red hawks, with the sound of tearing and bending steel, warped and compressed into useless bits of twisted metal.

Ingvild stared in astonishment but then, she drew her sword. "I shall not run." She rushed the witch.

Vanadis drew back another spell but before she could release it her mother's voice came from her lips. "I consign my entourage to King Siggeir." Suddenly, the seithkona stiffened and a horrendous choir of howls of anguish arose form her. It was so startling that it threw off Ingvild's thrust, the sword buried itself in Vanadis side rather than her heart.

The seithkona fell back on her ass, an expression of shock and terror on her face. "They're gone," she whispered. "My father, Bera, every last one of them... all of them... gone"

"I'm still here." her mother's voice cooed somewhere beside her.

Vanadis stared at her in disbelief. "H-how could you? My father, your husband, our family? I'm your child!" she proclaimed

Hanne laughed, "Oh, that ship sailed long ago. You should have been a good girl and consigned yourself to me. I have a new husband now and my loyalty to him will grant me far more power."

"My condolences." quipped Grave Shield and she swung her blade at the witch.

It rang against the Fire Wolf's. "Ah, ah, aah. One should not interrupt a family squabble."

Ingvild scowled and jumped back, kicking the chest open as she did so. Dorte tumbled out, her veiled face snapping up to regard Vanadis.

"Flee!" cried Vargeisa as she clashed with Grave Shield.

Vanadis did just that, though she was slowed by the bloody wound in her side.

***

Meanwhile, Hardegon slipped under Gamli's guard and sliced with Scorn, the blade cut through the smith's mail wounding him.

"Perhaps you should have given me the inferior blade?" the Nibelung hero chuckled.

"I did." Grunted the Volsung brother, he sliced down. Hardegon parried with his short sword and Fire Heart cut it in two.

The smith swung his blade but the swordsman stepped out of the way. The swordsman slashed and Gamli blocked it with his shield. He then heaved and threw Hardegon back.

The swordsman wiped sweat from his brow and smirked, then slid back into a fighting stance. Gamli rushed forward, chopped, Hardegon stepped out of the way again and stabbed wounding the smith on the side. Gamli spun around and elbow smashed the side of Hardegon's head, before swordsman could recover Gamli chopped down with Fire Heart and sliced the blade's edge deep inside him. Hardegon gasped and, with his remaining strength swung Scorn up and sliced the smith's throat.

Hardegon fell lifeless, an expression of victory was displayed on his face. Gamli dropped his blade and held his gushing throat. He fell to his knees, his blue eyes wide with panic.

The crowd, who had been cheering, hushed.

The smith held his bleeding throat, his face turning pale, his mind running with regret as thoughts of Lonija raced through them.

Suddenly Bjorn stood before him. He put a steady hand on the smith's shoulder.

"I just realized, you've been in Courland all this time, so you couldn't have committed crimes in Sveland. For your valor I declare you and your sister no longer vargs. If she lives she'll be a free woman." With that Bjorn drove his sword through the smith.

Gamli's eyes widened and he died.

***

Meanwhile, while the Fire Wolf and Grave Shield fought, Vanadis ran. As she did, so she reached out her will, seeking any spirit to aid her.

Behind her Dorte slowly rose. She gestured and barbed spectral chains enwrapped the seithkona. The Volsung sister cried out in pain and fell rolling onto the sand, her blood staining it crimson.

"This is how it should end, don't you agree?" chuckled Hane.

"No!" fumed Vanadis, with a focus of her will the chains shattered. She snarled and gestured at the approaching Haugbui, calling upon her own soul for the spell. Beams of black and white shot from her hands. Dorte merely knocked the spell aside shattering it. Within a moment she towered over the seithkona, staring down in silent malice.

Hanne brushed Vanadis' cheek. "You have no spirits and no strength left, poor dear. Goodbye daughter."

"I have one spirit." Vanadis said through gritted teeth. She grabbed Hanne's hand and forced her into a summoning. Suddenly the ghost materialized in plain sight.

"Dorte." Vanadis huffed. "Behold your true murderess."

The Haugbui turned to stare at Hanne.

"N-no." laughed Hane. "She speaks nonsense, how could I have killed you?"

"Focus Dorte, what face was the last one you saw? Mine or hers?"

The Haugbui considered them both.

Hane tried to pull away but Vanadis held her firm. In an unsteady tone the spirit said, "This is a desperate maneuver, clearly she wishes to save herself."

"Dorte, I owe you my life. Kill me if you wish, all I ask is you avenge yourself first.", stated Vanadis with no trace of fear.

Dorte let out a horrid shriek and dove for Hane, ripping her from Vanadis' grasp. The spirit screamed in fear and pain as the Haugbui tore her apart.

Vanadis held her bleeding side and tried to focus. 'This is a battlefield, surely I can rally fresh spirits.'

She glanced up to see that the Danevirke contingent had landed. Five warriors rushed towards her.

"Thor's balls." Vanadis cursed.

***

Meanwhile, it took all of the Fire Wolf's attention to fight Gave Shield. Her guard was perfect, her sword strikes quick and deadly. The Fire Wolf drove her back with cuts, jabs and hexes, but Vargeisa seemed to quickly be running out of breath.

"You are as much to blame for Drafli's death as the witch is." stated Ingvild.

"No," answered the Fire Wolf, "it was his own foolishness that did him in. If he had guarded the Barrow Bowl more wisely he would not have had to follow me into the Skane mounds."

Grave Shield shifted her stance and attempted to shield bash the Fire Wolf, but Vargeisa managed to jump out of the way, barely.

"Though you... you were suspicious of me from the start, were you not?" asked Louhi's daughter.

"Aye." answered Grave Shield, circling around for a better strike.

"Then, it was really your fault. You could have stopped me but didn't." The Fire Wolf paused as a thought struck her. "You meant for me to steal the Barrow Bowl, didn't you? You did to prevent further vile magic from infecting Danevirke. You betrayed Gorm for the greater good."

Ingvild's expression turned dark and she screamed, "I am no traitor." She swung but, in her rage, a little too far. The Fire Wolf smirked and suddenly, without an ounce of exhaustion stepped past her guard and gestured. The curse wracked Grave Shield, she screamed and dropped her sword and shield. Then the Fire Wolf jammed her sword deep into Ingvild's side.

The shieldmaiden paled and fell to her knees.

Vargeisa followed her down, guiding Ingvild's hand to the hit the blade inside her. She smiled, pulled a strand of hair form her shocked face and said. "I request you keep pressure on your wound. I wish you to live, to tell Gorm I send my greetings." She winked and strode away.

The sight that greeted her on the beach drove her forward. "Hel." she muttered.

Four Danevirke warriors lay twisted, burned, and completely broken. In the center of them, lay Vanadis, wounds ripped across her corpse, a sorrowful expression on her face, her cold, dead eyes staring into the starry heavens.

Epilogue

King Bjorn sat across from Malvis. They were in a closed pavilion. Five Curonain guards, armed with Gamli crafted axes, stood behind their High Chieftain. Behind Bjorn stood three of his men, a Kalevalen warrior and Ingvild Grave Shield.

"I shall repeat, so we all understand the terms. In exchange for Svealand, Danevirke, and Kalevala leaving our lands, we will use our holy magic to heal their wounded, this I have already done, and award them a gift a shipload of amber, twelve of our criminals which they may take back as slaves, and five weapons that my late husband forged. I trust this is acceptable?"

The Kalevalen representative, handsome Aku cut in. "Please know, we cannot control Lemminkäinen. We do not know where he lie. Even if we found him, though we are kin, he shall not heed us. I suggest you keep wary."

Lonija repeated his words for her father. Malvis nodded with full seriousness and responded.

"The High Chieftain hopes your Lemminkäinen has the wisdom to return home. The Reckless One has drawn the attention of our Gods, they if they find him in Courland they will do their utmost to kill him." Translated Lonija.

"I pray to Ukko it does not come to that." replied Aku with a respectful bow.

Lonija nodded cordially and then regarded the three. "With that out of the way, I trust we are in agreement."

"Aye." answered Aku.

"The vargs have been killed, Danevirke has no more business here." answered Grave Shield, Lonija's calm exterior cracked slightly at that. Ormir, trilled softly and rubbed his head under her hand, giving her comfort.

Bjorn regarded Malvis with a grin of comradery. "I'll see you on the sea old friend." He offered his hand.

Malvis snickered and clasped arms with his old foe. He responded with what sounded like a challenge of endearment.

***

A few hours later, the entirety of Bjorn's camp gathered around a field of funeral pyres. Placed on them were Svealand and Danevirke's fallen. The Kalevalens attended the dead with their own funerary rights. Bjorn stood on the hull of an overturned ship so as to be seen by the survivors. He regarded the small crowd, the remains of his massive invasion force, and felt a sharp pang in his heart. Though he returned with justice and treasure there would be great mourning in Svealand. Furthermore he'd have to be much more careful with his forces in the future. Bjorn smirked as he considered that the Curonians were in the same boat, he expected far fewer raids.

"Brothers." He called in a powerful voice. "On this eve of our return, we pay tribute to the fallen. We pay tribute to our dear friends," he waved his lit touch over Rodrekr and Hardegon, "and to to our foes." He waved his touch over Gamli and Vanadis.

The four had been cleaned, dressed, and laid on their pyres with what they carried into battle. Rodrekr had his axe and his horn at his side. Hardegon lay clasping a gleaming sword Bjorn gifted him, the expression on his corpse serine. Gamli wore his mail, his shield lay upon him, on his back were strapped both Fire Heart and Scorn. His death mask was solemn. Vanadis lay with her arms crossed over her chest. Lonija had given her a circlet of silver and bracelets of gold. A small, eerie smile was on her lips, she seemed almost alive.

"Some would ask, why honor our foes? It is because worthy ones open the way to Valhalla. I have seen the Serpent's valor with my own eyes. Though his crimes are steep I cannot judge him. I shall leave that for Odin." Then, harkened by the cheers of his comrades, Bjorn stepped down from the ship and lit Gamli's pyre, next was Hardegon's, then Rodrekr's and then Vanadis'. Then king walked amongst the other wooden mounds and personally lit each and every one.

The crowd followed solemnly, singing songs of glory to the heavens.

None noticed the masking spirit melt from 'Vanadis'.

The seithkona sat on a dune on the spit, watching the flicker of the pyre light across the river. Her own golden circlet adorned her temple, her spear Burning Mind sat beside her. Her cheeks were tear-stained, she hugged her knees looking wretched.

The ghost of Gamli stood beside her, hand on her shoulder. He glowered at the dancing motes.

Vanadis glared up at the spirit. "You had to be 'honorable.' What did that earn you? Tell me! Are you working in your forge? Is Lonija in your arms?" she laughed bitterly. "Of course not. You've only won the admiration of those who killed you."

The ghost shook his head evenly, glaring at his sister.

Vanadis pressed her face in her hands and wailed in sorrow. "Leave me." She sniffed, "You're not really him. He's gone, succumbed to his demandable valor."

Suddenly, a rush of flame erupted before the sandy mound. Vanadis opened her eyes but found the inferno too bright to see.

"Ah, there you are." called an amused, feminine voice.

Vanadis seized Burning Mind and stood. "What in Hel?"

"Nay, not Hel." With a sweep of her spear the Valkyrie dampened her flame. The black horse she rode, whose, mane was fire, stood on the air as if it were ground. The steed had burning wings. The woman on it was tall, crimson haired, beautiful of face and mighty in continence. Behind her steed lay Gamli's corpse, restored through Valkyrie's holy magic.

Vanadis stood flabbergasted and for a moment, even her sorrow was forgotten.

The Valkyrie kicked her steed and in a flash, darted around Vanadis, seizing Gamli's shade.

This snapped the seithkona out of her shock. She scowled and pointed the tip of her spear at the death spirit.

Her horse kicked up a little higher and the rider chuckled at Vanadis. She pushed Gamli's ghost into his husk, he did not rise out of it. Then she regarded the Volsung sister, "You would truly fight me? How amusing. Know that this,' she patted Gamli's form, "is your brother's true soul, the spirit and body once again whole."

"What does Odin want with Gamli? He was blessed by Surt." spat out Vanadis.

"You think I serve Odin?" The Valkyrie cackled. Her aura of fire flared once more. "Your brother will not be a Valhallan dog. I shall toss him into the burning lake of Glassisveller, there he shall be reborn to work wonders for the Sons of Muspelheim."

"I think not." fumed the seithkona. She reached out with her will and felt her new ghostly entourage stir. "You will return him to me."

The Valkyrie chuckled, "No. Once a life thread is cut, it is ours. You might see him again but only after the onset of Ragnarok." With that, the Valkyrie kicked her steed again and shot up.

Vanadis, flush with ghostly power, jabbed Burning Mind, a storm of shrieking skulls darted after the Valkyrie but far too short and far too late. The fiery steed raced into the heavens like a burning star. The seithkona screamed at it with impudent fury. When her rage was spent, she fell to the sands and wept deeply.

Unseen by her, another Valkyrie rose. She rode a white steed, behind her saddle lay Hardegon.

***

Hours earlier, Vanadis had also knelt in the sand, her soul calling to the ghosts of the battlefield. Then, she noticed the Danevirke contingent advance from the sea, four seasoned warriors and stout shieldmaiden.

"Thor's balls." she cursed.

"Finish the witch!" cried the one at their head and they charged. In the distance, Vargeisa fought with Ingvild Grave Shield, she would be no help.

Vanadis forced herself to her feet and lowered Burning Mind, if she were to die she'd at least impale one of them first. Then, she heard the sound of riders, many of them thundering across the beach.

"The Tuonela wasn't as nice, after all." she heard Ransu quip.

Suddenly, she was flooded with Ransu's spirit and all the spirits of Kintai. The force of their rush blew the sands up and lifted the seithkona off her feet. Black fire flickered around her.

Gerd's voice echoed in her mind, 'Our mistress took the liberty of summoning allies. Ransu will translate your will, the Curonians will follow your commands.'

Vanadis' sudden surge of magic caused her foes to pause. The seithkona gave them a patient, Ransu, smile and suddenly dashed towards them, as she did her obsidian aura flared. The Danevirke soldiers cried in agony as they lit like torches. The seithkona thrashed her arms, each thrash breaking enemy bones. The shieldmaiden and her partner struck the witch but when they withdrew their weapons Vanadis' wounds healed. She touched them both on the foreheads and their skulls imploded. With that, the last of her foes lay still.

Then, Vanadis drifted back to the earth, and the black flame dimmed to nothing.

'Why?' thought Vanadis in surprise, 'I know how much Laufey misses her child. Why help me when I sacrificed my own mother?'

'Hanne was not worthy of such a title.' Gerd answered tersely.

Vanadis glanced up to see Vargeisa jab her sword into Ingvild. Suddenly, she smirked as a clever idea struck. Vanadis brushed her fingers across the corpse of the shieldmaiden and then fled. As she did so the husk took on the torn and broken visage of the seithkona.

***

Three days later, Vanadis and the Fire Wolf sat on the dock of Klaipeda, their bare feet soaking in the warm Baltic.

"That's how I survived." Vanadis concluded.

Vargeisa applauded, "Well done. For a moment you fooled even I." She then regarded the seithkona quizzically, "So now that Vanadis the Cursed is dead, will you take up a new life? Become a simple Curonain jade prospector or perhaps a Pohjalander's buxom wife?"

The seithkona smirked, "I'm half tempted to go to Svealand with no guise at all. I'd put fear into the hearts of the people. They would think Vanadis the Cursed cannot be killed."

Vargeisa brightened at that and laughed, "Yes, do so, it would be most amusing." she then touched her arm, "In truth though, what will you do?"

"Return to Pohjola, I suppose." Vanadis answered. "I swore to your mother that I'd return."

The Fire Wolf smiled, "But, did you say when?"

The seithkona snorted, "What would you suggest I do? I can't look after my brother. I'm not strong enough to gain vengeance on King Siggeir. I don't belong in Courland, and it would be the height of stupidity to return to Alands."

The Fire Wolf, with an air of calm casualness seized Vanadis' palm and drew her dagger, with a swift slash she cut it open. As Vanadis cried in shocked pain. The Fire Wolf did the same to herself. "You have lost a brother," she commented and then pressed her bloody hand with the seithkona's, "but gained a sister." Her lip twisted into a smirk.

Vanadis stared at the blood mingling between them and back up at the grinning Face of the Fire Wolf.

"Join me. With my vision, your magic, and our cunning, we can bring about great things in Midgard and all the Nine Worlds." She leaned in and added, with frightening conviction, "I'm founding a society, one that will right the crimes of the Aesir. Our minions will be the Teeth of Loki. Krumr, Katla, and Wolf will be the Hands of Loki. And we two..." the Fire Wolf paused, searching for the right words, "we will be his eyes."

Vanadis considered her for a long moment. She then smirked and huffed, "Fine, Pohjola can wait. 'Mother' would wish me to look after her youngest, after all."

***

A year later, on a cold and windy night, the rocky shore of Kelifar was deserted. Nearby shone the dim lights of the fishing halls - the music and conversation behind the walls was loud and lively. The same with the Great Hall at the top of the hill. On this sort of night, the people of Kelifar sang and made merry for they wished to drown out the crying ghost who wandered the town.

Dorte did wander. Her veil had been lifted revealing her round, beautiful face. Her golden hair drifted on her shoulders. Her form was no longer long and gaunt, but the full, fine shape she had in life. Yet she drifted instead of walked. She breathed not. Her skin was snow white which accented her red lips and distant blue eyes.

On night likes those, none dared step out to meet her. They barely whispered about her. The sight of the ghost caused screams, even among the warriors. Kelifar was her home but crushing loneliness was her domain.

The spirit's attention was drawn by the hallow sound of a boat hitting the dock. She flew towards it, her eyes lit with an expectation of seeing someone, anyone.

The small skute had only two passengers. Wolf was at the oars. Before him was a woman draped in a long green cloak with a black fringe. She secured her vessel with a tight knot and stepped on to the dock the, butt of her gold ringed and gold headed spear thunked on the wood. She pulled off her hood and regarded the specter closely.

"Vanadis?" Dorte gasped in a hollow voice.

She was no longer the thrall Dorte remembered, nor the fleeing varg she had chased. This Volsung carried herself with an air of caution and strength. "The same." she answered evenly. "You look well, Dorte."

"This is well?" she laughed, gesturing to herself. "I am bereft of life, family, and I no longer even have revenge."

"You're no longer mad," suggested Vanadis.

"I would rather be." Dore sobbed.

The witch stepped closer and examined Dorte up and down. "You're not a shade. This is all of you, isn't it?"

"I have no idea what you mean." Dorte huffed.

The seithkona seemed to consider explaining but then she waved it off and asked, "Dotre, why haven't you passed on?"

Dorte laughed bitterly, "Where would I go, Vanadis? I will not freeze in Hel. I cannot ascend to Asgard. I am not welcome in the barrow of my Uncle. I have only this town, which is no longer my own." A question struck her and she asked. "Why are you here? You're even less welcome than I."

"I came for you. When you vanished, I assumed you'd met your final reward, but then, I heard the rumors of the Lady in White of Kelifar."

"You've come here to finish me off, haven't you?" Dorte snapped.

"That depends," replied the seithkona, "do you wish to finish me?"

Dorte snorted, "Hardly, my vengeance was fully spent on your mother."

At that Vanadis looked thoughtful and even, a hint hopeful. She extended her hand, "Then, come with me."

The spirit flinched back at that and asked, "What do you mean?"

To Dorte's phantom eyes Vanadis' form opened as if she were a portal. Within her was the light and warmth of a hearth. Within she saw many denizens, drinking, feasting and resting, their warm chatter was soothing to the ghost. Above it was Vanadis face, which smiled at her warmly, before her was the witch's open hand. "
Join my entourage. You'll share in their offerings and together, we can see the Nine Worlds."

"Why? Why would you offer this? When I have tried to slay you again and again?"

"You weren't in your right mind. Long ago, you saved me from the mill. I haven't forgotten that." Vanadis said with patience.

"I-I will not be your slave." the ghost cried.

Vanadis shook her head, "I don't keep slaves, Dorte. If you join with me, you will do so in friendship."

The specter glanced back at the empty streets and then forward to her former thrall's kind face. It brought to mind her childhood, happier days. Dorte steadied herself and with a smile answered "In friendship, then." She took Vanadis' hand and they left Kelifar together.

The Norns thread us in loops. | We circle over and over again.
That you cannot undo the past is true.
Your mistakes will haunt you. | They need not rule you.
To live and learn, that is the key to true contentment.

Also coming in 2015!

Fate of the Norns: Ragnarok
SAGA - FAFNIR'S TREASURE

Fate of the Norns: Ragnarok
CORE RULEBOOK

FATE OF THE NORNS

Fate of the Norns: Ragnarok
LORDS OF THE ASH

PENDELHAVEN PUBLISHING